LUTHER M. SILER

I0684870

SKYLIGHTS

PROSTETNIC
PUBLICATIONS

This is a work of fiction. Any resemblance to real persons, living or dead, is coincidental.

SKYLIGHTS

Copyright © 2014 Luther M. Siler

Cover art copyright © 2014 Casey Heying & Andrew Hibner

ISBN-13: 978-0-9906253-2-2
ISBN-10: 0-9906253-2-X

First Printing: September 2014
2nd Print Edition: April 2015

Skylights is dedicated to the crew of the Space Shuttles *Challenger* and *Columbia*, as well as to their families and friends.

Francis R. Scobee
Michael J. Smith
Ronald McNair
Ellison Onizuka
Judith Resnik
Greg Jarvis
Christa McAuliffe

Rick D. Husband
William C. McCool
Michael P. Anderson
Kalpana Chawla
David M. Brown
Laurel Clark
Ilan Ramon

TABLE OF CONTENTS

PROLOGUE

Flashbulb memory, they call it. It's when you remember exactly where you were when you first discovered something or saw something happen.

If you're younger than me, which a lot of you probably are, then your first flashbulb memory is probably related to terrorism somehow. Anybody in, say, their early thirties or older probably remembers exactly where they were on September 11, 2001. A little younger than that and your first flashbulb memory is probably one of the bombings in Chicago in 2018.

I was six years old when the space shuttle *Challenger* exploded. It was January 29, 1986, at exactly eleven thirty-nine in the morning. I was in first grade. For some reason-- I could look this up if I wanted, I suppose, but my first-grade self didn't know, so I'm not going to bother-- NASA had decided that it would be great if they put a schoolteacher on the Space Shuttle. Her name was Christa McAuliffe, and she'd been a middle school teacher, her students not a lot older than I was at the time.

There was a ton of publicity about her presence on the shuttle. Come to think of it, that might have been the reason that NASA put her there in the first place. Every single kid in my school was watching the flight launch on television. The *Challenger* took off, and we all clapped. Seventy-three seconds later, an O-ring failed on the shuttle's right Solid Rocket Booster. There was a little puff of smoke from the side of the ship.

Some of us were still clapping.

I remember noticing it and wondering, for the split second that I had, what had happened. And then the *Challenger,* with me and millions of other people around the country watching, silently blew apart. There were a few seconds of shocked silence in the room, and then every kid in the class-- every one in the building, probably-- started crying at once.

You know what? Writing that just now, I wondered what my teacher must have done afterwards. I can't even remember her name. I can remember the wood surface on my desk, because I dug my fingers into it so hard that day that they scratched it and I got splinters. I can remember the wood-grain on the television set they had us watching. I can remember being surprised that Rachel Douglas, the biggest butthead in the entire first grade, was crying as hard as I was. But I can't remember a single thing that our teacher did to try and bring everybody back to sanity after watching that happen. That's how flashbulb memories work; you'll remember the event itself forever, but that doesn't mean you'll remember anything else that happened around it.

Seventeen years and two days later, it happened again. This time, it was the shuttle *Columbia*, and I was twenty-four and no longer sitting in a classroom. In fact, when the *Columbia* was falling apart in the morning sky over Texas, I was stuck in traffic and late to work. I found out about it about ten minutes after I got in, when the smarmy dope from the office next door made some sort of comment about it to me. We had the Internet by then-- yes, there was Internet back then, although I think we might have still been calling it the World Wide Web-- and I saw the entire thing on CNN's Web site. This time there weren't any tears, just a dull sort of ache in the pit of my stomach. I spent the rest of the day on the computer, chasing down eyewitness reports and trying to devour whatever little bits of actual news managed to leak out. It was funny; I hadn't spent much time thinking about space flight since the first grade, but suddenly the families of the men and women on that shuttle were all I could think about.

I was working for the *Indianapolis Star* at the time, splitting my time between a biweekly column in the science section and general reporting on local news for the rest of the paper. It was a good job; I was happy enough, and making enough money, but I wanted something different from my life.

I decided to write a book.

A year later, I'd completed *Nothing to Bury: the Martyrs of the Space Race*, a look at the lives of the astronauts who had died on the *Challenger* and the *Columbia*, as well as a host of other lives lost in the pursuit of space, and a look at the culture of NASA in between the two disasters. I was pretty proud of it as a piece of work; I wasn't expecting it to necessarily sell well to the general public, but it was a good piece of writing. It did better than I'd expected, enough that I've been able to be comfortable with freelance writing since then. I'm still working for news sites and some of the few print papers that are left, mind you, but I can pick my own assignments and do my own reporting now as opposed to having people assign my projects.

You know where this is going, don't you? I imagine you do.

On August 15, 2022, after years of technical and political delays, the space shuttle *Tycho*, carrying four astronauts, launched on a six-month journey to Mars. They were to remain in orbit around Mars for thirty days, during which they would land on the planet's surface for the first time in human history, then to return to Earth. The run-up to the launch was the biggest public relations bonanza NASA had ever seen. Everything just *stopped* the day the *Tycho* launched. It was just like it had been for the *Challenger,* only times a hundred. They just weren't as good at hype in the eighties, I guess.

I was watching at home, with a couple of friends-- I actually had a little party for the launch. I didn't realize how tense I was until I looked at my hands afterwards. There were furrows in my palms from my fingernails. Then the shuttle took off, soaring into a perfectly blue sky, and I held my breath for a few moments.

The launch went off without a hitch, though, and pictures of the *Tycho* blanketed every website and print doc on the planet over the next few days. For the next six months, everyone was obsessed with Mars. The astronauts provided regular updates on what they were doing. You could get daily blink messages from them if you wanted to, and progress along their flight path was updated live on a map running at the top of CNN.com for the entire duration of the trip. Those six months, I'm convinced, inspired a whole generation of new astronauts, astrophysicists, and pilots. I've never in my life seen America more excited about science. It was amazing.

And then, on February 19th, 2023, when the long voyage was finally over, we... well, we don't actually know what happened. The *Tycho* was supposed to aerobrake into orbit around Mars, stay in orbit for a day or two, and then the astronauts were going to leave the ship to descend to the planet's surface in a lander. They were going to stay on the surface for two weeks or so, doing experiments, exploring the Martian surface, and making history.

There wasn't anything resembling photo evidence, not good evidence at least-- NASA had been sending a steady diet of pictures and video from cameras affixed to the outside of the *Tycho* for months, but they failed at the same time as the audio feed. But we were getting audio beamed back from inside the cabin. Right up until the point where the flight commander, a decorated Marine pilot by the name of Alondra Gallegos, spoke the last words that the *Tycho* sent back to Earth.

"Is that..." was all she said.

After that, nothing. No sound, no signals, no big explosion to be played on the news over and over again. Just nothing at all, and what started off as mild concern slowly morphed, over the next few days, weeks, months, into the certainty that, somehow, the ship had been lost. There was hope for a while that there had just been some sort of global communications failure, that the *Tycho* was still out there but had lost the ability to talk to us. Sadly, those hopes didn't make much sense in reality-- the *Tycho's* communication capabilities were among the simplest systems on the ship, something a talented twelve-year-old would have been able to repair, *and* there was a redundant backup system. Anything catastrophic enough to have completely crippled the ship's ability to talk would have caused fatal damage to the rest of the ship as well. We just couldn't figure out what.

Conventional wisdom eventually decided there had been some sort of asteroid or meteorite impact, something like that.

There was no flashbulb moment for the *Tycho*. The families of the four people lost on that mission-- Alondra Gallegos, Harrison Brown, Kassius Newsome, and Ai-Li Wu-- will never be able to move on. Many of them are convinced that their family members are still out there somewhere. There was no national mourning like there was for the *Challenger* and the *Columbia*. It was as if, after three high-profile ship losses, this time the country just wanted to forget about it.

I got a few calls for interviews after the *Tycho* lost contact, and a few more a few months later, once NASA officially stopped trying to reestablish contact with the ship. I turned them all down, though; I didn't want to base any more of my career on profiting from the deaths of people more heroic and important than I was. I didn't want to write about space any more.

Little did I know.

ONE

Someone please kill me, I thought, as the alarm in my ear bludgeoned me into consciousness. I was up earlier than usual-- I had an appointment for a phone interview with a doctor in New York City and a noon deadline for the article the interview was being conducted for, so waking up at Dear Sweet God on a Monday morning to call her was regrettably necessary.

I rolled out of bed, washed my face, and took my iLid out of sleep mode. A blink icon started flashing in the corner of my field of vision. That was weird-- nobody I know is the type to send a message in the middle of the night. I glanced at the icon for a second to bring it up. I didn't recognize the sender or the number. It looked international.

WANT TO GO ON AN ADVENTURE?

"It's too early in the morning for games," I said, staring at the REPLY icon while I spoke. The words scrolled across the inside of my phone lens, looking like ghostly, floating letters on top of my bedspread, and I blinked to send the message. Then I brushed my teeth and dug up my notes for the interview.

The response only took a few minutes. I HAVE A JOB FOR YOU, it said. PACK A BAG FOR A FEW DAYS. I'LL LET YOU KNOW WHEN THE PLANE LANDS.

This caught my attention. It had done so by being completely ridiculous, but it caught my attention.

"I've got some work to do right now," I replied. "Work for people who are already paying me, and whose names I know. If you can send blink messages, you can give me a call in a couple of hours and we can talk about details."

This time it was only a few seconds until I got the response. THIS WAY IS SO MUCH MORE FUN, it said. BRING A BATHING SUIT. YOU KNOW YOU'RE CURIOUS.

"Seriously," I responded. "You can at least give me your name."

FINE, my mysterious conversation partner responded. YOU CAN CALL ME ZUB. I'LL BE IN TOUCH.

"Noon," I said, sent the reply, and turned off blink messaging. I'd seen teenagers carrying on phone and blink conversations at the same time, but at 48 I didn't have the chops any longer, if I'd ever had them at all. This was already far too much excitement before noon anyway. I pulled up my contact's number from the notes app in my iLid and dialed. A bored-sounding secretary on the other side of the country answered the call.

"Dr. Kayla Gonzales, please," I said. "This is Gabriel Southern. She's expecting my call."

*   *   *

A few hours later, interview and article completed and sent off, I decided to take a few minutes and research my mysterious caller. I couldn't find anything specific on the number itself, which wasn't especially surprising, but I was right on it having come from an international number-- somewhere in the Caribbean, in fact. *No wonder he asked me to bring a bathing suit*, I thought. The funny thing was, the name "Zub" was familiar. I spent half an hour or so searching the Web on my iLid with little luck; there was a computer game from 1986 with that name that had had a belated sequel made five years ago, but that appeared to be a coincidence. I couldn't find any companies with that name, and it didn't appear to be an acronym for anything. Still, it felt familiar.

Right after I gave up looking, there was a buzz in my ear. It was him again. I set the iLid to record and answered the call.

"Gabe Southern."

"I know your name, dummy," the voice on the other end said. He was youngish, probably, his voice more high-pitched than it probably ought to be. Speaking fast, as if he felt like he had more important things to do than talk to me, or maybe he'd just been drinking too much coffee. "I didn't pick your number at random. Are you going to come see me today or not?"

The funny thing was, I'd actually checked my calendar and there wasn't a single thing I needed to be doing for the next few days. The next work appointment I had that required me to actually physically be somewhere was a good week and a half away. I had some things to do Thursday evening, but nothing that couldn't be put off if necessary.

"Do you have any plans to, I don't know, *explain* anything, or are you expecting me to just get on a plane and go? I don't even know who you are." He had me intrigued, I admit it, but... c'mon.

"I told you, my name's Zub. We met once, actually, but it was a long time ago and you probably don't remember. I'll give you a hint, but just one. Ready for it?"

I sighed. "Fine. Hint me."

"Mars."

He was right. That got my attention.

I'm kind of an idiot that way.

"What about it?"

"Pack a bag, my friend. Be at Indianapolis International in three hours. Look for a guy near the international terminal holding a sign with your name on it." He snickered, a goofy, girlish sound.

"And I wasn't kidding about that bathing suit."

He clicked off without another word. He hadn't bothered to wait for me to agree to meet him. I was vaguely impressed by the guy's moxie, if nothing else. I also felt kind of stupid. Some random stranger had blinked me at death o'clock in the morning and told me to catch a plane to *somewhere* based on nothing but the word "Mars," and, God, I was going to actually *do* it.

Like I said: kind of an idiot.

I spent much of the next hour trying to figure out what to put in my kit. Three days worth of clothes wasn't that hard to figure out. I didn't have a bathing suit. I thought about buying one for a moment, but then decided I'd made enough impulsive decisions for one day. I downloaded a few movies and novels to my iLid and sent out a global blink. MAKING POOR DECISIONS, it said. OUT OF THE COUNTRY TO PARTS UNKNOWN. SELL ORGANS FOR FOOD IF I DO NOT RETURN. A few friends sent back inquisitive replies; I ignored them. If Zub was going to have Mysterious Fun with me, I was going to have Mysterious Fun with everyone else I knew. A few minutes to sync files and make sure there was plenty of free memory in my iLid and I was ready to go. I didn't live far from the mag-lev to the airport; I had time to get something to eat along the way.

*   *   *

I'd been working in Indianapolis for years, but lived a good hundred miles outside the city limits. There was a train station an easy half-hour drive from my home and then the mag-lev took me the rest of the way. My iLid's IDchips were scanned automatically when I entered the train and my bank account dinged for the fare. I had been born in an era when we were still writing checks and keeping our registers updated; I couldn't even remember the last time I'd signed a charge slip. Modern life was good.

The train was virtually silent; the few commuters onboard mostly either sporting the glassy-eyed, thousand-mile stare of someone reading something on an iLid or were having mumbled phone or blink conversations with people. You could actually write text to people through your iLid instead of using the voice interface, which could be handy in public or whenever you wanted some privacy, but most of us didn't bother. Most people just learned how to subvocalize accurately and stopped worrying about it. With a few stops, it took about half an hour to get to the airport. I passed my bag through an ordnance scanner on the way into the building and headed toward the international terminal. There was a network of cabs to ferry people where they wanted to be; I preferred to walk, as the airport really wasn't all that complicated to get around in, particularly with my iLid on. Its GPS function worked in the airport, and the ghostly arrows imposing themselves on my field of vision were just never going to stop feeling cool.

Sure enough, there was a guy holding a placard with my name on it just outside the security checkpoint. I hung back for a few minutes to get a sense of the guy before announcing myself. He was a piece of work. He was in his early thirties, taller than me, with clean-cut, short-cropped brown hair. He was dressed like a Secret Service agent, with a dark, expensive-looking suit, dark glasses, and an ostentatious earpiece. The suit fit him well enough that it was probably personally tailored; it looked like he had a runner's body underneath it.

I was entertained by the earpiece. The one I was wearing was a few years old and was practically invisible; his actually still had a curly wire hanging off it that trailed down somewhere into his jacket. I had no doubt that the wire was nonfunctional; the Secret Service was big on *looking* the part, and at some point somebody had decided that those big clunky earpieces were part of looking the part. He was carrying the sign, but didn't appear to have anything else with him. I didn't see a bulge for a gun, but whoever Zub was, he'd have to have serious pull to get a gun into an airport even with a private security team.

The guy wasn't actually Secret Service, was he? That didn't make any sense. He had to be private security of some kind. It struck me that my mysterious benefactor might well be entertained by dressing his guys like government operatives.

Oh well. Nothing else to do but show myself, I suppose. I cut the clandestine act and started walking his way. He spotted me about three seconds later.

"I didn't think I was that famous," I said to him. "You knew what I looked like?"

He smiled and turned his placard over. The author photo from my book was taped to the back. "Good afternoon, Mr. Southern. May I take your bag?"

"Just as soon as you tell me what I'm doing here," I said. "Start with your name and then explain exactly where we're going."

He smiled again. He had annoyingly perfect teeth. "You can call me Mr. Green. I'm Mr. ben Zahav's personal pilot. He sent me to come pick you up and bring you to the compound; our plane is waiting outside. He didn't explain this to you in advance?"

Ben Zahav. I knew I'd heard the name before. I'd done a piece for the *New Yorker Online* several years back about the company the government had chosen to build the *Tycho*. It was Zahav International, a multinational aerospace company. The family was Israeli but had emigrated to the States in the nineties. But the CEO's name was David, and I hadn't heard anyone call him *Zub*. Plus there was no way that had been him on the phone; he would have to be in his eighties by now.

"How's David doing?" I asked. "I haven't spoken to him in eight or nine years; I'm surprised he remembers me at all."

Mr. Green looked startled for a moment. "I'm sorry, I wasn't clear. David ben Zahav passed away in 2021. Liver cancer. I'm here on behalf of his son, Ezekiel. He inherited the company from his father upon his death."

"Oh," I said. Man, I *had* met the kid. He'd been a teenager when I'd met him, probably not even out of high school yet. He'd wandered in while I was interviewing his father. I tried to bring his face to mind and couldn't do it. No wonder he'd sounded young on the phone; he was barely out of his mid-twenties. "I'm sorry. Did you know him well?"

"Never met him," Mr. Green said. "As I said, I work for his son. Who is, by the way, waiting for you. We should head to the plane. If, that is, you're coming with me."

Curiouser and curiouser. "Yeah, you've got me," I said, handing him my bag. "Let's see this plane of yours."

"Right this way," he said, and turned and strode away. I actually had to hurry to keep up with him.

As it turns out, flying on a private plane is *a lot easier* than flying commercial. I have to figure I'd been scanned, both obviously and clandestinely, probably two or three dozen times since entering the airport, and you learn quickly when you fly a lot to keep your ID on a lanyard around your neck so that even the people not standing near scanners can do a physical ID check on you without inconvenience. I didn't even have a *ticket* for this thing, but apparently the security people at the airport either knew Mr. Green or had been briefed not to bother him. The two of us were waved around a security checkpoint into a private waiting room featuring all-leather furniture and a thick plush carpet that probably cost more than all the furniture in my apartment. A bartender in a tuxedo stood guard over a bar that rivaled any of the expensive restaurants I'd been in during my life.

Unfortunately, it didn't look like we'd be staying, as Mr. Green continued through the room without stopping to sightsee and exited through a door in the back of the room. I considered protesting and demanding a drink and then followed him out. The plane was already at the gate, and he waved me toward the back of the plane and handed me my bag.

"Make yourself comfortable, Mr. Southern," he said. "It's just the two of us on the flight, so I don't have anyone to bring you drinks, but you'll find a minibar and some food to snack on at the back of the plane. We've got a fairly extensive collection of films and television programs for you to watch as well, if you're in the mood for that. We'll be in the air for about three hours. I'll make an announcement over the PA system when you ought to belt yourself in for takeoff."

He disappeared off to the left into the cockpit and closed the door behind him. There was a small corridor off to my right into the passenger cabin; I shrugged and went to find a seat. The plane was small, but ridiculously opulent. The walls were paneled in what looked like actual wood-- mahogany, maybe, or something similarly expensive-- and rather than rows of airplane seats, there were couches and recliners scattered around the cabin. There was a bar toward the back, with a nice-looking spread of fruits and vegetables and finger foods, enough for a party of ten or twelve people. No doubt the alcohol was behind the bar. There was storage for baggage discreetly placed along the walls and over some of the couches, and the windows to the outside of the plane looked bigger than I felt would be perfectly safe. All in all, it looked like a hell of a way to travel. I grabbed myself a plate of food and settled into one of the recliners. There was what looked like a set of TV controls built into one of the armrests; I pushed a button experimentally and a panel slid aside at the front of the cabin revealing a screen that had to be six feet wide.

Awesome, I thought. This guy's probably going to kill me and hold my brain for ransom once I get to wherever we're going, but at least I'm going to travel there in style.

"Pulling away from the gate in about a minute, Mr. Southern," said Mr. Green's voice over the intercom. "You'll find that wherever you're sitting, you still have a seatbelt. Please make sure you're belted in during takeoff. After that, you're free to move around the cabin as you see fit."

"Thanks," I said, not expecting him to hear me.

"You're welcome," he said. "The cabin's also wired with an audio feed to the cabin. If you need anything, say my name and then start talking. I'll hear you."

"Thanks," I said, resolving not to do that under any circumstances. I found my seatbelt pushed in between the cushions and put it on.

A blink icon popped onto my lens. It was from Zub.

DO YOU LIKE MY PLANE?

"It's pretty nice," I responded. "I've been on better." I was lying, but there was no reason to seem too impressed.

SO HAVE I, he responded. THAT'S MY GUEST PLANE. I DON'T FLY ON THAT ONE. BE CAREFUL, I THINK THE DUST BUNNIES BITE. I looked around; there wasn't a speck of dust anywhere on the plane, as I'm sure he was well aware.

"I'll forgive you this time," I said, as the plane started to move. "But don't let me catch you skimping on me again."

DON'T WORRY, he said. THIS IS DIME-STORE STUFF COMPARED TO WHAT I'M PUTTING YOU ON NEXT.

Now what in the world did *that* mean?

*   *   *

Mr. Green didn't lie; the flight took almost exactly three hours, moving steadily south across the United States and, as I'd thought, into the Caribbean. I'd spent a few minutes watching a movie, quickly giving that up in favor of spending most of the flight researching Zahav International and whatever I could dig up on Ezekiel ben Zahav. I was impressively successful on the first task and surprisingly stymied by the second. Zahav International had been founded by Zub's grandfather in 1950; he'd been one of the first emigrants to Israel after World War II and had immediately gotten into crafting his new country an air force. The guy was both a wickedly talented engineer and a tremendous businessman; when his planes were among those that wiped out the air forces of several neighboring countries during the Six Day War he'd become a billionaire overnight. His son David had left Israel and become an American citizen, but Zahav International still had close dealings with both countries and had several Israelis on their corporate board. They'd built the *Tycho* from the ground up, along with several of the most advanced planes the American governments were flying and about half of the components of the International Space Station. David ben Zahav had indeed died of cancer in 2021 after a short but brutal struggle with the disease; his funeral had been attended by presidents.

Zub, on the other hand, had done his best to keep specific information about himself off the Web; there was more about *me* out there to find than there was about him. Heck, at least I was relatively well-known within my field-- there was more about my *mother* easily available than there was about Ezekiel ben Zahav. *He's paying somebody to do nothing but scrub information about him off the Web,* I thought. Just keeping the Wikis clean alone would take a few hours a day. I had his birthday-- June 17, 2002-- and a fairly recent-looking picture of him, and a few scattered acknowledgments that, yes, he owned a really big company that made him a whole lot of money-- but other than that, nothing. No school record, no arrest record, no credit profile that I could track down, not even a freaking library card. The guy was a ghost.

This just keeps getting more fun, I thought. Privacy was an outdated concept and had been since I was in college. To be as wealthy as Zub ben Zahav was and not have your entire life available for ready dissection by others was unheard of. I was starting to wonder if he was even real. Maybe this was some sort of elaborate setup. I hadn't been kidnapped in a while; it would be a nice change of pace.

QUIT RESEARCHING ME, came the blink. EVERY SITE ON THE WEB THAT MENTIONS MY NAME HAS HAD A HIT FROM YOUR LID IN THE LAST FEW HOURS. YOU'LL FIND OUT WHAT YOU NEED TO KNOW WHEN YOU LAND.

That *sneaky little dork*, I thought.

"Good guess," I responded back. "I want your web monkey's job."

YOU DON'T HAVE THE COMPUTER SKILLS, he responded. I'D NEVER HIRE YOU. SERIOUSLY, I'LL EXPLAIN EVERYTHING SOON. SEE YOU THIS EVENING.

"Sure," I said, more to myself than to him. That said, he was right: I really was done looking around. My usual sources didn't have anything concrete and there really wasn't any point in doing any more digging when, one way or another, I was going to get some answers in a few minutes.

Right on cue, my ears started popping. "Mr. Southern, we'll be landing in a few minutes," came the announcement. "You should put your seatbelt back on if you've taken it off. We'll be on the ground soon."

Here we go, I thought.

TWO

Ezekiel ben Zahav's private island glittered in the Caribbean like a stolen jewel on a blue silk sheet. Even from the plane, I could see that he'd developed the place pretty extensively. The airport took up most of the eastern half of the island, and I could see what looked like an observatory at the island's highest point, as well as enough buildings to qualify as a small town scattered around. There was an enormous, square building dominating half of the airport. The thing looked big enough to see from outer space and I could actually read the Zahav International logo painted on the side from my seat.

What in the world does he need THAT for?

The entire island covered maybe nine or ten square miles at the most-- small enough for a private compound for an extremely rich man, but large enough that he had room to do whatever he wanted with the space. The plane banked steeply and turned toward the runway, eventually landing softly and gliding to a stop in front of a hangar. I could see several more planes in the hangar, including a couple of old biplanes and another luxury jet that, true to Zub's word, looked to be half again the size of the plane I was in.

Mr. Green exited the cockpit and extended his hand for my bag again. "I'm to take you directly to your quarters," he said. "There will be time for a tour of the island later, but my understanding is that Mr. ben Zahav wants to conduct it personally." As we exited the plane, a three-wheeled electric transport pulled up alongside the stairwell.

There was no one behind the wheel. Mr. Green noticed the surprised look on my face, and grinned that flawless grin of his again. "Automated. They notice when a plane lands and automatically dispatch next to wherever it stops. I radioed ahead that there was only two of us on the plane, otherwise there would be a larger fleet of vehicles plus a few for cargo."

"Ever had anybody run over by them?"

"No, not yet. They've got pretty sophisticated optical sensors on the front; they just stop if they encounter an unexpected object and try to either go around it or just wait until it goes away. You'll find that a lot of the vehicles on the island are unmanned." He put my bag into the trunk of the vehicle and got into the driver's seat. "I'll take us in myself, though. You'll find the ride perfectly comfortable. Please, have a seat."

I took his advice. For such a tiny vehicle, the back seat was surprisingly roomy. The back of the driver's seat also bore the Zahav International logo, a design I saw repeated all over the place. We pulled away from the hangar and onto an access road, heading steadily upward toward the populated area on the other side of the island. As we got a bit higher, I took a second look at the airport and got a closer look at the huge building I'd seen from the plane. It really was impressively large; you could easily fit two of the other hangars inside of it and probably still have room to spare.

"What's that building for?" I asked Mr. Green. "It looked like there was enough space for a few more planes in the other one."

Mr. Green nodded, not taking his eyes off the road. "You'll see that one tonight, I think. That's Mr. ben Zahav's special project."

"Fair enough," I said, and settled back, enjoying the ride. It was hot, but the transport was a convertible, and there was a pleasant sea breeze blowing in my face. The whole island just *smelled* good; there had been an expected gasoline odor at the airport but now that we were farther away the smells of the ocean were taking over everything. The sun was high overhead, it was midafternoon with plenty of daylight left. We pulled into the built-up portion of the island, which featured rows and rows of prefabricated housing, painted different colors but otherwise more or less exactly the same. There were numbers on each of the houses but I didn't see any street names. There probably wasn't a need for them. I figured the place probably had a single centralized post office and had few enough inhabitants that everyone knew where to find everyone else.

After a few minutes, we pulled up in front of a blue cabin and Mr. Green stopped the car. "This is it," he said. "Mr. ben Zahav will have you picked up for dinner in two hours. Feel free to unpack and relax."

"And if I decide to take a walk?" I asked. "What will he do if he can't find me?"

"There is nowhere you can go on the island where he can't find you, Mr. Southern," Mr. Green said. "That said, you're free to go where you want. There are a few places where you won't be allowed without an escort or a pass, of course, but the beach is immediately to the south if you want to swim, and you're welcome to explore what amenities we have to offer if you like. I suspect we'll be able to find you when we want to."

"One more question," I asked. "What's the island called?"

"I'm surprised it took you so long to ask," Mr. Green said. "We call it Eunostos."

"Eunostos," I said. "Sounds Greek. You named a Caribbean island after something Greek?"

"We did," said Mr. Green, "Or rather, Mr. ben Zahav did. I must be going now, Mr. Southern. I'll likely see you again soon. Do enjoy the remains of the afternoon, will you?"

"Thanks," I said, and walked into my cabin. There was no lock on the door, which didn't surprise me, and I spotted four security cameras on the corners of the house and on the lawn on my way inside, which did. Cameras were so easy to miniaturize, and had been for decades, that if you put one somewhere that was large enough for people to actually notice, it was because you *wanted* them to see it. And I saw four, which sent a pretty clear message: *nothing you do in this place is private.* I could probably expect that the bathrooms were clear of cameras, even in the guest house, but it was unlikely that anything else was free of surveillance.

Well, fine, then. Let him see me take the bait. I reactivated my iLid, which found a solid internet connection immediately, and did a search for *Eunostos*. It turned out to mean "safe journey or safe return." More significantly, it was the name of an albedo feature on the surface of Mars: in other words, basically a dark spot. As far as I could discover, we knew little about it. It seemed a little ominous.

Ezekiel ben Zahav's little mysteries were beginning to exhaust me. It was time to put other people to work. I sent a blink to an old buddy who had worked the business section for the *Star* with me for years. He'd always been better at chasing corporate money around than I was.

"AJ," I said, the words appearing on my lens as I spoke. "Got a few minutes?"

He apparently did, as the response came back quickly. FOR YOU, I CAN SPARE A FEW, the blink said. CAN WE DO THIS BY VOICE, THOUGH? YOU KNOW I HATE SENDING BLINKS.

"Nah, I'll make it quick," I said, knowing it was making him vaguely uncomfortable and rather enjoying the feeling. "I need you to ask around a little bit for me. See if you can find out anything interesting that Zahav International has been doing lately, or beyond that, if any of the aerospace multinationals have been working on Mars research in the last couple of years or so. Anything since the *Tycho* disappeared."

THAT'S A TALL ORDER, he responded. AWFUL BIG COMPANY. IS THAT WHERE YOU ARE RIGHT NOW? CHASING ZAHAV AROUND MARS?

"Sort of. Maybe. I'm not sure yet," I responded. "I spent most of the morning on a private plane and right now I have no real idea why. I'll let you know if I'm on to something."

I'M SELLING YOUR ORGANS ANYWAY, he responded. I CAN'T HELP IT, YOU TOLD ME TO. The letters were vibrating slightly, a sign that he wanted me to know he was laughing at me.

"Fair enough," I said. "I hear corneas are fetching thousands nowadays. I want a cut of whatever you get."

NO CHANCE, he said. BUT I'LL SEE WHAT I CAN DO. WILL SEND BACK IN AN HOUR OR TWO.

"Take your time. Thanks, man," I said. Quick calls to my mother and my sister, neither of whom had been terribly entertained by my blinks from earlier that morning, followed. Afterwards, I explored the guest house-- nothing too fancy, but not shabby, either. It featured a furnished living room with a decent entertainment center, two bedrooms with king-sized beds, a bathroom, and a fully-stocked kitchen. There was enough in the refrigerator for me to make dinner for half a dozen people or so if I had been inclined to do such a thing, which made me wonder how often the place was used. Surely bringing food out from the mainland was a bit of an inconvenience, and it seemed silly to keep the fridge so well stocked when it seemed unlikely to be used. I grabbed an apple from the crisper and wandered onto the back porch.

There was a monkey on the back porch. He was sitting on the rail, looking at me, as if he was wondering what in the world I was doing in his house. He had a black, furless face, with white rings around his eyes. Maybe two feet tall, with a tail about as long. He had his tail wrapped around the rail, and I suspected he was the type of monkey who could swing from things with his tail if he wanted to. He was mostly of a tan color, except for his arms and hands, which were black.

"Hello," I said, because I couldn't think of anything better to say to him. I'm not sure what the proper topic of conversation should be with a monkey.

He screeched at me and pointed at my apple.

"Hungry, are you?" Surely the monkey had somewhere he could get a meal around this place. He screeched again, reaching out a hand for some apple. I ducked back into the house, grabbed a knife out of the kitchen, and sliced him off a piece. I held it out to him, but he made no move to come close enough to take it from me.

"You're no fun," I said, and tossed the apple over his head.

He actually leapt from the railing, *caught* the piece of apple, and then jumped back up onto his perch to eat, all the while staring at me. *Yeah, what?* his facial expression seemed to say.

"Are there going to be a hundred of you here in a little while if I keep feeding you?" I asked. He finished his piece of apple and jumped up and down again a few times. I cut him another piece, and he repeated the jump-and-catch trick. *He's been here before,* I thought. *The guest house probably gets a fair amount of use, and he's used to being able to get food from the people staying here, whoever they are.* I looked through the trees behind the house, wondering if there was a nest of the things back there somewhere.

Monkeys don't have nests, do they? Probably not.

The iLid buzzed in my ear, ending my reverie. It was AJ again.

"That was fast."

"I like to be impressive," he said. "You busy?"

"I'm feeding a monkey," I said. "Absolutely fascinating. What'd you turn up?"

"Not much," he said. "First things first, though. Have you actually looked at a satellite map of Eunostos, by any chance?"

I hadn't. There hadn't been any reason to. "I just found out I was here about twenty minutes before you did," I said. "I didn't bother looking at a map because I didn't know to look for Eunostos in the first place."

"Give it a try," he said. "I'll wait."

"OK," I said, tossing the rest of the apple to the monkey and going back inside. I called up a satellite map of Eunostos, overlaying it on my normal field of vision.

"Whoa."

"Yeah. How do you think they managed to pull that one off?"

Eunostos was on the map, of course-- there wasn't a place on the *globe* that you couldn't pull up satellite imagery for nowadays-- but the version I was looking at was all trees and beachfront. The island, on the map, looked completely uninhabited-- except, I suspected, for apple-begging monkeys.

"How new is the development out there, anyway?" AJ asked.

"Everything's finished, as far as I've been able to tell," I said. "I haven't seen anything that looked like it might have been under construction, and there's a fully-functioning airport-- not just a helipad, an *airport*. One enclosed hangar and another building at the airport that's half the size of God. I haven't been inside yet. I'm not sure what they're doing in there. How long does it take to build something like that? Four, five years? Longer? There's no way that the satmaps for this area haven't been updated in *five years*."

"Right," AJ said. "Even the most desolate places on Earth get updated at least once a year, bare minimum. Yet there's not a trace of human influence anywhere on that map. Any theories?"

I thought about this for a second.

"Three," I said. "First, that ben Zahav is unimaginably rich. Second, that he has contacts who are willing to work with him in all the right places. Third, that he's invested in keeping whatever he's doing here secret from... well, *somebody*."

"I have more," AJ said. "Looking at the map was actually the first thing I did, and I wasn't actually thinking anything mysterious was going to happen-- I just wanted to know where you were. But once I realized that the maps were out of date, and I thought about what you'd said about *flying* into the place, I realized something was going on. I called a friend at the US Geological Survey. And guess what?"

"The government's maps don't have the place either," I said.

"The government's maps don't have the place either. He's now doing his best to figure out who Mr. ben Zahav's mystery hacker is."

That alarmed me. "Keep in mind I sort of need the guy to agree to fly me back to the mainland sometime soon," I said. "I can't really afford to make him mad at me at the moment." *And he's probably recording every word I'm saying right now*, I thought. If he was manic for secrecy in his own life, he certainly had a modern approach to privacy with regard to everyone else around him.

"Well, the thing is, he's effectively a sovereign country out there, if it's a private island," AJ said. "He's certainly outside US jurisdiction. It's not like they can do anything to him for screwing up their maps."

"Good point, I suppose," I said. "What else do you have? Anything?"

"Interesting that you should guess five years," he replied. "Take a wild guess as to how long there has been a major budget line in Zahav International's expenses that they're not telling anybody about."

"Five years?" I felt smart.

"Five years. Since, just to make sure it's clear, since just after Ezekiel ben Zahav's father passed away. The company's been channeling massive amounts of operating capital and virtually all of their profits into some sort of enormous, top-secret R&D project for the last five years. And, get this-- the budget has *tripled* since the *Tycho* lost contact."

"Fascinating," I said. "When did they get the contract for the *Tycho?*"

"That would be seven years ago," AJ answered. "They'd been working on it for two years when the new project started up. On top of that, it looks like there was a fair amount of friction between Ezekiel ben Zahav and David ben Zahav on how to best get human beings to Mars. David ben Zahav's ideas were apparently a lot more traditional, and Ezekiel had some other plan in mind. They were playing the dueling-engineers game for a while, and apparently David's ideas won out in the end."

"Did Ezekiel stop working on the project?"

"Not that I can tell," he said. "He didn't agree with the direction that they ended up going with the *Tycho*, but I think he's got either enough integrity or enough ego that he figured even if they were going about things the wrong way the project was better off with him on it than off. But two years is just about enough time to realize that something is going off the rails and to start laying groundwork for something else."

"Great," I said. "Thanks a lot, AJ. How'd you pull all of this together so quickly?"

"I'm *just that good,*" he said, and I could hear him smiling at me over the phone. "Plus I happen to know a gal who works in the aerospace industry and she keeps her ear to the ground. Other than the map thing, basically everything I just told you is hearsay and rumor that I picked up from her. I do have a copy of their last few annual reports here, which verified the budget line thing, but my friend gave me everything else. Sarieta Walker, you remember her? You guys met at the wedding a few years ago."

"Yeah, I think I do," I said. I didn't remember her. I was terrible with faces. But I wasn't about to admit that. "I'll fill you in after I've talked to Zahav. Any idea at all why he's dragged me down here?"

"That one's all you," he said. "I don't have the vaguest idea. But if I figure anything out I'll contact you."

"Blink me," I said. "Ben Zahav probably taped this whole conversation."

"Fine, fine," he said, sounding exasperated. "Catch you later, Gabe."

"Thanks, AJ." DISCONNECTED, said my lens.

I turned to go back on the porch, half-absorbed in digesting everything AJ had just told me. The sliding glass door to the porch was still open where I'd walked back into the house through it, and the monkey was on the countertop in the kitchen. He looked as if he'd been listening to the entire conversation.

"I hope that was as interesting for you as it was for me," I said, half talking to the monkey and half talking to ben Zahav. In response, the monkey leapt to the top of the refrigerator and stayed there, still staring down at me.

"What, you want another apple?" *Greedy little thing,* I thought. He reached down and slapped the front of the refrigerator with the palm of his hand a few times.

"It's too bad you're only two feet tall," I said. "Much bigger than that and you'd probably be able to open the fridge yourself." Still, it wasn't like it was my food. I fished another apple out of the crisper and held it up to him. This time, he took it from me, and started munching away right there on top of the fridge, not bothering to change his position.

"I guess I have a roommate," I said. "Great."

* * *

Mr. Green showed up maybe half an hour later. A muted bell started ringing as he pulled into the cabin's driveway. Either he was triggering the doorbell from the car or there were sensors built into the driveway. After spending more time than usual thinking about it, I'd changed clothes into something slightly more formal, if perhaps in need of an ironing board. The monkey, which had refused to leave the house on its own, followed me out the front door.

"Ah, I see Sajad found you," Mr. Green said.

"Sajad?"

"He's Mr. ben Zahav's monkey. He has the run of the entire island, and generally will come to investigate whenever anyone new shows up in the guest house."

Fascinating, I thought to myself as I got into the front seat next to Mr. Green. The little beast only reinforced the idea that I'd spent the last few hours being spied upon. The monkey clambered in through an open window and sat down in the back. "Do you often chauffeur him places, or is that a new thing?"

"He's smart enough to know where we're going," he replied, smiling that unnaturally perfect grin again. "He'll probably spend a good portion of dinner begging for table scraps and then disappear for a few days."

"Does Mr. ben Zahav have any other pets I need to know about?" I asked.

"Only the shark pit underneath the observatory," he said. Perfectly straight face.

"And where will Mr. ben Zahav and I be meeting?"

"The observatory."

"No wonder he asked me to bring a bathing suit," I said. At this, he allowed himself the very smallest of grins. I took it as a victory.

It only took a few minutes to reach the observatory, which was parked on the highest peak on the island, perhaps five hundred feet above sea level. The sun was just starting to set behind it, and the reddish evening light glinting off the bronze-colored dome was a stunning sight. Mr. Green parked the car in front of the place and the monkey leapt from the window, racing to the door and then looking back over his shoulder at us, clearly waiting for us to let him in.

Mr. Green did not move. "Are you coming in with us?"

"I am not," he said. "My wife and I have dinner plans this evening. You will find the door unlocked, and I suspect Sajad will be willing to show you to where you'll be eating, since he will need you to open the doors along the way." For the first time, I noticed the wedding band on his finger. For some reason, the thought of Mr. Green having a life outside of being a manservant for Ezekiel ben Zahav seemed strange to me.

"Thanks for the ride, then," I said, all the while thinking *How am I supposed to get back to the cabin?* The island wasn't that big, and the cabin was within relatively easy walking distance, but I hadn't paid a whole lot of attention to the turns the car had taken along the way.

Maybe the monkey would walk me back.

I opened the door to the observatory, which led into a narrow hallway. The hallway split into a T after ten feet or so, continuing off to the left and right, forming what looked like a ring around the central space. *Probably offices along the outside circle of the building,* I thought. The monkey charged ahead and dashed off to the right, returning after a few seconds to wave me along once he realized I hadn't rushed after him. He continued to stay ten or fifteen feet ahead of me, going perhaps a quarter of the way around the perimeter of the observatory until reaching a pair of double doors on the left. He leapt into the doors a few times, screeching, until I caught up with him and let the two of us into the central chamber.

I'd never been inside an actual observatory before, so I wasn't sure what to expect. I'd seen pictures and old movie scenes with observatories before-- always a giant telescope, generally built partially of clockwork and hanging from the roof, with a bunch of scattered tables or empty spaces around the floor. There would be a chair at the base of the telescope where the (generally) mad scientist would sit. He would be wearing a white lab coat. Probably weird, Coke-bottle thick glasses as well.

This was only very slightly like that. The room was dominated by banks of mainframe computers, which ringed the outside wall and took up a fair amount of floor space as well. The telescope was there, but obviously much more modern-looking than the (probably) inefficient and anachronistic version I had in mind, and the images didn't go to an old man in a chair, but directly into the computers. There was an immense monitor screen along one wall as well; the telescope could probably display directly to that.

And then there were the holograms.

The entire solar system floated about randomly in the air, starting with a few scattered stars that appeared to be nearly within reach and culminating with Jupiter, which probably took up a full third of the space in the room and was currently tucked into the highest point of the observatory's pitch-black dome. Saturn was drifting lazily over my head, its rings floating through the stars as it passed by, and I recognized the binary system of Pluto and Charon passing in between it and me. The occasional asteroid or comet drifted by as well. The overall effect was awe-inducing, and I'm sure my mouth was hanging open as I took it all in.

"Awesome, isn't it? This is where I take all my first dates."

"I just hope you don't expect me to put out," I said, as I turned and got my first good look at Ezekiel "Zub" ben Zahav. He looked much as he had when I'd first met him, if a decade and a half or so older— tall and slender, a couple of inches over six feet tall, without an ounce of muscle anywhere on him. He had a mop of straight, greasy black hair, a soul patch that looked like it was could very well be there by accident, and nervous-looking, intensely green eyes. He was wearing dirty jeans with a white t-shirt and, entertainingly, the scientist's lab coat that I'd been expecting and what looked like prescription eyeglasses. The eyeglasses were really unusual; as soon as communication technology had moved to a primarily visual interface, laser eye surgery had suddenly gotten very, very cheap. As a result, only the elderly, the technophobic, and the extremely poor wore glasses any longer except to screen out the sun. He surely still had a lens on underneath the glasses, though; he'd been blinking me all day. His voice, if anything, was even more thin and high-pitched than it had been on the phone. *He's using a bass boost on his voice*, I realized. It was the action of either a very vain man or a very practical one. It just didn't work when interacting with people face-to-face.

I got curious and checked the local wireless networks. My iLid filled with a list. It looked like every piece of clothing the guy had on was live.

Amazing.

"Nice to meet you," I said, extending my hand to him. "Gabriel Southern." He looked at my hand for a moment, as if not sure what to do about it, then shook my hand. Sort of. His handshake was not the most impressive thing about him.

"Call me Zub," he said. "Childhood nickname. No idea where it came from. It stuck, though. I hate *Ezekiel*. Do you like your name?" All of this rapid-fire, one breath.

"Fond enough of it," I said. "It's Biblical, like yours. Feels kinda old-timey nowadays; I don't often meet other people with my name."

"I suppose," he said. "We're eating in here. There's a dining table past the computers over here." He abruptly walked past me and past a few of the freestanding banks of computers toward the center of the room; I followed. There was an ornate round dinner table in the precise center of the room; Sajad was sitting in the middle of the table, an expectant look on his tiny monkey face. There were four chairs around the table; Zub sat in one of them and gestured at the one next to him. I sat. He flipped up a recessed panel on the top of the table and pushed a button. A few moments later a white-jacketed waiter entered the room and handed me a menu.

"Restaurant service?" I was surprised; I had been expecting him to have already decided what dinner was going to be. There were no prices on the menu, although the Zahav International logo adorned the cover, making it look charmingly official.

"I never have any idea what I'm hungry for until I eat, and the kitchen staff isn't exactly perfectly consistent in what they're able to obtain," Ezekiel said. "I started making them give me menus so that I had some idea what I could actually eat. The good news is that we're the only customers, so whatever we want, they cook *fast*. Ravioli," he said, handing the menu back to the waiter.

I scanned the menu quickly, not wanting to keep the man waiting. Interestingly, not only was ravioli not on the menu, I didn't see any pasta options at all. I decided on meat. "New York strip, the larger one. Medium well. Baked potato, and whatever vegetables you have handy," I said. If I'd been dragged thousands of miles for dinner, it was bloody well going to be a steak. The waiter nodded, took my menu, and disappeared the same way he came. He hadn't said a single word the entire time he'd been in the room.

Not exactly friendly with his employees, I thought.

"Tell me everything you know about the *Tycho*," he said.

Right to business, then.

"Well, you built it," I said. "Or at least your company did. I'm not certain how much of the design was yours versus your father's or some other engineer for the company. It launched from Earth on August 15, 2022 into low Earth orbit, rendezvoused with the International Space Station, then departed from the space station to Mars. It was scheduled for a six-month trip to the planet with a thirty-day stay, of which they were hoping that two to three weeks would be on-planet. The *Tycho's* lander was supposed to put down on the planet surface and rejoin the ship afterwards, and they would launch back to Earth directly from the Martian orbit. The *Tycho* itself was never to touch the planet's surface. Lost contact with NASA mission control very quickly after arriving in Mars orbit. Since then, enough time has elapsed that they did not seem to have turned around and come directly back. And if anyone has any idea what happened to the ship, they've not come forward to make it official. How's that?"

"Not bad," he said. "You've done your homework, especially if you've grokked that Dad and I didn't exactly see eye-to-eye on the mission design or the design of the ship itself. I loved my father, but when he went wrong, he went wrong *big*, and he got the *Tycho* wrong. So did the government."

"Is that why you called me here? To set the record straight?" *If I flew three thousand miles to take a pitch for a biography, I swear I'll choke him with his ravioli,* I thought. As if sensing my thoughts, the monkey, who was still sitting in the middle of the table, hissed at me and clambered up on Zub's spindly shoulder.

"Sort of," he said. "But probably not the way you're thinking. What do you know about the *Tycho's* crew?"

"Less than I just told you about the mission itself," I said. "Alondra Gallegos, Harrison Brown, Kassius Newsome, and Ai-Li Wu. Gallegos was the mission commander. Harrison Brown was the pilot. I think Newsome was the main engineer. Ai-Li Wu's main responsibilities were medicinal. She was also the chief science officer on the ship, if I remember right. Other than that and vague guesses at their ages, I don't know much about them."

"Ai-Li Wu was my fiancée," he said, a note of wistfulness in his voice.

"I'm so sorry," I said. "I didn't know."

"I'm bullshitting you, I barely knew her. *Super* hot, though," he said, a devilish grin on his face. I managed to keep my face straight. "This part's true though: did you know that they specifically screened for attractiveness among the crew as a prerequisite for going to Mars?"

"I didn't," I said. "I suppose they wanted everyone to be photogenic for television or something, right?"

"Not quite," he said. "Well, okay, that was part of it, but there was hard science-- well, *psychology*, at least-- behind it as well." An ugly sneer crossed his face at the word *psychology*.

"It turns out that attractive people, of either gender, tend to trigger more intense protective impulses from other people than ugly humans do. The theory was that if everybody on the trip was pretty, they'd do a better job of taking care of each other."

He paused again, chewing on his lower lip this time. The waiter silently brought us salads and a pitcher of water. He picked at the salad absent-mindedly as he spoke.

"I shouldn't have let them go. I shouldn't have let any of them go. I knew that the way they were going about getting to Mars was flawed in any number of ways, ways that I could see and could explain to people in short sentences, and I let it happen anyway."

"What happened to the ship, then? I thought that no one at NASA actually knew what went wrong?" The *Challenger* had been brought down by a faulty O-ring, the space shuttle equivalent of a faulty washer in a kitchen faucet. The *Columbia* had been downed by a missing piece of heat shielding the size of a bathroom floor tile. Any number of things could go wrong quite easily on such a complicated ship, especially on such an unprecedentedly long journey.

"It didn't blow up," he said. "I know it didn't blow up. I've got every second of the mission data that the ship sent back to NASA, every minute of communications between the crew and mission control. Nobody ever even *hinted* that there was anything wrong with the ship, which means that the ship hadn't given them any warnings that there was a problem. I wrote the diagnostics software on the *Tycho*, Gabe. I designed every sensor on that ship. If something was wrong, they'd have known about it. Ships don't just blow up."

"Rogue asteroid? Meteor shower? Something *had* to have gone wrong," I said.

"Neither," he said. "Nothing hit the ship. Proximity alarms would have picked up anything even close to a size that could have done damage well in advance, and there's not a whole lot of traffic through that part of space at that time of year anyway. Keep something in mind-- the ship ceased communicating *completely*. That means that if something had hit it it would have had to be large enough to have completely pulverized the entire ship. We're not talking about a meteorite punching a hole through the crew cabin; the *ship* would have reported that. If they got hit, it was by something larger than the ship was, big enough to completely crush it on impact. There's no way that was what happened."

He was perfectly calm while saying all of this. I got the feeling he'd gone over the details in his head a million times since the ship had disappeared.

"There was nothing mechanically wrong with the ship. Nothing hit the ship. And there wasn't a catastrophic failure of every single system that was capable of sending a message back to Earth at exactly the same time. We also know that the ship did not turn around and slingshot back to Earth, because they would have returned by now."

Oh, God, I thought. I knew where he was going with this, and I hadn't expected to have to deal with Big Crazy today. Not *this* kind, at least.

"What? Aliens?"

He blinked. I actually caught him by surprise.

"No, don't be an idiot. The only thing that makes sense is that they're still *on Mars,*" he said. "Or they have gone somewhere else. Have you heard the last communication Alondra Gallegos sent back to Earth?"

"She said '*Is that,*'" I said.

"Any idea how she might have been planning on finishing that sentence?" he asked.

"None whatsoever. There's a million and one possible ways she was planning on finishing that sentence, including something like "*Is that the most beautiful thing you've ever seen?*" or something similarly non-oh-my-God-aliens-are-attacking. Are you being serious right now?"

He leaned forward toward me, leaning one elbow on the side of the table.

"What if I told you that wasn't the end of the recording?"

I found myself completely at a loss for words. The waiter brought our entrées over, and I managed to register the thought *Geez, he's right, that really was fast* through the fog of incomprehension that had suddenly settled in on my brain.

"What was the rest of the recording?"

He leaned back and knit his fingers together behind his head, an immensely self-satisfied look settling onto his features.

"I'll play it for you after dinner. Eat up, it's going to be a long night. You don't want Sajad deciding you're done. I've seen him steal steaks before."

"I didn't think monkeys ate meat," I said.

"This one does. Or, at least, he's willing to steal it and run away, which might as well be the same thing."

"So what was the end of the recording?"

"Not telling," he said, the smirk back on his face.

"No, seriously."

"Not telling. I mean it. I am a Certified Mad Genius, in the sense that I have a literal certificate in a pile of paper somewhere around here declaring me a Mad Genius, and it has an embossed gold-foil stamp on it that makes it look very official. As a Certified Mad Genius I'm able to deny people simple requests arbitrarily any time I like and there is nothing that they can do about it."

For the second time in two minutes I found myself at a loss for words. Part of me wanted to strangle him. Another part of me was busy admiring the guy's sheer chutzpah, and was willing to let him get away with his nonsense just because he was so direct and open about it. The rest of me still strongly desired strangulation, possibly followed by stabbing and violation of the body, but was rational enough about it to be willing to wait until after he'd played the recording for me. *And flown me back to the mainland*, my reasonable brain-parts added.

"So, we're, what, eating then?"

"We're eating." He tucked into his ravioli with no small amount of gusto. It looked as if it had come from a can. More than one can, probably, since there was a fair amount of it. My steak, on the other hand, was absolutely delicious, and the baked potato looked too large to be natural.

I waited a few minutes before I started asking more questions.

"How long have you lived on the island?"

He thought about it for a second, a piece of ravioli perched theatrically on a fork halfway to his mouth. "I'm trying to remember what you were telling your buddy earlier this evening. Five years, right?"

"So you were listening."

"Funny thing about that cabin," he said. "Perfect acoustics. Especially if you say certain words, like *Zahav*, or *island*. If you happen to stand in the right other place on the island, the sound just gets piped straight there. It's amazing."

How does he keep managing to make ridiculous and offensive things sound acceptable? "Would that perfectly amazing bit of acoustics possibly involve one person standing underneath a microphone at one place and another person standing near a computer at the other place? And maybe wearing headphones while he did it?"

He didn't answer, just fed another piece of ravioli into his mouth and shrugged.

"So were we right or not?"

"Close enough," he said. "Five years or so for the place to be constructed, yeah. I've been here myself full-time for about two years."

"Why?"

"You'll see in a little while. The short version is that I needed private land where it was unlikely that anyone would be bothering me, and buying an island seemed like the simplest way to do it. I'm close enough to the mainland that getting supplies here isn't a problem, and other than the occasional hurricane the weather is nice. You brought a bathing suit, right?"

"Don't have one. You paid for the whole thing yourself?"

He'd lost every trace of the somber tone he'd had when discussing the *Tycho* and was beginning to speak more rapidly, the pauses between words virtually nonexistent. "That's reasonable. There will be one in the cabin when you get back. I'm assuming you prefer trunks to Speedos, right?" He didn't wait for an answer. "It depends on how you define 'yourself,' I suppose. I own Zahav International pretty much outright. And I have virtually nothing to spend my own money on. And make no mistake, *I'm rich as hell.* There are few markets that are as lucrative as manufacturing planes and weaponry for the United States government, especially if you're willing to be slightly unethical and charge a hundred dollars for the occasional replacement nut or bolt. And when you've been doing it for a couple generations, like my family has, well... I could own more than one island, if you know what I mean."

"That may be the first time I've ever heard that sentence," I said.

He laughed. "It won't be the last. I enjoy saying it. Your turn now, though. Tell me about yourself."

I snorted. "I'd be willing to bet good money you know more about me than I do about you, Zub. You still haven't actually told me why I'm here, or why you contacted me instead of any of the half-million other hacks in America. I mean, this is fun and everything, but I'd like to have a clue by the time I'm done with my steak."

"Fine," he said. "You're no fun at all, did anybody ever tell you that? Born in Fort Wayne, Indiana, March 17th 1979. Parents John and Corrie Southern, mother's maiden name Hixson. One sister, Nicolette, two years younger, who you don't see that often but is still probably the person you're closest to out of all your living relatives. One niece, Courtney, aged two and a half, one nephew, Joseph, aged six months. Father deceased, pneumonia, 2006. BA, journalism, Northwestern University, 2000. Master's degree in Journalism, Indiana University, 2002. One bestselling book entitled *Nothing to Bury: the Martyrs of the Space Race,* which I have read and found compelling, if saddled with a wildly morbid title, a relatively successful career in freelance writing, based mostly in Indianapolis. Engaged once, didn't work out, no wife or children."

"You're good," I said. He was trying to bait me with that abortion bit, and I wasn't going to let him.

"Most of that was on the Internet, actually," he said. "Nothing too fancy."

"We weren't so lucky on you," I said.

"True," he said, nodding. His plate was clean. He pushed it toward Sajad, who picked it up and started licking marinara sauce off the porcelain. "That's what happens when you're homeschooled for your entire life. I never went to college, so there aren't any records on me. Spent my whole life rich, so I've never had a credit card, or a car loan, or been in any debt at all. By the terms most people use to find things out about each other, I barely even exist."

He snickered.

"Finish your steak, Gabe. Let's go for a drive."

I finished my steak.

THREE

There was another of the three-passenger electric transports waiting for us outside. Zub clambered into the driver's seat, the monkey perched on his shoulder, and gestured at the back seat for me. Driving slightly faster than was strictly necessary, he headed back down the hilltop the observatory was set upon and turned toward the airport.

"I need you to understand something," he said over his shoulder as he drove. "What you're about to see is more or less a complete secret outside of this island. My company has thousands of employees, and the ones working here are the hundred or so who are the most talented and loyal among that group. Anything that I tell you tonight should be considered off the record and embargoed for the time being. You'll get to write about it-- I chose you for a reason-- but not quite yet."

"I'm not agreeing to that," I said. "What are you going to do, hold me hostage unless I agree to your demands?"

"No," he said. "But you're going to agree to my demands, don't worry." That should have sounded like a threat, but he said it with a smile on his face. *He's absolutely convinced I'm going to do what he wants*, I thought. *He's been convinced that I'd do what he wanted since he made that first phone call. This guy is either the largest narcissist on the planet or he knows me better than I do.*

On the other hand, it very well could be both.

We were heading toward the enormous building in the corner of the airport. The thing looked familiar from close up, but I couldn't quite figure out why. "Beautiful, isn't it?" Zub said. "The VAB is one of the largest buildings in the world. It can withstand a category 5 hurricane, piece of cake. The entire population of the island can fit inside of it if we need to."

"What's VAB stand for?"

Zub looked at me. "I'm kind of surprised you don't know, actually. No looking it up. And I don't want to tell you yet. It'll spoil the secret."

Zub pulled the transport into a parking spot near a side door. The door led into a small conference room, dominated by a large glass-topped oak table with several expensive-looking leather seats around it. Zub collapsed into one of the seats-- not, I noticed, one at either head of the table-- and gestured for me to sit opposite him. I took my place. Sajad jumped to the top of the chair at the head of the table. He screeched, which Zub took as the sign to start the meeting.

He tapped a button set underneath the table and the glass blazed into life. A holographic representation of the *Tycho* appeared a foot above the table.

"Understand something," he said. "The *Tycho* should have worked. There were a number of decisions made by NASA and by my father that I did not think were in the best interests of the mission, the company, or the astronauts. But the science and the engineering were sound even if the ideas behind them weren't perfect."

"What did you think should have been different?" I asked.

"For starters, the ship was launched foolishly," he said. "The *Tycho* launched from Earth to rendezvous with the International Space Station for refueling and cargofitting. This was almost completely unnecessary, and actually required the ship to burn *more* fuel than would have been used in a direct burn from Earth. The *Tycho* also carried enough fuel to relaunch from Mars back to Earth. What that meant was that the ship was absurdly heavy-- it carried enough food, water, and oxygen for the entire round trip, plus enough fuel for two burns-- one from low Earth orbit to Mars and one from Mars back to Earth. It wouldn't have even been *possible* with the fuels we were using as recently as a decade ago. The weight would have been too much. Even then, the ship was heavy, heavy, heavy, and it didn't need to be."

"Is that why it exploded?"

"No. It made the mission impractical compared to other alternatives, but not dangerous. These weren't bad people that built the ship this way, it was just... well, we'll say less than completely modern thinking."

Interesting. He's covering for his father. "It seems to me that carrying a couple thousand tons of rocket fuel a few million miles more than you need to would count as dangerous."

He shrugged. "Well, okay, you're right. There are other problems with a heavy ship-- braking into Mars orbit was a lot trickier than it needed to be, for example, since a ship with high momentum is a lot harder to stop and Mars' atmosphere isn't very thick, they'd have had to fire retrorockets to get themselves into orbit. That was tricky to program for, but in practice... well, we've done more complicated things, y'know?"

He reached out a hand, waved it through the image. "She was such a pretty ship."

"She was," I said. "What happened to her?"

"I'm getting there," he said. "The biggest problem I had with the *Tycho* mission wasn't the build model they used. It was the timing of the mission. How technical do you want me to get here?"

"I'm not that bright," I said.

He pushed another button, and a simplified map of the solar system replaced the *Tycho* hologram. "Simple version, then. The problem with going back and forth between Earth and Mars is that they're both moving. What this means is that the timing of the missions determines how long it takes to get from one place to another. It's not like going someplace on Earth, where two places are always the exact same distance apart."

He touched another button, and flight paths popped up on the hologram, traced in glowing blue light. "The ideal flight path to Mars is called a Hohmann transfer. It takes the least amount of time and energy but actually involves flying the largest distance. Takes about six months, give or take. The problem is getting back. The NASA mission design people had a few different possibilities to choose from as far as how long the astronauts were going to stay on Mars and how long the flight back was going to take. They decided to go with a short stay and a long return back. They were only going to be on Mars for thirty days."

"That's thirty days longer than anybody else has ever been there," I pointed out.

"It's also completely ridiculous. The mission cost billions of dollars and who knows how many man-hours to orchestrate. And they were going to be on Mars for a *month*. Mars has dust storms, did you know that? They can be planet-sized. If the *Tycho* had hit Mars during a dust storm, they probably wouldn't have authorized a landing until it cleared. There have been entire missions that have been completely scrapped at arrival at Mars because of dust storms. They've been crushed on the way to the planet's surface."

"So is that what happened?"

He waved a hand at me. "Nah, just bad engineering. My point is that if you're going to invest all of this time to get to Mars you should *leave some time to do something* when you get there. One or two minor snafus on the way into Mars and they lose the whole science part of the mission, just to spend over a year getting back home. It was completely stupid."

"So what should they have done?"

He pointed out another line on the map in front of him. "This trajectory is similar to the route they used to get to Mars, but the return trajectory is completely different. On this plan, the one I favored, it takes the same amount of time to get to Mars, but the time on-planet is much longer-- a little over a year and a half. The flight back is exactly the same duration as the flight in, just in the opposite direction."

Something didn't sound right. "Doesn't it add a whole lot more weight to the ship to have to pack that much more supplies? That's, what, two and a half years worth of food, water, and oxygen? The ship would have to be huge."

"There are ways around that," Zub said. "You're a step ahead of me. The point is, they didn't go that way. I lost the debate and they went with the short-stay, long-return mission. Like I said, stupid."

"But they never made it to the planet's surface."

"No, they didn't. Or, at least, we don't think they did." He held a hand out and Sajad placed a memory chip into his hand.

Did I just imagine that? No, I hadn't. The *monkey* had just given him a chip.

He put the chip somewhere underneath the table.

"If I play this for you, Gabe, you tell no one about it until I authorize it. I'm not playing around right now. There are less than a dozen people on the planet who know what was on the final transmission from the ship. Two of them are in this room with you and one is a monkey. Another is the President of the United States. You either agree to hold this in complete secrecy right now or I return you to the mainland tomorrow and you never find out anything."

God. He had me. The sneaky little jerk had played this exactly right, and he had me just hooked enough to agree to whatever he wanted me to do.

"Am I going to have government thugs chasing after me for the rest of my life if you play this thing for me? Is it actually legal?"

He shrugged. "Eh. Probably not. For all I know it's actually treason. But if you play your cards right, even if the government thugs decide to come after you you'll be so famous that you'll be untouchable."

Yep. He had me.

"Play the damn thing, Zub."

He grinned that snarky little grin of his again.

"I thought so."

*　*　*

The first ten or fifteen minutes of the audio file were the same stuff I'd heard before. I hadn't listened to the *Tycho's* descent into Mars orbit since watching the live feed on the day the ship lost contact, but I found that my memories of the event were pretty clear once I was listening to it again. Despite not really knowing what they were talking about half the time-- most of the conversation was either a time-delayed exchange of technical information between Mars and Earth or the crew basically chattering, keeping up a description of what they were seeing to accompany the video and images they were sending back to the billions watching at home. Most of the talk was between Gallegos, the mission commander, and Brown, the lead pilot.

And then, the final moment. Or, at least, the last moment that most of the world had heard. On the public version of the tape, you can hear Gallegos say "Is that" and then everything-- video, sound, everything-- cuts off. There's a couple of minutes of lag between Earth and Mars, so it was a little while before Mission Control figured out that anything was wrong in the first place, and a few minutes more before anybody really started to get concerned about it. On Zub's tape, though, there was no lag to worry about-- the audio seemed to be straight from inside the command deck of the ship.

I'd spent a fair amount of time imagining what she might have said. I'd never even come close to guessing what actually came out of her mouth.

"Is that... Code Ares, NASA, lock the doors and confirm a code Ares... God, is that a green spot?"

A bunch of things flashed through my head very quickly, even before any of the other crew members had a chance to react. Understand something-- they were probably forty thousand miles above the Martian surface when she said that. "Spot," in this case, would have to have meant something, at the minimum, several miles wide. And *lock the doors* was NASA code for *the shit has hit the fan.*

Lieutenant Harrison Brown's reaction, given the circumstances, was a marvelous example of restraint.

"Confirm green spot on Mars, Captain."

"The hell is that?"

I snickered at this for a second. Gallegos had already struck me as the type who had spent enough time around these people that she no longer felt the need to stick with typical NASA commander talk.   Between her and Brown, the second-in-command, she was by far the more informal.

"No idea, Commander.   We're too high up to get a good look."

Zub paused the audio.

I didn't waste any time.   "Do you have any video of this?"

"Not a single second, no.   The interesting thing is that they were actually *watching* video when they were talking about this. The *Tycho* didn't actually have any external windows.   It wasn't like they were watching through the windshield.   Gallegos was looking at a video feed from an external camera on the ship; the data never made it back.   Listen to the rest of this."   He hit play again.

"Are we locked into orbit yet?"

"Aerobraking completed, Captain.   I'm willing to begin panicking now if you want me to."

"Get the rest of the crew up here.   I'm going to take a closer look at the video."

I could hear the rest of the crew cram into the command deck-- which couldn't have been very big-- as Gallegos backed up the video feed.

"How far can we zoom in?"   This was Newsome's voice, not as deep as Brown's baritone rumble.

"Pretty far, I think."

At this point, a babble of voices.   Not a whole lot of it was distinct.

Zub stopped the file again.

"I won't bother you with the rest of it.   There's not a whole lot that's coherent.   They spend an awful lot of time talking over each other and there's quite a lot of yelling, some of it in Spanish and some of it in Chinese.   The point is, they'd located a patch on Mars-- as near as I can tell, somewhere around a hundred to a hundred and twenty-five miles wide-- that was green.   Mars is not supposed to be green, pretty much ever.   And then the audio cuts out.   We don't know what happened next."

"That's impossible," I said, fully expecting Zub to explain to me why I was wrong.

"You are completely correct," he responded. "It is impossible for there to be plants on Mars. It is, for starters, much too cold. The soil is actually relatively amenable to certain Earth plants-- basically anything that could grow in highly alkaline soil could probably take root on Mars. Or, at least, it could be theoretically possible if we wanted to do a whole lot of babysitting. But you can't plant ten thousand square miles of asparagus on a planet with hardly any *atmosphere* and not a whole lot of natural sunlight compared to Earth. It's impossible."

"Have you looked for it from Earth? We were in an observatory not half an hour ago."

"I have, yes. I haven't found it yet. It's harder to do than it seems, though, since it's difficult to calculate exactly where they were over the planet's surface when they moved into orbit. The green patch could literally be anywhere, and even a bit that size would be terribly difficult to resolve with Earth-based telescopes."

"What about the *Koothrappali?*" The latest-generation space telescope had been placed into low Earth orbit a year ago, and was supposedly high-resolution enough to count the freckles on a Venusian fly.

"Made a number of requests. All denied. There was a waiting list for the thing a million miles long, and believe me, they're all looking at the center of the universe or chasing new planets. Nobody's pointing *Kooth* at Mars, and I think even if it was my turn they wouldn't actually let me do it. Hell, I think Mars is probably actually too *close* for it."

I was flummoxed.

"I'm flummoxed," I said. You've got to take advantage of your chances to say that word; they don't come by all that often.

"You can't imagine how I feel. I've been studying this planet for decades. There aren't any damn *green patches* on Mars."

"So what happens when the file ends?"

"That's the bad news," Zub said, standing up from the table and beginning to pace around the room. "The part about the ship completely ceasing all conversation with Earth? That actually happened. About ten minutes, maybe, after she declares Code Ares."

"Wait," I interrupted. "I forgot to ask about that part. The original story was the team stopped broadcasting right before she said that. What's a Code Ares?"

"NASA security code phrase for the broadcast. As soon as NASA Mission Control heard her declare a Code Ares, they cut the live broadcast. She was supposed to call that if there was any sort of major problem or something they didn't know how to deal with. NASA didn't want another *Challenger*, didn't want another generation of kids scared out of their minds at the thought of going into space. They figured that if a Code Ares was declared, they cut the broadcast, which was on a time-delay anyway, and then blame sunspots or something like that once they'd dealt with the problem later on with no one the wiser. So they did. And then the ship went blank a few minutes later anyway."

"So what do you think is going on, Zub?"

"I think they're still on Mars, Mr. Southern. I think that after the broadcast discontinued, they decided to go ahead with the mission, probably entirely unaware that they'd stopped broadcasting. I still have no idea, by the way, how that happened. And I think that eventually they would have realized that they couldn't make contact with Earth anymore."

He waved a hand through the floating Mars above the table.

"And I think that there were four people on that ship who had literally risked their lives to be the first human beings to set foot on an alien planet. And I think that, if I were on that ship, that there was not a force on Heaven or Earth that could have prevented me from touching the surface of Mars once I had gotten so close."

"They didn't come back," I said. "They didn't blow up. So the only remaining possibility..."

"Is that they're still on Mars," Zub finished. "Which is impossible. But the impossible thing is the only thing that makes any sense right now."

"Why am I here, Zub?"

"You're going to Mars with me, Gabe. And when we get back, you're going to tell the world about it. We're going to find the crew of the *Tycho*. And then we're going to be famous."

FOUR

"Yeah, *right*," I said.

This seemed to deflate his grandiose mood. He collapsed back into his chair and shut down the holographic solar system floating above the conference table.

"No, really. I'm going to Mars. You're coming with me. Like, really soon."

"I'm not an *astronaut*, Zub. Perhaps you've not noticed the paunchy belly and the relative lack of skills in physics and basic science, but believe me, they're there." *Or not there, as the case may be,* I thought, but he blew past my grammatical confusion.

"I want a journo with me, Gabe. I need somebody independent who can chronicle the trip while we're on it and tell everyone what happened when we return. That book you wrote on the *Challenger* and the *Columbia* was incredible. Don't tell me you haven't thought about doing a follow-up on the *Tycho*."

I had, actually, but had dismissed the thought as too macabre. There are better things to get typed as than "guy who writes about spaceships after they blow up," and I didn't really want to be that guy.

"You're telling me that you've got a second *Tycho* stashed someplace? You built two of them? You've got NASA willing to back you up for a second mission? Congress? How did you pull all of that off?"

"What am I, Gabe?" The light in his eyes was almost manic. I had a feeling it had been a long time since Ezekiel ben Zahav had enjoyed a conversation as much as he was enjoying this one.

"A Certified Mad Genius?"

"Indeed. Come with me. I need to show you something."

He stood up and bounded out of the room, Sajad close behind. I took a moment and sent a blink to AJ.

DEAR GOD I AM STUCK ON AN ISLAND WITH A MANIAC. PLEASE SEND THE MARINE CORPS.

A moment later, he sent me a smiley face in response. *This is why friends are not worth the effort,* I thought, and followed the man and the monkey out of the room. We exited through a back doorway-- not the one we'd entered the room through-- into a concrete-floored, dark corridor. The corridor was surprisingly unfinished-looking compared to the rest of the buildings I'd seen; there were open pipes and electrical cables running along the walls and the ceiling hadn't been put into place yet. Everything looked very industrial, with racks of tools and other unidentifiable objects lining some of the walls. The hallway terminated with an enormous steel double door that looked thick and securely locked enough to stop a tank. *It would probably be easier to blast through the walls then to break through the door.*

Zub keyed in a long identification code—- fifteen or twenty digits, it sounded like-- into a keypad next to the door. A panel next to the keypad slid aside, revealing a retina and palm scanner. Zub set his glasses on top of his head, looked at the retinal scanner, and placed his palm down. A moment later, there was a chime and the huge locks on the door disengaged.

Zub had his High Drama look back on his face again.

"Do you know why the first ship was called the *Tycho*, Mr. Southern?"

I did, actually. "It was named after Tycho Brahe, who was one of the first astronomers to keep detailed records of the orbits of the planets. Mars included."

"Very good!" Zub said, beaming like a preschool teacher. "True fact about Tycho Brahe-- he lost part of his nose in a duel when he was twenty. He wore a prosthetic nose made of copper for most of his life. Most people don't know that about him. But anyway. The point is that the ship was named after an astronomer. Have you ever heard of Johannes Kepler?"

"I have, but other than knowing that he's an astronomer, I don't really know very much about him."

"Kepler was one of Brahe's students. He continued Brahe's work in mapping out the orbits of the planets, and also was the first person to realize that planets move in ellipses around the sun. He also helped to refine the refracting telescope, along with any number of other things. He did not have a fake nose. I like him *better* than Tycho Brahe."

"You asked me a little while ago what VAB stands for. It stands for Vehicle Assembly Building."

He laid a hand upon the door and pushed. It opened more easily than I would have expected.

"Gabriel Southern, I'd like to introduce you to the *Johannes*."

There was a full-size, honest-to-god spaceship in the bay behind the door.

*   *   *

"My God," I said. "She's beautiful."

And she was. The *Tycho* had been an evolution from the old-style Space Shuttles, but she had had little art to her. She had looked less like a ship than a gigantic white plastic dart or toy rocket, something you'd shoot at someone with an air gun or maybe throw at a rubber circle on your lawn. There were no windows, no decoration or ornamentation other than a NASA logo and an American flag, really very little that was visually interesting at all.

The *Johannes* was her complete opposite. She looked sleek and futuristic next to the *Tycho's* sixties-era lawn toy design, all brushed metal and cobalt blue and purple highlights. Her wings flared back behind her instead of jutting out abruptly. There was a cluster of windows near the front of the ship, which would allow the astronauts to see the Red Planet with their own eyes instead of being limited to a digital image on a computer monitor.

"How?" was all I could say.

"I am very rich," Ezekiel ben Zahav responded. "And I have been very clever as well. The *Johannes,* most of her at least, is officially and legally a prototype. She just happens to be entirely functional. I actually got the government to fund most of her, when we were submitting designs for what turned out to be the *Tycho.* The *Tycho* was my father's design. This one was mine. All I had to do was finish her. You're looking at the most advanced vehicle the human race has ever constructed. She will get us to Mars, she will land on Mars, and she will get us back home again, safe and sound."

"You're unbelievable," I said. "The ship is unbelievable. You did this *on your own?*"

"I had help," he said. "We moved most of ZI's best people to the island once we started working on her full-time. There's room for five crew comfortably, ten if we want to be on top of each other all the time. Enough cargo space to keep the crew eating, breathing, and drinking comfortably for a round-trip to Mars with a stop off at Venus along the way. She lifts off from Earth, not LEO, so no nonsense docking with the Space Station along the way."

"I don't see rocket boosters," I said.

"On their way," Zub responded. "We've got a pair of disassembled ATLAS-VI class solid rocket boosters and an empty external fuel tank on a barge that should be here tomorrow or the day after; they're the same class of booster that the *Tycho* used. One of them will lift the ship into orbit and fire her toward Mars. The second is a backup in case one of them is damaged in transport."

"How do we get back, then?"

Zub smiled, for once not looking snarky or sarcastic, just drinking in my elation. "Tomorrow. I've left a transport for you outside. It's programmed to get you back to the cabin; just sit in the thing and press the "Go" button and it will drive itself. Tomorrow, you can meet the rest of the crew, we'll talk more about what the mission actually entails, and we can explore the ship a little bit."

"What about now?" I asked. "Some other surprises in store?"

"Nope," he said. "I'm just tired, and I have a fair amount of actual work waiting for me. I figured I'd leave you here with the ship for a while. Take some time to get used to her, then go back home and relax. Be up and ready around nine or so tomorrow morning. Then we'll start."

He patted me on the shoulder as he left the hangar. "You can get out the same way we came in. The security system knows how many people there are in here. The door will lock behind you once all of us are out."

"What about the monkey?"

"I programmed it to ignore the monkey. The monkey does what the monkey wants to do."

"Good night, Ezekiel."

"Good night, Gabe. I told you I was going to change your life, didn't I?"

I don't think he actually did, I thought.

*   *   *

It took me twenty minutes before I could actually reach out and touch the *Johannes*. The events of the last 24 hours were almost more than my tiny man-brain could handle, and I found that just standing nearby and staring at her was about as much as I could take for a while. Once I did, an actual physical charge passed through me for a moment, and I spent a horrible second wondering if Zub had rigged the ship with some sort of electroshock security system before I realized it was just tension releasing. The main body of the ship was all gunmetal grey, cast in what looked like aluminum but was probably some sort of high-tech ceramic. None of the *Tycho's* staid ivory color here. It was cool to the touch, with a faint texture to it. It sat on three wheels, most of it-- *her*-- five feet or so off the ground. 150, 175 feet long, maybe.

Is this thing going to take me to Mars? Really?

I could doubt Zub's sanity for any number of reasons but I had trouble doubting his sincerity. He'd refused to tell me things on several occasions-- mostly out of his weirdly misplaced sense of drama and mystery-- but I hadn't caught him in a lie yet; at least not one that he hadn't himself admitted to immediately. And he'd had no reason at all to pluck me out of Indiana and offer to put me on a space ship if his offer wasn't genuine. The answer to *why me?* seemed to be a combination of having written the book in a way that caught his eye and pure, blind, dumb luck. I had no skills whatsoever to offer the crew. I was sure he was planning on training me to be useful *somehow*, but other than that it seemed like I was mostly sucking up oxygen and water.

This is stupid this is stupid this is stupid this is stupid.

This was *awesome*.

I hadn't ever wanted to be an astronaut. I was interested in science, sure; you don't get to be a science writer without a healthy layman's interest in and knowledge of the subject, but standing next to Zub I looked like a fifth-grader. And I hadn't ever *tried* to be an astronaut. But to go to *Mars?* Really?

It was crazy. And it was too big of a decision to make by myself. I needed to make a couple of phone calls.

Hell, can I even talk to anyone about this? He said I couldn't mention the mission. Surely I'm not expected to just drop off the face of the earth without a word to anyone.

The *Johannes* sat there, staring at me with her cobalt-blue eyes, as if daring me. *You know you want to.*

I sent Zub a blink. CAN I TELL ANYONE I'M LEAVING? IF I DECIDE TO DO IT?

He answered as quickly as usual. He wasn't *that* busy, whatever he'd left me to do.

GO AHEAD, blinked the response. UNLESS YOU MEAN YOU WANT TO TALK TO YOUR FRIEND AJ ABOUT ME AGAIN. I WANT YOU TO LEAVE MY NAME OUT OF IT, AND DON'T MENTION WHERE YOU'RE GOING. HE'LL PUT TWO AND TWO TOGETHER TOO QUICKLY, I THINK. YOU'RE SMART ENOUGH TO TALK YOUR WAY AROUND THAT DETAIL IF YOU NEED TO, RIGHT?

"Yeah, I am," I said, staring at the REPLY icon.

CALL YOUR MOM, THEN. OR WHOEVER. JUST DON'T SAY ANYTHING STUPID.

I left the hangar, lost in thought. As I walked out through the security door, it beeped again and swung closed behind me, the locks engaging with an intimidating metallic *thunk*. I walked through the conference room, where Zub had left a five-foot-wide hologram of Mars activated on the table, rotating slowly in the middle of the room. There was no mysterious green spot on the hologram. I left the room, and as I closed the door behind me I saw the table blink off as the door shut. *Everything in this place knows I'm here*, I thought. As promised, there was a transport outside, with a glowing green button marked GO on the dashboard. I pushed it and the transport silently started up and drove me back to the guest cabin. We didn't pass another living soul on the way back.

As we pulled into the driveway for the cabin, the porch light and the light in the living room turned on automatically. I ignored them and walked into the bathroom, trying not to be creeped out when the car turned a circle in the driveway and drove off with no one behind the wheel. On a whim, I took my iLid out of my eye and dropped it into a vial of cleaning solution, then took out the earpiece too and left it on the bathroom sink.

Completely cut off from modern communication for the first time in several weeks, I wandered into my back yard to look at the sky. Even at home, which wasn't an especially large town by any stretch of the imagination, light pollution often drowned out most of the night sky. On Eunostos, on the other hand, there weren't enough people for there to be light pollution-- "*real* dark," my grandmother used to call it-- and as a result the emerging night sky was incredible. There were thousands of visible stars overhead and the full moon was shining brightly, with not a cloud to be seen anywhere. My astronomy wasn't good enough to know if Mars was up there somewhere; for all I knew, it was on the opposite side of the planet from me.

I stared at the universe for a few minutes, trying to decide who, if anyone, I wanted to talk this over with. I could hear insects chirping in the grass and trees around me, but not a trace of human-generated noise. It was weird; I knew, intellectually, that there were people close by enough to hear me if I shouted, but at that moment it was like I was the only person on the island.

I thought back about what I knew-- just the raw facts-- about the *Tycho's* mission, and imagined what I would have to have given up to be on that flight. Round-trip to Mars and back was supposed to have taken just short of three years. Could I just *disappear* for three entire years? Ben Zahav hadn't actually mentioned paying me, but as wealthy as he was surely I wouldn't have to worry about making sure my bills were paid during that time. I wasn't seeing anyone; I had a few old friends, but it actually wouldn't be terribly difficult to stay in touch with them if I wanted to while I was on the trip. My mother and my sister would miss me; my niece and nephew were too young to notice I was gone. I didn't have any pets and I could put most of my stuff in storage for the time I would be gone. Heck, if I needed to, I could even file reports while I was on the ship and make additional money that way. Surely Zub wouldn't be too bothered so long as I waited until after we launched. Who was going to stop us?

Depressing, but true: I could disappear from the face of the planet for two or three years without tearing my life or anyone else's to shreds.

Man, the stars were *so pretty* out here.

You'll never get another chance like this again. Not once, as long as you live, ever again.

"I'm going to Mars," I said.

*   *   *

I went to bed about half an hour later, fully expecting to spend the entire night tossing and turning, and surprised myself by collapsing into sleep almost immediately. I dreamt of trees and grasses, and lying out in a field underneath a pale, cloudless red sky. I woke up early, which almost never happens to me. Even on my best days I was always a late sleeper. The island sun was bright but the heat hadn't settled in yet.

There was a pair of brand-new swimming trunks in my size on the kitchen table, with a plastic Christmas bow on top of them. I hadn't noticed them on the way into the house. I decided to take Zub's advice and go for a swim, since I had the time and the equipment. I didn't know my way around Eunostos all that well yet, of course, but finding the beach on an island wasn't the most challenging feat I'd ever attempted.

There were a few other people either running or swimming on the beach, all of whom seemed content to ignore me. This surprised me at first; surely the population of the island was small enough that the presence of a stranger would be noticed immediately. *He's probably circulated your picture on a dossier to everyone on the island already,* I thought, and lost myself in the water before I had time to pursue the idea any further. Swimming had been one of my favorite sports (in the interest of the strictest accuracy, the only sport I liked at all) through high school and college, and there had been a time when I could swim for two or three miles without stopping for a break. The beach didn't have lap lanes, though, so I satisfied myself by swimming out far enough that I couldn't reach the bottom and then floating around, enjoying the warm water.

No swimming on Mars, I thought. *Heck, chances are you'll go two years without so much as a good bath.* So be it, then. I could enjoy this while it lasted.

I lasted about 45 minutes before the word *sharks* floated through my head, followed quickly by the word *jellyfish,* and I decided to stick to pools with clearly delineated lap lines. Zub blinked me while I was swimming back to shore.

LOVE THE WATER THIS MORNING, RIGHT?

"Yeah," I replied. "It's fantastic. I wish I had a private beach back in Indiana."

THERE WILL BE A CAR WAITING FOR YOU IN TEN MINUTES. YOU'LL MEET PEOPLE WHO TAKE LIFE SERIOUSLY TODAY. DRESS WELL.

"Oh, goody," I said, and picked up the pace back to the cabin. I'd brought exactly one decent suit. I only owned two. Hopefully it would be good enough. I was mostly dressed by the time the car showed up, again with nobody behind the wheel.

The car brought me back to the hangar. Mr. Green, dressed in what looked like an identical suit to the one he'd had on the day before, met me at door and ushered me to the conference room. Zub's seat was empty, but there were three other people sitting at the table I hadn't seen before-- an older man with a sour look on his face and two women.

"Hi," I said, waving at them. "I'm Gabe Southern. I, uh, suppose you know who I am already?"

"They sure do," Zub said, managing to make a theatrical entrance again. *He had to be out there waiting for the right timing on that,* I thought. "Uncle Tsvika here doesn't think you should be here," this with an offhanded gesture at the older man, who was ostentatiously seated at the head of the table. "But I think the other two are on board. Gabe, meet the rest of the crew."

"Zvi ben Zahav," said the older man. He sounded as if he'd spent most of his life smoking cigarettes and swallowing glass. I'd never heard a deeper voice. If he was really Zub's uncle, I couldn't see it. He was very nearly Zub's polar opposite-- short, iron-grey hair instead of Zub's mop of black; rough, dark skin where Zub's was pale and smooth; barrel-chested and intimidating-looking, with arms that were bulging out of the pressed suit jacket he was wearing, where Zub was skinny and weak-looking, still wearing the exact same clothes he'd been wearing the night before. I wondered if he had actually slept since I'd seen him last.

Zvi hadn't bothered to stand or extend a hand to me, but he looked to be several inches shorter than average as well. *Isn't there a height requirement for the military?* Then again, he was almost certainly an Israeli. I was pretty sure they all had to join up over there at some point; he'd just stayed in.

"Uncle Tsvika doesn't mean to be rude," Zub said. "He'll warm up to you sooner or later, and I doubt he'll bite before then. At least not much."

The older man shot a glare at his nephew, but remained silent. "He's going to be our head pilot. Most of us will share duties on the voyage, at least to some extent, but Tsvika could fly a cantaloupe if you told him he had to."

One of the two women stood up, standing taller than me by an inch or two, and offered me her hand. She was my age, give or take a couple of years, African-American, with long, braided hair with a couple of shoots of grey in it and startlingly blue eyes. Cosmetically altered, maybe. She had an iLid on too, but the other eye looked natural. "Hi, I'm Dr. Celeste Flye. Ship's engineer. Zub will tell you he knows every nut and bolt on the ship. Chances are I'm the one who actually drilled the holes, though. I'm also the xenocartographer. I know Mars almost as well as I know the ship." She was dressed the part, too; not as informally as Zub was, but I got the feeling that the clothes she was wearing had sported oil stains in the past and were very likely to do so again in the future. Her grip was stronger than I expected, much firmer than Zub's had been.

"And this is Dr. Rosansky," Zub continued. "She's our medic and also our chief scientist. One of those MD/Ph.D dual types. She's the only person on the planet who is allowed to be smarter than me."

"Kathryn," Dr. Rosansky said, extending her hand. She was Zub's age or possibly even a little younger, all curves and blond hair. She was quite possibly the most attractive doctor I'd ever seen. Even for someone who was "allowed" to be smarter than Zub, she still looked way too young to have even one of her degrees, much less both of them.

Zub, as if reading my mind, blinked me.

UNDERESTIMATE HER AND SHE WILL EAT YOUR BRAIN, it said. I hadn't seen his lips or hands move, nor heard his voice. *How the hell did you just do that?* The guy was either some sort of ventriloquist or he'd managed to somehow install a cybernetic interface into his iLid lens. Zub was good, but capturing nerve impulses through his *eye* sounded slightly above his pay grade.

I SET IT TO SEND RIGHT AROUND THE TIME I'D BE INTRODUCING YOU, came the second blink. IMPRESSED? I'M IMPRESSED, YOU SHOULD BE TOO.

I glared at him. He grinned at me, both impressed *and* pleased with himself.

I ALSO SENT THAT ONE TO ARRIVE JUST AFTER THE FIRST ONE, came another blink. AND THIS ONE TO COME AFTER THAT ONE.

"Enough, Zub," I said, and Dr. Rosansky laughed.

"You're in on this nonsense that he's making me look at, then?"

"I've been getting the look you just gave me for my entire life," she said, still laughing at me. "I could either choose to get angry about it every single day or deal with it and move on. I don't have the time or the energy to get angry." Her accent was pure rural Texas, which didn't make it any easier to take her seriously.

"You're a more reasonable person than I am, then," I said.

"Plus she'll be ancient and wrinkled in, like, four more years, tops," Zub said. "She'll stop getting that *no way is she smart* look in no time."

Dr. Rosansky punched Zub in the arm, nearly knocking him to the ground. I made a mental note: *When Zub says "serious people," what he means is his uncle.* And he hadn't treated him with anything resembling deference, either. Only Dr. Flye seemed exempt from abuse.

"It's nice to meet all of you," I said. "I'm the hack, which means that I will be breathing your oxygen and eating your food for the next two or three years without providing much else of real value." *If she can roll with the punches, so can I,* I thought.

"This is the problem, of course," said Zvi, and he was *definitely* native-born Israeli with that accent, "my nephew thinks that with you he will make himself famous. But he is already famous, and more fame is not worth the risk. Each member of the crew for a trip such as this must be able to pull weight," and at this he turned to Zub, "and this man weighs more than he pulls."

"Gabe will be fine," Zub said. "He's smarter than he looks, and he's used to *noticing* things. We don't have the ground support that NASA does, where any problem has two thousand people and millions of dollars ready to work it at the bidding of the crew. We have the people *here* and the people on the *Johannes*. We need somebody who can think out of the box, somebody who hasn't spent their entire life either taking orders or doing experiments." His voice lowered, his tone suddenly softer. "We need him, Tsvika. Trust me on this. I know what I'm doing."

"How far away is the launch?" I asked. "I mean, I assume
you have time to train me to be useful *somehow,* right?"

"One month, basically," Celeste said. "Optimal launch path
to Mars hits in twenty-seven days. We've got a decent launch
window around that time if the weather turns bad, where it's
mostly a matter of how hard we burn on the way out of Earth's
atmosphere, but we need to launch within a month."

Zub jumped back in. "More importantly, I intend to proceed
as if the crew of the *Tycho* can be rescued. We're a bare
minimum of six months from touchdown on the planet's surface
if we launch *tomorrow.* We will launch during the window
unless a hurricane hits Eunostos. Nothing else stops us."

"How's that even going to work, though?" I asked. "You
said the ship was big enough for five. There are five of us. The
crew of the *Tycho* was four, which makes nine for the trip back.
How are we going to carry enough food for that many people,
not to mention water, air, and fuel? Does the ship have that kind
of cargo capacity?"

"Two answers to that," Zub answered. "First, we're not
bringing a lot of tonnage with us in terms of scientific equipment
and the like. There's more cargo space than you might imagine
available on that ship, and the ATLAS-VI boosters have plenty
of power to throw us where we need to go almost regardless of
what the ship weighs."

"And the trip back? Are we bringing a spare booster, too?
Is that even possible?"

"That's the awesome part," Zub said. "Everything else we
need is already there."

Knowing that he was planning on that statement eliciting
some sort of surprised response from me, I kept my face still and
tried not to react. He stood there for a few moments, then
shrugged his shoulders and kept talking.

"This plan has been in effect since the day after the *Tycho*
went dark, Gabe. The good doctors and I have been working
together for a good long time, and between the three of us we've
got this thing pretty well figured out. The *Johannes* will not be
the first time that Zahav International has launched a ship toward
Mars."

"Well, of course not," I said. "The *Tycho* was a ZI ship."

For a few seconds, I had the deep satisfaction of seeing Ezekiel ben Zahav caught off guard. I savored it.

"Okay, true, and also shut up. It's not the second, either, is the point. Nine months ago, we launched *this* into Martian orbit." He pushed another few buttons on his side of the conference table and the holograms reappeared. It looked like three solid rocket boosters and a fuel tank strapped together, with what looked like an oversized crew vehicle attached to the top of one of the boosters. The booster the crew vehicle was attached to was heavily modified, with a number of doodads and bits of machinery attached to the sides and base.

"Booster the First carried Booster the Second into low Earth orbit and fired it toward Mars. It arrived into orbit about a year ago, and began setting up everything that we will need in order to get back, including setting up a domicile for us to live in while we're there. The Earth Return Support Vehicle— the ERSV, for short-- will remain in orbit. Neither ship is manned, obviously. The ERSV contains enough supplies to get ten human beings back from Mars the hard way. The food's not tasty, mind you, and even Uncle Tsvika will be desperate for cheeseburgers by the time we get back to Earth, but we'll live. There's a ton of spare medical equipment as well in case any of the survivors are sick or injured."

"And the booster?"

"Is empty. And is, literally as we speak, sitting on the surface of Mars and finishing up the process of synthesizing a couple hundred tons of rocket fuel and stockpiled oxygen out of the Martian atmosphere. By the time we get there, it'll have filled itself with enough fuel to get us back and enough oxygen to keep us breathing the whole way. It's even got low-orbit launch capacity. It can rejoin the ERSV in low Martian orbit without human input, so we can bring it to us if we discover the green spot is on the other side of the planet from where we set it down."

Now *that* was impressive.

"That's brilliant."

"Yeah. But it's not my idea. It's been around since the 1990s, believe it or not, in one form or another. We've modified the particulars somewhat, since we don't intend to colonize the planet right now, but they could have done this twenty-five years ago with the tech they had then."

"He *wishes* it was his idea, though," said Kathryn.

Zub actually stuck out his tongue at her. "I wish a lot of things were my idea. Some of them even are."

"So what happens next?" I asked.

Kathryn stood up. "Fun stuff," she said. "First, I stick you with dozens of needles and make you do unpleasant medical tests to make certain that you're not going to suddenly die on me while we're in outer space. Then, after that, you belong to Celeste, who is going to put you through even *more* unpleasant testing. After that you go to Zvi, and he may just kill you."

"I will not," Zvi intoned portentously. "He may kill us. I will not hurt him."

"Tsvika's going to go over the basics of flying the *Johannes* with you," Zub said. "We want everybody along to at least understand where the giant Please Don't Press This button is, and the Please Take Me Home Now button, too. But that probably won't be for a few days. How long did you pack for?"

"Three days," I said. "So two more after today before I have to do laundry or be back somewhere Stateside."

"You've got time for the two of us, then," Celeste said. "Her today. Me tomorrow. Then you go back to the mainland long enough to organize your affairs and rejoin us here."

"Speaking of my affairs," I said to Zub, "we need to discuss certain issues, you and I. I mean, I haven't actually agreed to go yet."

He didn't hesitate even a moment. "Five million dollars, American money, right now, and one of my accountants makes sure all your debts and any outstanding bills get taken care of immediately while you're on the ship. Ten million in life insurance to your designated dependent or dependents if you die. You agree to not need the life insurance and to chronicle the trip, as well as whatever else we need you to do while offplanet. Oh, and eternal fame."

Holy Christ. "Right," I gulped. "Glad we discussed that. I'm in."

"I thought you would be," he said. "I'll have my guy give you a call this evening sometime."

Holy God, I'm going to Mars, I thought, as Zub, Celeste, and Zvi left the room, leaving me alone with Kathryn

.

FIVE

Kathryn turned out to have a small medical clinic all to herself on the "town" part of the island, and for the first time I got to see what life was like on Eunostos for the small group of employees that actually lived there. Most of the staff, it seemed, worked either at the small airport, mostly serving as technical support in some capacity or another for the *Johannes*, or at the observatory; I had just been there too late and too early, respectively, to have seen much activity. There was a small commercial district, too-- basically a Main Street-- that sported a couple of restaurants, a general goods and electronics store, a grocery, a movie theater that was showing the latest films and holopictures, and a combination bowling alley, arcade, and miniature golf course. I suspected there was probably a bar in there as well, but didn't bother to ask about it. We had taken one of the cars, but it looked as if most of Zahav International's employees got around by bicycle or on foot. Her clinic was nestled at the end of the street, across from the entertainment complex and next door to a restaurant called Rockwell's.

We made small talk on the way over, mostly about the island, and she kept up a steady stream of chatter, pointing out various features of Eunostos while the car piloted us to the clinic. It wasn't until we got inside that she turned suddenly businesslike.

A nurse met us at the door carrying two specimen cups. Kathryn took them from her and handed them to me. "Fill them both. One urine, one semen. Urine cup first, please."

"*Fill* them?" The semen cup, in particular, looked like it might take a week.

"Fill the first one. Do your best on the second. We don't need much. Once you're done with that, my nurses will take your vitals. If you have to wait, start to fill these out." She handed me a clipboard with what looked like twenty pages of questions on it.

"Why do you need my semen again?"

"To start with, in case cosmic rays make you infertile. We have other reasons, though."

Yikes. "Can I have a pen, or should I use blood?"

"Funny," she said. "There's a pen on the clipboard. Turn it over."

I turned it over. So there was.

"Thanks, I think," I said. The nurse pointed me to the bathroom, and I managed to take care of both required deposits without too much trouble. There was a rack of tastefully arranged adult magazines in the bathroom, which appealed to me as a writer, as I hadn't previously had the opportunity to think of such things using that particular phrase before.

I exited the bathroom and handed the cups to a nurse, who took them from me without a hint of distaste on her face. She beckoned toward a patient room, where I sat down and dug into the paperwork.

It began with a personal medical history. There wasn't much to report; I was moderately overweight, with a family history of diabetes and high blood pressure, but other than that had spent most of my life in remarkably good health. I still had all of my teeth, including all four wisdom teeth, and hadn't ever had even minor surgery. I'd made it through childhood without any broken bones, still with my tonsils, and had never spent more than 24 hours hospitalized.

The family history went back to my grandparents, and was just as detailed as the paperwork for me was. I considered myself lucky that I wasn't married; there were sheets for my spouse and enough for three children as well. I got as far as filling out my parents' names before the nurse came in.

"Good morning," she said. "I'm Amanda. Mind if I take your numbers?"

"Usually I have to ask women for their numbers," I said.

"Yes, very funny," she said, in a voice that said *you will get nowhere with me, old man,* in as clear and direct a fashion as I'd ever heard. "That's a yes, then, right?" I nodded, unwilling to make further attempts at small talk or humor, and proffered my arm. In rapid, businesslike fashion, I was weighed, measured, my blood pressure and temperature taken, my blood was drawn, saliva swabbed, and my fingerprints, teeth, and retinas were scanned. She also photographed me for a Zahav International ID card.

"I'm surprised that's part of your job," I said.

"We process all of our new hires through here," she said. "In a place this small, everybody ends up doing more than one thing. Doctors and security both need retinal scanners, so they figured we could take care of all the identification requirements while we were at it."

"Very efficient," I said.

"We try," she replied, and whacked my knee with a mallet. I got the feeling that she'd enjoyed it. She put me through a few other tests, mostly involving muscle control and balance, and then told me I could go back to my paperwork for a while.

I filled out what I knew about my parents' and grandparents' medical history, which wasn't a tremendous amount. I blinked my mother-- well, I sent her a text; Mom completely refused to wear an iLid-- to request whatever help she could give me and left the rest alone. Behind that was a form to fill out about my sexual history. Absurdly, it included a place to record the social security number of my partners. *Who in the world knows that,* I thought, and continued on, musing that the form hadn't taken me as long to fill out as I might have wanted and vaguely considering making a few people up. *Watch, Zub will catch me if I do that,* I thought, and decided against it.

There was a detailed questionnaire about my dietary and exercise habits and pages and pages of disclaimers and releases to sign. After a while my eyes glazed over and I just started looking for straight lines to put my name on, figuring that most of them were going to say some variant of *You're going to Mars, you're probably going to die, and it's not our fault,* and not particularly caring about what the variant might be.

There was a place to attach a resume. I hadn't thought to bring one with me, so I ignored that too.

Just as I was getting tired of paperwork, Kathryn came in.

"Sorry for the wait," she said. "We had a worker injured on the dock literally three minutes after you and I got here, and I've been stitching him back together. I was actually planning on letting you take tonight to put the paperwork together, but it looks like you've had time to finish most of it."

"I did," I said. "There's some stuff left blank right now, though. I don't know much about my grandparents' medical history."

"Not a problem," she said. "I'll put some of Ezekiel's researchers on it; they'll fill in the blanks." Interesting, that she'd called him *Ezekiel* when she wasn't in his presence; he'd been *Zub* more than once during the meeting in the conference room. "Come this way. We'll get the scans out of the way first, and then I need to put you through some stress tests. The scans will be easy. The stress tests won't." Her accent was suddenly entrancing. For some reason, it didn't make her sound dumb any longer.

"I was hoping to have to do something unpleasant today," I said, which got a grin out of her. She led me into a room with a full-body scanner in it and had me lie down. The machine passed over my entire body a few times from different angles, then moved back and forth twice over my head and torso, moving much more slowly.

She was watching the scan from an adjoining room. "Hold on," she said. "I'll be right back. Don't get up just yet."

That sounded ominous.

She returned a few minutes later, holding a cup with a few enormous pills in it and a cup of water. She held both out to me.

"Take these. Then I'll explain why."

Um. "Are you serious?"

"Yes. Trust me, take the pills."

I swallowed the pills. They were big enough that I actually had to do it one at a time, and I felt the last one for most of the tumble down my throat.

"Congratulations, Mr. Southern. You're officially a cancer survivor."

I nearly spit up my water. "I'm a what?"

"A cancer survivor. You had skin cancer."

"Had?"

"Skin cancer, yes. Had."

My brain was exploding, which was not, I think, her plan.

"Explain this in small words, please."

She smiled at me again. "Well, not really. These scanners are somewhat more advanced than what's available to the general public. It's part of the reason I like working here, frankly. You have what I'd term *pre-pre* skin cancer. In about ten years, you'd have been getting bad news from a doctor, if you'd caught it in time."

"But not anymore? You've actually *cured cancer* out here?"

"Not quite. What we *have* done, and which you'd probably already know about if you followed pharmaceutical news very much, is started working on ways to *inhibit* cancer before it starts. You just swallowed two million dollars' worth of experimental pills, there."

"Uh. Okay. Thanks?" This didn't make sense. "Why give me two million dollars worth of pills today when the cancer's ten years off?"

"We're going into outer space, that's why. The *Johannes* is pretty well shielded against radiation and cosmic rays, but there's no denying that spending much time in outer space is going to increase your risk of cancer by a small amount, particularly if we spend much time on the planet's surface. It's miniscule in terms of overall risk; perhaps a 2% increase in the chance of fatal cancer during your lifetime for the two or three years the trip will take, but the effect of the radiation is enough that the inhibitors won't work on you as well if you wait until we get home. Plus, since you do already show signs of precancerous cells, your personal risk would be elevated."

"Wow," I said. "What about, like, alien Mars bacteria or something like that?"

"There probably aren't any," she said. "We've done our damnedest to find any evidence of life on Mars and haven't had any success. There *should* be life on Mars, by all evidence, and there absolutely should have been in the past, when the planet was warmer and wetter, but we haven't found it yet."

"Bad luck, I guess," I said. The last several missions to Mars, even the unmanned ones, had been failures. We hadn't had a fully successful Mars mission since a run of good luck in the oughts and 20-teens.

"Even if we encounter xenobacteria, though, there's absolutely no chance of it being able to infect human beings with anything," she said, falling into a softer version of her drawl. "Bacteria evolve alongside their ecosystem. We're not a part of that ecosystem, and Martian bacteria wouldn't have evolved in a way so as to be able to do anything to human beings. There's truly nothing to worry about on that front. Plus, Zub and I would just end up finding a way to cure you anyway."

"Zub really takes care of his people, doesn't he?"

"He does," she replied. "He's terrible at face-to-face interaction, but he's incredible at taking care of his employees in an abstract sense. The pills aren't going to all of us, obviously, but he's spent some of his energy over the last several years encouraging medical research to drive costs down, as well. If Ezekiel has his way, these will cost less than a hundred dollars apiece by the time we get back from Mars."

And Ezekiel's very used to getting his way, I thought.

"Anything show up on the brain scans?"

"You have one," she said, reverting back into business mode again. "Nothing abnormal about it at all; congratulations." A nurse walked in holding a glass full of liquid.

"Here, drink this." I complied. It was terrible.

"And what was that?"

"Barium, mostly. We're going to do stress tests on you for a couple of hours, and then we're going to do another full-body scan, except by then your blood supply will be glowing. It makes it easier to make certain everything's exactly like it's supposed to be, or at least fixable enough that you don't catch cold and die in the cold of deep space. One aspect of Ezekiel's plan that I *don't* like is his approach to dealing with the dead respectfully; one of the papers you signed without reading it said that you were fine with either being jettisoned or actually *left on Mars* if you die during the trip. I think as a person that that's terribly disrespectful, and I don't want the first human beings to reach Mars to leave any corpses mouldering on the surface; it hurts my brain to think about what could happen."

She paused, then grinned. "Granted, as a matter of pure science, I'm interested in seeing what would happen to them after a while, since Mars lacks most of the organisms that would cause you to decompose on Earth, but either way, it's easier if you survive."

"Thanks for that," I said.

"Thank me after the stress test," she said.

As it turned out, there was *no chance whatsoever* that I was going to thank her after "the" stress test, which turned out to be several tests, each more horrifying and masochistic than the one before it. I ran on treadmills, walked on treadmills, crawled on treadmills, all at varying speeds and degrees of inclination. I stood in stress positions to see how long I could hold them without collapsing. I did a pressure test, where she put me into a barometric chamber and then increased the pressure in the chamber steadily until I thought my ears were going to explode. She even immersed me in cold water for a while to see how long I could stand *that*.

"There's no way that's a valid medical procedure," I said, just before I went into the water.

"Average Mars surface temperature is around eighty degrees below zero," she said. "There are places on Earth that are colder than that-- I've heard terrible stories about northern Indiana and Chicago, as a matter of fact-- and we need to see how much cold you can stand if your suit's climate control should happen to break down."

"I hate you," I said.

"You're not the first to say that," she said. "It turns out Zvi would literally die of frostbite before complaining about cold, by the way. Surprising, for an Israeli; he's from a place where it never snows. He might actually be tougher than God."

"I'm a Midwesterner," I said. "I can take him."

I couldn't. Not even close.

When she finally released me for the day, I felt as if someone had gone over every muscle in my body with a spiked bat, and couldn't mentally process any ideas other than going home and collapsing into bed for several months. The thought that I'd have to be up tomorrow to meet with Celeste Flye was a horror beyond imagining. Who knew what tortures she'd have ready for me.

*　　*　　*

Dr. Flye met me at my door at 9:30 in the morning. She'd given me fifteen minutes' warning that she was on her way, causing me to force my aching body out of bed and get cleaned up in what had to be world-record-setting time. I had been expecting her to send another car, but she arrived by herself and on foot, Sajad in tow. I remarked on my surprise and she shrugged.

"You can walk from any part of the island to any other part in 45 minutes, and that's if you don't have the benefit of roads and paved sidewalks. I like being outdoors, and I don't mind the exercise either. We can call for a car if you don't want to hoof it to my workshop."

"How long is it?" I didn't want to sound like a weakling, but at the moment, it was a perfectly accurate impression. I was surprised my legs were holding me upright.

"Ten minutes for me; I work out of my home, mostly, not the hangar, and anything we need for today is already there. Possibly fifteen in your current condition." She winked at me. "I've been through Dr. Rosansky's 'stress tests' too, you know. The woman is a sadist."

Sajad climbed up my pants and shirt and perched on my shoulder, managing to pinch me in at least six places that hurt along the way. "I can't imagine what the test session for Zvi must have been like. I'm surprised they're not still trying to break each other."

"I think Zub stepped in after a while, actually," she said. "Today will be much more pleasant. We're going to do some zero-G testing after we get you fit and trained in your suit, but that won't be terribly strenuous. It's disorienting at first, but it's not painful."

"I'll take it," I said. Celeste lapsed into silence, and after a few minutes I realized that I wasn't sure what day it was. *Amazing,* I thought, after thinking about it and deciding it was Wednesday. *This is only my second morning on Eunostos, and it's actually starting to feel natural.* For God's sake, I was taking a walk outdoors with a *monkey* sitting on my shoulder. Truth be told, the exercise felt good, which was also something that I wasn't completely used to. Something in my lifestyle had gone all sideways since I'd taken that first blink from Zub. I wasn't sure if I liked it or not.

"So how long have you worked for Zub?" I asked.

"Zub?" she said. "Since his father died. I was in on all of the arguments about the *Tycho.* Lost most of them, too. He promoted me when we started working on the *Johannes.* But I've worked for ZI since grad school. Twenty-three years."

I did the math. She was either older than she looked or had picked up her Ph.D awfully early. Given the caliber of everybody else around here, I figured the latter was more likely.

"Were you in aerospace the whole time?"

"Fighter jets," she said. "Unmanned drones, other things like that. I got tired of building stuff that killed people or spied on them and decided to jump when the company started working on space. I needed a new challenge, I guess."

"I'm surprised you were able to switch gears like that," I said. "I'd think it would have had to require an awful lot of retraining."

She shrugged. "I learn fast," she said. "Scarce resources as a kid, I guess. Never enough books to go around."

"Big family?"

"Twelve of us. And I was the jock, believe it or not."

I believed it. She had a basketball player's body, and I still remembered being surprised by her handshake the day before.

"So what brought you into engineering?"

"Wasn't good enough at basketball to play in college, and my older brothers were a doctor, a lawyer, a college professor, and an auto mechanic. Guess which one I looked up to the most."

"Where was college?"

"Michigan State," she said, suddenly looking a little defensive.

"Another Big Ten alum," I said. "I went to Northwestern for undergrad and Indiana after that."

"Yeah," she said, smiling again. "Nice to know. I actually grew up a couple of towns over from East Lansing. Eleven brothers and sisters means you go to state schools and you like it." She paused, a smirk crossing her face. "I occasionally find myself wanting to beat some of these East Coast private-school kids up and stuff them in a locker somewhere, too."

I grinned. I had a feeling Celeste and I were going to get along.

True to her word, it took about ten minutes to get to her workshop. From the outside, her cabin looked much the same as mine, right down to the conspicuously-placed security cameras and the paint job (the houses on Eunostos all seemed to be painted the same three colors) but once we got inside the differences became obvious. She had a basement, for starters, one crammed full of equipment I didn't have a name for or, really, a faint guess as to the purpose of. There was a door down there with a sign on it marked "HANGAR: BEWARE OF THE COUGAR," which both entertained me and disturbed me. The thought of Zub guarding a tunnel access to his hangar with a live cougar didn't seem entirely out of place.

"That really goes straight through to the hangar?" I asked.

"It does," she said. "There's even a high-speed tram in there, believe it or not. We can be at the hangar in less than a minute if the tram's at our end when we start. Two if it's at the other end. Zub likes for us to be at his beck and call when he decides he needs us, and he knows I prefer to not use the autocars."

I felt like this extravagance should surprise me, but despite having only known the man for two days I was rapidly reaching the point where little about Ezekiel ben Zahav's ability or tendency to throw money at a problem could surprise me any longer.

There was a portion of the wall near the door that had been covered with a grid of tiny squares, maybe a centimeter to a side. She pointed at it. "Strip down to your underwear and go stand over there by the wall. Brace yourself, too, I'm going to be pointing bright lights in your direction."

"You begin a sentence with *strip down to your underwear* and then act like the bright lights are going to be the problem?"

"The suit's skintight," she said, fiddling with some equipment and clearly not in the mood to humor me. "Or at least mostly skintight. It needs to be manufactured precisely to the dimensions of your body. The scanner I'm about to use can't see through your clothes."

I did as she said and she turned the lights on, which was indeed rather uncomfortable. She wheeled over a complicated-looking camera on a stand and took several pictures.

"Stand up straight, as tall as you can, and hold your arms out to your sides as far as you can." I complied, then turned to my right and my left when commanded as well. She pushed another button on the camera and a fine red line passed over my body in several directions. I had to turn a few times for the red line, too.

"Modern spacesuit tailoring," she said. "I'm feeding the pictures into a computer program that will measure you against the grid so that we know exactly what your measurements are. There are several places where the suit needs to be fairly precisely measured; it takes your vitals and such, for example, and it's best if those things are manufactured to the right size rather than being adjusted. We'll have one custom-fit for you in a couple of days."

"I'm not done already, am I?" I said. "That was easy."

"Not even close," she said. "We've got some that fit you well enough to try on and check out. We don't need to monitor you while you're getting used to the suit. You're not claustrophobic, are you?"

"Not a bit," I said. "At least, not that I've ever been aware of."

"Good," she said. She opened a cabinet, fished through it for a moment, and pulled out a garment bag. "Go try this on. It's pretty self-explanatory; if you have any trouble figuring out where something goes or if something is supposed to hook to something else, don't worry about it too much. What size shoe do you wear?"

"Eleven," I said. The garment bag was much lighter than I had expected.

"There's a rack of boots by the bathroom over there," she said, pointing. "They're not traditionally sized, but grab something toward the middle. They'll be close enough."

"One question," I said. "Do I, uh..."

That was as far as I got. "Nothing on under the suit," she said. "Unless you happen to be wearing bikini briefs underneath the boxers." I was not.

The thought that I was about to go commando in a space suit was kind of fun, to tell the truth.

I went into the bathroom and unzipped the garment bag. The suit inside was nothing like what I was expecting, even given the lightness of the bag. It looked like a full-body blue-and-purple Spandex suit, except with dozens of ellipsoid and semicircular shapes formed by what appeared to be cords or wires all over the body. The ellipses were smaller on areas of the body that moved a lot and larger away from joints. There were also several lines moving down the spine and along the shoulders, as well as the sides of my arms and legs. The thing unzipped along the back and covered my entire body except for my hands, feet, and head. The fit was reasonable enough, all told; I was a little too short, my arms a little too long, and my gut slightly larger than what the suit wanted for me, but for something she'd literally pulled off a rack it fit fairly impressively. There were gloves inside the bag as well; I pulled those on and tightened them, then stepped into the boots. It felt like there was wiring inside the gloves and something mechanical inside the boots as well, but I decided not to mess with that.

I opened the bathroom door and stepped out. I turned around and she finished zipping the suit up for me, then examined me with a critical eye.

"You'd be surprised how often people come out of there wearing the zipper in front," she said, a sardonic look on her face. "Once you make it past that hurdle you're generally good to go."

"How many people have you fit these things for?" I said. "I thought there were only five of us going on the trip. Did you have to audition a bunch of people for the other roles or something like that?"

"No," she said, "but I did design the spacesuit, so I've been putting them on people for quite some time. Graduate students can be surprisingly dumb sometimes."

"It feels like Spandex," I said.

"There's a good reason for that," she said. "It's Spandex. The cords are basically chicken wire. The real suits are probably about fifteen pounds heavier than what you're wearing and about thirty million dollars more expensive. I do not keep a rack of thirty million dollar space suits in a wooden cabinet in my office."

I suddenly felt very, very stupid.

"Don't worry," she said. "Zub thought his was the real thing too. I even kept him thinking he'd damaged it for a while when the Spandex tore away from the wire on his elbow. Went on and on about how if he didn't learn to be careful there was no way I'd let him on the flight. He was furious when I told him what I'd done. The point is, what you're wearing approximates the *feel* of the suit well enough that when you've got one on along with the helmet and everything, you should have an idea of what wearing the real suit is like. You'll get to wear the real one in a couple of days anyway. Here, put this on. And be careful, this one's real."

She handed me a helmet. It was smaller than I'd expected; the glass in the visor was fairly close to my face; I couldn't quite reach it with my tongue, but it wasn't much farther away. The back of the helmet had a number of digital readouts and soft lights on it and was the same color as the rest of the suit. And, it occurred to me, to the *Johannes*. Zub had designed his space suits to match his ship.

I put the helmet on. "Now ordinarily this would connect up with your suit," Celeste said, connecting it to wires that fed into a computer terminal nearby, "and be able to read information from it to give you real-time feedback on the condition the suit was in. Obviously this one's not going to do that. It's feeding you dummy data based on what I send it, but you can still get used to the interface. Ready for me to turn it on?"

"Go for it," I said. She pushed a button and the inside of the helmet exploded into light. There were a good half-a-dozen readouts on the inside of the thing. Air, external temperature, internal temperature, suit integrity, battery power, and suit pressure all displayed readings, all in pale green. My vital statistics were also available, although those weren't displaying yet. There was also a section called COMMS that didn't list anything underneath it, as well as a few other bits whose use in the interface wasn't immediately clear.

"Okay," Celeste said. "Your heads-up display-- your HUD-- should be showing you a ton of information about the condition your suit is in. Everything should be in green, which means that you're doing fine. Yellow is caution, red is *get your ass back to the Johannes*. Any other color means you're dead. Most of what's on there, honestly, you can ignore most of the time. You'll get plenty of warning if your oxygen starts to run out, for example, and a lot of it is also indicated on the back of your helmet-- so not only can you tell, so can anyone looking at you. If you're in atmo, you can pull condition reports on the air around you, and the suit can act as a gas mask as well, so if we end up with some sort of disaster on the *Johannes* that results in a loss of pressure, the suit can use up whatever's around us before it starts in on its own supply. You'll also get a readout on anyone else wearing a suit at the same time you are; it'll show up in the comm section."

"So far, so good," I said. Four names popped up in the comm-- Zub, Celeste, Zvi, and Kathryn. Their names also appeared at the top of my field of vision, with arrows pointing up.

"The HUD will also give you a location for anyone you're in communication with," she said. "Right now, it can't find them. If I fake it," and the names moved, gaining ghostly green body outlines at different points in my field of vision, "you can see what it would look like on planet surface if you were exploring. Turn around."

I did, and the outlines moved away to the sides of my field of vision. The names returned, with their arrows pointing off behind me. Distances also appeared underneath the names. Zub was three meters away, Kathryn 120.

"The distance readout is generally accurate to within an inch, and works up to five kilometers," she said. "Even beyond that, you'll get a general indication of direction for anyone your suit is linked to so long as everybody's aboveground. The color of the outlines gives a vague indication of their physical state, too; if someone's heartrate spikes or slows substantially or if they start running out of air, their silhouette will start redshifting."

"Interesting," I said. "What about communication?"

"The comm's pretty self-explanatory," she said. "If you want to communicate in general, just speak, and they'll all hear you. If you want to speak to a specific person, it works like a blink. Stare at my silhouette for a moment."

I did, and her name zoomed in on my HUD. "Hi, Dr. Flye," I said, and the words appeared on-screen. "So is this actually sending a blink, or is it actually sending you audio?"

"You can do it either way," she said. "It generally defaults to verbal communication, because there's generally no need to send a blink when you can do private two-way radio communication, but if you start off by saying the word "blink," it'll appear as a text message on the screen of whoever you're sending to. It can be useful for keeping instructions or objectives for people on screen if they need them."

"Got it," I said.

"Incidentally, the thing holds about a hundred gigabytes of music. Playlists are stored in the note icon in the lower-right corner. Zub absolutely insisted on being allowed to bring a soundtrack along with him. You can worry about that later."

"I was concerned about that," I said. "I can't operate without my music."

"Here's the fun part," she said. "Reach up and find the tab for the visor shield at the top of the helmet." I did, and found the tab she was talking about. I pulled the visor down, and the inside of my helmet went completely dark. The green glow of the HUD elements were all I could see.

"The visor shield is generally user-deployed. The visor will darken in bright-light situations, and the shield will close on its own if you're ever exposed to sudden bursts of light that could be blinding-- and it does so impressively fast under those circumstances. You can also deploy it with an icon from inside the HUD," and as she spoke the words, the icon began softly pulsing in the corner of my eye, "or just by pulling it down like you just did. You can still navigate even without being able to see out of the helmet, however."

I heard her pressing a few buttons, and a digital version of the world around me appeared in my HUD. Everything looked slightly unreal, almost like a video game from when I was a kid.

"The graphics in this game are terrible," I said.

"That's intentional," she said. "The HUD gives you enough information to operate with without providing full realism because you want to never forget whether you've got your visor down or not. It'll notice if you're staring at something and bring that into natural resolution, but otherwise it's video game world."

"Why is that?"

"Power consumption. On the real suit, there's a network of cameras all over the place, but they don't fire up and start recording unless you tell them to or unless the visor drops. If they're recording in a low-light environment, or in the middle of a Martian dust storm, where you've got light but no visibility, the batteries on the suit that keep you nice and toasty warm and alive start to take a hit. They're long-lasting; you can actually stay in the suit for about a week if you don't mind drinking recycled water and food paste while you're doing it, but you still don't want to wear the batteries down unnecessarily."

"GPS?"

"Yep, that too," and a swarm of coordinates flooded onto my HUD, "with automapping capability so that even on the Martian surface the suit is constantly scanning the geography around you and updating its maps. You'll even have the ability to slave your suit to anyone else's in your group, so that if someone is away from you and looking at something interesting, you can see what they're seeing. All in all, it's an awesome little piece of technology."

"You built this?"

"I came up with the physical design for the suit," she said, "but some of Zub's software engineers designed the software that powers the HUD and the suit's communication suite. Officially, you're wearing a Flye exosuit running the Otero-Overmyer user interface program. Congratulations."

"What's going on with my hands and my boots? It feels like there's something beyond the normal wiring in there," I asked.

"We'll get to that when we've got you in a fully working suit. The boots are designed for easy maneuverability in a weightless or low-G environment, and the gloves have all sorts of interesting stuff built into them."

Holy God I'm wearing rocket boots.

"Dr. Flye, am I wearing rocket boots?"

"No," she said, crushing my tiny soul. "But they're very, very close to that. The boots are fun. But we need to get you into zero-G to test them, and we're not going to be able to do that in my office. Ready for the next step?"

I was.

"Let's go check out the tram to the hangar, then," she said, and unhooked me from the computer.

*   *   *

The tram did indeed move very fast-- alarmingly so, in fact, and without what a normal person might have thought of as useful safety features such as seatbelts or full-body suits of armor. It had six seats with handholds and a windshield and that was about it; I had the feeling that if we happened to hit a bug along the way that it was likely to cause a fatal accident. There were apparently no insects with death wishes in the tunnel between the workshop and the hangar, however, and we arrived without incident-- but also without my stomach, which had stubbornly refused to leave the workshop when the tram had first taken off.

"You look a little green," Celeste said to me, a look of concern and barely-veiled mockery on her face. "You recognize that the tram ride to the hangar was *not* either the zero-G or the motion stress test?"

"I'm going to throw up today, aren't I?" I asked.

"That depends," she said. "Did you have breakfast before you came over?"

Funny thing about throwing up-- you can do it on an empty stomach. I hadn't been aware of that fact before this morning, but it rapidly became salient to me as my stomach began somehow spontaneously generating material for later expulsion not long after we began what Dr. Flye referred to as the "disorientation test." This was surprisingly simple; they sat me in a rotating chair and asked me to roll my head around my shoulders as the chair turned, then slowly increased the speed of the chair. Had you asked me beforehand, I'd have suggested that such a thing would not, in fact, be remotely disorienting.

It turned out that I have a low tolerance for motion sickness, and that there was a very good reason why most of the surfaces in the testing rooms we visited were either concrete or stainless steel. I did not fare better on later tests involving larger and more chaotic amounts of motion. Yet, somehow, my stomach never emptied. The high-G test, where they checked my reaction to high gravitational force by strapping me into a fast-moving centrifuge, was perhaps the most unpleasant three or four minutes of my entire life.

"I don' like you either," I said after one test. "I thought I jus' didn' like Zub and Kathryn. An' Zvi. I don' like *you* either."

"But we *love* you," she said, the mockery now having fully overtaken the concern on her face.

"Wannaknowwhazzisfor," I slurred.

"Nothing, really," she said. "We're just hazing you."

We're outside any nation's jurisdiction, I thought. *I could kill them.*

"Thassajoke." *That had better be a joke.*

She smiled. "Mostly," she said. "Zvi said it was okay if we were a little rough on you. But I do have to make sure you're not going to black out under disorienting or high-G environments. Vomiting we can deal with by putting you on anti-nausea meds before liftoff and touchdown. You'll probably be a little seasick, for lack of a better word, while adjusting to gravity on the ship and gravity on Mars. But you'll come through all right."

I sat there and panted for a few minutes, not deigning to respond to her.

"There's still weightlessness, though," she said. "That's Zvi's area. And the plane is actually *called* the Vomit Comet. You'll love it."

SIX

As it worked out, the elder ben Zahav was not my appointed tormentor for the day. Dr. Flye returned my clothes to me and told me to go have lunch and meet her back at the hangar in a few hours for the Vomit Comet flight. I wasn't able to eat much, especially knowing that it was likely that I was just going to lose it soon anyway. I considered trying to nap, but after the events of the last two days I was too tired to sleep. I ended up walking along the beach with Sajad, trying to figure out how I was going to write the first few chapters of the book once I'd survived all of this nonsense. If nothing else, it managed to distract me from what was sure to be my impending vomiting, exploding, plane-crashey doom later on that afternoon.

The pilot, a young (younger than me, anyway) guy in an honest-to-God cowboy hat that clashed with his flight suit, met us at the plane, which was a sleek-looking jet done up in what I was starting to recognize as Zub's favorite colors, dark blue and gunmetal grey.

"Douglas Myers," he said, shaking my hand. "I'll be your tormentor this afternoon."

"I thought Zvi was taking us up?" Dr. Flye, in full Flye suit minus the helmet, had just arrived as Myers was introducing himself. She had a backpack of some sort on, too, that seemed to be part of the suit, and was carrying a gym bag full of equipment. The real suit was closer to purple than the ones that I'd seen at her place. I found myself wondering if Zub had complained about the color scheme.

"Something came up," Myers said. "He asked me to take over. I always enjoy taking newbies up in the Comet. You're the writer?" This last to me, of course.

"Yeah, that's me. Why is everyone on Eunostos so interested in making me feel bad?"

"Orders from the boss," Myers said. "He said to treat you like family, so everyone's treating you like crap. He told me to wear the cowboy hat, too. I can take it off now, right?"

God. "Yes. I am suitably impressed with your maverickness." I was pretty sure the guy wasn't old enough to remember *Top Gun*, but I couldn't help it. He tossed the hat into the back seat of a nearby transport and waved us over to the plane.

Dr. Flye handed me the gym bag, which turned out to contain a second backpack like hers, along with a pair of boots and gloves. "You don't need the full suit on for this, but you'll want the maneuvering equipment," she said. "The three items work together as a unit, so we'll need you to have everything on for your training today. Gird your loins, my friend; this will take a few hours." I left my shoes in the transport with Myers' hat and changed into the boots and gloves. The backpack, which looked like a solid piece of material covered with some sort of grey metal mesh, strapped across my chest twice as well as under my arms; it wasn't very heavy, and I wondered for a moment if they expected the thing to attempt to fly off my back if it wasn't strapped into place.

The inside of the Vomit Comet was a featureless, padded cylinder, with no furniture or protruding pieces that you could injure yourself on. Everything was a uniform dark brown in color.

"Go ahead," Celeste said. "Take a flying leap or two onto the floor. You'll be spending most of the next couple of hours bouncing off it, so if you have any sort of fear of impact you should probably test it right now. It's really, really hard to hurt yourself in here unless you try." Obligingly, I took a flying leap onto the floor. She was right; the padding was thick enough that I didn't even come close to making contact with the metal outsides of the plane. Rather enjoying the spectacle of it all, I tossed myself around a couple more times, with the same results.

There were a couple of hidden, recessed seats on the side for take-off and landing. Celeste showed me how to move the padding aside to reveal the seat and the two of us strapped ourselves in. "We'll be taking off in a few minutes," Myers said, entering the bay from the cabin. "We're doing eighty weightless spells. I'll let you know once we're at altitude and ready to begin the testing."

"*Eighty?*" They really were trying to kill me.

"Eighty. We're going to be flying in a series of giant parabolic shapes, basically. At the top of the parabola and the beginning of our dive, you'll be effectively weightless. That part will last for about 45 seconds at a time or so, then you'll undergo some time at roughly twice Earth's gravity as we pull out of the dive. Think of it as the world's largest roller-coaster ride, except you won't be strapped into anything."

"It's fun," Celeste said. "Really."

"I *absolutely promise* that if I get sick I'm going to aim at you," I said.

"About two thirds of first-timers will get sick, to some degree or another," Myers said. "There's a reason we don't use white cushioning in here. If you feel yourself starting to get ill, let me know and I'll wait a while before the next dive. Puking in a weightless environment is a unique experience, but not the kind you look forward to."

"The video's going to be downloadable half an hour after we get home, isn't it?"

"Ten minutes, if Zub has anything to do with it."

I'm throwing that man out of an airlock. I swear I will.

"Let's get this over with," I said.

"You got it," Myers said, and headed for the cockpit. A few moments later, I heard the jet's engines roar to life and we began taxiing to the runway.

"How many times have you done this?" I asked Celeste.

"Two dozen times, maybe," she said. "Unfortunately, it's difficult to test a zero-G maneuvering system on Earth because you can't really create a weightless space. What we've done is adapt systems that we put together for maneuvering *underwater*, which in a lot of ways is very similar. But nearly all of the testing had to be done either at the Space Center or on dives like this. Mostly on this, since even the Space Center has artificial gravity and if something goes wrong on the Comet you're not as likely to be blown out into deep space. So I've been up a few times."

"So how do the boots work?"

"Feel that thing underneath your toes?"

"Yep."

"Don't push that unless we're weightless."

"Gotcha."

A few minutes later, we were at altitude.

"Beginning the first parabola in sixty seconds," came Myers' voice over the PA system. "I'm leaving the microphones on back there, so if you need something from me, just shout; I'll hear it."

And you'll be recording it, too, I thought.

"Okay," Dr. Flye said. "For the first several parabola, we're going to just try and get used to the physical feelings of weightlessness and two-gee gravity. There is *nothing* that I want you to do, other than to experience the feeling and do whatever you want. If you want to float around, go ahead; if you feel like trying to zoom around the cabin, you can do that too. It's entirely up to you. Just make sure you're lying comfortably when we pull out of the dives; two-gee should be perfectly okay, but it can be harsh if you're not positioned right."

"That's about the strength of a roller coaster ride, right?"

"Yeah, most of them top out at two or three g. Most people can handle five before blacking out."

A moment later, I was floating. There was a brief moment of panic when I realized my feet weren't touching the ground but I still wasn't falling, but that didn't last long. As it turns out, being weightless was remarkably relaxing. I pushed my feet off the walls and shoved myself toward the front of the plane, turning lazily in the air as I went, using my arms to spin myself through the space in the cabin.

"Coming out of the first dive," came Myers' voice from the speaker, and I drifted to the ground as gravity's force took control of my body again. I'd been expecting to fall to the ground abruptly; as it turned out, it was a pleasantly gradual experience. The pressure of the two-gee recovery from the dive wasn't that bad, either. I'd been through worse in tight turns in my *car*.

This isn't that bad, I thought, as the plane climbed back to altitude and regular gravity took over.

Three minutes later, Dr. Flye was holding an airsick bag to my lips and Myers was crowing over the PA system about getting a "kill." I was, according to him, his fiftieth such victory, and he felt that I should be proud of him for it.

Can't murder pilot until we land, I thought, and focused on getting everything into the bag. I suspected that weightless vomit would likely not make the trip any more pleasant. Myers kept the plane level until I'd recovered, and then we dove again.

"Okay," Dr. Flye said, "push the button in your boots." I curled my toes, depressing the little nub under my feet, and with a loud *hiss* my boots propelled me into the wall on the other side of the cabin. I caught myself with my hands and relaxed my feet, and the boot propulsion stopped. I tried it again, this time orienting myself lengthwise on the jet, and made it all the way across in a couple of seconds before the jet began pulling out of the dive and gravity dumped me onto the floor again.

"That was fun," I said.

"It is," Dr. Flye said. "There's not a ton of gas built up in the boots when you're not in atmosphere, but you don't need as much propulsion in outer space anyway since there's less gravity. If you're in an environment with an atmosphere, the boots will repressurize themselves more or less constantly. Listen."

I did, and I could hear a slight hissing from my boots and from the backpack as they sucked in air to repressurize.

"This time, try and change direction in midflight," she said. Gravity went away as the jet pulled out of the climb. I aimed my body at the far end of the Vomit Comet and triggered the boot jets, sending me flying across the cabin. Just before I reached the other side, I pulled myself into a somersault, trying to point my feet in the direction that my head had been pointing. I ended up crashing into the floor face-first as the boots pushed me into a curve.

"Ow," I said, turning the bootjets off.

Dr. Flye glided to a stop next to me. "Turning is where the gloves and the backpack come in," she said.

"So you knew that was going to cause me to land on my face," I said in my most accusing tone.

She laughed. "I was mostly checking to see if you had any idea how the physics worked. There was always the chance that you would disengage the bootjets before trying to spin. That would have worked, too. Leaving them on while you're turning isn't the best possible solution to that problem."

"So now my face hurts *and* I'm stupid," I said, feeling slightly nauseous again.

"Quit whining, newbie," she said. "You're having fun and you know it. Wanna know how to turn, or should I let you figure it out?"

I chose the option least likely to be painful. "You can show me."

She held up her hands and curled them into what looked like a gang sign, with her index and middle fingers pointing straight ahead and her thumb touching her ring and pinky fingers. "Try it again," she said. "Only this time, when you want to turn, do this with your hands and point back the way you came from." I mimicked the gesture, and she nodded.

The jet went weightless again and I repeated the maneuver, rocketing my way along the length of the cabin. I gave myself ten feet to make the turn, making the pointing gesture with my fingers and pointing back toward my feet.

The backpack roared into life, firing a blast of cold air along the back of my neck that slowed my momentum and played havoc with my hair. Then a number of other jets of air fired in a precise sequence that forced my upper body into a turn. I brought my legs back underneath me, keeping my hands pointed in the direction that I wanted to go, and the boots fired again, propelling me back in the other direction. I'd made the turn with a good four or five feet of space left in the cabin. Experimenting, I pointed at Dr. Flye, and the braking jets fired again, slowing me down so that I was able to stop gracefully by taking my toes off the ignition sensor and stopping the jets entirely.

"That's impressive," I said.

"So were you," she replied. "I've seen plenty of people panic when they get their hair mussed the first time they try to turn. They assume the backpack's malfunctioning."

She'd gotten me thinking about the physics. "That's why it's strapped down so securely to my torso. You can't turn with the boots, since they're so far from your center of mass."

"Right, they'd just put you into a spin," she said. "The boots can do some directional movement instead of just straight up and down, but using them to make you turn when they're so far from your center of gravity is more trouble than it's worth. The backpack can do anything but stop movement perpendicular to your body orientation; it would have to fire jets into your back to do that. You have to point your feet ahead of you or turn your body to stop something like that. It's remarkably versatile once you get used to it."

I wasn't wearing jet boots. I was wearing a *jetpack*.

"Awesome," I said. "Let's play some more."

*   *   *

By the time the Vomit Comet landed back on Eunostos, I'd forgotten that it had ever made me nauseous, adrenaline from the exhilarating feeling of learning to control myself in flight overwhelming any other signals my body was trying to send me. I'd taken to maneuvering with the jet boots and the backpack in record time, apparently; once I'd gotten the hang of understanding which way the pack and boots might push me when I pointed in a certain direction, I was able to make turns as fast as if I were swimming. It took a few minutes to get my "land legs" back even after such a short time in weightlessness, but once that was taken care of I was ready to get right back in the jet again.

"Not so fast," Celeste said. "You'll have plenty of opportunities to play around in weightlessness once we're on the

Johannes, remember. You'll be looking forward to Earth gravity after not too long, I think." She'd commented on how impressed she'd been with my progress. By the end of the flight I was almost as good at maneuvering around as she was, and she'd invented the propulsion system.

"That was still fun," I said. A thought struck me. "What's Mars gravity like, anyway?"

"About forty percent of Earth's," she said. "Enough that the difference will be quite noticeable at first, but not enough that you won't get used to it fairly quickly"

"Anything I can do to get ready for it? We're going to be spending a tremendous amount of time on-planet, aren't we?"

"You'll be working out with a trainer or two for a couple of hours a day once you come back to Eunostos for good," she said. "And there is actually a fully-functioning gym on the *Johannes*. I suspect by the time we get to Mars you'll be in the best shape of your life. Your body's going to have enough to worry about dealing with unfamiliar gravity; we don't want you to have to bring any health problems along with you that we can't fix on Earth. Not the brightest ideas. And there will be bone supplements to take and things like that as well, but that's Rosansky's department, and--"

Dr. Flye was interrupted by a shout from behind us.

"So how'd he do?"

The high-pitched, whistly voice was a dead giveaway. Zub had just arrived, pulling in behind us in one of those unnaturally quiet electric transports while we were talking.

"He barfed," said Myers. "I got it on tape."

Celeste punched Myers in the arm. "Mr. Southern did *just fine*, thank you both very much," she said. "He's taken to the maneuvering system as quickly as anyone I've ever seen, actually. And the Vomit Comet only got to him for a few minutes."

"Great," Zub said. "Listen, sorry about my uncle. He was supposed to take you through the *Johannes* this afternoon before going out on the Vomit Comet, and he's been sulking in his office working on something all day instead. I'll try and get him to act more like a human being by the time you get back. Want to have dinner before we dump you back to the mainland for a few days?"

"Sure," I said. *Why not?*

"Great," he said. "Celeste, are you coming along?"

"Can't," she said. "I've already got plans this evening."

"Cancel them," Zub said.

"No."

"Cancel them or I'll fire you."

"Fire me and I promise me your spaceship will smell of rotten eggs and spoiled milk for the *entire trip*, and that you will never, ever be able to figure out where the smell is coming from."

Zub considered this for a moment, a thoughtful look on his face.

"I've decided you should take the night off," he said. "In fact, that's an order. You are not to do any work for me or do anything I tell you to do-- except this-- until tomorrow morning."

"Learn how to work with him," Celeste said, smiling at me. "It'll make your life so much easier when you're stuck on a space ship with him for three years."

"Thanks, doc," I said.

"I'll see you when you get back," she responded. "Try and relax for the next couple of days. You're going to be awfully busy all the time once you get back."

I handed her the gym bag with my flight equipment in it and watched her drive away.

"So what's for dinner?" I asked. "The restaurant at the observatory?"

"Nah," he said. "I'm done impressing you for right now. I thought we'd go to the place on Main Street, where everybody else eats. Did you drive by Rockwell's at all while you've been here?"

"Yeah," I said. "On the way to the med clinic yesterday. What kind of food?"

"Classic American diner," he said. "Annoyingly healthy most of the time, but it's good stuff. You can get basically whatever you want."

"Sounds good to me," I said, as he drove us out of the airport.

*   *   *

Rockwell's turned out to be a slightly classier place than I would normally expect from the description "classic American diner," coming off more like an upscale sports bar than a diner. The restaurant was full of dark corners and secluded tables, but also sported a dance floor and a number of wall-mounted and ceiling-mounted television screens showing current sporting events. There were a fair number of customers present when we went in, most of whom acknowledged Zub as we were led to our table. I found myself wondering if he had a regular table there or if we'd have had to wait along with everyone else if there had been a line at the door. A moment later, the waitress answered my question for me by seating us closer to the bathroom than I'd expect the owner of the entire island to be placed if he'd expected special treatment.

The hostess handed Zub two menus. He gave her one back and tossed the other one to me. "Whatever you're in the mood for," he said. "Most of the food is pretty good." The menu did look diner-like, with most of the food being of the boiled or fried variety. *Open-faced turkey sandwich*, I thought to myself, and as if on cue a waitress appeared.

"Hi, I'm Alayna," she said. "I'll be taking care of you tonight." I wondered if she was the daughter of one of Zub's regular employees, as I couldn't imagine anyone moving to Eunostos just to work at the local restaurant and I doubted she was moonlighting as an engineer. "Have you guys decided what you want yet?"

"Ravioli," Zub said. I hadn't seen ravioli on the menu. Again. The waitress nodded, though, not making any mention of that fact. I ordered and she went along on her way.

"Why don't you just have these places put ravioli on the menu, if you like it that much?" I asked.

"It is important to me that no others be allowed to consume my ravioli," Zub said, using his Mysterious Voice, and I decided not to pursue that line of questioning any further. He probably wanted me to keep asking him about it anyway. He could keep that particular idiosyncrasy to himself.

"Your accountant didn't call me last night," I said. "Is there going to be a contract for me to sign or anything like that?"

"Technically, you already signed everything I need you to sign," he said. "Yesterday, at Dr. Rosansky's. She blinked me and said that you'd looked awful beaten up when you left her office, so I figured the dotting of I's and crossing of T's could wait for a day or two. I'll have everything drawn up when you get back to the island, I think."

"Fair enough," I said.

"You'll get the first deposit before you leave," he said. "I'll have it transferred to you tomorrow morning, before Mr. Green flies you back to the mainland."

"Speaking of that," I said. "When do you expect me back?"

"How long do you need?"

I thought about this for a minute. There were some phone calls that needed to be made, to my agent and a half-dozen or so different editors and job sources that deserved to find out from me personally that I'd be unavailable for a little while. I'd have to talk to my mother and my sister in person, and that would take a couple of days. Any number of other miscellaneous wrapping up of things and tying off of loose ends.

"A week, maybe," I responded.

"That should work," he said. "That gives us three weeks for the incredibly intense and soul-crushing training regimen I intend to put you through when you get home, and it gives me a week to convince Tsvika to treat you like a human being at least most of the time."

"How much of this training regimen will *you* be doing?" I asked. Skinny and pale as he was, even in my current less-than-optimal shape I was pretty sure I had beaten him in every single one of the stress tests I'd been through in the past 48 hours.

"The mad genius needs no training," he said, reverting back to Mysterious Voice.

Our waitress walked past. I gestured, catching her attention.

"If it's not too late, I think I'd like the ravioli after all," I said.

"Oh, I'm sorry," she replied, a faint blush touching her cheeks. "I'm actually not your waitress."

I looked at her again. I'd been guilty of misidentifying my waitstaff in the past, when I was focused on something or someone else, but I was absolutely certain this was my waitress.

"Yes you are," I said. "You're my waitress. You introduced yourself five minutes ago. Your name's Alayna. It's right there on your--"

The name tag said *Alyssa*.

"My sister," she said. "We both work here."

Christ. *Twins*.

"Well, if you happen to *see* your sister, could you ask her to bring me the ravioli instead?"

"Sure," she said, as her sister glided in next to her, carrying two plates full of food. "Alayna, your customer would like to change his order, if it's not too late."

Alayna shot me a disapproving look and put my plate in front of me. "You don't like the turkey? C'mon, try it. I made it myself." I glared back and ate a spoonful of mashed potatoes. *Everything conspires against me on this island*, I thought.

"Your tip just tripled," Zub said, and the twins both dissolved into a shower of giggles and walked away.

"So, tell me about yourself," I said. "If I'm going to be expected to write a book about you and your glorious trip to Mars, I probably ought to know something about my subjects."

"You'll have plenty of time for interviews during the trip to Mars," Zub pointed out. "Six month flight, remember. But it's a fair question. The thing is, I'm not that interesting."

Oh, NOW you're not that interesting, I thought.

"How do you figure?"

"I'm a scientist," Zub said. "I'm a wealthy scientist, as I've made sure to reinforce with you periodically, which means that everyone around me is willing to put up with what I refer to as my charming quirks and they refer to in less charitable terms. But ultimately? I got raised by fairly absentee parents in an environment where there wasn't a ton of stimulation from other people but where I had access to literally any piece of human knowledge I wanted. I went into aeronautics because that was where my parents were and it was expected of me. But if I'd decided to be an archaeologist or a surgeon or a businessman instead of an engineer, I'd still have been able to do it. But none of that makes me interesting. It just makes me brilliant and wealthy. And incredibly, sickeningly lucky."

It was the most self-aware thing I'd ever heard him say. Somehow, I didn't expect the mood would last terribly long.

"Why Mars?" I asked. "Zahav International was never really into outer space until you started taking over a large role within the company; your father and grandfather were content with making fighter jets and passenger aircraft."

"It's *there*," he said, pausing to eat some of his ravioli. "And my father and grandfather had more or less cornered the market on ways to move people or kill people with planes. I wasn't too interested in the killing people part, and the idea of spending my career designing the newest Airbus to take tourists from Kansas to Disney World sounded more like a death sentence than a life decision. My options for real exploration were limited to the deep sea or outer space, and outer space is... well, it's *bigger*."

"And more lucrative," I pointed out.

"True," he agreed. "If we land on Mars, we immediately become the most famous people in human history, and if we manage to bring back the crew of the *Tycho* we become even more famous than that. There's no opportunity that compares to that in deep-sea exploration. And I don't see the ocean every time I look up. Maybe I'll become the first person to reach the bottom of the Marianas Trench when we get back from Mars."

"The Johannes II?" I said.

"I'd have to come up with a better name for a deep-sea vessel," he said. "But yeah. Want a contract for the second book?"

"Let's get the first one written first," I said, and dove into my food.

*   *   *

The conversation for the rest of the meal was mundane, for the most part. Zub turned out to have a passion for football, and commanded that the staff at Rockwell's "find something" for him to watch once he was done with his food. We spent the rest of the evening discussing the developments that the last decade or so had brought to the National Football League, and whether arena football was ever actually going to catch on or whether its brief flirtation with worldwide popularity in the late twenty-teens was as good as it would ever get. I decided to walk back to my cabin, enjoying the warm weather and the night air.

There was a paper deposit receipt on the kitchen table-- the same kitchen table I'd found my new swim trunks on the previous morning. *Funny*, I thought. *Zub said this would show up tomorrow morning.* His accountant must have felt bad about not having called me the previous morning.

My bank account, which, naturally, I hadn't provided Zub with any access to, had swollen by five million dollars. I hadn't done a single thing yet.

Then again, I thought, *he wants me 24/7 for the next three years for this.*

I did the math. $190 an hour, every hour, for three years. And, realistically, I wouldn't have a chance to spend any of it until I got home, so it would be earning interest for that entire time. *Yeah, I can work for that.*

As of tomorrow morning, I had a week to put my entire life to bed. And then I was going to Mars.

SEVEN

It was amazing to me how alien Indiana felt after my four-day trip to the Caribbean. For starters, it was freaking *cold* outside. My apartment, which was probably twice the size of the cabin I'd been staying in on Eunostos, felt tiny and confined. After all, there was no beach in my backyard. No monkey, either, come to think of it. It was a strange thing, to look around at your home and know that you wouldn't see almost everything in it for the next two and a half years. *Or longer, if I'm dead at the end of the trip.*

No use worrying about that, though.

I spent most of my first day back making appointments-- with my bank, my creditors, and with my editors, and arranging for my mom and my sister to come by and pick through my things. Everything else was going to go into storage. I didn't see any reason to keep my apartment, so I also needed to tell my landlord I'd be moving out. I'd lose the security deposit I'd given him, but for five million dollars I figured I could absorb the loss.

The week passed in a blur. I'd expected it to be painful, but other than saying goodbye to my mother and my sister, neither of whom quite believed that I was doing what I said I was doing and both of whom seemed to think it was more likely that I'd fallen in with the mob or some sort of drug cartel, everything went surprisingly well. I gave each of them part of the money, enough to ensure that neither of them had anything to worry about while I was gone.

And that was it. I packed up my whole life in a week and went back to the island. In a way, it was almost depressing.

* * *

My first tour of the interior of the *Johannes* was six days after I arrived. I was surprised that it had taken so long, but Zvi was still being difficult and Zub was off the island for part of that time taking care of last-minute business of his own. Since Zub refused to allow anyone other than the technical crew on the *Johannes* without him or his uncle present, there was nothing to do but wait. I spent most of my time in intensive training-- both general physical conditioning to improve my health, something Dr. Rosansky assured me I'd be continuing while on the ship, and training for whatever rigors the space trip might hold for me. My stomach eventually adapted to high-G and weightlessness; by the second trip on the Vomit Comet Myers wasn't able to get a "kill" out of me any longer. Celeste's team finished manufacturing my Flye suit, and I got my first look at myself in an honest-to-God space suit. I had her take pictures immediately and we sent them to my mother and sister for posterity.

I also did a fair amount of studying. While Dr. Rosansky was the official ship's medic, every member of the crew was expected to be able to provide basic medical care in an emergency, and while I'd had simple CPR training and could probably bandage a wound successfully, I spent a couple of hours a day in the presence of one of her nurses being instructed in medical procedures. By the time the ship launched, I was expected to be able to set a simple bone fracture and stitch a cut. I couldn't stitch in fabric, much less in human flesh, so that was going to be a bit of a hurdle for me. I also resolved to spend some time with Celeste and learn to make myself useful, if not indispensible, as a backup mechanic.

In my copious spare time, I read up on Mars, space exploration in general, and tried to rough out the structure of how I was going to write the book. There was little point to doing much planning at this early a stage, before the ship had even left Earth, but I wanted to have a few ideas in mind before I had to start taking notes. Well, *more* notes, at least, since transcribing everything I could remember about my first visit to Eunostos had been my first order of business upon returning to Indiana.

Anyway, on Day Six I got a blink from Zub. BACK ON EUNOSTOS, it said. HANGAR. NOW.

"I might be busy," I replied. "Lots to do around here, you know."

He was succinct, for once. LIAR.

"On my way."

* * *

"Welcome to your new home," Zub said, escorting me through the airlock onto the *Johannes* with a theatrical bow. The interior of the ship was as stylish as the outside, with as much attention paid to form as to function. Luckily, it didn't continue the outside's color scheme-- staring at dark blue and grey for the entire time we were inside the ship would have blinded me eventually-- and was instead decorated in ivory white and earth tones. The floor, unlike every NASA spacecraft I'd ever seen the interior of, was actually carpeted, with subtle running lights along the sides.

I'd seen the interior of the Space Shuttle. The interior of the Space Shuttle was pure science; no attention had been paid to making anything look pretty, and every square inch was used for function. The *Johannes* wasn't like that at all; this ship resembled something more suited to a movie or a science fiction program than the much older design of the *Columbia* and *Challenger*.

"There's a floor," I noted.

This was actually unusual. The previous Space Shuttles were designed for flight in zero gravity, so it wasn't always clear what the "floor" in any given area was supposed to be. The entryway to the flight deck was literally a hole in the floor, and the passageway from the mid-deck to the rest of the shuttle was in the center of the wall, meaning that if you weren't floating it was difficult to step into. The *Tycho*, similarly, had obviously been designed with zero-G in mind, with the different decks stacked on top of one another and movement up and down achieved with ladders or weightless maneuvering. The *Johannes* was laid out more like a luxury aircraft; horizontally oriented, with a clear floor and separate rooms accessed by doors instead of portals.

"We'll have gravity," Zub said. "The *Johannes* is designed to spin on a counterweighted tether while we're in flight. I tried to get the *Tycho* built on the same principle, but they decided that the weight of the tether was going to be a problem. One of the stupider design mistakes."

"The weight of the tether *won't* be a problem?" I asked. It didn't look like the *Johannes* had really been built with the weight-to-thrust ratio in the forefront of the designer's minds.

"No," he said. "We'll release once we're in transit. Most of the non-mission-critical scientific and mapping components, the lander, and some of our nonessential cargo will be at the other end of the tether, which is how we'll generate enough centrifugal force to give us gravity on this end. The thing weighs tons. Once we extend the tether, with the weight at the other end, we fire rockets that put us into a spin and, voila, gravity."

"And if something hits the tether while we're in flight, or if it breaks?"

"It's not going to break. The thing is stronger than God. It's probably the single strongest object on the entire ship. And if something hits us hard enough to break off the weight or snap the cables, well, we're probably dead anyway." I was starting to get Zub's curious fatalism about many aspects of the trip. His method seemed to be to design the ship as well as he possibly could and then stop worrying about it. This was not the type of guy to have forty different backup plans covering every eventuality; he seemed to trust in his own ingenuity and that of his crew much more than his own imagination.

"I understand. Continue," I said, and he closed the airlock door behind us. The airlock was small-- just barely enough space for the five crew to move through at a time, but only if we were willing to crowd into each other. The interior airlock door opened into a hallway that extended in both directions.

"Crew cabins on the ground floor, plus a conference room," Zub said. "Conference room doubles as a mess hall. Cabins are built for two at a time if necessary. They'll be very tight for two people but will provide a private space for one, so that we're not chewing each other's heads off while we're on the trip. Beds can be configured as sleeping bags in case we're forced to go zero-G during the flight at any point." The astronauts on the Space Shuttle had actually slept in what looked like a vertical position, in sleeping bags strapped to the "walls" to keep them from floating about while they were sleeping.

I poked my head into one of the crew cabins. It was small, but functional, with two bunk-style beds, a desk, a computer console, a number of cabinets for storage and, surprisingly, an enormous television screen built into the wall that had to be seven feet across.

"I insisted on the TVs," Zub insisted. "You'll be able to view any movie produced from about seventy years ago through *last week* on the television screens on demand, and they'll beam new stuff to us periodically. In addition, there's a library full of novels, nonfiction books, and periodicals in digital form stored in the ship's mainframes. Hundreds of thousands of volumes, and all the music you can steal, too. No one will lack for digital entertainment on this trip. It will keep us from killing each other."

"Wow," I said. I'd chosen carefully what books and music to load my own iLid with; storage was substantial but it wasn't unlimited, and most of my reading material was still physical books sitting on shelves anyway. I'd never gotten used to reading books on my iLid.

"It gets better. Once a month we'll be receiving a heavily compressed signal from Earth containing major television programs and sporting events. I'm actually paying a guy just to watch and prepare television programming for us at home. On top of that, we'll get daily updates for any Internet site any crew member has visited in the past 24 hours. When we launch, the ship will be taking most of the Internet with it. The console will allow you to communicate with family members, too, either with recorded video or sound messages or directly, if you don't mind the lag between us and Earth. You like video games?"

My head was reeling. I'd be leaving Earth behind, but it didn't look like I'd be leaving behind many of the things I *liked* about Earth. "I used to," I said.

"Got those, too. Most of 'em in emulation, but you can play about half of all the computer and video games released since the seventies. You could spend the entire trip playing video games if you wanted to."

"I don't think I want to do that," I said.

"Probably not a good idea. If nothing else, Katie will insist you get more exercise than that."

It was the first time I'd heard Zub or anyone else refer to Dr. Kathryn Rosansky as *Katie*. It did not escape my notice that he had done it while she was not in the room.

We left the bedroom. "Bathroom and shower facilities on this floor, too, across from the conference room. Get used to sponge baths most of the time; you'll get about five minutes for a shower twice a week, since they use recycled water and we won't be able to take a huge amount for washing with us. The good news is we get a new supply once we reach Mars."

Sponge baths sounded fun. "Bathrooms are set up for zero-G too, I assume?"

"Yeah," Zub said. "We thought about installing zero-g and traditional models but ended up cutting the traditional models to save on weight and water. There's running water in the bathrooms, mind you, and you can get it from a sink if you want to, but the toilets use forced air instead of flushing. You'll get used to peeing into a hose pretty quickly. Just be glad you're not one of the girls."

The conference room looked exactly similar to the one in the hangar, right down to the holographic table, except the chairs were bolted to the floor.

At either end of the hallway was a tight spiral staircase. Zub pointed toward the one to his right.

"Fore end, up to the command module. Aft end, to the recreation and medical deck. There's an elevator back there, too, in case we need to move anybody upstairs on a stretcher. Port to the cargo bay is on the second floor. Which do you want to see first?"

"Rec and medical, I think. I imagine Zvi will try and hurt me if I end up in the captain's chair before he decides it's okay for me to be there."

The staircase led up another hallway, not as lengthy as the one downstairs, no doubt due to the presence of the command module at the far end of the hall. There was another airlock-style door immediately behind the staircase; this no doubt led back to the cargo bay. Both the medical bay and the rec area were walled in glass; you could see both areas from the hallway, although I could see privacy curtains available in the med center. You were apparently doomed to be a spectacle if you decided to use the recreation area, though. It was full of equipment, the purpose of most of which I was unclear on.

"Full weight room with machines, plus two treadmills, plus a court for what I'm calling spaceball," Zub said, pointing at a metal hoop affixed to the ceiling in the rec area. "No room for a basketball court, so we put the hoop in the middle and put a court around it. We'll figure out the rules once we're in flight."

"No free weights?" I didn't actually care, I just felt the need to say something.

"You want stacks of forty-five pound weights floating around in here? Too much work to keep everything locked down. We won't be under gravity for the entire flight, remember. Just most of it. Plus, again, *weight*. When the choice is between lifting chunks of metal weighing two hundred pounds or pushing on a machine designed to resist you with the same force, you don't bring the actual weight along on a space ship."

"Fair enough," I said, feeling rather foolish. The medical suite was about what I expected; two separate sick bays, what looked like a surgery table, and cabinets full of medical supplies that I was only beginning to learn the use for.

"We can actually fully quarantine the medbay if we decide we need to," Zub said. "It's got its own air supply and everything, although it can share the ship's and will most of the time. Katie makes fun of me every time I mention alien pathogens, but I figure the flu getting loose among the crew is probably just about as bad."

There he went again with that *Katie* thing. It would be interesting to see if he ever called her that to her face.

"Can I see the cargo bay?"

He shrugged. "Nothing to see, really, but yeah." He opened the airlock door-- using some effort, I noticed-- and left it open behind us while he opened the second door. The cargo bay was just that; a wide open space, with a few scattered catwalks and metal walkways to aid in moving around.

"The tether's getting installed in the back here, and the counterweight will take up about forty percent of the available space. Most of the rest of the space will be food supplies, some essential spare parts like CO_2 scrubbers, and water tanks, which haven't been installed yet. Sometime in the next few days we'll start putting that stuff in."

"What *will* we be eating, anyway?"

"Mostly wet food, believe it or not," Zub said. "We went back and forth on the trade-off for nutrition and quality vs. weight, and ended up deciding to go with the extra weight to keep everyone happy. We'll likely be eating dehydrated for the way back, though, especially if we find the crew of the *Tycho*. But we'll have McDonald's to look forward to for the whole way home, so it won't be as bad." A wistful look crossed his face for a moment.

"Don't let yourself forget about that, Gabe. We're going to be famous, yeah, but that's not why we're doing that. I really do believe that the Tycho's crew is still out there. And we're going to bring them back. I'm not about to let Mars make a liar out of me."

I nodded. There didn't seem to be much I could say.

"I think I'll let you see the command center some other time. We'll make Tsvika do it. I'd like to be alone for a while, if you don't mind."

I left him alone there, staring into the empty cargo bay of his ship.

EIGHT

I didn't sleep for two full days leading up to the launch. Nobody did, it seemed, and the entire island was abuzz with activity-- supplies and equipment moving in, last-minute tweaks to the systems on the *Johannes*, endless testing and rehearsal of emergency procedures, even a dry run on the launch itself-- for the entire three weeks before we left. Zub seemed to be everywhere at once, even helping out the dock workers in physically unloading cargo.

As it turned out, there was a reason the VAB was so enormous. The solid rocket boosters had to be assembled from components on-site, and then attached to the external fuel tank, which was larger than the *Johannes* was. It hadn't occurred to me that every space shuttle I'd ever seen had launched from a vertical position, so I hadn't wondered how they *got* the ship into that position to begin with.

Cranes. Really, unbelievably, impressively large cranes, that grabbed the ship, hauled it into a vertical position, and kept it in place while swarms of crew took several days to make sure it was properly attached to the fuel tank and the boosters. Then the entire assembly was lifted into the air and placed on top of a giant crawler that moved the components into place at the launch site. Even in slow motion, watching it happen was impressive, and did strange things to my sense of scale-- seeing a *crane* lift something the size of a space ship three stories over my head was one of the more incredible sights I'd seen in my lifetime. I found myself wondering how long it had taken for the building itself to be built.

How long had AJ said they'd been diverting funding to the island? Five years? That, in and of itself, seemed incredible. For all of this to have been put together in half a decade seemed impossible, even for one of the richest families on the planet. I briefly considered digging more deeply into the company's finances and decided against it. I'd been given a specific job to do here; I didn't get the feeling anything *illegal* was going on, I just didn't have the whole story. Plenty of time to worry about that later.

I had finally gotten a few moments with Zvi just before the *Johannes* was moved into position before the launch. He'd continued avoiding contact with me for the first two weeks I was on the island, at which point Zub had lost all patience with him and insisted that he give me at least enough training on the *Johannes'* controls that I knew how to turn on the autopilot and the life support if I needed to.

He was already in the cockpit, his back to me, as I climbed up the spiral staircase behind him. There were five seats, enough for the entire crew, with the main pilot's seat in a slight depression toward the nose of the ship and the other four in two rows, theatre-style, behind it. The seats were oriented facing forward, but they could be rotated to interact with banks of monitors and switches and indicators running along either side of the cockpit. There were also a few switches on the ceiling, within arm's reach. The control panels for the pilot extended fully three-quarters of the way around him; only the back quadrant was free of equipment so that he could get into and out of his seat.

"Looks complicated," I said, assuming he wasn't about to start the conversation.

"Yes," Zvi said, his voice like broken glass. Hostile, angry broken glass.

I stood there waiting for a couple of minutes. Zvi didn't say anything.

Screw this guy, I thought. I hadn't done anything to him, and I was already tired of his attitude. "Anything in particular I ought to know, or should I just start pushing buttons and see what happens?"

He turned, finally lowering himself to face me. He was wearing military fatigues, of all things, and a beret with the Israeli Defense Force logo on it. He'd had a business suit on the last time I'd seen him; I wasn't sure if this was an improvement or not.

"I do not dislike you," he said. Between his thick accent and his voice, even that sentiment came off as mildly terrifying.

"I... don't dislike you either?" I wasn't sure where he was going.

"No," he said. "I need you to understand. If I have been unwelcoming to you since you have been here..."

"*Unwelcoming* doesn't quite cut it," I interrupted. "*Frighteningly hostile* would be slightly more accurate."

He waved a hand, cutting me off. "If I have been unwelcoming to you, it is not because of you. It is because I do not think that my nephew should have involved outsiders in this... *mission*." He said the word *mission* like it was an epithet.

"Why?" I asked. "I know I'm not a scientist, but..."

This time he interrupted, speaking slowly, as if sounding his words out in his head before saying them. "Science has little to do with it. I am a soldier, and Ezekiel is my brother's only son. I am obligated to look after him as best I can. Dr. Rosansky and Dr. Flye understand the risks. They have worked with my nephew for many years, and they know his... let me call them his *foibles*. You have not, and you do not. I fear that you may be placing yourself in danger for no good reason."

"There's a good chance I don't come back alive," I said. "I understand that."

"But you believe that you *will* come back alive," he said.

"Of course I do. I hope I will, at least."

He stared at me, fingers steepled in front of his face, obviously thinking carefully about what to say next.

"I do not. And I do not believe that either of the other crew members do either. Nor, I think, does my nephew."

This was unexpected.

"Why not? The plan seems sound to me. The other ship should have worked. What do you think Zub is doing wrong?"

He stared at his fingers.

"My nephew is a very talented man. If he says that this ship can fly to Mars and back, then this ship can fly to Mars and back. If he built a device to take me into the very center of the Sun, I would fly it for him without regret. But man was not meant to set foot on the surface of Mars."

"What do you think happened to the *Tycho?*"

He shrugged. "The wrath of God, perhaps. Or something else. I do not know. But that is the difference between Ezekiel and his Uncle Tsvika. I see a mystery where people have died, and I resolve not to repeat the mistakes of those who have died, if I can. Ezekiel repeats them with glee and trusts in his own cleverness to save him."

"And the others?"

"They trust in his cleverness as well. And they are motivated by other things, I think. The doctor, I believe, loves him in her way. The engineer pursues challenge above all else. But you? You are here by fate. You may turn away from this. And I think, Gabriel Southern, that you should do just that."

I didn't know what to say. At the very least, he'd changed tactics; he had been trying to scare me away at the meeting earlier, or perhaps to convince Zub not to bring me along after all. Now his affect was all about concern.

"More than two thirds of the missions sent to this planet have failed," Zvi said. "None successful for nearly fifteen years. Every person sent there has died. It may be that this is not a place mankind is meant to be. I go because I must. The others go because they must. You need not repeat their mistake."

"I'll think about what you said," I replied. "But until then, I probably ought to know what you can tell me about the ship."

He sighed. "So be it. The first thing to learn, then, is how to operate the console you can reach from your seat..."

Five minutes later, my brain froze over. In what I later discovered was typical thoroughness, Zvi walked me through every lever, button, dial, switch, warning light, and monitor in the command module, giving me detailed instructions on the use of and care for each, and then, most of the time, warning me to never touch them once he'd explained what they were for. It was an intensely dizzying experience, and by the time he was done I was still fairly certain I knew where I was supposed to sit and how to belt myself in, but there was little else about the command module that I felt certain about.

"Any questions?" he asked.

"I can't think of a thing," I replied. I was speaking literally; I'd lost the ability to think. He thought I'd meant that that I didn't have any questions, though.

"Think about what I said," he told me, patting me on the shoulder with his hand. "I have no real hope that it will change your mind. But my conscience would not let me not speak to you. *Ad machar*, Mr. Southern." He left me in the command module and walked down the stairs. Not sure what to do, I sat down in the pilot's seat. *He's convinced we're all going to die*, I thought. *He doesn't think he's ever coming home, and he's going to go through with it anyway.*

"And so am I," I said to the *Johannes*. So was I.

* * *

Nobody spoke much while we were preparing for liftoff. I was expecting Zub to be in his usual expansive mood, but even he was subdued, changing into his Flye exosuit without much of a word to anyone. I'd spent my life watching video of the Space Shuttle taking off from Cape Canaveral. This wasn't the same thing at all; for starters, no one knew we were doing it. There were no crowds to watch the liftoff, no cameras, nothing. Every available person on Eunostos was at work. There wasn't even much chatter over our radios; there was a Mission Control, but they weren't actually there for much. Zub had designed the *Johannes* so that they weren't necessary.

Getting into our seats turned out to be annoyingly complicated. The problem with Zub's decision to design the *Johannes* with an identifiable floor was that it left us with no good way to get to the cockpit and into our seats when the ship was in launch position. Zub had solved the problem with temporary scaffolding inside the ship, to be uninstalled and stowed in the cargo section once we were underway. We hauled ourselves up through the central corridor of the ship and across the staircase, then pulled ourselves into our seats.

"Strap in," Zub said. "And make sure your HUDs are on in your helmets. It's going to get loud in here in a few minutes." It was the first sentence I'd heard him say in over an hour. We strapped ourselves in. Zub and Zvi ran the ship through some diagnostics while the rest of us watched our monitors. Everything checked out.

The final countdown before liftoff was in Hebrew, Zvi's voice piped through the microphones into our helmets.

I'd never been so scared in my life.

"Eser... tesha'... sh'moneh... sheva..."

A *whump* as the *Johannes'* three main engines lit.

"Shesh... tamesh... arbah... shelosh... shtayim... achat... ephes. Launch."

A roar from outside, and the entire ship vibrated as if it was being shaken by God. Numbers and symbols and graphs started flashing across all of the monitors. I had no idea what any of them meant. Then gravity hit me in the chest and for the next few minutes I couldn't think of anything at all. It seemed to last forever, but it couldn't have been more than a couple of minutes.

THIRTY SECONDS TO SRB JETTISON, read a blink from Zub. Half a minute later, another small jolt as the solid rocket boosters fell away from the ship. Ordinarily, they would land in the ocean to be recovered later. These would land in the ocean, too, but I had no idea if Zub was planning on having them brought back to land. The pressure on our bodies lessened as the three main engines took over.

TEN MORE MINUTES, came another blink. The solid rocket boosters had given us most of our thrust, and the three ship's main engines would consume the rest of the fuel in the external fuel tank, angling slightly as we flew to point us on the right trajectory toward Mars. Once the fuel in the external tank was consumed, it would fall away from the ship, and any additional course corrections would be provided by the limited fuel supply the *Johannes* had onboard.

I looked over at Dr. Rosansky, who was sharing the back row with me. She had her head tilted back in her seat, eyes closed, murmuring to herself about something. I found myself wondering if she was saying a prayer. I tried to get a good look out of the front of the ship, but the windows were set for visibility from the pilot's seat, not from mine.

A few minutes later, the external fuel tank finally fell from the underbelly of the *Johannes*. With the external fuel tank gone, the final impacts rattled through the ship as the maneuvering rockets pointed us toward Mars on a Hohmann trajectory. With inertia no longer shoving us back into our seats, weightlessness finally took over.

"We're getting well away from the planet before we release the tether and establish gravity," Zub said. "Another couple of hours, at least. We need to make sure we're on the right trajectory before we complicate things further." It was possible to adjust our flight path even while spinning, but it was a lot easier to adjust things beforehand, when our angular momentum didn't need to be taken into account. He reached up and disengaged his helmet from his suit, which floated away when he let go of it.

"Stow your helmet," Zvi said. "I don't need anything floating around the cockpit." Zub shrugged and released himself from the restraints in his chair, then floated up and recovered his missing helmet.

"Let me know when it's time to release the tether," he said. "Let's go enjoy weightlessness, everybody." The three of us unbelted ourselves from our seats and one by one maneuvered our way down the stairwell to the main corridor. We threw ourselves up and down the hallway for a few minutes, enjoying the idea of being weightless for more than the few seconds we'd been allowed on the Vomit Comet, then adjourned to the rec room upstairs to see what Zub's spaceball game was like without gravity. As it turned out, it was virtually unplayable if you intended to take it seriously. It was too easy to just float up to the hoop, grab hold, and wait for a teammate to throw you the ball. *No rocket boots* quickly became a house rule as well. I'd half expected Zvi to eventually leave the command module and join us, but he stayed in position, no doubt constantly monitoring for anything that could possibly go wrong.

After we all tired of the game, Zub cleared us all to remove our space suits-- which, incidentally, had done an excellent job of keeping everyone cool despite the physical activity-- and I went back to my cabin to relax for a bit. At Zub's suggestion, most of the clothes I'd brought were loose-fitting, relatively shapeless, and warm; lots of sweatpants and hooded sweatshirts, with a few pairs of baggy jeans and a dozen or so T-shirts thrown into the mix as well. There were a couple of crates of standard-issue replacement clothes in the cargo bay somewhere, too; after all, we'd had to pack enough clothing to last us for three years, and a lot of what we'd initially brought with us was going to get awfully threadbare in that time; we were also hoping we'd need extra clothes for the *Tycho* refugees. We were going to spend nearly all of the trip looking awfully casual, though.

I'd selected one of the cabins farthest from the front of the ship, figuring that if I stayed away from the command module and the conference room/mess hall that that would provide the closest thing to privacy that it was actually possible to get on the ship. All of my possessions were stowed in cabinets at the moment, there being no point to doing any actual unpacking until the ship had established gravity.

I hadn't actually spent much time in the cabin-- other people had packed everything away for me-- so I took a few minutes to look around. Walking in from the corridor, the room stretched out ahead of me and to my right, with the long side of the rectangle being the wall along the corridor and along the outside of the ship. The wall opposite me was blank, completely featureless. The bunk beds and the desk were to my right, on the short wall on the fore side of the room, and to my left was the large television screen I'd noticed before. The rest of the wall space was taken up mostly with storage cabinets.

That blank wall caught my attention, for some reason. It looked as if it was made of a different material than the rest of the room; something smoother and more regular than the slightly pebbled texture the walls in the rest of the *Johannes* had. I walked over and touched it.

A split second later, the wall *disappeared*, replaced with the blackness of space. I shrieked like a girl and threw myself away from the vacuum, trying to remember what I'd been told to do in case of explosive decompression and wondering how long I had to live. The panic lasted until I slammed into the wall behind me and realized that decompression would have thrown me into space by now.

FORTY SECONDS, came the blink. WHO'S GOT LESS THAN A MINUTE IN THE POOL? It was Zub, the bastard.

IT WAS ZVI, Celeste responded. THAT'S $500, CONGRATULATIONS.

The damn thing was an enormous viewscreen, camouflaged to look like the wall. I was watching a feed from cameras on the outside of the ship-- Zub's way of giving us windows in a place where they wouldn't be structurally possible.

It was actually pretty freaking cool, once I got over the initial terror. Earth was the largest thing visible on the screen, with the moon just starting to peek over the horizon. I could actually see my home planet receding on the monitor as we pulled away.

VERY FUNNY, I responded, including everyone. ANY OTHER SECRETS NOBODY TOLD ME ABOUT? WHOOPIE CUSHION ON MY BED? SOMETHING HIDING IN THE CLOSET? In return, I got nothing but a burst of laughter over the suit radio.

If I was going to spend the entire trip in the company of practical jokers, I was going to have to start coming up with ideas for revenge.

I fished some clothes out of a plastic sack (I'd shown up with a suitcase and been mocked for it; suitcases only added weight) and touched the monitor again, turning it back off. I thought about it for a moment and decided to take the bottom bunk; I had a lingering fear of heights and a tendency to roll around a lot at night, which made the idea of sleeping five feet off the ground something to be avoided. I took the t-shirt and sweats I'd selected out of the bag and set them down on the bed, then laughed at myself when they immediately floated off the bed on their own private mission. *No point in setting anything down anywhere for a little while,* I thought, and simply let go of my helmet. There was a special cabinet for the suits which kept them on but powered down at all times, avoiding wear and tear on the batteries, and also ran diagnostics on them to avoid any chance of us missing small tears or other defects in the suit.

I stashed the helmet, gloves, boots, and backpack in their assigned places in the cabinet and wormed myself out of the suit. It fit much the same way that the Spandex unitard substitute had fit, with one exception: I'd stepped into the unitard through an opening in the back, which just closed with Velcro once I had the suit on. Velcro was, for obvious reasons, considered unsuitable for use on pressurized spacesuits, so this suit's seal was reinforced electrostatically somehow. Dr. Flye had given me an explanation; the two flaps on the seal were charged in such a way that they stuck to each other, and with the backpack on the seal was probably the single strongest part of the suit. I was more likely to accidentally tear open the suit at the joints than to lose the seal in the back.

Naturally, though, you had to issue a command to the suit to disengage the seal, and that was only available through the helmet, which I'd just stowed away. For the first time in my life, I'd failed at getting undressed. I put the helmet back on, released the seal, and climbed out of the exosuit.

Getting dressed in zero gravity took a little bit of getting used to, too, but I managed to figure that out after a few minutes as well. Putting my shirt on was simple enough, but I discovered quickly that it was better to try to put both legs into the sweat pants at the same time rather than one at a time.

I got a blink from Zvi a few seconds after I finally got dressed.

OPTIMUM TRAJECTORY MET. BEGINNING TETHER RELEASE PROCEDURE IN FIVE MINUTES, it said. Our brief flirtation with zero gravity was about to come to an end, then.

There was a knock at my door. It was Celeste.

"Sorry about that," she said, a big smile on her face. "Zub was actually supposed to point out the monitor wall to you when he gave you the tour of the ship, but he forgot. Once he realized he hadn't said anything about it, it was my idea to do the bet. You don't hold grudges, do you?"

"My revenge will be painful and unavoidable," I said.

"No, then? Okay." She floated over to the monitor wall and touched it, turning it back on. "The tether release is almost entirely automated other than touching a few buttons, so we don't need to do anything to help, but I thought I'd show you something." She reached for the wall again, but instead of simply touching it she dragged her hand across its surface. The image rotated in the direction her hand had moved, until the *Johannes* emerged into view. The cameras were obviously set on the top of the ship; I was looking at the same view everyone else had access to instead of the view through "my" window, but had some ability to point the thing where I wanted. We could see the aft portion of the ship, which included the entire cargo compartment.

"We can watch," she said. "This actually ought to be pretty neat." Without asking, she turned the chair away from my desk and took a seat. With no other options, I sat down on the bed. A second later, we both floated out of our seats, leaving us feeling silly again. "Takes some getting used to, doesn't it?" she said.

"Seriously, I'm not going to run into any other surprises in the room, am I?"

"None that I'm aware of," she said. "And the only parts of the ship that I'm not aware of are currently inside those cabinets. Somebody could have stashed something strange in one of them, I suppose, but I kind of doubt it. Like I said, finding out about the monitor wall wasn't supposed to be a joke."

"I will consider forgiving you someday," I said. "Until then, fear my wrath." It would be interesting to see how our day-to-day lives during the trip would go. We really had little to do other than derail each other's lives in more and more disruptive ways. I entertained myself for a few minutes by contemplating the opportunities for mischief on a space shuttle.

A screeching sound from one of my cabinets cut short my reverie. Both of us jumped, my leap propelling me into the ceiling of my room before I could react to my motion. Celeste hadn't been within reach of the floor, so her reaction was more comic but less painful.

"What the hell was that?" she said.

"I have no idea," I said. "Please tell me you were kidding about stashing something strange inside of the cabinets."

More screeching and rattling. The door to the cabinet shook back and forth.

Suddenly my blood turned cold as I realized I recognized the noises I was hearing. "Wait a second," I said. "I know that sound." *There is no way Zub is this dumb,* I thought, and opened the cabinet.

Eight pounds of screeching monkey launched itself at high speed out of the cabinet directly into my face. Eight pounds of screeching monkey wearing a tiny, monkey-sized white space suit.

"My God," Celeste said. "Tell me that isn't *Sajad.*"

It was Sajad. "In a space suit," I said. "He made a space suit for his monkey." The thing even had a Zahav International logo on its ridiculous little helmet.

"He brought a *monkey* with us to *Mars,*" Celeste said. "I'm going to *kill him.*" Sajad kicked me in the shoulder and launched himself for the ceiling, where he grabbed a corner of one of the cabinets and screeched at us again. There was a miniature command chair inside of the cabinet. He'd managed to get himself out of the restraints somehow.

"Zub! Get down here *right now.*" She hadn't bothered to blink it, opting to send the message over the ship's PA system, using an access point by the door. A few seconds later, the response arrived by blink. FEED MY MONKEY, he said. THERE'S FOOD IN THE MESS FOR HIM. BE DOWN ONCE THE TETHER IS OUT.

It was actually a little scary how aggravated Celeste was. "He's insane. He's *insane.* What are we going to do with a freaking *monkey* on the ship for the next six months? How are we supposed to deal with him on Mars? Is that... God, is that one of *my* suits?" It looked like it was, actually; just minimized and reworked to fit Sajad's less than human anatomy. There was even an extension of the suit for his tail. I couldn't imagine when

Zub had had time to have the thing manufactured, much less gotten it past Dr. Flye or gotten Sajad trained to wear it without flipping out.

"Hey," I said, "they're releasing the counterweight." The cargo bay doors had slid open in the aft portion of the *Johannes,* and the enormous counterweight was slowly sliding free of the ship. The counterweight was more or less exactly what Zub had described it as; a large cargo container, full of heavy supplies that we wouldn't be needing during the flight to Mars, including our lander, a motorized rover, and a number of other items, and it was slowly unspooling a thick, multistranded cable as it gradually floated away from the ship. I could see a few cameras on the outside of it, as well as what had to be maneuvering rockets. They would have to fire in precise synchronization with the rockets on the ship to get us spinning, a procedure which would provide artificial gravity to the *Johannes* if Zub and his engineers had done the math right and spin us completely out of control if they hadn't. I kept my fingers crossed. Physics was easy, right?

The counterweight gradually drifted to the extent of the tether's reach, putting it what looked like the better part of a mile away from the *Johannes.* As it reached the end of the cable, maneuvering rockets fired, slowing its movement, and I could see the cable retract slightly, providing tension along its length without a jerk that could pull the ship slightly off its trajectory.

Maneuvering rockets along the sides of the *Johannes* and the counterweight all spat at the same time, providing just a moment of propulsion. From my perspective, it didn't look like either moved, but the field of stars in the background started shifting off to the right, slowly. The rockets fired again, this time for a few seconds, and our angular velocity increased. I started sliding toward the floor as centrifugal force began to assert a hold on us. Sajad, who had grown quite comfortable in his perch on the ceiling, began screeching again as his grasp on the cabinet grew more tenuous. He launched himself at me again; I caught him this time, depositing him on my shoulder. Figuring out how to get him out of his space suit was going to be an interesting challenge. The rockets fired a third time, and for a moment I felt much too heavy as I hit the floor and my knees had to support my weight for the first time in a few hours. All over the ship, I could hear soft *thumps* as every person and object in the cargo bay and in the living quarters drifted to the ground. A moment later, the maneuvering rockets gave one final burst of propulsion-- this time in the *opposite* direction, slowing our spin by an infinitesimal amount, and the world felt normal again.

"Gravity restored," Zub's voice said over the intercom. "Please enjoy your flight."

"I swear I'm going to kill him," Celeste said.

*   *   *

To Dr. Flye's great credit, her first reaction upon seeing Zub in the *Johannes'* conference room was not to launch herself at him and tear off his face. She did, however, throw a metal pot at him, the first portable object she could get her hands on upon walking into the room.

"What?" was all he had to say.

"There is a *monkey* on my *ship*, Ezekiel," she said. I was a little surprised she wasn't foaming at the mouth.

"Your ship? That's interesting." Zub, on the other hand, was remaining remarkably calm for a man who had just had to dodge flying cookware. "I thought it was mine."

"You know what I mean, you idiot," she said. "Are there any other living things on the ship that the rest of us should know about? Much less share our oxygen, water, and food with? Is there a giraffe or a flock of geese hiding in the cargo bay somewhere?"

"The cargo bay's not pressurized," Zub said placidly. Sajad leapt off my shoulder and ran over to him. He removed the monkey's helmet and backpack and Sajad did the rest, sliding out of the space suit as if he'd been doing it since the day he was born. "If there was a giraffe in the cargo bay, it would have asphyxiated by now. And I can't imagine the g-force from launch would be good for something with those legs."

Celeste hit the intercom button by the door. "Everyone to the conference room," she said. "Ezekiel's got a surprise for all of us."

All of us, as it turned out, only meant Zvi, as Kathryn betrayed no surprise whatsoever at Sajad's presence on the ship. Zvi was, rather predictably, also annoyed with the sudden revelation that we had a pet, although he limited his displeasure to giving Zub the same glare he'd had on his face when he first met me. I found myself surprisingly neutral about the entire thing. Sajad would provide some comic relief on the trip, at least, and while his presence certainly meant some logistical strangeness once we got onto the planet's surface, I didn't think he'd be eating or drinking enough to really make that much of a difference during the trip.

"The first living thing in outer space was a monkey," Zub said. "I thought having one with us was appropriate."

"First, Ezekiel, it wasn't a monkey, it was a *dog*," Celeste shot back, a contradiction that Zub appeared unconcerned with. "And do you know the difference between that dog and this monkey? Everybody *knew* there was going to be a dog in space, and nobody was *surprised* when it jumped out of a cabinet and attacked them. I cannot believe you've done something this irresponsible."

"We'll be fine," he said. "The monkey's spent as much time aboard the ship as you have, believe it or not. He can get into and out of that suit in about five seconds. I've even got him wired into your HUDs so that he'll show up when we're outside the ship. He's even been toilet-trained." He looked at me as he said this; my first experience peeing into a tube had been a bit messier than I'd wanted it to be. "He poses no health risks of any kind. You have no valid argument against me bringing him along other than not knowing about it in advance."

He stared at Celeste, then at Zvi, clearly daring either of them to continue arguing. Celeste opened her mouth to say something else, then closed it, made an exasperated sound, then started talking again.

"Air and food," she said. "He's breathing and I assume he's going to eat while he's on the ship, since you ordered me to feed him a few minutes ago. How much of our fuel are we burning to overcome moving the supplies to keep the monkey alive?"

"Nothing," Zub said.

This took all of us by surprise. "Nothing?" Kathryn said. "I'm not a veterinarian or anything, but I don't see how that works."

Zub signed. "Fine, spoil my game. C'mere, Sajad."

I'd seen the monkey respond to verbal commands once or twice before, but it was uncanny the way the thing spun on a heel and darted toward Zub at the sound of its name.

Then Zub grabbed him by the neck and yanked his head off.

Everyone screamed at once. Zub tossed the monkey's head at me. In a state of numb shock, I caught the thing. It screeched at me and tried to bite my thumb.

Parts of my brain decided they'd had enough for the day and simply shut themselves off. The rest of me noticed that there was no blood on my hand and that there seemed to be some sort of metal *joint* attached to the bottom of the monkey's head.

"Christ, it's a robot."

Kathryn was still hollering. Zub placed Sajad's body on the table and it ambled over to me to recover its head. I handed the head over and the monkey put its head back on.

"The *monkey* is a *robot*, Zub." I couldn't believe how real it looked. The thing had spent who knows how much time crawling all over me; it had *body heat*.

"I know it's a robot," he said. "I built it."

"Robot?" Celeste said, starting to come around.

"I've seen it *eat*," I said. "And I'm pretty sure it threw poop at me once. Tell me this isn't the same Sajad as the one on the island." It looked *exactly the same* as a real monkey.

"Nope, he's always been a robot," Zub said. "Pet project of mine."

I suddenly regretted not still having Sajad's head in my hands. I really, really wanted to throw something at him. "You built a digestive system into a robot? And built a space suit for it?"

"And wanted me to *feed* it?" Celeste said, having replaced her former aggravation with utter bewilderment.

"Sure," Zub said. "I wanted it to look real. And Sajad actually draws a fair percentage of his power from food and water, believe it not. On that note: ha ha, fooled you." The monkey screeched at us and made a gesture at Celeste. I was about halfway certain it had given her the finger.

"That's the most insane idea I've ever heard, and I'm on a space ship right now which is *headed to Mars on a rescue mission*," I said.

"Welcome to the *Johannes*," Zub said to me. "This will be life for the next six months. I hope you guys are ready for it."

I hoped I was too.

PART TWO

ONE HUNDRED AND SEVENTY-EIGHT DAYS LATER

NINE

"Right there," Celeste said, pointing at a bright red star in the center of the wall monitor in my room. "That's Mars." She circled the planet with her finger, leaving a yellow circle around the dot. It wasn't anything terribly special that Mars was visible from the ship's cameras-- after all, for a good portion of the year the planet was visible with the naked eye from *Earth*-- but after months of travel it was good to occasionally remind ourselves that our destination was actually out there somewhere and that we were finally going to reach it soon. Mars was the largest thing in the sky at the moment, but at this distance that still only amounted to a few times larger than your average star.

Little of any real importance had happened during the trip, which we all felt was probably the best news the mission could possibly have had. We'd received word from Eunostos soon after leaving that a number of foreign governments had detected our launch, that none of them were especially happy about not being told about the mission in advance, and that only the speed of our launch had prevented the Russians from launching missiles at us. Zub had left instructions for a press conference to be held 24 hours after the launch, both to reveal the existence of the mission and to announce Zahav International's upcoming line of startlingly real artificial pet monkeys. The press conference had initially sent Zahav International's stock prices into a nosedive, a nosedive that had been reversed rather quickly once word got out to the general public that a rescue and recovery mission had been launched for the survivors of the *Tycho*. My suggestion that the recovery in stock price was primarily due to legions of frustrated prospective monkey owners was met with derision.

Apparently the five of us were already worldwide heroes in absentia, and most of our living relatives had been tracked down and interviewed by someone or another. A photo of my own mother had adorned the front page of *People's* website within a week of the launch. Zub refused to send back frequent radio updates the way the *Tycho* had, however, which only fed the mania for information. I could only imagine how our families were putting up with it.

But little of the excitement reached us on the ship. I spent most of my time reading, watching movies, generally with Celeste, and playing occasional two-on-two games of spaceball with Zub and Kathryn or free-for-all games with the entire crew. Zub and Kathryn had become, if not a couple, at least a *duo*, much the same way that Celeste and I had.

Zvi continued to hold himself aloof from the rest of us, frequently spending his time in his room, often reading religious scripture, or working out in the recreation room by himself.

Sajad did whatever he wanted. He'd built himself a nest of sorts in Zub's room and another in mine, and he split his time between the two of us. I occasionally tried to examine him to figure out how he worked, but the monkeybot seemed to know when I was in a curious mood and either avoided me or fled whenever I tried to examine him. I still could barely believe he was artificial; I'd likely have never figured it out if Zub hadn't told us.

I had learned to work out, too, and was probably in the best shape of my life. It was difficult *not* to work out regularly when the equipment was one of only two good ways to get any sort of physical exercise on the ship; I'd learned quickly that I didn't like cycling or running on the treadmill, so whenever I had physical energy to burn off I did it with the weight equipment. The food was nutritious, I suppose, but there was little to recommend it other than that. I had a strong suspicion that once cheeseburgers and French fries were available to me again, I'd rapidly lose what gains I'd made on the trip. We were all required to have a medical and psychological consultation with Dr. Rosansky once a week, too. As the only part of my schedule that was guaranteed to happen on a fixed schedule, I found myself looking forward to it.

But now, with only two days of travel left, everyone, even Zvi, was in a happy, relaxed mood. None of us really knew what to expect once we reached the planet's surface, but at least *looking for something* was going to give us some variety.

"Mind if I work in here?" Celeste asked.

"Not at all," I said, reading something on my iLid and not bothering to look directly at her. I was halfway through the last story in a compendium of *Tarzan* stories, and I had no intention of landing on Mars before I'd finished it. Celeste had spent at least a day or two a week since we'd left poring over enhanced images of the Martian surface, trying to find the "green spot" the crew of the *Tycho* had referenced just before their ship went dark. She'd had no luck at all, despite having gotten at least one good look at nearly every corner of the planet at some point or another during our trip. This was our biggest problem, of course; we'd established contact with the automated ship Zub had sent in advance of the *Johannes* soon after launch, and planned to land near it as a backup plan, but everyone on board preferred to at least know *where* the green spot was, if not what it was, before making touchdown.

No luck, though. From everything we'd seen so far, if there ever had been a green spot on Mars, which was vanishingly unlikely to begin with, it was gone by now.

"Holy God," Celeste said. "Gabe."

"Hmm?" I asked.

"Gabe, *look*," she said.

I looked. She'd zoomed into the Martian surface from one of the scopes in the *Johannes'* nose. What we were looking at was unmistakable: a large green spot standing out from the red of the Martian surface, with an oval-shaped black spot directly in the center of it.

"Holy crap," I said. "You found it! I knew if you looked long enough, it'd turn up."

"That's not it, Gabe," she said. "I just looked at this part of the planet *last week*. There was no green spot here last week. Now there is. That's got to be twenty or thirty miles wide and it *wasn't there* a week ago. What the hell is going on?"

I had no idea, and told her so. "What's that thing in the middle? It looks like the telescope is missing a spot or something like that."

"That's... wait a minute," she said, waving her hands over the monitor, the image flying by underneath her fingertips. A moment later there were two more green spots visible on the planet's surface, both with nearly-identical black circular shapes in their centers. A few more minutes of searching produced a total of seven of the circles. Five of them had green clouds around them.

"The skylights," she breathed, her voice almost a whisper. "The green spots are around the skylights."

"Skylights?"

She pulled back the view, showing all seven of the green spots in one view. "It's a nickname," she said. "What you're looking at is an extinct volcano near the Martian equator. It's called Arsia Mons. It's not far from Olympus Mons, which is the largest mountain in the solar system. The skylights were seen for the first time in 2007. They're literally *giant holes* in the side of the planet. This one, the largest, is called Dena. They're named after the wives of the people who discovered them, I think. Anyway, they're huge-- you could fit a football field inside of the openings-- and the other six are so deep that we've never been able to see to the bottom. Dena's about a hundred and thirty meters deep, meaning you could stand a football field on its *side* and still not be able to get out. A couple of the missions of the last few years, the ones that have failed, were supposed to drop a probe into them. We don't have the *slightest idea* what's down there."

"Holes. In Mars."

"Holes in Mars. The best guess is that they're entrances into some sort of subterranean cave system, thus everyone calling them *skylights*. But, again, they're probably at least a hundred meters deep, each. I don't know how we'd get down there even if we wanted to."

"Have you looked at them before now?"

She shot me an annoyed look. "I just said that. I was looking at them *last week*, and I'm telling you they *weren't green* six days ago. And now five of the seven have a green halo around them. No idea what it is or where it came from, or how it got there so fast."

"How close can you get to them? Any idea what the spots *are?*"

"None," she said, chewing her lower lip. "The scope doesn't have the resolution to pull out details on surface features just yet. But now we know why we hadn't seen them before or why the crew didn't notice them until they were on approach to the planet. Chances are, the feature *wasn't there* when they were looking before."

"We should get Zub," I said.

"We should get *everybody*," she agreed. "We've got to decide what we're going to do about this. Meet me in the conference room in ten minutes." She killed the display on my screen and hurried out the room. Sajad, sensing something exciting happening, leapt from the top bunk and ran out after her.

*   *   *

"Fascinating," Zvi said. Celeste had just spent ten minutes showing everyone previous satellite imagery of the area around the skylights, including the first images recorded in 2007, and comparing them to the images she'd just taken from my room a few minutes before. That one-word reaction could well have been the most excited I'd ever seen Zvi get about anything. Kathryn, clearly in disbelief, was sitting in her seat with her mouth hanging open comically. Zub's eyes were wide, clearly entranced.

"They're real," he said. "The green spots are real. I can't believe it." This last sentence got him an irritated look from Zvi.

"I'm wondering something," I said. "Didn't the recording you showed us only mention a green *spot?* These are close together, aren't they, Celeste?"

"They're basically in a line, all within about 160 miles of each other," she said. "All on the side of the same mountain. If you're close enough to see one, you're close enough to see all of them."

"So they were either all surrounded by the green, or only one of them was," Zub said. "And then it went away, and now it's back. That about the idea?"

"That's about the idea," Celeste said.

"So which one do we land on?" Zub asked. "And where?"

"I am not convinced that that is a wise course of action," Zvi said. "The domicile module and the return fuel tank are perhaps a hundred kilometers away from these green spots. We should land there first and establish a base. Landing too close to the green areas seems incautious to me."

"That's my middle name," Zub said.

"Your middle name is Shlomo," Zvi replied evenly. "We are still perhaps 35 hours from planetary orbit. I will begin scanning to see if there are any signals from orbit or the planet surface that might originate from the *Tycho*. If we can find them, I will entertain the idea of landing on or nearer to one of the green spots; one of these so-called skylights. If we do not, unless you plan to relieve me of my duties as pilot, we will follow the original plan and land near the domicile module."

"Both of the rovers can do a hundred-klick round trip easily," Celeste said. "Even if we don't find a signal, we should be able to drive over once we're on the planet's surface and check the place out by ourselves. I don't know that I like the idea of landing there either."

"Kathryn? Gabe?" Zub looked at the two of us. "There's a reason I brought five people along. No tie votes."

"We are not *voting*," Zvi said.

"Yes we are," Zub said.

"I vote we land at the domicile module," I said, putting a rest to the argument before it began. "That's three votes not to land on the mysterious green stuff. Dr. Rosansky?"

"Four to one," she said. "Sorry, Ezekiel. We've come too far to throw caution to the winds now. We're not far from the point where we lost contact with the *Tycho* altogether. I don't think we should tempt fate any further than we have to."

"Fine," Zub said, accepting defeat. "Gabe, do me a favor, though, before we get much closer. Gather up any notes you've taken for the book, plus a recording of the conversation we just had and all of the images Celeste showed us, and tightbeam everything back to Earth. We found the green spots well before the *Tycho* did. It's time everybody knew about them."

"I can do that," I said. It would take a couple of hours of work, but it wasn't like I had a whole lot of other things I needed to be doing. "We were recording this conversation?"

"Yep," Zub said, producing a chip from underneath the table. "I recorded just about every important talk held in this room. Figured you'd need backups later."

"Glad to see you're so thorough," I said. "This is a copy, right?"

"Of course it is," Zub said. "Now get to work. If we disappear tomorrow, I want people to know what we were doing."

*   *   *

The *Johannes* was built to be capable of landing on the Martian surface, but in the absence of paved runways, this was considered to be a rather unwise idea unless there was grave danger to the ship or its inhabitants. The previous flight had deposited on the surface a small domicile module, two solid rocket boosters and an external fuel tank which had mostly filled themselves, synthesizing rocket fuel out of the Martian atmosphere (there was no need for the solid rocket boosters unless the *Johannes* actually landed; their power mostly being necessary to escape the planet's gravity) and a rover with enough range to get us to around a third of the planet's total surface area. The fuel tanks had their own rockets on them and were able to rendezvous and hook up with the *Johannes* in orbit once they'd fueled themselves. The rest was for us. The *Johannes* would remain in orbit, certainly with Sajad and possibly with Zvi on board (this point had been debated endlessly on the trip out to Mars, with Zvi and Zub both switching sides a number of times) and the rest of us would descend to the planet's surface in the lander currently stored in the counterweight storage container at the other end of the tether. Once we'd gotten ourselves into orbit around Mars, the counterweight would be hauled back in and unloaded. The *Johannes* would be weightless for the duration of the orbit around Mars.

Since it had turned out that they had chosen more or less the perfect place to put the domicile module, it didn't end up being terribly difficult to get Zub to come around on the idea of not planting ourselves directly on top of the green area. As we came closer to the planet's surface, the green areas mysteriously receded as quickly as they'd appeared, and when we woke up the morning we were to insert the ship into orbit, they were gone. This didn't reassure anyone. Zvi, in particular, had convinced himself that the green spots were hostile in some indeterminable way.

I'd sent the tightbeam back to Earth with all of the information Zub requested, only to be bombarded with demands for additional information from our little Mission Control outfit on Eunostos. We beamed back that we didn't have anything in particular, but agreed to send a signal back home every fifteen minutes for the duration of our stay on the planet. We'd found the green spots, but we still didn't have any idea what had caused the *Tycho* to lose contact. Nor had Zvi's attempts to track down a signal from the *Tycho* borne any fruit. There was no sign of any wreckage on the planet's surface, either, although it was far from clear whether such a thing might be visible from orbit.

"Mars doesn't have a single human-made satellite right now, other than the ERSV that we put there," Zub said. "There used to be a few in orbit, but they're all decommissioned now, and none of them are still orbiting the planet. If the *Tycho* had blown up in orbit, I don't think there's any way that there wouldn't still be some pieces of junk floating around the planet."

"That leaves two possibilities," I said, thinking it through. "The *Tycho* is either on the planet's surface, or it's... well, anywhere else in the solar system or out of it, actually. If they'd done a burn out of orbit, or had been knocked out of orbit somehow, they could be almost anywhere."

Zub thought about that for a moment. "It would be hugely unscientific of me to say that I don't feel like that happened, wouldn't it?"

"Turn in your Mad Scientist badge, ben Zahav. You filthy hippie."

"What's a hippie?"

"Never mind." *God, he's young*, I thought. "One huge mystery at a time, I guess."

"There's one more possibility, you know," Zub said, settling into his Mysterious Voice, which I hadn't heard in a while.

"Probably more than that, but from your tone of voice you really seem to want me to know what it is." *Please don't let this be horrible*, I thought.

"If the ship was vaporized, they wouldn't have left anything behind."

"Ah, great. I'm glad I have that idea in my head now, Zub. Thanks. Now I get to add vaporization to the list of things I don't want to happen to me in the next 48 hours. Really, that's great."

"Sorry," he said. "If it helps any, it occurred to me first and I'm as freaked out by it as you are."

"I doubt it," I said.

*   *   *

"So now what?" I asked. We'd gotten close enough to Mars that the planet looked bigger than Earth's moon through the "windows" built into our rooms, so it was time to figure out for certain exactly who was going to land and how we were going to do it.

"We reel in the counterweight," Zvi said. "That removes our local gravity. I put the *Johannes* into orbit. And then we descend to the planet's surface. Or, at least, some of us do. I believe I will stay on the *Johannes*. There is much that needs to be done here."

"I still think you should come to the surface with us," Zub said. "Why would you come all this way and not finish the trip?"

Zvi shrugged. "Someone should stay with the *Johannes*. It may as well be me." He entered a series of commands into the computers in front of him. "Dr. Rosansky, Gabriel, you should go to the cargo bay and make sure everything is secured properly. We will begin bringing in the counterweight when you give us the all-clear."

We got up and headed down the stairs. The check was routine and completed in a few minutes; the cargo bay was currently pressurized and under gravity, as was the rest of the ship, and it was important to make sure that nothing would go flying out of the cargo bay when we pulled the tether back in. We tightened a few lids on crates, but there was little else that needed doing. We locked the airlock door to the crew portion of the ship and radioed back to Zvi that the job was done. A few moments later, we heard a loud hiss from the cargo bay as the atmosphere was sucked from the cargo bay and back into the storage tanks for our use. There was no point in venting good air out into the Martian atmosphere.

"Prepare for loss of gravity," Zvi's voice said over the intercom, and the maneuvering rockets fired. Kathryn and I went into my quarters to watch the procedure on the monitor wall. It was necessary to stop the spin first before bringing in the tether; to do otherwise would *increase* the rate of our spin, possibly damaging the ship and definitely making life for the inhabitants highly unpleasant. I said goodbye to gravity as the ship's angular momentum slowed and everything floated off the floor again. A few moments later, the winch in the cargo bay activated and the counterweight began its slow descent back to the ship. A robotic arm on the back of the *Johannes* would ensure that it ended up precisely where it belonged, at which point we would repressurize the cargo bay, unpack what we needed from the storage bin, and descend to the planet's surface. It promised to be several hours of hard work, even without the onus of having to lift everything. Weightlessness did have some advantages, I supposed.

A few hours later, everyone converged into the *Johannes'* control center as Zvi inserted the ship into orbit. Everyone, right down to Sajad, who was in his usual spot atop Zub's shoulder, was in their space suits in case something catastrophic happened to the ship. No one wanted to miss whatever was going to happen or, worse, to be alone when it did.

I'd been ambivalent about this idea. If something happened to the ship that was so severe that I'd need my Flye exosuit in order to help me survive, I wasn't sure that I actually wanted to live through it. A quick death seemed vastly preferable to slowly expiring on, or in orbit around, an alien planet. But I wore the suit anyway.

It was almost anticlimactic when Zvi put us in geosynchronous orbit above Arsia Mons without a single trace of a problem. The planet lay forty thousand miles beneath us, adding a serene red horizon to Zub's forward view port and filling the monitors the rest of us were using. Zub sent a transmission back to Earth confirming our success, and several minutes later we received a response message mostly consisting of whooping and hollering. It seemed that Mission Control had been chewing on their metaphorical fingernails as badly as we had.

"Let's go build a lander," Zub said, and we filed out of the bridge.

*   *   *

"Are you ready for this?" Celeste asked. She was tightening bolts and making other minor modifications and adjustments to our lander-- which, to my surprise, had shipped to Mars mostly *disassembled* in the crates. She and Zub had spent four hours wiring and bolting everything together, the last part accomplished outside of the *Johannes* itself, as the assembled lander became too unwieldy to put together in the cargo bay. The living space on the lander was astonishingly small-- there was room for the five of us, but only barely; the entire lander was barely the size of the airlocks on the *Johannes*, with two benches and no individual seating. As Zub had explained, all the thing needed to do was to get us to the ground and back without killing us, which meant that it needed some shielding against the heat of reentry and a propulsion mechanism; the rest of it was just storage space. We'd actually ride down on top of the domicile module and not inside it as I'd expected; the part we were inhabiting was the only piece designed to be able to return to the *Johannes* afterward. Everything else would stay on the planet's surface once we were done with it. Once we were back on the *Johannes*, the ship would grab the ERSV out of orbit, thus ensuring we had supplies to live on during the trip back, and off we would go. My job had mostly been to keep an eye on everything and make sure no essential components drifted away from the ship. In that, I was successful.

"You're not trying to talk me out of going down with you, are you?" I asked. "It seems like every member of the crew has tried to talk me out of this at some point except for Zub. I'm kind of getting tired of insisting on coming along."

"That's not what I meant, no," she said, a slightly wounded expression on her face. "I mean that we're about to enter human history, here."

"We're already there," I said. "We have been since we got noticed leaving the planet. We're the human race's first interplanetary refugees." That got a laugh out of her, which was gratifying.

I thought about the idea for a moment. "Honestly? No. I'm not ready for this at all. None of us are. There's *no way* to be ready for something like this. What I am, mostly, is impatient. I'm tired of not knowing what's going to happen and ready to be surprised by it, y'know?"

"I think I feel the same way," she said. "This thing's as ready to go as I can make it, I think. Zub," she said, moving to the group channel on her suit's radio, "fire it up and run the diagnostics. I think we're golden, here." There was a burst of static from Zub in return, and lights began blinking on as the lander powered up for the first time. I could see the evidence of machinery whirring on the inside, but there was no sound, even if I hadn't had my helmet on. It had taken a while to get used to the utter silence of being in space.

"Green to go," Zub said. "Last chance, Tsvika."

"Acknowledged," Zvi said. "I shall remain. Good luck and Godspeed to the rest of you."

"We'll let you know when we're inside," Zub said. "Katie, do you have everything?"

Zub had this faint hope that we were going to find survivors-- this I was aware of. It was only in the past few days that he had admitted that he was hoping that the survivors would actually be located *inside* the very domicile module that Zahav International had sent to Mars two years previous, so he had dispatched Dr. Rosansky to pack a kit of emergency medical supplies just in case. The rest of us found this scenario incredibly unlikely, but none of us were willing to argue that we shouldn't be bringing medical supplies with us just in case, so we let it pass.

Dr. Rosansky entered through the airlock a few minutes later, medical supplies in tow, and the four of us entered the lander.

"We're in place," Zub said. "Toss us."

Zvi manipulated the *Johannes'* robotic arm to push us to maximum distance from the ship, then disengaged the arm smoothly, causing the lander to fly on a trajectory away from the ship. We had to achieve a certain distance before attempting to land so as not to inadvertently damage the *Johannes*.

"Disengaged," Zvi said.

"Initiating thrusters," Zub said, and pushed some buttons on the control console. There were no external windows on the lander, and no camera views either, so we were reliant entirely upon the lander's sensors to land us properly. The ship could be piloted remotely from the *Johannes* just as easily as from inside; I think the only reason that Zub insisted on doing it was that he liked to be in control.

"It's going to get hot in here," Dr. Rosansky said. "Crank up the air conditioning in your suits now, before it's necessary." I obliged, staring at the INTERIOR TEMP gauge in my HUD and sliding it down to sixty degrees. The temperature change took place almost immediately, and I started shivering in my suit. That didn't last very long, as the heat of entry into the Martian atmosphere kicked in. This wasn't supposed to be as bad as entering Earth's atmosphere, not by a long shot, since Mars had such a thin atmosphere, but it was still uncomfortably warm in the lander in a matter of minutes.

"Halfway down," Zub said, and the lander started rattling.

"You did finish putting this thing together, right?" I asked, mostly kidding.

"She probably left the parachute off," Zub said. "The good news is that the crash will kill us instantly."

"This thing lands by *parachute?*" I asked. Nobody had mentioned a parachute.

HE'S MESSING WITH YOU AGAIN, came the blink from Celeste. THIN ATMOSPHERE, REMEMBER? PARACHUTE JUST SLOWS US DOWN A BIT; MANEUVERING ROCKETS LAND US.

"Two minutes to planet surface," Zub said. "One minute, thirty seconds to braking rockets. Make sure you're strapped in, please. We're on target within half a klick of the planned landing zone. That's not bad."

"We're not landing *at* the landing zone?" I asked.

"Do *you* want to plant an overheated lander on top of a tank full of rocket fuel?"

"Point taken," I said. "Half a klick is fine."

"Learn to enjoy walking," Kathryn said. "It's good for you."

The braking rockets fired, throwing us into our seats as we decelerated and ending any pretense at conversation. The lander began rattling again, just long enough for me to notice a look of concern on Celeste's face, and then we touched down with a *whump*.

"You thought something was about to break off just then," I sent on our private channel. "Admit it."

She turned to me and stuck out her tongue, which I suppose was as clear a response as I deserved.

"Zvi, we're down," Zub said. "Everybody okay?" We all were. "Last-minute diagnostics on your suits, folks; make sure nothing tore or got bumped out of place while we were landing. If we need to, we can drop the dom and head straight back to the *Johannes* if there's a problem." I activated the diagnostic mode on my suit; a few minutes later, everything was glowing green. I had enough oxygen stored up for three days of running and enough water to keep me alive for three days after that. No problems there.

"Clear," we all said at the same time.

"Zvi, anything we need to know about?"

"Negative," came the response.

Without another word, Zub stood and opened the door to the lander. There was a stairwell down the side of the lander that would give us access to the outside world. A second later, and we all got our first glimpse of the Martian surface.

It was much as I had imagined, I suppose. I'd seen enough pictures sent back from Mars to know, more or less, what I should expect from my first sight of alien soil. The ship had landed in what looked like a salt plain. Everything was flat and featureless, nearly as far as the eye could see, with scattered rocks on the planet's surface. It was daytime, giving the sky its typical butterscotch hue; the sun was visible as a large white star in the sky. The sky around the sun took on a bluish hue, almost like the sky on Earth.

Celeste and I had discussed what this moment might feel like. It was a given that Zub was going to be the first one out of the lander, the first human being ever to set foot on an alien planet. We'd gone back and forth for hours about what he would say when he first touched Martian soil, about how much time he'd spent thinking about it, and whether he'd discussed his first words with anyone or had kept everything to himself. Kathryn had been remarkably coy on the matter when we'd brought it up with her, and we'd mutually agreed that it was unnecessary to discuss it with Zvi.

For myself, I was as excited as I'd ever been about anything, to the point where it was almost fatiguing. My suit was actually blinking warnings about my heart rate and perspiration at me; apparently my blood pressure was elevated as well. *Hey, looky, my suit knows I'm excited,* I thought. Zub gave little time for contemplation, bounding down the stairwell toward the planet surface. Not willing to miss seeing him touch the planet's surface, the rest of us followed him.

The planet Mars had not truly been "discovered;" as a stellar object visible with the naked eye from Earth, the honor had gone to the first human being to lift questioning eyes to the skies. The Egyptians had named the planet, as had the Babylonians and the Greeks before the Romans chose the name that stuck. For literally all of human history, human beings had wondered what might be on this "wanderer," this planet; had wondered what it would be like to live there.

Ezekiel Shlomo ben Zahav took the first steps onto the Martian surface, the first steps any human being had ever taken on another planet, at 12:07:32 Greenwich Mean Time, June 4th, 2027. Moments later, his first words were broadcast into our ears and back to the *Johannes,* where they would be relayed via tightbeam back to Earth.

"Dudes. Mars is *awesome.*"

The next several hundred words spoken by human beings on planet Mars were not publishable on any mainstream newsfeed back on Earth, as everyone started yelling at Zub at once. There was utter cacophony in my helmet. I killed the feed and took my own first steps onto the planet. The place seemed incredibly peaceful; I caught myself thinking *I could live here*, then reminded myself that I had little choice, at least for the next year and a half.

Then I turned around.

I turned my comlink back on. They were all still bickering.

"Guys."

The bickering continued. I changed my comm setting to PRIORITY and tried again.

"GUYS."

Everyone stopped, wincing at the sudden spike in volume in their ears.

"Turn around," I said, pointing behind the lander.

My first view of the Martian landscape had been awe-inspiring. There was no way it could be anything else. But in some ways, what we had seen when we exited the lander had not been terribly different from some of the bleaker vistas available on Earth. I'd been to Death Valley; Mars really wasn't terribly different in a lot of ways.

The view in the other direction was entirely different.

We could see the original domicile unit and the fuel tank off in the distance; as Zub had promised, it looked to be less than half a kilometer away from us; easy walking distance.

Behind it, though, rose the peak of Arsia Mons, three kilometers higher than Mount Everest, the second largest volcano in the solar system. And behind that, Olympus Mons, the largest mountain in the solar system, so big that the curvature of the planet itself made it impossible to see the mountain's peak from our vantage point. To the north, two more volcanoes, sisters to Arsia Mons, named Parvonis Mons and Ascraeus Mons.

Olympus Mons was three times the height of Mount Olympus. It literally disappeared into the sky.

Complete silence on the comm channel, for nearly two full minutes, as everyone took in the view. The moment was eventually broken by Zvi asking us if something was wrong.

"No," Zub said. "No, we're fine. Just... enjoying the view." He sounded choked up, and when he turned around I could see tears streaming down his face.

"Let's get the rover up and running," he said. "Then I want to go check out the other landing site. Zvi, still no signals, right?"

"Nothing," came the response. "I will notify you immediately if I discover a signal."

Once again, I discovered that I'd made an incorrect assumption about how things were going to work on Mars. I'd assumed that we would need to set everything up more or less exactly where we landed; that didn't turn out to be quite true. The domicile unit was extremely lightweight, and the rover was capable of actually *towing* the entire thing across the 500 meters or so between us and the other site. It took about half an hour to deploy the wheels on the domicile and detach the rover from the assembly; once that was done, we were quickly underway.

I didn't feel like we'd been working very hard, but I found myself out of breath quickly. I opened a channel to Kathryn to tell her about it.

"I'm going to blame your emotional state right now," she said. "Increase the oxygen mix your suit is giving you, if you want to. Everything still green?" I checked; it was. She walked over, bouncing slightly in the lighter Martian gravity. "Let me do a visual check." She pored over the outside of my suit, joined after a moment by Celeste, and both of them pronounced my suit in acceptable condition.

"I'm a little tired too," Celeste said. "It's been an exhausting day, remember. I'm not surprised that we're getting winded easily."

"Ride on the rover, if you want," Zub said. "We want to be at the site before the sun sets, I think, and this thing isn't exactly fast when it's towing weight."

I shrugged and grabbed a seat on the rover, which was already rumbling toward the first landing site. We rolled along for several minutes, everyone silently taking in the novelty of being on another planet.

"Stop. Stop *now*," came a sudden warning from Zvi, breaking the quiet. Zub hit the brakes on the rover. We were perhaps a hundred feet from our destination.

"What?" Zub shouted. "What's the problem now?"

"I'm getting a signal from *inside* the domicile unit," Zvi said. "There's someone in there."

TEN

"No way," Zub said.

"I am telling you the truth," Zvi said. "There is a signal coming from inside the primary domicile unit. It is not a distress signal and I do not recognize its origin. You should proceed with extreme caution. Zub, perhaps the measures we discussed should be put into effect here."

"You think it's something that bad?" he asked.

"Zub, what's that mean?" This was Kathryn; I found myself mildly relieved that she hadn't immediately known what he was talking about.

"He wants us to use these," Zub said, opening a container on the side of the rover.

There were four laser guns inside.

"You're kidding," I said. "Are those what I think they are?"

"They look like laser guns, don't they?" Zub said. "They're not, not really. That's mostly styling. They're basically longer-range Taser guns. I considered bringing something more destructive along, but we decided electrical shock would be bad enough. I wasn't comfortable with lethal weaponry." He handed me one. "Point and pull the trigger. Try to make sure you hit what you aim at."

"We left the military veteran on the ship for what reason, precisely?" I asked.

"He insisted," Zub said. "Look, the chances are there's nothing alive in there. If there is something alive, chances are it will be the people we're here to *rescue* and we won't want to shoot them. If there is a person in there that we want to shoot, there are four of us here, and only one of us has to hit him or her to put them on the ground for long enough to restrain them. We do not need a Mossad commando in order to do this."

"Zvi's Mossad?"

"No. I didn't say that. Shut up."

"You *just said* he was Mossad."

"I said we didn't need a Mossad commando. We're lucky that we don't need a Mossad commando, because all we have is my uncle Tsvika, my uncle Tsvika is *not* a Mossad commando, and my uncle Tsvika who is not a Mossad commando is *forty thousand miles away* right now and cannot help us at all anyway. So *shut up* and point your *new laser gun* at *anything that moves* once we get inside." I'd not actually heard Zub angry before. This was a new feeling.

"I'm surprised you're not in more of a hurry to get in there," I said.

"If any of them are in there, they have survived for years without any help from us," Zub said. "They'll make it for five more minutes while we take our time. I want to do this right."

"Fair enough," I said. "Lead the way."

"Gabe, you and I are going in first. Kathryn, Celeste, you *stay outside* the domicile unit. You only come in if you hear us clearing you to do it. If you hear any combat, you lock yourselves into the lander and prime it to return to the *Johannes*."

One of the women-- I think it was Celeste-- started to protest, and was silenced by a blast of static from Zub. He clearly wasn't in the mood.

"Let's go, Gabe."

He raised his Taser to shoulder level and crept toward the domicile unit, doing a credible imitation of someone who knew what he was doing. The domicile unit was a large hexagonal dome with an airlock on one side; there was only one way in. Zub punched a number into a keypad next to the door and it unlocked. He put one hand on the door handle and counted from five down to one with his other hand. I went in first when he pulled the door open.

The airlock was empty. Moving quietly, he shut the door behind him and sent me a blink.

NO TALKING, it said. SUBVOCALIZE A BLINK IF YOU NEED TO TALK; EVEN THE HELMET COMMUNICATION SYSTEM MIGHT BE TOO LOUD. THE INSIDE OF THE DOM IS ONE CENTRAL ROOM WITH FIVE CHAMBERS AROUND IT. IF THERE'S NOTHING IN THE MAIN ROOM, I GO LEFT, YOU GO RIGHT, AND CHECK ALL THE ROOMS. THUMBS-UP IF YOU UNDERSTAND.

I gave him a thumbs-up. There was a window on the inner airlock door into the central room of the dom. It looked unoccupied.

This time I opened the door, letting him into the central room first. The room was unoccupied, featureless; all five of the doors were closed. We each moved to our first door. Gabe counted down again, and both of us opened the doors and moved into our room. I saw nothing other than storage crates, and the lack of sound from Zub showed that he'd seen nothing different. We repeated the process, with the same result, in the second set of rooms.

Zub pointed at me and mimicked opening a door. The communication was clear: *You open the last door; I'll go in first.* If there was anything alive hiding in the domicile unit, it was going to be in this room.

On three, I yanked the door open and Zub charged in.

There was nothing in this room either. A few storage crates, sterile aluminum walls, nothing--

"What's that?" Zub asked, pointing.

There was a device of some kind sitting on top of one of the crates. Zub walked toward it and a light started blinking.

I got as far as "I don't think--" before he spun on his heel, a panicked look on his face.

"Run. RUN!"

I didn't need any more encouragement. I turned and fled the room as fast as I could. We made it out the inner airlock door before the bomb exploded. Zub threw the door closed just in time; the airlock doors were of thicker material than the rest of the domicile unit, and the shrapnel from the explosion either embedded itself in the door or glanced harmlessly off it.

Chaos on the comm units, everyone yelling at once. Zub looked at me. YOU OKAY?

I was. He was still showing green in my HUD, too, so if he'd been hurt his suit hadn't noticed it yet. We did a quick visual check on each other. There didn't appear to be any damage to either of us.

"We're fine, everyone," came Zub's voice across the comm. "Stay where you are. Coming out now." He shoved the outer airlock door open, revealing Celeste and Kathryn on the other side, both looking very concerned. The back third of the domicile unit was blown to bits. I had been expecting flames and smoke, but in the thin Martian atmosphere this was unlikely.

"The tank," Zub said. "Did anything hit the tank?"

"No," Celeste said. "We'd be dead by now if it had. What happened in there?"

"There was a bomb in the back room," Zub said. "It armed when we entered and blew a few seconds later. Some sort of plastic explosive, I think. That was probably where the signal was coming from. The whole thing was a trap."

We all paused a moment, letting that sink in.

"A trap," Kathryn said.

"Meaning that someone *left it*," I said. "For us. How long has that domicile unit been on Mars?"

"About a year and a half," Zub said.

"I think that you should all return to the *Johannes* immediately," Zvi said through the comm. "I have detected another signal. This one is from the *Tycho*."

"That's impossible," I said.

"It began a few minutes ago," Zvi said. "Ezekiel, the signal is coming from *inside* one of the skylights. It is not far away from you. I strongly suggest that all of you return to the *Johannes* immediately. We have to assume that you are not safe on the planet's surface."

"No," Zub said. "We don't have enough fuel to go back to the *Johannes* any time we want. We stay here and regroup.

Let's lock down the domicile from the lander here and think this through."

Kathryn spoke up. "I don't think--"

"And I didn't ask," Zub said, cutting her off. "We're not going back unless all of us go back, and since I'm not going back, *none of us are.* Conversation's over, kids. Get the domicile set up."

Kathryn looked shocked. Celeste had a stony look on her face-- she wasn't happy, but she was keeping it to herself for now. I actually found myself looking forward to doing some work. No one had ever tried to blow me up before, and I thought an hour or two of hard work would keep me from a full-blown panic attack. It didn't seem like it would be a good idea to have a panic attack in a space suit millions and millions of miles from home. For now, I would compartmentalize.

* * *

It wasn't actually that complicated to set up the domicile, which was one of the tasks we'd trained for and practiced a few times on Earth. No one wanted to be consulting an instruction manual on Mars. We lowered the domicile off its wheels, pulled the lander off the top of the thing, and secured everything in place. Winds on Mars weren't especially strong due to the thin atmosphere, so the domicile was basically staked to the ground like a really robust tent. There was little chance that anything short of an earthquake was going to move the thing.

Two of the crates inside the dom contained basic furniture for the central room. We set up some chairs around a table to talk, then sat down to discuss our options. We kept our suits on. The dom would be pressurized eventually but that took time that we didn't have at the moment.

"Zvi, is the signal still coming?" Zub said.

"It is consistent," Zvi said over the comm. "The signal is an audio clip. It is a distress signal from the *Tycho*. It's the same clip every time."

"Saying what?" I asked.

Zvi didn't answer, playing the clip instead.

"This is a distress signal from the USS TYCHO," a voice said. "Please render us assistance."

"That's not Alondra Gallegos," I said. "Heck, that's not any member of the crew at all." The voice was androgynous. I had thought that it was female at first, but after the second sentence I wasn't sure any longer.

"It's definitely not Wu either," Zub added. "And both of the men had pretty distinctive voices. What the hell's going on?"

Celeste spoke up. "It's a distress signal, though. It doesn't have to have been a live recording from a crew member. We're asking the wrong question. Why in the world does the *Tycho* even *have* a premade distress signal? Who would they be broadcasting to? This doesn't smell right. That can't be coming from the actual ship."

"I built that ship," Zub said. "We didn't pre-record a distress signal. And we also didn't set up the ship to begin autobroadcasting anything under any circumstances. Somebody on the ship would have had to set that up deliberately."

"Or someone *pretending* to be on the ship," Dr. Rosansky added. "We have no proof that the signal's coming from the *Tycho*. It's just *claiming* to come from the *Tycho*."

Zvi cut in. "I can confirm that it cannot be coming from the *Tycho*," he said.

"What's it from, then?" Zub said.

"That I do not know," Zvi said. "But we missed something. Listen to the recording again." The clip streamed through our earpieces again. I paid close attention to the voice, trying at least to nail down the speaker's gender.

"This is a distress signal from the USS TYCHO. Please render us assistance."

Then again. "This is a distress signal from the USS TYCHO. Please render us assistance."

There was about a three-second pause between repetitions. "This is a distress signal from the USS TYCHO. Please render us assistance."

"I can't believe I missed that," Zub finally said.

"Care to let the rest of us in on the secret?" Kathryn asked, still looking rattled.

A fourth repetition, and it dawned on me as well. "The name of the ship's wrong," I said. "USS is a *naval* designation. The *Tycho* was just the *Tycho*. It wasn't the *USS* anything."

"And just saying *render us assistance* sounds funky," Celeste said. "No information at all about what's actually wrong? Or *how* to render assistance? None of this adds up."

"The message cannot be from the crew of the *Tycho*," Zvi said. "Too much does not add up. This recording must be fraudulent."

"Zvi, what kind of signal is it?" Celeste asked. "Can you tell us anything about what it's coming from?"

"Standard ship-to-ship radio," Zvi said. "Much like planes would use to communicate with each other or with control towers on Earth. But with the signal boosted enough that it can be received in orbit. I suspect you can set your helmets to pick up the signal if you experiment. There is no location data with the signal, and the strength appears to be constant, which suggests that the source is not moving."

"Zvi, take the *Johannes* out of geosynch," Zub said. "Do a few planetary orbits and see if the signal gets stronger or weaker over any particular part of the planet's surface. We might be able to figure out where it's coming from that way."

"I will be happy to once you are back aboard," Zvi said, steel in his tone. "I will not put this ship any further away from you than it already is."

"That's an order, uncle," Zub said.

"Nonsense," Zvi replied. "It is no such thing. I am the pilot of this ship, not you, and I am in control of it and you are not. I cannot force you to return to the ship, but you cannot force me to abandon you either. Return to the *Johannes* and we can orbit Mars at your command. I will not put an entire planet in between you and rescue. This is not negotiable. Do not fool yourself into believing otherwise, nephew."

Zub said nothing.

"Aren't we missing something important here?" I asked. "The issue isn't whether the signal is really from the *Tycho* or not. The issue is that there's a signal at all. And, oh, the bomb.

Can we talk about how somebody just tried to kill us, please? On Mars?"

"That shouldn't be possible," Zub said.

"Robot monkeys shouldn't be possible, Zub," Kathryn said. "Bombs are possible. I've seen them."

"Not what I meant," Zub said. "It looked like plastic explosive, and there wasn't anything even similar to plastic explosives on the *Tycho*. Nor was there any in the supplies for the domicile. Whoever set a plastic explosive bomb for us did *not* get to Mars on the *Tycho*."

"God, I was hoping you weren't going to say something like that," I said. "Any chance that somebody smuggled something onto the ship?"

"None," Zub said. "I don't know if the rest of you were aware of this or not, but there were an incredible number of terrorist threats made against the *Tycho* and the crew before the ship launched. Religious nuts, mostly, who thought God wanted us all to stay on Earth, but a few other crazies as well. ZI's security teams intercepted two or three teams of saboteurs just by themselves, and I'm sure the FBI and CIA were kept busy chasing down threats too. There had to be a hundred bomb sniffing terminals operating around Cape Canaveral in the weeks up to launch, not to mention a half-dozen teams of dogs. The idea that one of the *crew* could have just loaded some plastic explosive onto the ship is ludicrous. There's just no way, unless there were *dozens* of people involved, and then... well, why wait until *now*? It's not like they knew we were *coming*. It doesn't make any sense."

Kathryn looked unconvinced. "So where did it come from, then? Aliens?"

"Aliens using *plastic explosives?*" Zub snapped. "Does that make sense to you, Katie?"

"Absolutely nothing makes sense to me right now," she replied. She reached for the sides of her head as if she was going to run her hands through her hair, then looked surprised when they ran into her helmet instead. "We have two possibilities: the crew of the *Tycho* set the bomb, or *no one* set the bomb. You've told us the first one is impossible. The second one is impossible. But there was still a bomb. So, somewhere, we're wrong."

"We're going in circles here," Celeste said. "Let's think for a minute. If somebody left a bomb for us-- if *anybody* was here *at all* other than us-- they have to have left some traces somewhere. I imagine footprints last an awfully long time on Mars. Let's get the dom set to pressurizing itself so that we can get out of these suits and go inspect the landing site more closely before we start losing light. If we're not going back to the ship, we're sleeping in here tonight, which means we have an awful lot of work still to do. It's going to get cold once the sun goes away." With little atmosphere to speak of, Mars' surface temperature could fluctuate wildly from day to night. It was a little after noon Mars time. The Martian day was about 37 minutes longer than an Earth day, so we had a good seven or eight hours of daylight left.

"Sounds good," Zub said, his old temperament suddenly back. "You and Gabe go check out the blast site. Gabe, you're a journalist, go *notice* some stuff. Katie and I will stay here and get the dom running."

"Not a bad idea," Kathryn said. "I'm starting to feel claustrophobic inside this thing. Let's start unpacking. We can at least get the beds set up."

I nodded at Celeste and the two of us left the dom, locking Zub and Kathryn behind the airlock.

*　　*　　*

We walked to the exploded dom in single file, carefully scanning the ground around us, trying to be careful not to accidentally step on anything that might be evidence. The Flye suits, luckily, had fairly distinctive boot tracks, and we were all wearing them. We only needed to find a single bootprint, or evidence of someone trying to get rid of them, to find evidence of our mysterious bombers. Unfortunately, scattered debris from the explosion had torn up the pristine ground around the domicile for dozens of feet in every direction around the back of the building. Strangely, comparatively little of the shrapnel seemed to have shot toward the front of the building.

"Shaped charge?" I asked Celeste over a private channel. "That would explain how Zub and I both escaped without a scratch." We'd gotten the airlock door in between us and the explosion, but that could only help us so much.

"Maybe. Or maybe it's just where they placed the bomb. I don't know enough about explosives. Maybe we should ask Zvi," she said.

I sent Zvi a blink. PUT ON A HELMET, I told him. YOU HAVE MILITARY EXPERIENCE. NONE OF THE REST OF US DO. WE NEED YOU TO LOOK AT THIS.

IT WON'T WORK AT THIS RANGE, the response pointed out. I BELIEVE THAT YOU CAN SET THE CAMERAS ON THE SUIT TO RECORD, HOWEVER. LOOK AROUND CAREFULLY AND SEND THE FILE BACK TO THE SHIP.

Right. He was forty thousand miles up. I could send messages back and forth, but the direct connection between the suits wasn't going to be functional at that range. I turned the recorder on and carefully inspected the blast area, verbally describing what I was seeing to help Zvi interpret the images I was sending him. Other than twisted bits of metal and wreckage, however, I couldn't see anything that looked helpful.

"Anything?" I asked Celeste.

"Other than the blast pattern, no," she said. "Nothing that looks salvageable, either. Everything got blasted to powder except for you two, apparently."

"Let's spread the search out, then," I said. "We haven't really taken a look at the tank yet. We probably ought to."

The fuel tank was set up perhaps a hundred yards from the domicile unit, lying on its side. There was a bank of machinery hooked to one end of the thing. Those, no doubt, were the distillers; equipment designed to synthesize rocket fuel from the Martian atmosphere and pump it into the fuel tank so that we'd have something to fly back to Earth with. I didn't really have any idea what the machine was supposed to look like, but there were green lights in what looked like appropriate places and I could feel the thing thrumming when I put my hand on it. It didn't look like any of the debris from the explosion had hit it or even landed anywhere nearby. There were two enormous rocket boosters on a Y-shaped wheeled flatbed next to the tank. The SRBs would be used to get the *Johannes* back into orbit if we had to land it for some reason.

"We got really lucky here," I said.

"I wonder," Celeste said. "The thing's *unmarked*, Gabe. The entire tank is, in fact. And look how far we are from the dom. The installation process was automated once the ship touched the Martian surface. Hold on a second," and I could hear a few clicks over the comm as she switched over to a global broadcast.

"Zub."

"You find something?"

"No, but I have a question. Where does the robotics from the fuel tank go after everything gets set up?"

That caught his interest, judging from his voice. "What do you mean?"

"I mean that the dom and the fuel tank are a good hundred yards apart, which I'm pretty sure is farther than there's any reason for the installation 'bots to have dragged it. The fuel tank is *on its side*. It's supposed to be vertically oriented. And the robots that moved the dom and set the whole thing up are nowhere to be found."

"Tank on its side is intentional," Zub said. "Late change in the plan, since we didn't want the thing to tip over and leak or explode. You don't see the bots anywhere?"

"Could they have been blown up along with the dom?" I asked.

"Only if they were right behind it," she replied, "and there's no reason for them to be."

"You're right," Zub said. "There's no reason they're supposed to be that far apart. I didn't think anything of it on the way in, but the dom and the tank were supposed to be pretty close together. Hell, I don't think the robots that dragged the dom into place had enough *juice* to get the thing a hundred yards. Something else to wonder about, I guess."

I went ahead and wondered about it. "So somebody else-- the same person who put a bomb in the dom, maybe-- also moved the dom farther away from the fuel tank than it needed to be? And then made off with the robots that were supposed to have moved it? The same person who can't be on Mars in the first place, since it's impossible for them to be here?"

"That's what it looks like," Zub said. "Somebody who wanted us dead but didn't want to disturb the fuel tanks. That's... unexpected."

"Gabe, get over here," Celeste said on the two-way. I saw on my HUD that she'd gone back behind the fuel tank.

"Hold on, Zub," I said over the global line, then hurried to join Celeste on the other side.

"Look at those," she said, pointing at the ground.

Footprints.

"Those aren't ours," I said. "This is the first time any of us have come back here."

"Look at the tread pattern," she said.

I did, recording the image to send to Zvi. "Zub, link our suits, right now," I said. The treads didn't match our boots. A few moments later, an image appeared in the corner of my HUD.

"These are the boots that the *Tycho* crew was wearing," Zub said, sending me an image. "They look the same to you?"

It was hard to tell. Our boots had a fairly distinct tread pattern, with the bottom of the boot almost resembling the stylized look of an athletic shoe. These were much more simplistic, with a dozen or so evenly spaced straight ridges across the bottom of each foot. Superficially, the tread patterns on these boot prints looked the same. But it was hard to tell; the prints had degraded since they'd been made. Even in Mars' thin atmosphere, the wind was always blowing, and the prints weren't as crisp as they could have been.

I counted the treads, down on my hands and knees. "It looks like the treads on the print are one short," I said. "But it's hard to tell. That last tread is pretty small. It might have just worn away in the wind. Should we follow them?"

"Let's follow for a while," Celeste said. "I don't think there's much point-- I mean, you can see for *miles* out here. There's nowhere for anyone to hide. But we can look."

There appeared to be tracks from multiple people, maybe four or five different sets of boots, but they crossed over each other all over the place and very few of them were very distinct. Whatever these people had been doing here, they seemed to have been here for a while.

"You check the tank out," I said. "There might be another bomb. I'll see if the tracks head anywhere."

"Check your oxygen first," Celeste said. It was still green, plenty of air left. While she looked at the tank, I walked away, trying to find the spot where the crazy tangle of tracks ended. Eventually I found a group of them that appeared to be moving in a straight line away from the domicile and the tank. I followed them for several minutes, where they joined another set of tracks.

These were clearly treads.

"They got into and out of a vehicle back here," I said over global. The vehicle had headed to the northwest, toward Arsia Mons and, behind it, Olympus Mons. "I'm heading back. If they took a rover who knows how far away they could be."

"That's another thing that's missing," Kathryn said. "There was supposed to be a second rover, right?"

"There was," Zub said.

"This one can't be ours," I said. "There aren't any tracks coming *from* the dom. It looks like they drove a rover here from somewhere, walked to the fuel tanks, then walked back to the rover and drove away. The tracks are pretty deep. We'd notice them if there were any near the tank or the domicile."

"Did the *Tycho* have a rover?" Kathryn asked.

"Yes," Zub replied. "Same kind as ours. As both of ours, actually. Come on back to the domicile. We'll spend the night here and head out in the morning to follow the tracks."

Instant objection from Zvi. "I still think you should return to the ship," he said. "We should abort the mission and head back to Earth."

"We can't abort the mission right now, Zvi," Zub said. "We don't have a good trajectory back to Earth right now. We're stuck in orbit for thirty days, bare *minimum*, before we've got a good path home. And, let me remind you, we don't have a Hohmann transfer for a *year and a half*. We have enough time to figure out what happened here and then some. There's *no way* to speed this up, so we might as well follow it through." There was a click as he switched channels, no doubt to continue berating Zvi on a private line.

I rejoined Celeste back at the tank. "No evidence anywhere of anybody tampering with the fuel tank," she said. "There's a fine coating of dust on it everywhere back here. I think we'd be able to tell if anything had been changed. The boosters aren't any different."

"Good enough for me," I said. It didn't seem likely that there was another bomb hidden somewhere in the dom or on the fuel tank. I figured that our biggest problem was likely to be cameras, and there was just no way that we were going to find those with a visual search, particularly if they were just recording and not transmitting anything. Whoever was out there did seem to have wanted us dead, but if they'd had multiple bombs, they would have set them all off at once. That hadn't happened.

"Anything else we should do out here?" I asked.

Celeste merely shrugged in answer, not bothering to say anything. I was suddenly reminded of Zvi telling me, back on Earth, that he didn't think anyone going on the trip really expected to return home alive.

ELEVEN

By the time Dr. Flye and I returned to the new domicile unit, Kathryn and Zub had unpacked enough equipment to get us through the night without too much hardship. Just having a place that was heated and pressurized was good enough for me, even though "heated" was a relative term at best. It was well below freezing outside, and inside, after the heating units had run for a few hours, it reached perhaps fifty degrees. This meant moving around in heavy clothing and wrapped in blankets, and eventually sleeping in tight, winter-weight sleeping bags, but it was much better than any of the available alternatives. It would take a day or two to get everything set up well enough to make life in the dom not seem like a winter camping trip. Among the most important of our tasks would be setting up solar panels so that we could start generating our own energy instead of relying on what we'd brought with us. The four of us spent the rest of the daylight hours packing what equipment we could salvage from the first dom onto the rover and bringing it back to our unit. Much of what was in there was not anything we needed duplicates of-- we had ten cots, for example-- but extra air, food, and batteries were going to be absolutely essential.

There was little conversation once the sun set, a process that was substantially less impressive on Mars than it was on Earth. The sky went from butterscotch to pinkish-red, except around the sun, which was as blue as the sky on Earth. Phobos, the planet's larger moon, had sped overhead earlier in the day; the other moon was too small for any of us to bother looking for it. Once the sun set, it took forever to get truly dark. I'd been looking forward to this, and actually wriggled back into my Flye suit once it got properly dark outside to go out and look at the night sky on an alien planet. Zub looked like he was considering forbidding it, but then apparently decided against it.

I was a bit surprised, at first, that I couldn't easily pick out the running lights on the *Johannes*, circling in orbit high above us. There were no external lights around the domicile-- Zvi had asked if we'd thought to bring any night-vision cameras with us that we might set up to guard against anyone attempting to infiltrate the camp, a suggestion that Zub had scoffed at over the comm and then immediately tried to put into effect once the conversation was over. Sadly, we had nothing with us that could be used. The Flye suits themselves had night vision capabilities but we hadn't anticipated needing to remotely monitor any part of what was supposed to be a dead planet. Short of leaving one of our suits outside, powered on and empty, there was no good way to survey the area short of posting one of us as a sentry.

The night sky on Mars, truth be told, wasn't much different from the night sky on Earth. Or, at least, wasn't much different from the night sky outside of civilized areas. It wasn't quite pitch-black. There was no moonlight to light the night sky, but there were plenty of stars. It was still darker than any night sky I'd seen in years.

"There's no constellations," Celeste said through the comm, nearly causing me to jump out of my skin. I hadn't set the suit to receive external audio, and had turned off the silhouetting feature, since all of my companions were supposed to be in the dom, so her sudden appearance at my side startled me enough to send her into obvious spasms of laughter. She was nice enough to not bother piping that over through the comm, though.

"Sorry," she said. "I wasn't expecting-- God, you had *no idea* I was there, did you?"

"Shut up," I replied. "Can't a man try to enjoy a little peace and quiet on Mars without somebody coming out and ruining my mellow mood?"

"You're not mellow," she said, and she was right. I was stressed out to an incredible degree, honestly. I'd been putting it off by working for the several hours since the explosion, but with nothing left to do until morning it was creeping back up on me again.

"I'm trying to be," I said. "And that's not true."

"What's not true?"

"That there's no constellations," I said. "We just haven't found them yet."

"You'll never pick out the Big Dipper without a star map," she said. "And that's assuming we're even facing the right direction. The stars won't look the same. We're millions of miles away."

I laughed. "You scientists have no imagination," I said, and pointed at a rather suggestive-looking cluster of stars in the skies northwest of us. "Look over there, that bunch of stars above where Olympus Mons ought to be. As their discoverer, I dub that constellation the *Naked Man*."

"How is that-- oh, *God*," she said, as the image suddenly resolved itself. Her HUD cast a pale light onto her face through her visor, and I could see her blushing. "The Naked *Lucky* Man, maybe."

"Or maybe we need to find a constellation that looks female and call her the Lucky Woman," I suggested, which got both of us laughing. I picked out another bunch of stars at random. "What's that going to be?"

She squinted. "The Wrench," she said. "Those four in the straight line are the handle, and that bunch at the end is the business end of the thing."

"Figures you'd pick a tool," I said.

"I'm not the one that looked out at the three billion stars of the Martian sky and immediately managed to locate a naked *guy*, Dr. Freud," she replied. "That one's on you."

"We could keep this up all night," I said. "My turn. Pick some stars, I'll tell you what they are."

"We might as well," she muttered, suddenly sounding vaguely unhappy for some reason. "Zub suggested we keep watch for a few hours, then come back in and wake the two of them up. I shudder to think about what might be going on behind us."

"Nothing, I'm sure," I said. Zub and Kathryn had grown close, but I hadn't gotten the feeling it had developed into a bona fide relationship. "Taking watches isn't a bad idea. Speaking of, remind me of how to set the chronometer on this thing to Mars time." There had been raging arguments about how best to keep time on Mars given that the days on Mars and Earth weren't the same length, arguments that I'd done my best to stay out of. At the end of it, Celeste had simply integrated a dual clock into the HUD, one showing local Martian time and another showing time on Eunostos. There was also a calendar, which was terrifying enough that I avoided ever looking at it.

"You look at it," she said. "It'll bring up the options." Sure enough, a two-second stare at the chronometer allowed me to put Mars and Earth time on the HUD at once. It was currently 24:08, which meant we were in the witching hour, the extra thirty-seven minutes that we had placed between 12:59 and 1:00 AM. On Earth, it was slightly past midnight, and thus tomorrow.

"Got it," I said. "How long's our watch supposed to be?"

"You've got the first two hours, and I've got the last two hours," she said. "*We* don't have one, technically. Although I'll keep you company if you'll keep me company. It'll be a lot easier to stay awake if there are two of us." *And to notice space aliens or bomb-wielding maniacs creeping up on the dom,* I thought.

"Fair enough. You might as well go ahead and pick me some more stars, then, since it's going to be a while."

"Those," she said, and we started the game again.

*   *   *

By the time my watch was up, we had found constellations for half of the stars in the sky, and Celeste had managed to find a star-mapping application in the exosuit's HUD software that she'd forgotten she left in there. She assured me that discoverers had virtually impregnable naming rights, but I didn't think that it was too likely that the constellation that we'd named the *Flatulent Jackass* was going to stick. We'd wanted to name it in Latin and refuse to explain the meaning to anyone, but neither of us knew the Latin word for "flatulent." The *Naked Man* was also probably unlikely to become permanent, and there were several others that I didn't even want repeated in mixed company.

And we hadn't seen or heard a single thing. I'd turned on external audio soon after Celeste surprised me, and other than the weak sounds of our feet kicking up dust on the Martian soil there hadn't been a single sound. Mars' thin atmosphere meant that sound didn't carry nearly as far as it would on Earth. I'd actually had to check a few times to make sure the microphone was still on, mostly by stomping my feet. We'd tried throwing rocks, but with Mars' weak gravity both of us could throw them much farther than the sound from the impact would travel. Had Celeste and Kathryn been much farther away from the dom when it had blown up, they likely wouldn't have heard it. We relied mostly on our suit-assisted night vision to scan the surrounding area.

"We need thermal imaging," Celeste had said. "If there's anything living around, that's going to be the easiest way to find them. Even if they're wearing exosuits like ours, they're going to show up as a huge bright spot against all the cold." I had the feeling she was already designing the things from spare parts in her head, since we hadn't brought any thermal lenses either.

After her two hours ended, Celeste and I went into the domicile, not at all sure what we might find going on inside. In between naming constellations and low-g rock-throwing contests, we'd speculated wildly on what might be going on inside the domicile behind us. As it turned out, it was nothing we had expected: Dr. Rosansky was sound asleep in one of the domicile's tiny rooms, and Zub was working at a table, surrounded by electronic equipment.

"It's warmed up," he said over his shoulder, not bothering to turn around. "Can't see my breath anymore, which is awesome. I put a few things together. This," he said, holding up an object with one hand, "is a three-hundred-sixty-degree thermal imager. Anything hotter than thirty-two degrees Fahrenheit comes within about five hundred yards of the domicile, it's going to send a signal to this."

He pushed himself away from the table, revealing a receiver. "The thing only beeps, no visual image," he said. "Haven't been able to put that together yet, but if we turn the dial here we can figure out which direction trouble is coming from. We should be able to get dressed and out of here before they get too close to us."

"And then do what?" I asked.

"Fight back. Zap them. Hide. Wet ourselves. Whatever we feel like we ought to do. The guns are stored in the airlock, in case you didn't notice." I hadn't.

"So we just took a watch and now you're going to wriggle out of yours, huh?" said Celeste.

"Nonsense. I have Mad Scientisted myself a way to perform *all* of the future watches. Your mere and weak human eyes are nothing compared to my command of the laws of mechanics." He picked his Flye exosuit off the floor, where he'd cast it when he changed into his regular clothes. "I need but install this masterpiece atop our lovely home here, and we may rest in comparative safety for the rest of the evening."

God, I wish he hadn't said that, I thought, and I noticed Celeste cringe in anticipation as well. I'm not sure what we were expecting-- another explosion, maybe, or possibly just the Rapture-- but whatever it was, the moment passed without comment from Fate or any other celestial organism.

"Do you need a hand?" I asked. I hadn't taken my suit off yet, and it didn't seem like installing the thing was too likely to be an easy one-man job, seeing as how it was pitch-black and way, way below freezing outside.

"Sure," Zub asked. "Then you can get up early in the morning and take over part of Katie's watch, too, you *watch hog*." I wasn't sure what to make of that, and briefly considered whether it was likely that Zub was on something. I hadn't seen him this silly and manic since Earth. His megalomania and determined silliness had seemed to cool a bit while we'd been on the trip. I shrugged at Celeste and put my helmet back on.

"Celeste, see if you can find a way to patch the receiver into our suits," Zub said. "The transmitter emits a signal, after all. It shouldn't be too hard to rig the exosuits to capture the signal and transmit the data on our HUDs. We'll be back in ten minutes. I expect a full status report at that time. And a glass of lemonade."

At least he didn't ask for ravioli.

"I'll take a look at it," Celeste said. She recovered an interface cable and a tablet from somewhere and plugged it into a small port on the inside of her helmet. "Security," she said in response to my questioning look. I was surprised she couldn't interface with the suit's programming wirelessly. "I didn't like the idea of anyone being able to hack my air supply from outside the suit, even just in theory, so you have to be hardwired. The cord's proprietary. I thought I was being weirdly paranoid at the time, but damn if it doesn't seem like one of the best ideas I've ever had right now."

"Less chatter, more following," Zub said, and I followed him into the airlock.

Nothing about the Martian landscape had changed in the few minutes since we had last been outside. There were ladders built into the side of the domicile to allow easy access to the roof-- they were necessary for the solar panels that we were going to install in the morning. Zub and I each climbed up one of the ladders and, working in a comfortable silence, managed to get the thermal camera affixed to the highest point of the domicile in just a few minutes.

"Celeste, you ready?" He sounded impatient already.

"Not even close, Zub," she said. "This is going to take a little while, especially since you have the broadcaster and I can't get a good look at it. It would help if I wasn't guessing about the signal. The good news is that the receiver is up and running and beeping like crazy, since the two of you are so close by. Thanks for not warning me you'd left it on, by the way, I needed to be frightened out of my mind. I'm surprised I didn't wake Kathryn up."

Zub and I both reacted the same way, by looking down toward the room Kathryn was in, and I could tell he was turning on the locator feature at the same time I was. I had a brief moment of panic when she didn't show up on my HUD, then felt sheepish when I realized she'd likely taken the exosuit off before going to sleep.

"She's fine, guys," Celeste said, reading our minds. "I just stuck my head into her room a minute ago."

"Stop tempting fate, Dr. Flye," I said.

"Quit being so paranoid, *Mister* Southern," she replied evenly. "Besides, tempting fate is Zub's job. It barely even counts if I do it."

"Speaking of that," he said, and we both groaned. "We need to test this thing. Celeste, Gabe and I are going to both start walking in opposite directions. Turn the dial on the receiver; you should notice that the volume and frequency of the beeps should start increasing when the dial is pointed toward where one of us is. Let us know when it stops going off."

"All right," she said. "But be careful."

"Of course," he said. "Gabe, you go that way," and pointed back toward our landing spot. "I'll head out past the fuel tank. Flye, let us know when you lose the signal. With some luck, it'll take a few minutes at least." He dropped off the ladder onto the ground and began walking. I did the same, periodically turning around to check Zub's progress and make sure we were both walking at roughly the same speed.

"Still have both of you," Celeste said after about twenty seconds. "You're both about twenty-five yards from the domicile. Strong signals on both of you. Will report back on one minute."

I kept skip-walking. It abruptly hit me that I was *used to* walking in Mars' weak gravity already. It didn't take her a full minute to come back onto the channel.

"Just lost a signal from one of you. Zub, what did you-- oh, *CRAP*. Gabe, get over there! Something's wrong! He's--" and then a burst of static cut off our communication.

I whirled around. Zub's silhouette had turned yellow since I'd last looked back and was rapidly transitioning into orange. At this distance it wasn't clear what position he was in, but it looked like he was either crouching or actually prone.

None of those things were good.

I poured on speed as best I could, considering that I had only just gotten the hang of walking in the low Martian gravity and had a terrible time getting the traction necessary to run.

"Get Kathryn up!" I shouted, switching over to global. She almost certainly hadn't gone to sleep with her helmet on, and I knew she'd taken the suit off, but there was no reason not to try. I didn't get any detailed information on Zub's condition through the HUD, but *red is bad* was clear enough, and his color was steadily deepening. It took me under a minute to reach where he was-- lying face down on the ground with his hands at his sides. As I rolled him over, it occurred to me that I had no reason to think I was safe from whatever had put him down, a thought that froze my blood in its veins. I looked around quickly, seeing nothing, and cranked up the sensitivity on the external microphone to maximum. Nothing.

"Whatever got him, it's not around here anymore," I said. Then I looked down. Zub's eyes were rolled up into his head, his teeth clenched together, saliva running down his lips. His entire body shook furiously.

Christ. "He's seizing," I said. I ran my hands over the front of the suit. "No sign of damage to the suit. I don't think he got hit with anything."

"Get 'im in here right now," Kathryn growled over the comm. Her accent was thicker when she was scared. I knew basic procedure to deal with a seizure-- just enough to know that there was absolutely nothing I could do as long as he had the suit on. I picked him up from the ground and threw him over my shoulders, fireman-style. For once, gravity was working to my advantage, as his weight barely slowed me down at all as I double-timed it back to the dom. Celeste and Kathryn barely waited for me to lock the external door on the airlock before throwing the interior door open, stripping Zub's helmet and suit off him in record time. He didn't appear to be actively seizing any longer, but he was still unconscious.

"Somebody find my bag," Kathryn spat, peeling back an eyelid and looking at his pupils. "And dim the lights in here, if you can. He's going to be photosensitive when he comes around." Celeste dove into Kathryn's room while I tried to turn down the lights in the dom. This turned out to be impossible; our options were "off" or "on." I grabbed a blanket for him instead, figuring that at worst we could cover his face with it.

"What happened to him?" Celeste asked, coming back into the room with Kathryn's medical bag under her arm.

"No idea," I said. "He'd just gotten past the fuel tank. As far as I know, he just *dropped*. He didn't say anything beforehand. I don't think he ever saw whatever hit him."

"Nothing hit him, Gabe," Kathryn said, now shining a light from her bag into Zub's eyes. "He's epileptic. Has been since birth. This happened all on its own."

*   *   *

A few minutes later, Kathryn satisfied herself that Zub's vitals were all right and that he would be rejoining the world of the conscious in a few more minutes. We wrapped him in a few thick blankets and put him in a cot to sleep.

"How long have you known?" I asked.

"As long as I've worked for him," she said. "He controls the seizures with medication. He hasn't had one in about a year, and I've never seen him have a grand mal seizure before. It's probably the stress. Was he acting funny before it happened?"

"A little manic," I said. "He kludged together a thermal camera while Celeste and I were keeping watch outside. Full-blown Mad Scientist mode. I was actually thinking he was back to his normal self."

"I can't believe he didn't tell any of us," Celeste said. "Full-blown epilepsy should have disqualified him from the trip in the first place. Hiding it's practically criminal."

"He also brought a robot monkey and didn't tell you," Kathryn hissed. "I'm the doctor. I knew. It's controllable. And I can't believe you can start a conversation about *Ezekiel* with the words *I can't believe he didn't tell us* in the first place. Withholding information is practically his *motto*."

A muscle twitched in Celeste's cheek. "That doesn't make it okay!" she said, barely keeping her anger in check. "Kathryn, what if he had *died* out there just now? Do *you* know how to pilot the return vehicle back to the *Johannes?* Because our other pilot is kind of forty thousand miles up, and I'm a little rusty on my flying skills."

"Isn't it automated?" I asked.

"Shut up, Gabe, that's not the point," Celeste spat. "He's endangered all four of us. The robot monkey was at least kind of funny. This is madness."

Four. "Wait a minute," I said. "Where the hell is Zvi?" The first part of the conversation, before we'd gotten into the dom, had all been in global. Even without his suit on, the conversation would have been broadcast throughout the *Johannes*, and Zvi was a famously light sleeper. I put my helmet back on and opened a channel straight to the ship.

"Zvi? Southern to the *Johannes*, please respond." It felt weird to be using such official-sounding calls, but I figured Zvi's military training would make him react to me faster this way.

I let about thirty seconds pass before trying to hail the ship again. Nothing.

"New problem," I said. "Can't get through to the ship."

"No way," Celeste said. "He's just asleep."

"Try it," I said. She put her helmet back on. I saw her try the ship over a private channel, then again over global. No response.

"Try a blink," I said, and I could see her eyes focusing on the interface in her lens.

"Nothing," she said. "What the hell is going on?"

"He's waking up," Kathryn said. Zub was indeed stirring in his cocoon of blankets, swearing softly as the bright light in the room got to his eyes. He rubbed his face with his hands, then let his arms fall down limply at his sides.

"How bad was it?" he asked Kathryn.

"Grand mal," she said. "Looked like a pretty bad one. And me with no EKG. Gabe brought you back into the dom. How do you feel?"

He lifted his arms up again, wiggling all of his fingers, then lifted his blanket-wrapped feet from the cot and, no doubt, wiggled his toes as well. He started to sit up. "I'm okay, I think. A little woozy. I haven't... owww, crap, my head," he said, falling back into the cot.

"You were on your face when I found you," I said. "Maybe you hit your head on the way down?"

"Wait, he fell *forward?*" Kathryn said. "People don't do that when they pass out. They always fall backwards."

"They usually pass out in Earth gravity, though," Zub said. "I think I was in midstride when it hit. That was momentum that put me on the ground, not just the seizure."

"You don't have any marks on your head," she said, ruffling his hair and examining his scalp. "You probably knocked it pretty good, but I don't think you did any lasting damage."

Zub looked at Celeste. "Don't yell at me, please," he said. "At least not until tomorrow. My head hurts too much for you to yell at me."

"That's the first time I've ever heard you use the word *please*, you *giant jerk*," Celeste said. "This wasn't a joke, Ezekiel. This wasn't a *minor thing*. This is a huge problem that is relevant to all of our safety that you decided not to tell anybody."

"It's controllable," Zub mumbled. "And you're yelling."

"I'm not even close to yelling. You'll know when I'm yelling. And I can't imagine what it would be like if your seizures *weren't* controllable. You might, I don't know, be going into convulsions on the surface of Mars or something like that. That would be *much* worse than what actually happened."

Something clicked in my head. "No wonder Zvi's been so concerned about you," I said. "He's a relative. He knew too, right?"

"Actually, he didn't," Zub said. "My family isn't actually that close. We've kept it a pretty tight secret. I'm surprised he's not on the comm yelling at me right now."

"Can't raise him," I said. "We tried. He's asleep or something."

Zub sat up. "What?"

"We hailed the *Johannes* two or three times while you were out," Kathryn said. "Sent a couple of direct communications to Zvi, too. He didn't respond to any of them. We figured he was sleeping; it's three o'clock in the morning up there, too, remember."

"Bull," Zub said. "I dropped a wrench once in the cargo bay and it woke him up *in his room*. Through who knows how many walls and an airlock door. No way is he just *not awake*." He opened a line to Zvi.

"No response. That's a priority line. It rings *in his ear* on top of the iLid lens. Something's wrong." He pulled himself up to a seated position and rubbed his eyes again. "You already hailed the ship, right?"

All three of us nodded.

He tried again. "Zub to *Johannes*, come in *Johannes*." There was no response. "Anybody think to send a ping?"

"We didn't have time," Celeste said. "You woke up before we had a chance to start brainstorming any new communications ideas."

Zub stabbed at a bunch of buttons on his tablet, his fingers flying. "Even if something's gone wrong with communications, we still ought to be able to get a pingback if we're connecting *at all*." He stared at his screen, a look of disbelief on his face.

"Nothing. There's no response at all. It's as if the ship's not even there."

"The *Tycho* lost communication after a little while in orbit, too," I said.

"Get outside," Zub said. "There's binoculars around here somewhere. Zvi wouldn't have broken orbit even if he couldn't communicate with us. We should still be able to *see* the thing up above us."

The receiver on the table started beeping. The receiver for the thermal camera that the two of us had just installed on the roof of the domicile unit.

Something was coming.

TWELVE

"Help me get dressed," Zub said. "We've got to get out there."

"No chance," Kathryn said, putting a hand on his chest and pushing him back into his cot. "You just had a seizure. There's no way I'm letting you back outside right now! We should stay in here anyway!" I decided to let the two of them argue and grabbed my helmet, heading for the door.

"Wait, Gabe," Celeste said. "I'm coming with you." She hadn't gotten around to removing her suit either, so the two of us were ready to go in moments.

"We should think about this," Kathryn said, sounding frantic. "Guys, you have *no idea* what's out there right now. Stay in here, where it's at least safe."

"And let them put another bomb on the outside of the dom?" Zub asked. "We're *blind* in here, Kathryn. Out there at least we can see what's coming. God, who talked me out of putting cameras all over the outside of this thing?" He glared at Celeste with this, who had her back to him and didn't notice.

"Where are they coming from?" I said. Celeste ran to the receiver and started adjusting the tuner.

"Northwest," she said. "Where they came from before. They're back behind the fuel tank. Let's go." She opened the inner airlock door, then found the crate with the Taser guns in it. She pulled it open and tossed two of the guns back to Zub and Kathryn, then handed me the other two.

"Both of you get your helmets on," she said, "and turn on your locators. If you see us go down, come out shooting." Before Kathryn could protest, she closed the inner airlock door.

"You ready for this?" she said, turning the lock on the door.

"Not remotely," I said. "What exactly are we doing?"

"I have no idea," she replied. "Okay, we're finding out where the heat signature is coming from. I think once we know that, we'll know what to do about it. You airtight?"

I checked my status monitors. Everything was green. "I'm good."

"Me too," she said. "Opening the airlock."

My external microphone picked up the *hiss* of the air inside the lock escaping into the Martian atmosphere. Outside, everything was still.

Celeste's voice took on a rather surprising aura of command, as if she'd been giving orders all her life. "Pull down your visor. Let the cameras show what we're looking at. All they need is a low-intensity laser through these faceplates and they've blinded both of us."

"Are we sure we want to rely on technology?" I asked. "They've been awfully good at shutting the ships down." I didn't like the idea of suddenly going blind when my suit's cameras got cut.

"We don't know that the two things are connected," she said. "If you go dark, just pull the visor back up. Zub, Kathryn, you there?"

"Yeah," Zub said, sounding sullen.

"Slave your suits to ours."

"Already thought of that," he said. I noticed Kathryn's name in the corner of my HUD. Zub had slaved his suit to Celeste's. They would see everything we saw as we investigated the alarm from the camera.

"Signal's still to the northwest," Zub said. "Head toward the fuel tank. You can use it for cover."

"They already know we're here," I said, whispering even though the suit was soundproofed. "I mean, they have to, don't they? I don't think we're going to be able to sneak up on someone who knows we're here and is walking straight toward us."

Celeste and I crept toward the fuel tank, eyes peeled for anything out of the ordinary. The vague unreality of the projected landscape inside my helmet kept shifting, the level of focus changing as I looked around. I hadn't done much training with the suit's virtual mode engaged-- it had been one of the few areas where Zub and Celeste felt like it was okay to cut corners-- and, naturally, I found myself wishing I had. After a few minutes of walking, it was enough to make me sick.

"I'm going to puke inside the helmet," I said. "That can't be good." There was actually a crude vacuum built into the helmet in case of exactly those circumstances. We couldn't exactly remove our helmets in low-atmosphere situations or in deep space to clean them.

"Calm down," Celeste said. "If it's that bad, just switch back to regular visuals. But don't complain to me if something terrible happens to you in a couple of minutes." I decided the certainty of eventual mockery and the slight potential health hazard were outweighed by the sheer horror of having to vacuum my own vomit off my face and pulled back the visor shield. The blessed normalcy of the Martian landscape without any digital effects applied to it was refreshing, and I spent a moment being startled that I'd just thought of looking at the landscape of *Mars* as "normal."

"Guys, I *really* don't like the readings I'm getting here," Zub said over the comm. "Can you hear anything?"

"Can't hear or see anything," I said. We were creeping up on the fuel tank, but thus far there had been no indication of anything going on. "What's going on?"

"Heat signatures *everywhere* around you right now," he replied. "The detector starts going crazy about twenty degrees to your right and stops about another twenty-- no, make that thirty-- degrees to your left. It's like there's an *army* coming toward you.

"We're at the tank," Celeste said. "Zub, there's nothing. Unless your army's in single file--"

As she walked around the outside of the tank, nearly in the exact place where Zub had collapsed into an epileptic seizure just half an hour or so before, Celeste stopped talking and froze.

"Unless your army's in single file *what?*" Zub shouted into the comm. "Celeste, I'm seeing everything you see. There's nothing there. What's wrong?" I rushed over to her side. There was nothing behind the tank, and nothing beyond it, either. Unless her suit was manufacturing and putting something that wasn't there onto her visor, I couldn't tell what the problem was.

Then a red light started blinking in the corner of my HUD. The external temperature, which had been hovering around sixty degrees below zero moments before, had started to spike. It was at twenty degrees and rising, an eighty-degree swing in a matter of seconds.

"Warm air," Celeste said. "The camera's picking up a *warm front.*"

"What?" Zub asked, clearly not believing what he was hearing.

My external thermometer hit forty degrees. Still rising. A hundred degree temperature change in under a minute.

"Do you hear that?" she asked.

At first, I almost said no. I couldn't hear anything but the wind. I listened for the sound of creaking metal-- perhaps she thought the metal on the tank wasn't going to react well to the sudden temperature change.

Then I realized what the issue was. I could *hear the wind.* On Mars, which barely had any atmosphere to speak of. In the distance I could see an enormous plume of Martian soil building up. There was an enormous dust storm headed our way. Mars was well known for occasionally having dust storms, storms that were sometimes large enough to cover the entire planetary surface. And it looked like the mother of all of those storms was heading our way, powered by an impossible spike in air temperature.

Fifty degrees outside. If I'd been able to breathe the air, I could have taken my space suit off.

"Look," Celeste said, and pointed toward the bottom of the dust storm in the distance-- a distance that looked like it was rapidly decreasing.

The storm was taking on a new color-- it had been shifting from the butterscotch color of the sky in the early Martian morning to the red color of the sandstorm, but underneath all that a new hue was emerging.

Green. The sandstorm was turning green.

Sixty degrees and rising.

"We need to get back to the dom right now," Celeste said.

Over the comm, Zub screamed for someone to explain what the hell was going on.

We turned and sped back for the domicile. Halfway back, I lost my footing-- turns out I *wasn't* used to running in one-third gee-- and took a header into the ground, tumbling head-over-heels, landing on my back, and then rolling to my feet and continuing to run in one fluid motion. If it hadn't *hurt* to do it, I'd have been proud of myself.

"Sandstorm coming, coming *quick*," Celeste said over the global comm. "External temperature's spiking, too. There's a wave of obscenely hot air washing over us right now."

"I got it," Zub said. "Get in here." The front edges of the front must have just hit the dom, or at least he'd just noticed the temperature spike outside.

Seventy-five degrees. Mars probably hadn't been this warm in thousands of years. Warm enough that the permafrost in the soil was probably going to start melting soon, if it hadn't already. If this lasted too long, the dry, dusty ground we'd been walking on could very well turn into a morass of red mud.

We both hit the airlock at a dead run, Celeste actually overrunning the door by several yards when she wasn't able to stop a leap in time. She threw up a dust cloud of her own skidding to a stop and spinning to come back to the door. We got inside in what felt like the nick of time, with the huge cloud of dust no more than half a kilometer from us.

I tried to hail the *Johannes* again. "Zvi? We need eyes down here, man. We've got a dust storm coming and I'm pretty sure another one of those green spots is erupting even as we speak. You up there, man?"

Silence. I looked over at Celeste, who was shouting something into her comm as well, but not over a channel I could hear. When her face fell after waiting for a response for a while, I figured she'd had the same idea that I had.

We were stranded on Mars, unknown assailants had tried to blow us up, our camp had been invaded and carefully examined by *someone* (and, it occurred to me, all traces of their presence were about to be obliterated by the wind and sand) and we were about to be hammered by a dust storm from hell *and* a heat wave of unprecedented and frankly impossible proportions.

Life had been better.

*   *   *

"We need a plan," Kathryn said. We'd been in the dom for five hours, listening to the constant, rain-like tapping of particles of Martian soil thudding against the outside of the dom and watching the external temperature like hawks. Each of us had tried to get some sleep at some point. I don't believe anyone other than Zub, who wasn't fully recovered from his seizure, was actually successful. The high temperatures had crested at eighty degrees Fahrenheit about two minutes after Celeste and I had reentered the domicile unit, and had remained there for a good hour. Since then, the temperature had been dropping. While the drop wasn't nearly as precipitous as the sudden temperature increase, by the time morning rolled around it was well on the way to average Martian temperature-- that is, slightly colder than most of Earth outside of Siberia, Antarctica or Chicago ever got.

The statement was the first words any of us had spoken in several hours.

"A plan to do what?" Zub asked.

She shot him a withering look. "In no particular order, figure out how we're going to eat, drink, and breathe, how we might find the *Johannes*,"

"...and the *Tycho*," Zub added.

"Screw the *Tycho*," she shot back, her accent flaring up. "How we might find the *Johannes*, and how we might then get back to Earth, and how we might find out what the hell else is going on. We trained to go to Mars, Zub. We didn't train for a *murder mystery*."

"Is someone dead?" he asked. "Sure, a whole lot of people are *missing*, but that's not the same thing."

"I could kill *you*," Kathryn suggested.

"Then it wouldn't be a mystery," Zub said. "There's two witnesses here. And the cams in our suits. No doubt who did it. Doubt and uncertainty are absolutely essential parts of a murder mystery. You have neither."

"I'll make do," she said, practically hissing at him.

"Enough," Celeste said. "Kathryn's right. Zub, any idea how much food and water we have available to us?"

"Food? Maybe two weeks," he said. "Everything else is on the *Johannes*. Water's a little trickier. We've got maybe a week's supply stored, but finding more should be possible. There's got to be some decent-sized ice flats underneath the soil around here somewhere."

"Is that safe?" I asked.

"Safe enough," Katherine responded. "There's no risk of bacteria or microorganisms, so that just leaves trace elements in the water, and we can test for that. Martian water ice isn't likely to be contaminated with anything that can actually hurt us."

"So where's the *Johannes?*" I asked. "And what was... *that?*" I gestured outside as I spoke, not really knowing what to call what we had just seen happen.

"Absolutely no idea," Zub said. "Once the temperature is back to normal, we'll go check and see what's changed outside. We know one thing: even if those were people who put a bomb in the dom and who left those footprints all over the place, there's no technology I'm aware of that could have blanked the *Johannes'* communications."

"What about jamming *ours?*" I asked. "That seems a lot easier."

"It's not us, it's the ship," he replied. "Person-to-person communications work fine. And I'm assuming that whatever happened to the *Johannes* is the same thing that happened to the *Tycho*, which had virtually exactly the same communications systems. That was absolutely the ship being prevented from communicating, as opposed to NASA being prevented from hearing the communications. I assume the same thing's happened here."

"What about the dust cloud?"

"Bits of it make sense and bits of it don't," Celeste said, "although the bits that don't make sense *really, really* don't make sense. We're within spitting distance of Arisa Mons right now. That volcano has a history of extremely strange local weather phenomena-- giant funnel clouds and the like. Dust storms happen all the time. But the green cloud and the heat wave are flatly impossible. There's no way they arose from natural causes."

"Fresh volcanic eruption?" Kathryn asked. "That could have heated the air."

"By nearly two hundred degrees, for several hours, miles from the eruption? Not too likely."

"And there's no human technology that can do *that*, either," Zub added.

"So you're suggesting *Martians*," I said.

"Nope. I'm suggesting aliens of non-Martian origin," Zub said. "There are no Martians, or there haven't been for millions of years, and they didn't live on the surface if they ever existed. It doesn't make any sense for the phenomena we've witnessed to have a Martian origin."

"You could have stopped after the word *sense* and that sentence would have been just as correct," I said. "Were the aliens wearing space boots?"

"If they're anthropoid, there's no reason to assume they can move around on Mars without space suits," Kathryn added helpfully.

"Great," I said. "So what we think happened is that aliens from outer-space-but-not-Mars have come to Mars to blow up our space ships and put bombs in our domicile units. Have I nutshelled this correctly?"

"No," Zub said. "There are other people on Mars who are not us. That's undeniable."

"I look forward to hearing this explained," Celeste said.

"The bomb. It was Earth tech," Zub said. "I *recognized it.* If there are aliens on Mars, they're from outside our solar system. That means that they're using propulsion technology that is so far from what we can do that it might as well be magical. I don't believe that beings like that use plastic explosives. If they were going to blow us up, they wouldn't have failed. It would be like us squashing a bug."

I considered countering with some anecdotes of resilient insects I'd tried to kill and failed-- several came to mind-- and decided not to.

"So," I said, rubbing my forehead and trying to avoid a migraine, "the following are on Mars: other human beings who tried to blow us up, possibly the crew of the *Tycho*, but likely not, as they have no reason to attempt to blow us up, possibly also the crew of the *Tycho*, plus aliens, wielding magic-like technology and from some other galaxy, plus plastic explosives. That's what we're dealing with here."

"Yes," Zub said. "Except probably no on the aliens. It's possible but I still think it's ridiculous."

"I'm glad we've cleared that up," I said. "I feel so much better now. This trip was a wonderful idea."

"Wasn't it?" Zub asked, a twisted little giggle escaping his lips. "I've don't think I've ever had this much fun in my life."

Everyone ignored that.

"So we have two weeks to explore the entire surface of the planet Mars for two space ships that might not be there," Kathryn said. "We're dead, in other words. We're dead and we just don't know it yet."

"And orbit, too," Zub said. "The ships might still be in orbit."

Kathryn didn't respond at all. I wasn't even sure she'd heard what he said.

"I don't think that's what we have to do," Celeste said. "I think I know where to look for the *Johannes*."

"What do you mean?" I asked. "How could you possibly know that?"

"The skylights," Zub said.

"The skylights," Celeste repeated. "The first thing the *Tycho* did that was remotely out of order was report the green spot. We know now that the green spots are clustered around the skylights. We're not far from the skylights now. It stands to reason that whatever is causing all of these problems is *inside* the things. The ships may even be inside one of them as well. I say we hook up the lander to one of the rovers and go exploring."

"That's crazy," Kathryn said. "We're going to go *toward* the problem?"

"Unless you have a better idea?"

"Orbit," she said. "We can put ourselves into orbit with the lander."

"And then we can run out of fuel, air, food, and water up there, and die of any of the above," Zub said. "Celeste is right. The *Johannes* is capable of landing on the surface and taking off again, remember. So was the *Tycho*. It's far from optimal, but they could both *do* it. They could both be on the ground somewhere, maybe even inside the skylights. And whatever is causing the green stuff and the heat is *definitely* inside of them. Our options are the skylights or the *entire rest of the planet's surface*, which is roughly the same size as every continent on Earth rolled together. I know how I'd like to start."

I opened my mouth to respond, but didn't get a chance to.

"Do you hear that?" Celeste asked. I hadn't. It fell silent instantly inside the domicile unit.

Scratching, from by the airlock doors. There was something outside of the dom. And it was trying to get in.

"I hear it," I said. "The hell is *that?*" I reached for one of the taser guns, which I'd left on the floor when I sat down.

Zub got up from his cot, the first time he'd done so in hours. "Gimme my helmet," he commanded. I handed it to him. He put it on, fiddled with a button, and then launched himself at the airlock door, giggling insanely as he did so. I was surprised that, in his current state, he could move that fast.

Before anyone could stop him, he'd opened the inner airlock door and was scrambling through. He locked the inner door behind him before we could get to him and punched something into a keypad, locking the door behind him. Not slowing down any, he scrambled into his space suit, then searched around for his boots. Celeste tried to override the lock on the inner door, with no success. Kathryn was still sitting in her chair, head lowered, not responding to anything that had happened.

We watched through the window of the inner door as Zub kept looking for his boots. He looked back at us, then shrugged, a giant smile on his face, and opened the outer airlock door.

"He's trying to kill himself," I said.

The door was thrown open, and something came through, leaping onto Zub from the outside. He staggered back for a moment, nearly losing his footing, then recovered himself and shoved the outer door closed with a stocking foot. There was a *hiss* as the airlock repressurized itself.

"Oh, God," Celeste said. "What was that?"

Zub finally turned back around to face us. There was something hanging from his neck.

Sajad.

The robot monkey.

The robot monkey who was, last I'd seen him, forty thousand miles above us, in geosynchronous orbit over our campsite. And while Zub had built him an entirely unnecessary space suit, I didn't think he'd go so far as to make a lander just for his monkey robot.

"Is that the monkey?" Celeste said, incredulous.

"Yeah," I said. "That's the monkey. Which means that the *Johannes* is on the planet surface somewhere after all. Nothing else makes sense."

"Don't say that," Celeste said. "You're tempting fate again."

I decided to close my mouth as a triumphant Zub unlocked the inner door and brought his pet into the domicile unit with us.

"Sorry," he said. "I turned on my locator feature when I heard the scratching. He didn't show up earlier. He was *right outside.*"

"How did he find us?" I asked.

Zub grinned. "Another of my little tricks," he said, pointing to a spot on his forearm. "There's a locator chip embedded underneath the skin of my arm there. Sajad's keyed to it. It's how he was always able to find me on Eunostos. I think I must have overpowered the transmitter in the thing, though, if he found us on *Mars*. Who knows how far away he was."

"Can we find out?" Celeste asked.

"Not sure," Zub said. "I didn't exactly build him for espionage, you know. That was going to be Monkey 3.0. He doesn't have a ton of onboard memory or anything like that. Monkeys don't need hard drives, y'know?"

"3.0?" I asked. "He's not the first one?"

"Nope." Zub said. "The first one was terrible, though. A mop with a monkey hat on it would have been more convincing."

"Wait a second," I said. "Guys, look at him."

Sajad's space suit, formerly pristine white in color, was dotted with reddish Martian mud and patches of green dust. He'd walked through who knows how much of the stuff in order to get back to us.

Zub set him down very quickly.

"Think it's safe to touch that?"

"If it's not, we're... wait, we're dead anyway," Kathryn said, her voice flat and expressionless. "I wouldn't worry about it too much." She put her hand down close to the ground and snapped her fingers a couple of times. Sajad ran over to her. She picked him up and wiped some of the green dust off with her fingers, then looked at the residue on her hands carefully.

"No idea what this is," she said. "Do we have a microscope handy, Ezekiel?"

"Somewhere," he said. "Just a minute." He disappeared into one of the adjoining rooms and I heard boxes of equipment being rustled around. A minute later he emerged, holding a small microscope over his head in a victory pose.

"Nothing too terribly high-powered; that was what the ship was supposed to be for. But it'll do," he said, putting the microscope in front of her, then producing a box of slides from a pocket and handing her that as well. She collected some more of the green dust from Sajad, then prepared a slide and peered through the lens at it. She made a few adjustments to the microscope, took a long look, then sat back.

Everyone stared at her, waiting for some sort of verdict.

"Take a look yourselves," she said. "Wait, no. Gabe, you go first. You noticed the dust before the rest of us did. Take a look at this and tell me what you see."

"I'm not a scientist, remember?" I said.

"You graduated *high school*; that ought to be enough," she said, drawing out the words *haaaaaaaah schoooooool* at me. I figured that was probably Texas for mockery. I looked at the microscope.

It took me a second to figure out what I was looking at. And I realized she was right.

It didn't take much more than a high school education to recognize plant cells when you looked at them.

THIRTEEN

"Plant cells," I said. "The dust cloud was spewing plant cells into the atmosphere."

"That's impossible," Zub and Celeste said in unison. I smiled, but no one else did.

"Everything that has happened in the past six months has been impossible, the last 24 hours most of all," Kathryn said. "And you can look for yourself. What I can see looks consistent with terrestrial plants. There's definitely a cellular wall, and the cells are all rectangular and regular in shape. Plus they're green. That all says *plant* to me. And I'm the biologist."

"Any theories on why xenobiological organisms might look so similar to something terrestrial?" Celeste said.

Kathryn thought for a moment. "Panspermia," she said, snapping her fingers as she spoke. "Exogenesis. Or, more likely, a form of parallel evolution. Perhaps this sort of cellular structure is just more useful than we'd imagined."

"Panwhat?" I'd heard the word before, but I couldn't remember where. *Exogenesis*, on the other hand, was entirely new.

Her accent got thicker when she was excited. "Panspermia is the idea that the universe was seeded with life, by some unknown source, in a wide variety of places. This would lead to life evolving with certain vague similarities everywhere it exists."

"*Star Trek* syndrome," I said. "Millions of alien species with different-looking foreheads."

"Basically," she said. "Exogenesis is related-- the idea that life on Earth was originally transported there from somewhere else. Think about bacteria hitching a ride on a comet or a meteorite somehow. Theoretically, that other place would have green plant life much like we do. Parallel evolution just suggests that, since life can only arise, as far as we know, on planets with a fairly restricted set of characteristics, that the life that arises on those planets *must* share certain traits-- in other words, some life will inevitably evolve *eyes*, for example, or cell walls and a chlorophyll-based method of gaining nutrients, which leads to plants. The plants could look wildly different from what we have on Earth and still share an underlying cellular structure."

"The most important thing to remember is that panspermia and exogenesis are nonsense," Zub added.

"But parallel evolution in this case depends on a pretty impressive string of coincidences," Kathryn replied pointedly. "The first xenobiological organism the human race discovers and its cell structure matches human plants so well that a nonscientist recognizes them? That's astounding."

"So we're back to *every possibility makes no sense* again," I said. "Par for the course, I guess."

"Give me a few more minutes," she said. "Maybe I can find a clearer example to look at somewhere on the slide. While I'm doing that, you should probably look to see if Sajad is okay. Maybe he's got a note from Zvi or something like that."

"I hadn't thought of that," Zub said, and in response to a hand signal the monkey stripped out of his space suit and went into what looked like a sleep mode, standing creepily still. It took me a moment longer to realize that he'd actually stopped breathing. I'd accepted that he was a robot months ago, but he continued to be impressively realistic, and seeing him in a way that broke the illusion of animation made me surprisingly nervous.

"Some more dust caked into his fur," Zub said, looking at his fingers. "Red and green, it looks like. And there's a singed patch here on his elbow. Gabe, check the suit." Sure enough, there was a small patch on his elbow that looked like it had been burned through. Other than that, it didn't look like he had a scratch or a dent anywhere on him.

"I've got him running a self-diagnostic, too," Zub said, fiddling with something concealed in the fur at the base of Sajad's skull. "He seems to be behaving normally, but if there's something going on with his programming, the diagnostic ought to catch it."

"Got something," Kathryn said. "Take a look."

Zub snatched the microscope away from her before either Celeste or I could get to it.

"Huh," he said.

"That's about right," she replied. "Gabe, Celeste, take a look yourselves, if you want. That's as clear a view of one of these organisms as we're likely to get with this microscope. Look in the lower right corner. That's a chloroplast, or I'm the monkey. They're plant cells. I don't know what kind yet, but they're plant cells."

"How useful is chlorophyll going to be this much farther away from the sun?" I asked. "Mars can't get nearly the amount of sunlight that Earth does."

"You'd be surprised at how hardy green plants are," Kathryn answered. "They grow nearly everywhere on Earth, and there are Earth environments that are just as hostile to life as most of Mars. Remember, the soil's not far from Earth soil, chemically speaking."

"We're back to the impossible field of asparagus again," I said.

"It was impossible six months ago," she replied. "Now we're looking at it and it seems a little more likely."

"Wait," Celeste said. "Right now what we've got is plant matter being spewed into the atmosphere for some reason. Sajad's covered in green stuff. Plant cells don't reproduce on their own, though. Are there any *seeds* on him? That would be... well, I don't know what it would mean. But it would make more sense than random green *stuff.*"

Zub had put down the microscope and gone back to poring over Sajad. "He should be done with his diagnostics in a few minutes. Other than this singed patch and the stuff on his suit, I don't see anything out of the normal at all."

I picked up the suit and looked at it more closely. Zub was right; there was mud and dust caked into it, along with a few tufts of what looked like monkey fur, along with the green dust. If there were any seeds on him, or anything else out of the ordinary at all, they were too small for me to see.

"If he had the suit on, there's not going to be anything matted into his fur anyway," Zub said, losing interest in the search. "If he-- wait a minute."

He looked at us, a broad smile on his face. "Guys. He's *wearing the suit*. Wherever the *Johannes* is, it *landed*. It's not crashed."

"Explain," Celeste said. Kathryn and I just sort of stared at him.

"It's his programming," Zub said, talking at top speed, his voice cracking a bit. "If the ship had crashed, he wouldn't have his suit on. He's only supposed to put the suit on in response to a direct command or if the ship is landing or taking off. If the ship had *crashed*, or come down accidentally or been, I don't know, *lassoed* down to the Martian surface... well, there's nothing in his programming to deal with that situation. No reason to put the suit on. He *knew* the ship was landing. Which implies, logically, that it *landed*. We just have to figure out where."

"If only we had a xenocartographer," I said.

"Shut up, I'm thinking about it," Celeste said.

"She's about to say *nowhere*," Zub said.

"Nowhere," Celeste said. "The *Johannes* is designed to be able to land and take off under its own power. If we needed to, we could bring it down onto the planet's surface for repairs or whatever reason we might have. But depending on where we landed, we might have to prepare an appropriate landing surface for it first."

"No runways on Mars, you mean," Kathryn said.

"Basically, yeah. Under the right circumstances, the ship doesn't necessarily *need* a runway. If we had had time to survey the planet's surface closely, we'd probably have been able to find an appropriate place-- and, honestly, the plains areas we're in right now are probably the best landing zones for hundreds of kilometers in every direction. There's a reason so many of the previous missions have landed near here. But if Zvi landed the ship nearby, we didn't notice it happen and we can't establish communications with his suit. I don't think he's nearby, and if he managed to brought the *Johannes* down, on his own and without communications, on any of the rockier parts of the planet, then he's the best pilot who ever lived."

"So are we back to the skylights again?" I asked.

"Pretty much," she responded. "There's no better place to look, at least that I can think of, so we might as well stick with the previous plan."

"And yet we have the monkey," I added.

"We have the monkey," Zub said. "Now what we need to do is find the pilot. Look, he's done with the diagnostics." Sajad had indeed recovered from his trance state, and flashed a double thumbs-up at me in what had to be the single creepiest gesture I'd ever seen from him, even in his more anthropomorphic moments.

"Make him never do that again," Kathryn said.

Zub just grinned in response. "Let me see if I can figure out where he's been," he said. He fiddled with something in his helmet, producing a thin cable that he attached to a hidden port in the back of Sajad's neck.

"Anything?"

"Not really, since he doesn't have any local maps built in. He's been moving in a pretty straight line, but I'm not sure what direction he came from."

"How far could he walk in a day?" Celeste asked.

"Oh, about thirty, forty miles, maybe, if he doesn't stop or worry about his batteries," Zub answered.

"Chloe is about that far away," Celeste said. "That's the closest of the skylights."

"It's settled, then," Zub said. "Everybody pack up everything we might need for a few days. We're going to load up the rover and go for a trip."

*   *   *

Everything we might need for a few days turned out to be a startling amount of equipment. I spent most of the packing time acting as heavy labor while the three scientists brainstormed out every single bad thing they thought could happen to us during the trip and every piece of equipment that we could carry that they thought could be of some use. I had suggested simply packing up the domicile and bringing it along with us, a suggestion that was rejected on the grounds that we could take shelter in the lander when we needed to sleep. Failing that, we had several two-man tents that could be pressurized and heated in a pinch. They wouldn't be comfortable, but they'd keep us alive.

We were bringing the entire lander along. Zub and Celeste hadn't been able to come up with any other way that we might be able to get down inside of the skylights once we got to them, since we weren't exactly expecting there to be stairs. The rover was entirely capable of towing the thing, of course, but it took time to bolt everything together correctly. We'd not found a trace of the second rover. It would have come in handy.

Our first view of the planet's surface post-heat-wave and post-green-dusting was less exciting than we'd thought it might have been. The heat wave had turned the permafrost into a sea of red mud, but it had quickly re-frozen once Mars' typical far-below-zero temperatures had had a chance to reassert themselves. Other than the obliteration of the footprints, there was little visible change. There was little trace of the green dust. Kathryn speculated that everything had quickly died once being exposed to the elements on the surface.

Between that and a Dr. Rosansky-mandated four hours of sleep for everyone, since none of us had gotten any real sleep the previous night, it was early afternoon before we were able to get underway.

There had been no communication from Zvi. Our sporadic attempts to contact the *Johannes* were similarly unsuccessful.

Moving at a reasonably cautious pace, Celeste estimated it would take several hours for us to reach Chloe. Once we got there, we'd have to determine somehow whether that skylight was a good candidate to investigate further.

"One of them should be as good as the rest," Zub had said during the discussion. When we'd first seen the green spots from orbit, it had appeared that five out of seven of the skylights were spewing out the plant material. However, if for some reason Chloe didn't look like an auspicious choice, we'd just move on to the next closest one. Nobody was really sure what we'd do if we didn't find anything useful at any of the skylights. We really didn't want to think about what we should do if we really were stranded on Mars.

* * *

"That... is a *really* big hole," Zub said.

Since only two of us could ride in the rover at a time, we'd alternated on which of us rode and which of us walked as we made the journey to the first of the skylights. With as much weight as it was towing, the rover was actually slightly slower than the top speed any of us could reach on foot. Zub had managed to get ahead of us, and as a result, got the first look at Chloe.

It was a really big hole. I hadn't spent a lot of time on football fields, but I was pretty sure that you could fit three or four into the surface area with some room left over. The ground was flat enough here that we hadn't gotten a lot of warning. One minute everything was fine and the next minute there was this enormous yawning black pit stretching out in front of us.

"Stop where you are," Zub ordered, his tone suddenly sharper. "In fact, back up a few hundred yards. We don't know how thick the crust is here. Don't get the rover too close."

"You're probably too close yourself," Celeste pointed out.

"Which would be why I'm coming back," Zub said, and in the distance we could see him pivot and head back in our direction. "Get the cords out and prepped while you wait."

Celeste and I climbed out of the rover. Kathryn was already hip-deep in one of our cargo crates. Among the items we'd brought along were several hundred yards' worth of what was basically superlight bungee cord. We'd considered using it as support while we climbed down into the skylights, but none of us

felt confident enough in our physical conditioning to attempt
something like that when we didn't have any idea how far we'd
be climbing. That said, one end tied to us and the other tied to
the rover would do a dandy job of safety backup if the crust
around Chloe suddenly crumbled underneath us.

"Should we all go at once?" I asked.

"We might as well," Celeste said. "This is still soil
underneath us, not bare rock. I think the skylights go straight
down for a while before they start curving out. The four of us
would weigh a bit over a quarter-ton in Earth gravity. Surely
whatever's out there can take our weight on Mars."

"That's what I was thinking," Zub said. "Wasn't willing to
risk it without the safety cords, though."

"I'll stay behind," Kathryn said. "Fear of heights. I don't
want to look into a canyon I can't see the bottom of."

"I thought we screened for that before we left Earth," Zub
said. "You're afraid of heights? We were *forty thousand miles
up* when we were in orbit."

"Call it a new discovery," she said nervously. "It looks deep
enough from here. I'll be the one that hits the winch when the
rest of you fall in."

Zub considered this for a moment. "That's reasonable," he
said. "You're right, somebody ought to do that. The luck we've
been having, the rover will get stolen the second we stop looking
after it."

"Just make it fast," she said. "I'm not too keen on being
alone out here either."

"The speediest," Zub said. "Let's go, guys."

We all strapped into our safety harnesses and double-
checked each other. "Don't forget the boot jets," Celeste said.
"They're mostly for maneuvering in zero-G, but they'll slow you
down if you fall here too. If we do fall and it looks like there's
something to land on, fire the jets a few seconds before you land
even if the cords are working. Safe as houses."

I thought about mentioning how one of the two houses we
had on Mars had blown up three minutes after we entered it and
decided not to.

Moving slowly, alert for any shift in the ground underneath us, we made our way to the edge of the enormous cave opening.

Have you ever been to the Grand Canyon? I first went there as a young man. It's one of the most amazing sights on Earth, I think, and the couple of times I've been back have only reinforced that view. It's amazing to think that such an immense hole in the Earth was carved by something as fundamental and simple as water.

This was nothing like that at all.

Chloe simply stretched out to infinity in every direction. And at the bottom was... nothing. A couple of generations of high-tech outer-space science-type doohickies had pointed high-powered cameras at the bottom of this thing and received not a single pixel of useful data. Our eyes, even aided by the automapping feature of the exosuits, could see *nothing* at the bottom of the pit. I could see, much as Celeste had thought, the ground stretching away more or less straight down under our feet, and the sides of the pit, just as steep, on the other side, both plummeting into sheer darkness. The vertigo was overwhelming. On the plus side, it seemed incredibly unlikely that the cliff face was going to be collapsing underneath us anytime soon.

"Dear God," I said.

"*Wenn du lange in einen Abgrund blickst, blickt der Abgrund auch in dich hinein.* When you gaze for long into the abyss, the abyss gazes also into you," Celeste said.

"Well, I hope the abyss sees more than I do," Zub said. "Because I can't see a freaking thing. Figure there's enough room in there to land the *Johannes?*"

"There's enough room in there to drop the entire Vehicle Assembly Building and still have trouble finding it," Celeste said.

I nodded.

"We are *not* trying to climb into that thing," Celeste said. "It's the lander or nothing."

"Correct," Zub said. He activated the external lights on his suit, which did nothing to penetrate the total darkness. "But not quite yet. You ready, buddy?"

Sajad came scampering up behind us.

"Oh, hell no," I said.

The monkey was wearing a parachute.

"I thought about tossing a couple of strobe lights into the pit," Zub said. "Maybe we could illuminate it from the bottom instead of from the top; if nothing else, we could see if we *saw* the light once it hit the bottom. Problem is, I can't just toss one down there. The fall will destroy it. And if we put a 'chute on the thing, it'll just obscure the light. Thus the monkey."

"That's not going to do *him* a whole lot of good, is it?" I asked.

"Not really," he said. "It's mostly just for kicks. He's got the same bootjets that you do. He could probably survive if he just jumped into the thing."

"Wait," said Celeste. "Zub, if he came from the skylight-- if the ship's in there-- how did he get out?"

"Dunno," Zub said. "And he hasn't been much use on that front either. He can't explain it because he wasn't programmed to do stuff like that. I promise Monkey Robot 3.0 will rectify this problem. If only I had a lab here to build one."

"How's he getting back out again once he's down there? I mean, if we don't follow him."

"The bootjets will get him a good distance off the ground," Zub said. "I figure we can lower the cord down the rest of the way if we need to. He'll be fine."

"Your monkey, I guess," Celeste said. "We have a camera to send down with him?"

"You forget," Zub said. "You can slave your suit to his, too. Works the same way."

I could think of no other objections. Zub was right. Even if we lost Sajad sending him down into the pit, it was certainly much better than wasting precious fuel to take the lander down, to say nothing of the possibility of losing one of the humans on the mission.

"Off he goes," I said.

"Everybody connect up your suits," Zub said. "Sajad, whenever you're ready." The little monkeybot padded over to the edge and, down on all fours, peered comically over the edge, then looked back at us, a suspiciously human mix of abject terror and other kinds of terror mixed on his face. A moment later, he flashed a smile and tossed himself headlong into the pit.

*   *   *

A word of advice: if you're ever given the opportunity to slave your visual input to the exosuit worn by a robot monkey as it throws itself headfirst into a bottomless pit on an alien planet, *don't*. If someone had asked me, I would have thought that the slow-motion fall caused by Mars' low gravity would have made falling into an almost pleasant process, perhaps something akin to swimming into the deep end of the pool.

I thought that because I'm an *idiot*.

Let me make this clear: when it looks like you're falling, the thought *you fall slower in Martian gravity* is absolutely not helpful in any way. If you're falling, you're falling *much too fast* as far as your body is concerned.

Within just a few seconds, the sight of the rock wall rushing past Sajad's visor as he fell into the dark was enough to induce vertigo that was almost physically painful. Kathryn, already uneasy around heights, shrieked behind me, and I had to drop to the ground to convince my body that I wasn't the one falling. *Thank God I'm not close to the edge*, I thought. I'm convinced I would have tumbled in after him.

After some amount of time-- it's hard to tell when you're terrified-- the rock wall curved back out underneath us and disappeared from Sajad's view, cutting down on the vertigo but replacing it with blindness, which wasn't much of an improvement. After probably no more than ten seconds of falling, apparently relying on robotic eyes more precise than our own, he turned on his boot jets and decelerated. A few seconds later, he landed on a gray rock floor. The light shed by his exosuit showed us little in the way of detail around him; the sheer wall was out of sight, and all we saw was the ground. Chloe's floor, at least this part of it, looked as nondescript and uniform as the rest of her.

"Nothing," Celeste said. I decided not to respond, choosing instead to catch my breath and not fall off the ground.

"Maybe," Zub said. "Give him a couple of minutes to explore a little bit before we give up." The little monkey stood up, looked around for a moment, then scampered off away from the wall. Curious, I killed his feed to my suit and crawled to the edge of the skylight, looking carefully to see if I could see any trace of his light deep beneath us. His outline showed up on my HUD, showing him as a full hundred and fifty meters away. *God, this thing's deep*, I thought. I could just barely detect a hazy nimbus of light around where my suit said he was if I squinted at it. Then again, it could very well have been my imagination.

I switched back to Sajad's visual input to discover that he still hadn't found anything. Interestingly, the floor was a solid gray in color, almost the color and texture of bare concrete, only obviously not artificial. Occasional small rocks, most of the grayish color but some of the traditional Martian red, spotted the landscape.

And then, abruptly, a glint off something at the very edge of the pool of light. Something reflective.

"Tell me someone else saw that," I said.

"I did too," Zub agreed. "Sajad, check it out."

Sajad had moved perhaps fifty meters farther into the pit from his landing spot, putting him a sizeable distance from the rock face that formed the edge of Chloe's deep pit. He turned toward the reflective area, shining a high-intensity light beam on it. Much of the light was bounced back at him, and my visor temporarily darkened in response to the sudden burst of luminosity. As it returned to normal, it became perfectly clear what Sajad had discovered.

Sixty meters from where he had first touched down, there was a sheet of some sort of metal. It rose perhaps a foot from the ground and well off into the distance from Sajad's point of view.

"My God," Celeste breathed, coming to a realization a split second before I did.

It hadn't taken a biologist to recognize what were obviously plant cells ground into Sajad's suit. And it didn't take an aeronautical engineer to recognize a landing pad.

FOURTEEN

"No way," I said.

"Way," Zub said. "That's a landing pad. We just found a goddamn landing pad on Mars. For spaceships. A landing pad for spaceships is on Mars. On *Mars*." Sensing that he was enjoying his babbling and would likely not stop for a little while, I turned down his audio feed.

"Zub, have him walk the perimeter of the thing," Celeste said. "Get its dimensions."

"What if the *Johannes* is down there?" Kathryn asked. "I still can't get a fix on Zvi's exosuit anywhere."

"Mental note," Celeste said over our private channel. "Put a fix on the ship in the next revision of the suits."

"I'll remind you once we get home," I said.

Zub blinked me. TURN ME BACK ON, YOU JERK. I turned him back on, wondering sheepishly how he'd noticed.

"I noticed because I was *talking* to you," he said immediately, showing off his annoying ability to read my mind. "When someone ignores direct questions from me, it's generally because they've not heard me. There's only one way you could not have heard something I was saying."

"So what were you saying?" I asked.

"None of your business," he fired back. "Now you'll never know. And it was an awesome thing to say, too. Too bad for you. And don't the rest of you go telling him, either."

"My lips are sealed," Celeste said.

"He asked if you--" Kathryn started saying, and was immediately silenced by a burst of horrifyingly loud static.

"Huh," Zub said. "That's what it sounds like if I lick the microphone in my suit. Do not make me do it again."

"I could just tell him over a private channel," Kathryn said, sounding annoyed.

"But you won't," Zub said.

"Enough," I said. "Monkey. Giant pit. Landing pad. Mars. Scientific discovery of a lifetime. Focus, guys."

"Right," Zub said. "Sajad, go black." I switched back to the monkeybot's visual feed and was rewarded with the suit's closed-visor HUD. He hadn't moved much since discovering the landing pad.

"Anybody who is paying attention has probably already noticed we're here," Zub said. "But I figure it's better to be careful. He's as close as I can get him to not emitting any signals of any kind right now without compromising communications. We can cut the visual feed, too, if we want to, but I don't think that would be as noticeable as the flashlight he was using a couple of minutes ago."

"Send him around the perimeter of the pad," Celeste suggested again. "We should find out how big it is."

"Go," Zub said, and Sajad started slowly edging around the outside of the pad. The four of us sat in breathless silence as he slowly made his way back to his starting point. The landing pad was hexagonal in shape, perhaps fifty yards across. The pad itself appeared to be a single enormous piece of featureless gray metal, with no seams or other disruptions marring its surface.

"No dust," Kathryn noticed at one point. "Look at the thing. Everything else on Mars is coated with a hundred million years of red dust, and everything around here's probably got a load of those plant cells on top of them too. It might be the resolution, but the thing looks spotless."

Sajad, obligingly, climbed onto the surface of the landing pad and looked at it carefully, and everything swam into clear focus. Kathryn was right; there didn't appear to be a rock or a speck of dust anywhere.

"Head across," Zub ordered. "Right through the middle." Moving quickly, Sajad did as commanded. The landing pad was unoccupied.

"What's amazing is that there's still an enormous expanse of space down there that he hasn't explored," Celeste said. "There's enough room for another half-dozen of those things down there, at that size. In fact, given the amount of room they've got, if that's the size of the landing pad there's almost certainly something else down there taking up the rest of the room."

"How much time do we give Sajad to look around before we go down ourselves?" I asked.

"As long as we need," Kathryn suggested. "Why risk our necks when we don't have to?"

"Because that way is much more fun," Zub said. "Seriously, do you want to wait around up here while a robomonkey becomes the human race's most famous explorer? We came all this way; I want to be *famous*, not the answer to a trivia question on a game show."

"So you admit that was the reason," Kathryn said.

"Part of it," he said, his voice growing heated. "And don't you pretend for a second that you're surprised by that or that you feel any differently. Besides, *oh no it might be dangerous* is somewhat of a silly thing to say. Consider our situation for a moment. You can't honestly say that it's any more dangerous down *there* than it is up *here*. I mean, either way we're pretty much at the *do something or die soon* stage, aren't we?"

"I like the way you think, where doing the riskiest thing we can imagine is considered exactly the same as the safe route," Kathryn said evenly, ignoring Zub's tone.

"This is why you signed up," Zub responded. "Because I am insane and you all love me. Fire up the lander, Flye. We're going down."

*   *   *

Surprisingly, no one argued with the order. Even Kathryn, who had been by far the most cautious among us, seemed to give in to the inevitable: Zub was going to get his way. In a weird way he was right anyway. We had no good reason to hide out on the planet's surface and wait for danger to come to us. Whatever we were up against, at the moment it had a virtually unsurmountable advantage over us, and there was no reason not to at least *try* and discover what had happened to the two ships that Mars had swallowed up in the past four years.

We hauled the lander as close as we could get it to the edge, hoping to conserve as much of our fuel as possible. The plan was to burn just enough to pop the lander out over the surface of the pit, then a controlled descent onto the landing pad below. The lander, as it turned out, featured a smaller version of the atmospheric condenser that the solid rocket boosters were using. Zub figured that between that and the reserves, we'd be able to get into the skylight and back out again... so long as we only had to do it *once*. It was entirely possible that there wasn't going to be anything other than the landing pad down there. We didn't want to close off any of our options completely until there was no other choice.

After instructing Sajad to move to the center of the landing pad, Celeste used his coordinates to program a descent into the lander. It only took a few minutes. The lander would effectively toss itself off the side, free-fall for a few seconds, then fire the landing rockets to glide to a relatively smooth landing.

Relatively smooth, of course, being in the eye of the beholder. "I wish I knew exactly what the surface was made of," Celeste said. "Make sure you're strapped in, everybody."

She looked around. "Zub, we're sure about this?" It was as close as she was going to come to expressing reservations.

He nodded. "We are. Punch it."

My stomach dropped into my toes as the lander's launch rockets kicked the ground out from underneath us. Then five seconds of vertigo as we fell toward the landing zone, punctuated by a couple heavy bumps as the maneuvering rockets threw us in the right direction. Then we were lifted out of our seats by the retro rockets firing and just as quickly slammed back into them as the lander crashed into the ground. The whole trip had taken less than fifteen seconds.

"Worst roller coaster *ever*," I said. No one laughed.

"Everybody okay?" Kathryn said. I felt fine, if perhaps a little bruised. On the HUD, everyone was blinking green. Heart rates were elevated, but our hearts had all been dancing a tarantella since we landed, so that was no surprise.

"We're good," I said. "How are we doing this?"

"Split up," Zub said. "Stay on global channel, but everybody pick a direction and look around. Separate for ten minutes then meet back up here at the lander. Anybody finds anything interesting, let the rest of us know so we can come running."

"Are you sure that's safe?" Celeste asked.

"I am not even vaguely *theorizing* that it's safe," Zub said. "But I don't think we'd be any more safe together, really, so we might as well break up and get some exploration done quickly. Keep everybody up on your HUDs. Anything strange happens-- *anything*-- we all converge on whoever went funny. Agreed?"

"Fair enough," I said. Celeste nodded. Kathryn didn't say anything. The four of us did an awkward little fist-bump in the enclosed chamber of the lander and then Zub sprung the door.

I wasn't prepared for the darkness. I'd been told that the skylights were so deep that light wasn't able to penetrate to the floor, and I'd just spent several minutes piggybacking off Sajad's visual feed, a visual feed characterized mostly by staring intently into the small pool of light generated by his suit. I knew there wasn't any light out there, but seeing *absolutely nothing* when Zub opened up the hatch was still jarring.

"Get your lights on, kids," he said, and led the way out of the lander. We all took a moment to kneel down and touch the surface we'd set down on-- it certainly felt like metal, or at least it did through the gloves, and was weirdly slippery. Celeste and I both nearly lost our footing when we first stepped onto its surface.

"Not a trace of residue on my hands," Kathryn said, looking at her gloves. "Nothing I can see, anyway." She reached out and gave the lander an experimental push, shoving herself a few inches away from it in the process. "If I was a little heavier, I think I'd be able to move the lander around if I wanted to. And look, there's no scorch marks where the rockets were firing. I bet there's no scoring underneath the legs of the thing, either. What the hell is this stuff?"

"Plenty of Earth alloys that the lander wouldn't scratch," Zub said. "Let's worry about what else is around here. Let's go."

I picked a direction, heading the opposite direction from Zub, with Kathryn to my right and Celeste to my left. It was tougher than I'd expected to keep my footing on the metal of the landing pad, and since I had little interest in slipping and breaking my skull on anything, I walked slowly until I reached the end of the pad. There was little to be seen in any direction, with the edge of the pad transitioning into the flat gray rock surface and little else. Curious, I scraped a bit of Martian dust off the ground and tossed it at the metal.

The handful of dirt hit the surface, bounced, and *kept going*, the particles skittering away manically until they were out of my field of view.

"Be on the lookout for runaway Mars dust," I said on the global channel. "The landing pad's actually repelling the surface material. I don't think it's going to stop until it falls off the other side."

"Do me a favor and don't do that again," Zub said.

I kept walking, watching the chronometer on my HUD. Zub had said we were to explore for ten minutes then head back; half of that time was gone and I hadn't found the other side of the pit yet, much less anything else interesting.

"Huh," Zub said.

"What does 'huh' mean, dear?" Kathryn said, using what I'd learned to think of as her Patient Voice.

"Second landing pad," he said. "I'm maybe, what, a couple of hundred yards away from the first one? It looks exactly the same."

"Weirdly redundant," Dr. Flye said. "Maybe these aren't landing pads after all. Why would they put two separate pads right next to each other like that instead of one larger one?"

"No idea," he said. "I'm going to skirt the outside of the thing and see if there are any structures attached. Unless somebody finds something more interesting, everybody head toward me in three minutes."

"I've got one too," Kathryn said. "Same exact thing."

"I've hit the cliff face," Celeste said. "If we've found three of them this quickly, there are probably a ton of those things down here. They're probably all over the place. Heading your way, Zub. I'll stay along the cliff face until I can't any longer."

A minute later, I found my own landing pad. I saw the reflection from the metal first, a bright burst of light flashing back into my eyes from the spotlight on my suit. "Got another one," I said. That was four. Celeste was right; there were surely more.

Then I noticed something. The reflection of the light didn't look like it was coming from a uniform surface.

"Something funny about this one," I said. "Give me a minute to check it out, then I'll head over."

There was a minute crack in the surface of the sheet of metal. It was tiny, probably less than a millimeter wide, but it looked like it stretched across the entire surface of the pad. Perfectly straight, too.

"This one's in two pieces," I said. "Either that or it's broken. There's a seam or a crack in it." Lights blipped in my HUD as the other three members of the crew switched their visual input to mine.

"Get a light in there," Zub said. "See how deep the thing is, if you can."

"I knew I should have built a zoom function into the helmets," Celeste said. "Something else for the next revision." I leaned closer and peered into the crack, but I couldn't see anything other than darkness inside.

Suddenly warning monitors started bleeping madly in my HUD, and a blast of wind hit me in the face. The external temperature spiked fifty degrees in a second.

Oh God. We'd already known that the skylights were the source of the green clouds the crew of the *Tycho* had witnessed, and that they were also the source of the blast of heat that had turned the surface of Mars to a sea of mud only a few hours earlier.

These things weren't landing pads. They were *vents*.

"I'm in trouble," I said, watching the temperature continue to spike as the crack in the "pad" grew wider. "Anybody else's acting up?"

"Gabe, *run*," Zub said. "Run *now*."

"Where to?" I yelled, turning away from my pad and cursing my slow movement speed in low gravity. "Back to the lander?"

"Toward me!" Zub shouted. "All of you! There's a structure over here! And the door's open!"

That was all I needed, even if it sounded like jumping from the frying pan into the fire. I spun toward Zub, overcorrecting in the low gravity and almost rolling off my feet, then ran toward him as fast as I could. I could see Celeste, Kathryn, and Sajad's ghosts in my HUD all speeding in his direction as well.

The temperature outside was already at eighty degrees Fahrenheit and climbing. Not dangerous yet, but it had gotten hotter than that at the base site, miles from the skylight. It was going to get much, much hotter very fast. I had spent the last ten minutes walking in the exact opposite direction from Zub. I was going to have to close that difference in a tiny fraction of that time. *Thank God I was walking slow,* I thought, bounding ridiculously across the Martian landscape.

"Gabe, use your maneuvering jets!" Celeste shouted. "Point your feet behind you when you're in the air!" Judging from the HUD, she and Sajad had already found Zub, with Kathryn only a short distance away. *Man, I wish I had practiced this in low gravity,* I thought, bounding up in the air, pointing my hands in the vague direction of safety, and hitting the toe trigger to activate the boot jets. The boots and backpack fired, tripling my speed and hurling me on my way in a manner that was not at all entirely terrifying. I curled my legs underneath me, planning on cutting the boots and hitting the ground at a dead run.

This worked well, bouncing along and trying my best to ignore the rapidly increasing temperature outside (a hundred and fifty degrees Fahrenheit, still rising) until I realized that my next jump was going to land me squarely on top of the first landing pad.

Oh, hell. I was about to hit a virtually frictionless surface at an unsafe speed. This was not going to be fun. I tried to land on my feet again, which flew out from underneath me, dropping me hard onto my shoulder. *If the suit tears, I'm dead.* The impact knocked the wind out of me for a second, leaving me gasping for air as I skidded across the pad's metallic surface.

The lander. If I was crossing the middle of the thing, I was bound to slide by the lander at some point. Unfortunately, that meant that I was probably going to also have to cross the gap that was most likely opening up ahead of me as well. A burst of light from in front of me caught my attention, and I craned my neck to see what I was careening into.

Fire. This just kept getting worse. I was heading straight for the seam in the vent, and there was honest-to-god flame coming out of the thing now. A hundred and eighty degrees outside, and the fire was going to be worse.

"Gabe, roll onto your back!" Celeste shrieked into my ear, and I noticed she had her suit slaved to mine. "Point up out of the crater and fire your boots!" I rolled over, and the jets built into the backpack fired just in time to carry me out of the reach of the flames. My suit temperature jumped to five hundred degrees for a split-second as I flew over the blast of superheated air coming up out of the vents.

"How hot can these suits get, Celeste?" I asked.

"They were built for Mars, not for Venus," she said. "They're not built for reentry, either, Christ, Gabe, *shut up and run!*" I shut off the external sensor, figuring there was no need to keep terrifying myself.

"Gabe, *don't* turn around," Zub said into my ear, cutting off everyone else's feed. "Run toward us as fast as you can. Exhaust the fuel in the jets if you have to. The door to the structure you're headed toward is on the *back* side of the thing, so you'll have to get around it. We're holding it open for you, but it's getting too hot for any of us out here. Move it."

I heard the unspoken message in his voice, which he was doing his best to keep completely calm. *I will let you broil out there to save the other two* was what he was telling me. It felt like the middle of the Amazon inside my suit. I was sweating freely, and my vision was starting to be obscured by steam that was rolling out of the vents. I cranked the maneuvering jets up to maximum, throwing my hands ahead of me like Superman and praying there was enough juice left in the things to get me to the structure they were hiding in before they had to close the door.

I was a hundred yards away, skidding uncontrollably over the surface of what must have been Zub's vent, before I even saw the thing. "Structure" was probably doing it too much justice. The thing was a bunker at *best*, a squat, low thing that I might have mistaken for a small hill were there not clearly a window in one side of it. No need to go around it, I slammed a foot into the ground for lift then tumbled *over* the building, hitting the ground hard on the other side and rolling to my feet.

My HUD darkened immediately as I took in the view behind me. At some point, the spotlight on my suit had become pointless. There was clearly *air* venting from the innumerable vents behind me, and that air was on fire. My eyes hurt from the sudden change in brightness, and that was *with* the darkened visor. The blast shield visor slammed into place, and the only thing I could see was the outlines of my friends and the entrance to the weird, utterly out of place building that Zub had discovered. With red warning lights flashing in every corner of my HUD, I covered my head with my arms, dove through the door, and blacked out entirely as I hit the floor.

FIFTEEN

I was still alive. I was pretty sure of that much. I just wasn't at all sure that I wanted to open my eyes. *I'm on the beach,* I thought. *I'm on the beach, at Eunostos, and there are friendly, beautiful, ever-so-slightly-indecently too young for me serving girls nearby who will bring me fruity drinks and rub my shoulders.* I was certainly not locked into an underground bunker on Mars, millions of miles from the nearest serving girl, with a raging inferno outside and quite possibly a melted space suit.

I opened my eyes. Zub, who at least was making an effort to look concerned, made an extraordinarily poor substitute for a serving girl. His face was green for some reason.

"You could at least have been Celeste," I said.

"He's whining. Means he's better," Zub said, and yelped as Kathryn shoved him out of the way. She leaned toward me, pulling my eyelids back and staring intently at me, apparently checking my pupils for something. Her hair brushed my face.

It took a minute for that to sink in. My reaction, shoving her away and scrabbling madly for my helmet, which was nowhere to be found, elicited laughter from my companions, none of whom had headgear on.

"I'm breathing," I said, wishing the screaming in my head would stop. "I'm breathing *air*. Why am I not dead? If I was dead, none of you would be here, unless this is Hell. And then I don't think I'd be breathing."

"The air's oxygenated," Kathryn said, still trying to examine me. "Not quite a perfectly habitable Earth mix—it breathes more like what you'd find at the top of Everest-- but it's survivable. The tunnel we took shelter in pressurized the second we shut the door." She sounded excited.

"With *Earth air??*" I said. "That's..."

"Impossible!" the other three shouted in unison. "We know," Kathryn said. "Everything around here is impossible."

"Yeah, it's official," Zub said, a crazed grin on his face. "We've completely eliminated human origins as even a remote possibility for this place. You're in a building built by aliens. Awesome, isn't it?"

I nodded, still a little weak and not entirely interested in talking.

"The breathable air actually makes some sense," Zub said. "Or, at least, I can justify it. Whoever built this thing—and as I said I think we can definitively eliminate humans at least for *that* responsibility—seems to have wanted to terraform Mars into something with oxygen and photosynthetic plants. *That's* where the crazy coincidence lies, not that the fact that their buildings are filled with an air mix that we can breathe. It's not quite Earth air anyway, like Kathryn said. We're probably all going to die soon."

Wonderful, I thought. "So we don't need the suits any more?"

"Oh, we're still using them," Kathryn said. "Just because the air has enough oxygen for us to not die from breathing it doesn't mean that there aren't plenty of other toxins for us to worry about. Once we move on into the complex, we're putting the helmets right back on again and using the external filters to pull in the air around us. Between that, the built-in air supply and the rebreathers we shouldn't have to worry about O2 for a while."

The word *complex* caught my attention, and I took a moment to look around me for the first time.

We weren't in a building.

For an alien complex on Mars, the entryway—- whatever it was—- looked surprisingly mundane. There was nothing about it that would have been out of place on Earth. I was lying on a landing, with a steep ramp on one side of me leading up to the door to the surface and another ramp parallel to that one heading farther down. The floor and walls were a uniform dark gray in color, the same shade as the rock outside-- in fact, it wouldn't have surprised me to learn that the passageway was simply hacked out of the bedrock were it not for the fact that everything was perfectly smooth. From what I could see of the door, it looked like it was on sliders, disappearing into the wall on one side when opened, and probably locking mechanically.

Wait. "I can see," I said. "Where's the light coming from?" It wasn't just that Zub's face was green, now that I could see; everything around us was lit in a sickly green light. He picked up a glow light from the floor and waved it at me.

"Worried about batteries," he said. "I figured we might be here a while so I used one of these instead." It left me wondering how much we had squirreled away in supplies.

I stood up, inspecting my suit and taking my helmet from Celeste. I had some scorch marks here and there, but it didn't look like the suit had been breached anywhere.

"How's my back?" I asked, figuring I wouldn't like the answer.

"Your suit held up ridiculously well, considering it wasn't built for surfing," Zub said. "Do I hire awesome engineers, or what?" I grinned at Celeste, who shrugged.

"Some of the accelerant nozzles on your backpack have seen better days," she said. "You're going to be handicapped if we have to do any more low-G maneuvering, especially anything precision. But other than that and some superficial scrapes and scorches, you're fine. It helps that the metal surface was so smooth; if that had been even as rough as the walls here you'd have been in trouble after that long of a skid." She walked up to me, her eyes suddenly turning to obsidian and her hands going to her hips.

"Don't go *breaking my suits*, Southern. You don't make enough to pay me thirty million dollars, do you?"

"No, ma'am," I said, keeping my eyes down.

"That's what I thought," she said.

"So what now?" I asked. "I'm guessing I wasn't out very long."

"Ten minutes, maybe," Kathryn said. "Zub pulled the door shut after you got in here. It locked itself and the next thing we heard was the place pressurizing. I checked on you. We haven't explored at all."

"Any idea if all hell is breaking loose outside?"

"None," she replied. "Zub tried to listen at the door. It's either completely silent outside or the door's too soundproofed to hear anything. One is safe, one gets us killed. We decided against opening the door."

"So we go down," I said.

"We go down," she agreed. "That is, if you're feeling up to it. You took a couple of pretty hard knocks there. I don't think you're concussed, but it's a risk."

I thought about it. I had a headache, and I really wanted to curl into a ball and sleep for a million years, but neither of those seemed sufficient to keep everybody else waiting on me.

"I don't see that we have a choice," I said.

THAT'S GOOD, BECAUSE WE WEREN'T REALLY GIVING YOU ONE, Zub blinked. I looked at him, startled by the blink, and realized that he'd put his helmet back on. I wouldn't have been able to hear him talk anyway. PUT YOUR GEAR BACK ON AND LET'S MOVE OUT. SAJAD'S SCOUTING AHEAD FOR US.

He was right, as usual. I put my helmet back on, Celeste checking to make sure everything sealed properly, and we all turned on our spotlights and moved into the dark.

*   *   *

There's a line in an old movie I used to like a lot when I was a kid. A wall has just come crashing down in a building, revealing a set of old stairs behind it. One of the characters looks at the stairs and asks where they go. Another one answers him.

"They go up," he says.

The ramp? It went down.

Steeply.

More steeply than human beings would ever have designed a ramp or a stairway on Earth, with a landing and a change of direction every 25 feet or so. It was difficult going, and I wasn't looking forward to climbing back up them later. The low gravity helped, since we could sort of bounce down each of the landings, but we had to be careful not to crash into walls or into each other on the way. The walls were entirely featureless for the first fifteen minutes or so, then what was unmistakably writing began appearing on the landings.

"Not human, right?" Celeste said. "I've seen a lot of Earth scripts, and that doesn't look like any of them to me." If anything, the letters had the look of a more military version of Arabic, since there were lots of words that looked like they'd been drawn with a single line, with dots and dashes above and below the "letters," but everything was at precise geometric angles. I'd never seen anything like it. There wasn't much there, only a single line of text each time, perhaps a place name or a "you have two more hours of walking" sign.

Zub stared at the script for a long moment before moving on. "No use spending too much time with it," he said. "Everybody record everything interesting. Maybe we can see if there's something to compare it with later on. For now we might as well-- wait a minute."

His hand went to the side of his head, almost as if he was trying to concentrate on listening to something. "It's Sajad. He says there's something weird a few turns beneath us."

We all slaved our suits to the monkeybot's.

"Please tell me that isn't blood," I said.

"It sure looks like it," Kathryn responded. Sajad was scouting ahead, three turns of the ramp beneath us. It looked as if he'd wandered into a slaughterhouse. The landing beneath him, as well as the walls around them and bits of the ceiling, were all coated in a thick layer of what looked suspiciously like dried blood.

"He's going to stay put until we get to him," Zub said. "As quiet as we can, people. Let's go."

We crept down the passageway, turning through another two landings before we reached Sajad's level. He was waiting for us at the beginning of the landing, unwilling to go any further. The amount of blood was immense. There were sprays all over the walls and what looked like dried pools of it on the floor. A few spurts had reached the high ceiling.

"Okay," Zub said. "No bodies. No bits of bodies, either. The blood's red. That says *mammal* to me. So something got killed here, and then... what? Taken away?"

I shined my spotlight down the next ramp. He was right. There was what looked like a drag trail and then more droplets of blood heading down into the darkness.

"The spray patterns are pretty high on the wall," Kathryn pointed out. "People don't bleed *up*. Something was attacking them from below, it looks like."

"So we had one group of people, or aliens, or *something* moving down this passageway before us," Zub said, "and they were attacked by another group down below. Then either the group up here won, and took their wounded further down, or they *lost*, and the second group made off with the bodies."

"Encouraging," I said. "Any way of telling how long ago this happened?"

"Not really," Kathryn said. "The blood's dried, but that could have happened nearly instantly if this place were exposed to outside temperatures for more than a few seconds. Without a body, there's no good way to check."

"And decomposition requires microorganisms anyway," Celeste pointed out. "Not many of those on Mars except for what we're carrying inside us. I doubt a dead body rots on Mars the same way as on Earth."

"Yes, they'd probably mummify first," Kathryn said. "And there's no good way for us to--"

"God, *enough*," Zub said. "We don't know. That's good enough. I don't need a forensics lecture. Let's look around here and see if there's anything else to find, then move down to the next level. Whatever was involved in the fight, it's obviously not here now."

"There's writing on the wall here," I said. It was nearly invisible underneath the blood, but it was there. I ran my hand over it, sweeping a cloud of dried flakes of blood off the wall's surface, showing the writing more clearly. It looked the same as the writing a few levels above us.

"90% match," Zub said. "I'm guessing they read from left to right, the same way English speakers do. The only parts that are different are the last portion here." He pointed to a cluster of symbols on the far right side. "All of the open symbols point to the right. Hebrew's the opposite, and it reads from left to right. I bet these are floor numbers, or something similar. This last bit is probably a number."

"There's something else down here," Celeste said, interrupting Zub. She had started down the ramp to the next level, leaving the rest of us to continue examining the blood smears. "I think our guys up above won."

There was less blood on the second landing, but there was still evidence of a fight. The walls were chipped, there were scorch marks on the floor, and, most interestingly, the floor was scattered with pieces of damaged machinery of some kind. Everything had been thoroughly wrecked, making it difficult to determine what the pieces had been part of before the fight had occurred.

"I think I've got it," she said. "Whoever was coming down ran into some sort of defense system for the building we're in. Everything down here was *mechanical*. Some sort of sentry robots, maybe. There's not nearly enough blood for the defenders to have been biological. All the blood is up above. And look at the walls here. This looks like damage from projectiles, or perhaps from shrapnel."

"There's no holes in the walls on the top level," I said.

Celeste shrugged. "Maybe they didn't miss."

She bent down and picked up something from the floor, then tossed it at Zub. It was strange watching the object fly through the air in the Martian gravity. It seemed to move slower than it ought to on Earth. This didn't stop Zub from failing to catch it, of course, but he recovered it from where it fell quickly enough.

"That's a bullet casing," he said.

"There are hundreds of them down here," Celeste said. "Casings, bullets, and-- judging from the marks here-- probably a grenade or two as well." I watched the engineer in Zub take over as he bounded down to her level. Kathryn and I shrugged at each other and followed.

"Okay, then," Zub said. "There are people coming down the ramp. They are attacked-- surprised, probably-- by some of whatever is down here, the sentry-bot things, they fight back, and destroy at least some of them. Whoever wins drags off the bodies. Any way of knowing who won?"

"That's an *awful lot* of blood up there," I said.

"One exsanguinated human being could have done that," Kathryn replied.

"What happened to the you who didn't want to come down here in the first place?" I said. "You seem awfully gung-ho now that there's blood all over everything."

"I'm as terrified as I've ever been in my entire life," Kathryn said, obviously annoyed with me. "But the choices I have are to deal with this clinically or shut down and curl up into a little ball and *die,* and by this point that's not really an option any longer. The fact is, one human being could have produced that much blood. That person is *very very dead now,* but it's still possible. The only question is whether the body was dragged off by his companions or by whatever attacked them. I don't think we have any evidence for that one way or another."

"Yeah, we do," Zub said, and everyone stopped to look at him. "We have tracks, and a bomb in one of our domiciles. There are still living human beings on Mars. They came down here at some point. We just don't know if they're *still* here. Oh, and they have guns and grenades, which we didn't bring any of."

"Better them than aliens," I said. "I'm guessing there were no guns on the *Tycho.*"

"None," Zub said. "I still say it's impossible."

"Keep moving?" I asked.

"We keep moving," Zub agreed.

*   *   *

The pieces of wreckage kept showing up for another couple of levels. Whatever had hit the mechanical sentries, it had hit them hard, and thrown pieces a few floors down. The blood spatters continued until we hit the bottom of the rampway. It took another ten minutes of climbing before we saw anything else.

"Light," Zub said. It took me a moment to realize it, but he was right. In addition to the greenish glow from our chemical lights, it looked like there was white light shining from somewhere beneath us. He held up a hand, and everyone froze.

"Hold on while Sajad checks it out," he said, and the little monkeybot crept down to the lower level. Once he got there, he was greeted with a door.

Like the one at the top, this one was unlocked and just barely cracked open, where a sliver of light penetrated into the rampway. Unlike the one at the top, it had obviously been forced open. It looked as if something-- an acetylene torch, perhaps, or something similar-- had been used to burn out the locking mechanisms and then the door had been opened afterward.

"That's too bad," Zub said. "I'd like to have gotten a look at how the locks worked. Apparently they're not exactly advanced technology, if they can be burned out."

"Doors are doors," Celeste said, inspecting the ruins of the lock. "They're pretty universal. I don't see why they would be all that different with an alien technology. If it's a physical lock you can cut through it."

Kathryn crouched down in the corner. "There's more blood pooled here," she said, tracing her fingers along a discolored spot on the ground. "They must have set him down while they burned the door out."

"Which means that the humans won," Zub said. "The aliens wouldn't have needed to burn through the lock, would they?"

"I can't imagine so, no," I said. "Unless there are three different groups involved, and the aliens didn't build the place."

"Shush," Zub replied. "Quit making things complicated. Everybody kill your lights." We all complied, tossing the rampway into darkness and activating the virtual environments in our helmets. Zub took the lead, creeping down toward the door slowly, keeping close to the wall. He reached the door and tested it, easily sliding it open another few inches without making any additional sound. For a long moment, he peered inside the room beyond the doorway. I slaved my suit to his, taking in his view.

The virtual environment generally didn't pick up a ton of detail-- just enough for the user to be able to move around without inadvertently hurting himself or herself. Since Zub wasn't looking at the same things I was, I wasn't benefiting from the increased resolution when I directed my attention at something. But I was able to get an idea of what lay beyond the doorway.

It looked, for all the world, like a factory floor. Giant vats of *something* dotted the floor, and the space on the upper levels was filled with storage tanks and catwalks, all suspended from somewhere hundreds of feet above us. It looked as if the entire area underneath the skylight might be accounted for, or at least a sizeable percentage of it. From our vantage point, I couldn't see that there even was a wall on the other side. The scale was immense. Whatever they were making or storing here, there was an extraordinary amount of it. There were grates all over the floor, too, meaning that as far underneath the surface as we'd traveled, there was more underneath us as well.

"It doesn't look like there's anyone in there," Zub said. "Or anything. Suggestions on how we move in?"

I found myself wishing we'd practiced SWAT tactics before leaving. I had no idea how to clear a room successfully, much less one as big as this. And it looked as if we were a nontrivial distance from the closest wall, so there wasn't even an obvious place to move to once we got inside.

Then again, it occurred to me, perhaps we were safer than I thought.

"Zub, we didn't get attacked," I said. "If there was some kind of automatic sentry on the place, whoever got here before us destroyed it. It may be that there's nothing in there to attack us."

"Except for the survivors, who have already tried to bomb us to death," Zub said. "Think this through, Gabe."

"Then we either follow the blood trail or go the opposite direction," I said, feeling foolish. "The opposite direction might lead to more sentries. Following it leads to wounded or dead human beings. Your call."

"Let's follow it," he said. "Or, at least, I think so. Celeste, Kathryn, do either of you have better ideas?"

Both of the women shrugged. "Knowing where the other people are seems like a good thing whether they're hostile or not," Celeste said.

"I *am* a doctor," Kathryn added. "If there's someone in need of medical attention nearby, I should at least try to help them."

"There you go," Zub said. "We follow the trail. Move as quietly as you can, and point before you talk. Everybody watch everything. Don't forget to look up once in a while."

"And if something attacks us?" I said.

"Run like hell," he answered. "But try to run slower than me."

Kathryn laughed. I didn't.

*   *   *

It took longer than I had expected to find the first blood spot. Either the wounded person had died in the rampway or they'd received some medical attention while the lock was burning out, because a few steps away from the doorway what had been a consistent trail of drops of blood suddenly dried up. No one wanted to get out of anyone else's line of sight, so it was a few minutes before one of us spotted anything. We appeared to be in some sort of chemical or processing factory. It didn't seem like any of the mechanisms were on. There were control panels or workstations for every second or third vat, but no lights were lit on any of them. The room itself was lit from *somewhere*, though. The ambient glow in the room came from no clear source. We cast shadows in several different directions, none of them especially dark. Other than our muffled footsteps and my own heartbeat thudding insistently in my ears, it was terrifyingly, overwhelmingly silent.

The first splash of blood was on a handrail-- or what would have been a handrail if I was a bit taller-- a few yards away from the door. My internal map said it was north. I'd lost all sense of direction. A few minutes later, we found a partial handprint on a control console. Zub stopped us, taking a closer look at it. I couldn't make heads or tails of the thing; it had a bunch of dials and buttons paired with a large screen, all covered with the strange alien script. The handprint was in the middle of the screen.

"Could that be a touch interface?" Celeste whispered. "It's at the same level as the controls, and in a weird place for a monitor."

"For us, at least," Kathryn said. "We don't know what the aliens look like. It could make perfect sense for them. But yeah, it could be a touch interface. It looks like the others thought so, too. Maybe it was on when they came in."

I spotted more blood on the floor, still stretching off to the north, and pointed it out. Zub left the control console alone and led us off, picking his way around the storage tanks and vats on the floor and resolutely avoiding stepping on any of the grates. I thought about asking him why and decided that the increased noise was probably good enough of a reason.

Fifty yards later, we found the scene of another battle.

This one looked as if it had gone worse for the invaders, whoever they were. We could see two bodies piled awkwardly in the middle of a pool of blood, with what looked like bits of a third scattered around them. *Don't throw up in the suit*, I thought to myself, and I could see Kathryn's hand going to the front of her visor in what was no doubt the same thought.

The second attack had been a massacre. It didn't look like the people had even gotten a shot off. There were no shell casings scattered around this time and no sign of the scorching or the wreckage that had been produced by the first attack. Only carnage, and there was a shocking amount of it.

"Oh, God," Zub breathed.

"Don't go near them," Kathryn said. "They're... they're *arranged* over there. Whatever did that put them like that on purpose. This is a trap, Ezekiel. Let's go back."

"Kathryn, those are people over there. We don't know that they're even dead. We've got to check it out."

"We *don't*," Kathryn said, her accent coming through and her voice rising in pitch. "We can go somewhere else. We do what you said and we *run*."

"There's nowhere to run to," Zub said. "Katie, you're a *doctor*. We've got to take a look."

I watched her, then, silently fighting with herself. We all felt the same way; everyone was terrified; Kathryn was just having more trouble controlling it than the rest of us. I felt the same way she did-- I wanted to run, to be anywhere other than in this terrifying, awful, blood-soaked place. But there was nowhere to go, and if we could help any other survivors while we were there, we didn't have any other choice. Her shoulders slumped as she recognized the inevitable.

"I hate you, Zub." She'd laughed at his joke a few minutes before; this time, it sounded like she meant it. She took a deep breath, calming herself, a professional façade falling over her features like a sheet. She and Zub moved toward the bodies, Dr. Rosansky taking the lead, Celeste and I covering our backs.

Once we got close enough, we knew two things for certain right away: whoever these people were, they had been human beings, and there was no chance that any of them were still alive. The two bodies were wearing the shredded remnants of space suits-- bulkier, more complicated models than the sleek, skintight Flye exosuits we had on, red in color. There was a shattered machine gun on the floor next to one of the bodies.

They had been cut to pieces by a blade-- or possibly by several blades. They looked mummified. Who knew, the way the atmosphere worked around here, how long they had lain here. One of them was male, split from stomach to shoulder by a single fatal blow. His insides spilled out over the concrete, looking as if they'd frozen in place. He was Asian, perhaps in his mid-forties. It was difficult to tell anything else about him without removing what was left of his space suit, and none of us felt especially inclined to try and do that.

The second body belonged to a woman, probably a little bit younger, but it was hard to tell. Her head had been split nearly in half, one arm hacked from her body. She could possibly have been Asian too, from her long, straight black hair, but from the wreckage her face had been turned into it was impossible to tell with certainty. The third body was in pieces and scattered about. I couldn't bring myself to look carefully for anything identifiable.

"What... what *does* that?" Celeste asked, clearly shaken by the gore. "Why cut them up? Why not... God, *anything?* What did that?"

"Blades," Kathryn said, inspecting the male's wound, her voice expressionless. "Big ones, and incredibly sharp. These cuts are as clean as if they'd been inflicted with a scalpel. Even the ribs and sternum are sliced, not broken. I've never seen anything like it."

"The sentry robots use *blades?*" I said. "Why in the world would that be?"

"Look around," Zub said. "The things are guarding a factory. These tanks are probably all pressurized, or supposed to be. And who-knows-what might be floating around in the air when the place is fully active. They don't want anything punctured, and they don't want anything to cause a *spark.* Like a sugar factory on Earth. The whole place could go up. So they arm their guards with close-combat weapons. It's really very ingenious, when you think about it."

"I'll make sure to let them know how much I admire their handiwork, Ezekiel," Kathryn said. "Or perhaps you could do it, once they're done decapitating you."

"Zub, is that Ai-Li?" I asked.

"No," he responded. "Although it just about gave me a heart attack at first. I don't think this is her. I have no idea who either of these people are. They aren't from the *Tycho*."

"China," Celeste said. "Look at this." She passed us a broken piece of helmet from somewhere on the floor. The helmet had the Chinese flag clearly emblazoned on the side, along with some text in Mandarin underneath it, probably a name.

"They're yuhangyuan," she said. "Chinese astronauts. What the hell are they doing here?"

"So the *Chinese* are here," Zub said. "Nobody told me that there were Chinese nationals on Mars. Nobody told *anybody* that there were Chinese nationals on Mars. How the hell did the Chinese get to Mars without anyone noticing?"

I considered pointing out that we had done just that and decided to keep my mouth shut.

"Maybe they kept it a secret," Celeste said. "Perhaps the government was afraid of being embarrassed if the expedition failed."

"I think they've been here for quite some time," Dr. Rosansky said. She had partially stripped the male body of his space suit and was inspecting his torso. "This man doesn't look like he's been eating well. You can see his ribs; there's some malnutrition here. And there are bruises all over him; they all look too old to have been inflicted by whatever killed him. He doesn't look like he was healthy enough to have been an astronaut in the first place, especially one chosen to go to Mars."

"Let's conduct the autopsy someplace else;" I suggested. "I'm really not liking being out in the open like this."

It turns out it wouldn't have helped; the sentry bots had already noticed us.

The first one appeared from between two storage tanks ten or so feet in front of us. Zub shouted something incoherent, alerting the rest of us, and turned to run. There were already two more behind us, and one more coming from the left and the right.

We were trapped.

SIXTEEN

"Need Plan B," Zub said. "Right now would help."

I looked around wildly, trying to find an avenue of escape. The sentries weren't attacking yet. They'd taken position around us, but they were set up in such a way that there was no way to escape them short of scrambling up on top of one of the storage tanks or fighting our way through.

Fighting our way through didn't look like much of an option.

The sentry robots were huge-- taller than man-sized, and broader and thicker than a man would be as well. They looked almost centaur-like, with a rotating humanoid-style torso, head and arms set on top of a wheelbase that looked like it would allow them to move in any direction without turning around. Four arms, two ending in grasping claws, and two ending in heavy blades-- surely the same impossibly sharp blades that had sliced up the three Chinese astronauts. The triple photoreceptors in their heads glowed yellow.

"No way out," I heard myself say. The four of us drew closer, our backs pressed together, as the robots closed the gap in between us. Sajad, screeching, scrambled up my back and on my shoulder. For no good reason, I found myself wondering what the hell he thought he had to worry about.

Moving as one, the five sentry robots folded their grasping arms in tight to their chests, the bladed arms twirling alarmingly. Sajad screamed in my ear again, making me wish I could shut off whatever speaker was passing for his vocal cords. Abruptly giving up on me, he dove off my shoulder and streaked toward the robot in front of us. He cut to his left, and the robot smoothly shifted over to intercept him.

What the heck is he doing?

Sajad dodged back over to his right, and the robot pivoted to reach him again-- or, at least, it tried. The thing lurched over to the side, the treads in its wheels suddenly stuck, and I noticed a row of bullet holes scored into the armor plating surrounding the wheels. Sparks flew as the mechanism whirred uselessly.

"It's stuck!" Zub yelled, realizing what was wrong as soon as I did. "Everybody, past the one ahead of us! *Move!*" We all hightailed it past the disabled sentry robot, racing at top speed in the low Martian gravity. It still came dangerously close to taking my head off, whipping a blade at my neck and missing as I sped past it. It took no more than a few seconds for the thing to get turned in the right direction and begin chasing after us, but that was all the time we needed to escape the trap. All hope of quiet, inconspicuous movement was abandoned as we fled across the cavernous room, Zub taking the lead and zigging and zagging back and forth among the machinery. I was completely lost in seconds, hoping that Zub's sense of direction was better than mine or, failing that, at least his luck would be. I spared one look over my shoulder before we stopped running.

Our pursuers were as fast as we were, though, and they were on our tails in moments, the disabled one eventually getting itself turned around and after us as well. They had the advantage of knowing where they were going, too. My panicked glances over my shoulder showed them fanning out and cutting off any chance of doubling back on our route to lose them. Soon they started showing up ahead of us, each time far enough in the distance that we could change direction before they reached us. Occasionally we lost sight of them for a while, each time leading to hope that we'd outwitted them altogether, but it was never long before we saw one again, and they moved silently enough that we never heard them coming before they were on top of us. Who knew what they had tracking us down there. There was nowhere we could go that seemed like it could be safe.

It wouldn't be long, at this rate, until we were surrounded. All four of us were tired and hungry, and while we were all in decent shape, only Celeste would ever be mistaken for an athlete. Ahead of me, Zub was barely missed by a flashing blade that lunged at him from a side passageway. He tried to turn away from it, losing his footing and crashing to the floor, coming to a stop at the foot of another one of the control consoles that were scattered around the floor.

And then he did something entirely unexpected, hopping up to his feet and wildly pushing buttons and throwing levers on the control console in front of him.

All hell broke loose.

From somewhere high up above us, an alarm klaxon began sounding-- a booming, world-shattering noise that temporarily killed my ability to do anything other than try and shut out the sound. I killed my external microphone, which wasn't especially helpful-- the sound was powerful enough to cut right through my suit. Whatever had designed this place, they clearly had much weaker hearing than ours.

There was a massive explosion above us, showering the floor with bits of metal. I looked up, just in time to witness the last throes of the fireball that had appeared toward the top of the room. A thin, shimmery mist, a phosphorescent forest-green in color, was drifting down toward the floor. It seemed that one of the storage tanks had ruptured. As I watched, the material caught fire, filling the vista above us with rolling flames. A moment later, there was a second explosion, then a third.

Oxygen-rich environment, I thought to myself. *Tiny particles of flammable material.* We'd speculated that the sentries used blades because setting off a spark could be dangerous.

It seemed the worst possible time imaginable to be right.

One small bit of luck: the sentry robots had disappeared, perhaps losing interest in us in favor of putting out the fire or returning to whatever safe haven they had emerged from to attack us.

We fled again, trying now just to stay ahead of the fires. Just as I was starting to think my heart might explode if I had to run any further, Zub called us to a halt, holding a fist in the air like a SWAT captain. We'd finally gotten to a point where we could see where the walls hit the floor. There was a ramp leading up to one of the innumerable catwalks above us. This one hugged the wall all the way around the room, with offshoots like spokes leading to the equipment that hung above us. We'd run past one or two other access points to the upper levels during our flight from the ambush as well.

THERE'S A TUNNEL, he blinked to us. OUT OF THIS ROOM. LOOKS LIKE IT GOES DEEPER INTO THE COMPOUND. AUTOMAP SAYS IT LEAVES THE BORDER OF THE SKYLIGHT. HOLD UP A HAND IF YOU THINK WE SHOULD TRY IT.

Automapping, I thought, feeling like a dummy. That was how he'd seemed to know where he was going. He'd probably set the map as an overlay on his HUD.

He lifted a hand. The three of us followed suit, me mostly thinking that there were, as usual, not many more appetizing options. With the sentries still out there and the upper levels mostly in flames, we had nowhere else to go. Our lander had surely been destroyed when the vent opened, leaving our only choice to go farther in and take our chances. Zub turned his outstretched hand into a thumbs-up and took off again, not at quite the blistering pace we'd set before but fast enough. We were all looking around this time, keeping our eyes peeled for anything that might be chasing us or keeping pace with us at our flanks. The sentries had clearly decided we were no longer worth worrying about. We had to get out of the room before the entire thing blew up around us.

Zub apparently had better eyes than I did, because it took me a while to locate the tunnel entrance we were running toward. There was good reason, though. The thing was the exact same color as the surrounding wall, and it was *closed*.

"The tunnel isn't open," I said, not wanting to make Zub read a blink while we were running. "Why isn't the tunnel open?"

I'M HOPING WE CAN GET IT OPEN, Zub blinked back, the letters bouncing around crazily on my lens as I ran. I had to fight the sudden impulse to stop running to make reading the text easier. IF NOT, WE HIT THE CATWALKS AND SEE THERE'S ANYTHING SAFE ABOVE US, OR IF WE CAN

GET UNDERNEATH THE PRODUCTION FLOOR SOMEHOW. *Fine, good enough,* I thought. Hopefully he had a good idea for how to open the thing. If not, the imminent explosion would probably do the job for him.

As it turned out, he didn't need one. Once we got within about ten yards of the gate, it slid open noiselessly, revealing a featureless, fifteen-foot-wide hallway behind it. It looked like some sort of access tunnel, wide enough to bring vehicles through if necessary, but not leading immediately to any other rooms or chambers.

Just so long as it slides closed once we're through it, I thought.

Naturally, no such thing occurred.

We all stumbled to a stop once we got into the tunnel, hoping that the gate would slide shut once we were through it. It would just reopen again if the sentries got too close, but at least we'd have time to put some distance between us and then before that happened. Obstinately, the gate refused to budge, the flames in the room beginning to descend to where they could reach us, and Zub began frantically looking for a control panel.

"There!" he shouted, pointing at a small instrument panel unobtrusively set into the wall just inside of the tunnel. He sprinted to the panel and, after considering it for a moment, began pushing buttons at random.

"Zub," Celeste cautioned. "Maybe you don't want to--"

That was as far as she got before three things happened in rapid succession: first, the gate slammed shut, moving quickly enough that I was glad it didn't collide with any of us on the way. Second, the lights in the tunnel winked out, pushing us into perfect darkness. Third, a massive explosion shook the outside room, rattling the door but not opening it. I began wondering what the smoke would smell like if I took my helmet off. The alarm continued clanging.

I didn't feel like any of that was an improvement, personally.

MORE RUNNING? There was no point in sending voice communication; I couldn't hear myself think even with the outside microphones turned off. I turned on my suit lights; at least we weren't going to be running around in the dark.

YES, he blinked back, and the four of us headed deeper into the unknown.

*   *   *

I had just decided that the alarms would go on forever when they finally cut out. The chronometer would probably show that they had been sounding for less than ten minutes, but those ten minutes had felt like an eternity, leading to Zub twice uselessly trying to cover his ears with his hands and Celeste sending me a series of blinks about exactly how simple it would have been for her to build noise-cancelling software into the exosuits had only one of the idiots involved in planning this trip managed to think of it before they left.

SPACE IS SUPPOSED TO BE SILENT, the last one said. JUST ONCE ON THIS TRIP I WANT SOMETHING TO HAPPEN THE WAY PHYSICS SAYS IT WILL.

WEREN'T YOU THE ONE THAT SAID WE WERE ALL GOING TO DIE? I asked.

THAT WAS ZVI, she replied. OTHERWISE KNOWN AS THE ONE WHO WE HAVEN'T SEEN ALIVE IN A COUPLE OF DAYS. SEE WHERE NEGATIVITY GETS YOU.

Then, a few seconds later:

THAT WASN'T FUNNY. SORRY.

WE'RE ALL STRESSED OUT, I sent back. I'M NOT GOING TO GET ON YOUR CASE FOR BEING MORBID.

We'd been running for the entire time the sirens were going, and when they stopped we all slowed down without really bothering to discuss it, taking a moment to figure out where we were and where we were going. Our way had been lit by the lights on our suits, the glowsticks not being as practical when we were running. I hadn't seen much other than the floor. It didn't seem likely that we were being followed any longer, and no combination of filters or settings on my suit allowed me to see far enough into the darkness behind us to pick up any traces of pursuers. The sentry robots either hadn't seen us go into the tunnel or hadn't cared when we did.

Looking around now, we appeared to be in some sort of service or maintenance tunnel. Other than a few pipes running along the ceiling, there was next to nothing in the way of ornamentation or even functionality. The tunnel just stretched off into infinity in front of us and behind us. The unearthly light that had pervaded the previous chamber was nowhere to be seen here. It was possible that there was no light source in the tunnel at all.

"Are we going somewhere?" Zub asked.

"We're headed directly toward Abbey and Nikki right now," Celeste said. "But we'll pass all of the other skylights along the way, so there might be side passages, and those last two are much farther away than I like to think about ever trying to walk. If there's nothing in this tunnel in between the two I don't want to think about what kind of shape we're going to be in when we get there."

"Surely there's *something* in between," I said.

"No good reason to assume that," Zub said. "We just found one large complex underneath a skylight and now we're in a tunnel headed toward one of the other ones."

"Dena's the closest," Celeste added. "But it's still sixty miles away."

Zub continued. "We could go back and see if there are other tunnels heading somewhere other than the other skylights, but that would involve dealing with the sentry robots again. I'm not keen on doing that unless we're armed. And unless Celeste can cobble together a rocket launcher from one of those pipes, I don't think we're going to be arming ourselves anytime soon. Oh, and there's the minor matter that everything is blown up behind us. That might be a problem, too."

"What's that?" Kathryn asked.

She was pointing down the tunnel ahead of us, away from where we'd entered.

Pitch black.

"I don't see anything," I said.

"Everybody hide," Zub said. "Get-- hell-- get against the walls or something. Maybe it won't notice us."

And then I saw it. A single point of light, off in the distance. It had been small enough that I'd taken it for a glint on my visor or a glitch in my HUD at first. But there was something with a light off in the distance. And it was coming toward us.

We all split for the walls-- Celeste and I to one side, Zub and Kathryn to the other. There was no point in running back. I flattened myself against the cold concrete wall, killed all the lights on my suit and even the internal ones in my HUD, and waited.

The light slowly grew, and after a while the sounds of whirring machinery reached my ears. Whatever it was, it was mechanical and it was rolling. Nothing that sounded like footsteps.

The light grew larger, bright enough that the protective screen dropped down in front of my visor. The virtual HUD flared into life on the screen.

It was a vehicle. And as far as I could tell, it was empty. It stopped perhaps twenty feet in front of us and stayed there, the engine still on and idling, frozen in place.

"That's not what I was expecting at all," Zub said.

"I'm taking a closer look," Celeste said. She looked back at me, and I killed the virtual HUD and followed her.

"My God," Celeste said. "Is that what I think it is?"

It was a rover. A four-seater, but otherwise the same exact style as the one on the *Johannes,* which was currently sitting at Chloe's edge waiting for us to come back to it.

"Is that our missing rover?" I asked. The question brought Zub and Kathryn out from hiding to inspect the vehicle.

"It sure looks like it," Celeste said. "At least from-- oh, God. Zub, get over here."

She was on the opposite side of the rover from me, and all three of us raced to her side of the rover to see what she was looking at. She was pointing at the door of the rover. At first, I was expecting bullet holes, bloodstains, something indicating death and disaster. There was nothing like that anywhere I could see, on the door, the windows, anything.

Then I saw it. In small letters, at the top of the door. I hadn't seen them before because they weren't very prominent.

The word "TYCHO," with a tiny American flag painted next to it.

SEVENTEEN

"The ship didn't crash," Celeste said.

"The ship's *on the planet somewhere*," Zub said. "I was right. I was *completely right*. Do you know what this means? They're here somewhere. They could *all* be here somewhere. Somebody *sent* this thing to us."

"Maybe," Celeste said. "Let's not get too far ahead of ourselves." She reached for the door handle.

"Wait," Kathryn said, and Celeste's hand froze above the door. "What if it's another trap?"

"What do you mean?" I said.

"You haven't forgotten that there was a *bomb* inside the first domicile unit, have you? The door could be wired to something," she replied.

"It would have blown up by now," I said. "There's no reason to make us open the door to blow us up."

"That said, go *slowly*, Celeste," Zub said, and I noticed him backing away from the rover. Celeste, not entertained at all, cracked the door open and carefully inspected the edges and the seal. There was a hiss and a rush of air as the atmosphere inside the vehicle dissipated.

"No wires, no strange contact plates, nothing that's not supposed to be there," she reported. "And it's pressurized above the level of the tunnel, so if there was an aerosolized virus in there or something we're doomed already. Can I open it now?"

"Go for it," Zub said. Kathryn shrugged.

The control console for the rovers was uncomplicated in the extreme; anyone who could pilot a bicycle on Earth, much less a car, would be able to operate one of these vehicles without trouble. I wasn't expecting there to be very much for us to look at inside.

Other than the note on the dashboard, I was right.

GET IN, it said. THE ROVER WILL DO THE REST.

"That's encouraging," I said.

"It's in English," Kathryn said.

"There's *food* in here," Celeste said. "And water. A fair amount of both."

I was suddenly ravenously hungry. I wasn't sure at all how long it had been since the last time we'd eaten, but I knew I'd been subsisting off of my suit's recycled and reclaimed water supply for the better part of a day. I was getting tired of it.

"Let's just agree that this is the latest in a series of terrible ideas and do it anyway," I said.

"I agree," Kathryn said, surprising me. "This is the first thing that's happened since we landed that seems straightforward. Whoever sent it is friendly. They sent food and water and a preprogrammed rover to get us somewhere. I doubt they did it so that they could kill us afterwards. And I'm hungry, and I'm tired of the helmet. Let's get in."

She took the lead, climbing into one of the back seats, quickly followed by the rest of us. There was a buzz as the locks clicked shut on the doors and the atmosphere pressurized and warmed. Green lights inside my HUD blinked, declaring the environment inside the rover to be sufficiently Earth-like, and I took off my helmet, savoring being able to breathe relatively unprocessed air. Kathryn handed me a foil-wrapped package that presumably contained something to eat and a cylindrical object that, after some investigation, turned out to be nothing more complicated than a heavy-duty Thermos. I considered tearing the package open with my teeth, then thought better of it and took my gloves off as well.

Jerky. My favorite. There were a few examples of freeze-dried Something Else inside the package-- slices of what looked like dried fruit, for example, and something that might once have been a vegetable-- but beef jerky had never looked more appetizing. I dug in, almost not noticing when the rover started moving again.

"Where are we going?" I asked Zub. "Back down the tunnel?"

"You ask me like I'm driving," he responded from the front seat. "The thing's running itself. We're just along for the ride."

"Could these things always do that?" I asked. "Could we have set our rover to go back to camp once we went down into the skylight?"

"Not automatically," Celeste responded. "Although programming the thing to drive itself wouldn't actually be all that complicated. Either of us could probably do it in a day or two."

"It wouldn't take me that long," Zub said. "And it would only take you that long because you'd insist on using three times as many safety protocols as I would."

"You say that like it's a bad thing," I said. "Let's hope someone more like Celeste programmed this, since we don't actually know where it's going."

Just then, the rover hit a bump, jarring us up out of our seats. I looked back to see what we had hit, but the rover's design and the utter darkness of the tunnel around us made that impossible. There was just no way to see anything around us.

"See?" Zub said. "If Celeste designs the software, we don't hit whatever we just hit and it takes an extra day. If I design the software, we hit the rock and everything's fine anyway. It's all about priorities."

Celeste decided to ignore the boss' obvious attempt to provoke her and concentrated on her food. I looked out the front viewport, trying to figure out if the tunnel really did just head straight on forward forever. If there were any branches or changes in direction, I didn't notice them. The lack of any markings on the tunnel made it really difficult to estimate how fast we were moving, but judging from the way the automap in my HUD was busily sketching out the tunnel as we moved through it, forty or fifty miles an hour didn't seem unreasonable. Twice we passed what looked like industrial equipment: large vehicles designed to move earth or cargo. They were unoccupied and, I had a hunch, probably automated anyway. There was nothing else in the tunnel.

"I'm going to make a suggestion," Kathryn said. "This thing looks like it's going to be going on for a while. Everybody get some sleep."

She looked as if she was going to try and justify her suggestion a bit, but I decided it wasn't necessary. I was out before she finished her next sentence.

* * *

My chronometer showed I'd been out for nearly four hours when Kathryn shook me awake.

"We're slowing down," she said. "Wherever we're going, we're almost there. And the lights are back on."

I checked my automap. We hadn't proceeded on a straight line; it looked as if the tunnel had taken a few gentle bends and turns as we'd been traveling through it, but we were almost directly under the summit of Arsia Mons by now, closest to the skylights called Abbey and Nikki.

We'd travelled 160 miles, entirely underground. I'd thought the facility was immense when we were just underneath the skylight. I'd had no idea. For all we knew, it spanned the entire planet. There was no way to tell from the tunnel that we'd gone anywhere, though; the newly-visible expanse of grey wall was as unexciting at the end of the trip as it had been at the beginning.

Celeste pushed more food and drink into my hands. "Hydrate yourself again," she said. "And eat something else. We all figure that we're going to have to walk soon, so we're going to take everything with us that we can. Hopefully there will be more food wherever we're going." I shrugged and tore open another foil package. At this point, I couldn't imagine anything surprising me. Starvation seemed equally as likely as discovering that our destination was somehow entirely edible.

After a few minutes of chewing, the headlights on the rover illuminated the end of the tunnel. It looked as if it had originally been similar to the one where we had started; a large gate that came down from the ceiling, with a control panel to one side.

Unfortunately, the control panel had been damaged beyond repair, and the end of the tunnel was filled with rubble. There were piles of garbage two or three feet above our heads, not reaching the ceiling but coming close, mixed in with what looked like debris from an explosion or two and, notably, more than a few damaged sentry bots.

"That's not what I was expecting at all," Zub said.

"You were hoping for caviar?" Kathryn asked.

"I was hoping for something less... I don't know, *destroyed*," he replied, as we all suited back up and exited the rover, parking it next to the tunnel wall. "Something sent the rover to us, right? It stands to reason that whoever it was did that for a reason. Bringing us to a dead end doesn't seem like a very good reason."

"There's a passageway over here," I said. It was narrow enough that we would just barely fit through it. *And a sentry robot wouldn't,* I realized. The passageway was concealed well enough to be nearly invisible to someone who wasn't specifically looking for it. It was slightly lower than my own height and irregular in shape, but it looked as if one of us would just barely be able to fit through the thing, even in our spacesuits, so long as we were careful about it. Zub pointed and Sajad hopped through the gap, clambering over loose rubble and out of my field of view. I considered slaving my suit to his, then decided that given our circumstances I wanted to see my own field of view. I'd find out soon enough what he was looking at.

Sure enough, a moment later I heard a chitter over the comm system that Zub interpreted as an all-clear. "He's through," Zub said. "It looks like it broadens out to a door after a few feet." Presumably there would be some way to open that door when we got to it.

Zub turned himself sideways and went in first, edging past the sharp metal edges of blown-up sentry robots and the constricting piles of steel and concrete.

"Stay out there," he told us. "It doesn't look like there's room for more than one of us in here until we get the door opened. The tunnel takes a sharp bend right before the door."

Then nothing, for a few seconds.

"Celeste," he said. "Take a look at this and tell me what I'm looking at." Curious, I abandoned my caution and pulled up his HUD view.

The tunnel proceeded parallel to the pile of rubble for about half the length of the gateway beyond it, then took a sharp turn to the left. A hundred and sixty miles away, the other end of this tunnel had ended in a gate that spanned the width of the entire tunnel. This looked to be much the same-- I could see the top of the gate above the piles of garbage in front of me-- but someone had cut a human-sized doorway out of the gate. The hinges, if there were any, were on the other side. But on this side--

"That's a palm lock," Celeste said. And it was. There was a jury-rigged palm lock crudely soldered to the wall next to the door. It looked, unsurprisingly, wildly out of place.

"What's a palm lock doing here?" Zub asked.

"The same thing we are," Celeste replied.

"I don't think the palm lock is busy being scared out of its mind," I added. No one seemed to think that was helpful.

"Those are magnetic locks, aren't they?" Zub asked, pointing a light at something on the door. I couldn't figure out what he was looking at.

"Looks like it," Celeste said. "Have you tried the lock yet?"

"No," Zub said. "Do you think I should take the gloves off? There's still a thin atmosphere down here; it's probably okay--"

"No," Kathryn cut in. "Not unless you absolutely have to. Try the thing with your hand in the gloves first. You never know how sensitive it is."

"That makes sense," Zub said, and put his hand on the palm lock.

With a *whump*, the locks on the door disengaged and the door swung open, away from Zub and into the chamber beyond.

"No lights," he said. "It's pitch-black in here." This end of the tunnel had maintained the same vague glow that permeated the rest of the facility; apparently it had either been turned off or damaged in the room beyond the gate. "Follow me through, guys. I'm not going into the room alone."

I could see him switch to the Flye suit's virtual environment-- safer than using the external lights, since it didn't make the wearer visible-- as I brought my own display back up. Kathryn and Celeste, both smaller and more nimble than me, followed Zub through the passage in the rubble and through the door. I went last, maneuvering carefully to avoid damaging my suit. I wasn't exactly a weightlifter, but the passageway still seemed sized for people skinnier than I was. After a few minutes of determined effort, though, I managed to squeeze through without incident.

The room on the other side of the door was big. Unfortunately, other than "dark," that was the only word I could use to describe it. Neither our virtual environments or, after a few minutes of looking around, our suit lights could penetrate the dark well enough to reveal any actual structures. It appeared to be a gigantic empty black space-- as featureless and silent as the skylights had been.

"Could this be Abbey or Nikki?" I asked. "Maybe we're at the bottom of one of the other skylights."

"I don't think so," Celeste said. "Our position's off slightly, and we were actually going on a slight downward slope while we were traveling as well. My best guess is that we're at least a kilometer or two underneath the surface. Chloe wasn't even close to being that deep and I doubt the smaller ones are. We're right underneath the mountain. This should be an entirely enclosed space."

I had to fight off the urge to scream at the thought of all the rock that must have been hanging above me.

"There's always the chance that Arsia Mons is hollow," Zub said, reading the look on my face and no doubt feeling much the same way.

"Yeah, it's only, what, the second-largest mountain in the galaxy? That's not alarming at all."

"Only by volume," Celeste said.

"No one is being helpful," I complained. "People should be helpful when we're on alien planets."

Right about then was when everything went wrong, naturally.

There was a bright flash-- bright enough to trigger the blast shield on my helmet-- and something slammed into me from the side, knocking me sprawling to the floor. The virtual environment came up in my HUD, but just as quickly exploded into static and gibberish, then shut down completely. I was blind and on my back, with no idea where anything was or what had happened. I started reaching up to pull my visor out of the way and something landed on me. The suit radios died with a shriek, leaving me virtually deaf as well, with only ambient thuds and crashes barely making it through the helmet. Something hit me in the head, hard, putting me back on the floor again as I tried to stand up.

The gunshots a second later convinced me to stop trying.

My blast shield was wrenched up and off my visor, providing me with a clear look straight into the business end of a somehow more-dangerous-than-usual-looking machine gun. There was a flashlight on the end of the barrel, blinding me and making it impossible for me to see the face of whoever was holding the gun.

There was something strange about the weapon. I couldn't quite put my finger on what. That may have been because I'd just been hit in the head. I wasn't sure about that either.

"No one moves," said a voice over my comm system, which suddenly burst back into life. I didn't recognize it. I didn't argue with it, either.

"Which one of you is in charge here?" the voice demanded.

"I am," Zub responded. As he spoke, my HUD began rebooting. I still couldn't see well, but the outlines of my friends started appearing on my display. All four of us were prone. Zub was raising a hand. There were three other people, all identified with blinking purple outlines.

"Is anyone injured?"

I wasn't expecting that question.

"One of you punched me in the head," I said.

"I think that was me," Celeste said. "Sorry about that."

"Are you bleeding?" the first man asked. I didn't think I was, so I shook my head.

"I want any weapons you have placed on the ground in front of you," he said. "Hide nothing. There will be consequences if you resist." None of us had anything that would do us any good.

We'd left the closest thing we had to weapons back on the rover, hundreds of miles behind us.

"Nothing," Zub said. "We're unarmed."

And then a very unexpected thing happened, as all three men lowered their weapons and activated ambient lighting on their suits, killing the flashlights. They were wearing red, bulky, presumably Chinese-issued space suits. One of them slid back a blast visor similar to ours, exposing the face of a male yuhangyuan of perhaps Zub's age.

"You need to follow us," he said. "Welcome to Mars."

* * *

The yuhangyuan did not, at first, appear interested in answering any questions. Keeping the four of us in between the three of them, we moved quickly along the wall of the chamber we'd entered at a fast clip, not quite running but close enough. My head hurt from where Celeste had accidentally pounded on me-- I'd never been happier to have been wearing a helmet-- and keeping up had started to become challenging when they finally called for a halt. We'd reached another door, this one clearly part of the original facility, without seeing anything of note in the cavernous room we'd been racing through. There was more of the alien language above the door, which slid aside easily as we moved through it. One of the yuhangyuan pulled the door shut behind us, pressing a button that activated a lock. The door led into a stairwell, which climbed upward for several flights before terminating in a landing with another door. This one had another jury-rigged palm lock next to it. There was a chronometer just above the palm lock.

"We will stop here," the lead yuhangyuan said. "There is much that we need to discuss, but not just yet." He gestured at the other two, who collapsed to the floor, breathing heavily. I'd had the idea that these men had managed the jog around the room effortlessly. I was wrong. It looked as if they'd barely made it.

"California," Zub said.

The surprise in the man's face was obvious even through the mask. "What?"

"Your accent. You sound like you're a Californian. You either grew up in the United States or you learned to speak English there. I thought you were doing all the talking because you were in charge. You're the only one who speaks English, aren't you?"

The man laughed, a short, bitter sound. "Close. My name is Mengyao Yang. And I grew up in Arizona, not California, although I did go to Berkeley. Good guess. I'm not the only one who speaks English. All of us understand it, but I'm the only one who speaks it well. We haven't exactly had much opportunity to practice our skills out here."

"Are we prisoners?" I asked.

Mengyao looked surprised again for a moment, then looked down at his gun and blinked, as if he'd forgotten that he had it. "You are not. Please forgive us for our... *abrupt* appearance. We had thought to disarm you quickly so as to avoid unnecessary bloodshed between our two groups. How surprising to learn that you were not armed."

"You flashbanged and EMPed us because you thought we'd shoot at you if you didn't?" Celeste asked, incredulous. "Aren't you the same people who just fed us?"

"Yes," Mengyao said. "But we were not certain that you would react positively to our appearance. It was determined that it would be best to make certain that you were not hostile when we first made contact."

"We should have shot you," another of the yuhangyuan said. "Those were our orders."

Mengyao said something in response over a private channel. He looked angry. The four of us sat very still. I found myself wishing I'd taken Chinese in college instead of Spanish.

"You are not in danger from us at this time," he said, speaking slowly and carefully. "We are all in great danger, but we have agreed,"-- this with a quick glare at the other man-- "that we should work with you and not against you."

The other yuhangyuan said nothing, his face impassive. I began wondering if "agreed" meant the same thing in Chinese that it did in English.

The chronometer on the wall began beeping, and all three men pressed their hands into the palm lock in quick sequence. The lock disengaged with a heavy *clank*, and Mengyao gestured to us to enter the room.

It was on a timer, I thought. We'd waited in the stairway because they'd had no other way to get into the room. I wondered what would have happened if we had been late.

The room we'd entered appeared to have, at some point, served as a security station or control room of some sort. The walls were covered with monitors, with banks of machinery underneath them. The consoles seemed similar to the machinery on the factory floor, with banks of buttons and levers surrounding another screen. One wall was piled high with storage crates, all labeled in Chinese. The floor was scattered with trash and debris. There were half-a-dozen or so mattresses piled in a corner. It looked as if the yuhangyuan had been living in this room for some time.

Mengyao gestured to the floor. "Sit. You will find the air in this room perfectly breathable. We will eat, and then we will talk. I can imagine that you have many questions. So do we." He and the other two yuhangyuan removed their helmets. Mengyao and the second one, who hadn't spoken yet, began busying themselves with the crates, pulling out food packages similar to what the rover from the *Tycho* had been outfitted with. The third man did nothing, glaring at us warily but not quite standing guard over us. None of us spoke as the three men gathered the meal together.

We ended up with an assortment of dried foods and water, which Mengyao heated and poured over tea leaves. A surprisingly refreshing smell filled the room. It hadn't been long since we'd eaten-- indeed, we still had the leftovers from the rover with us-- but it wasn't difficult to find our appetites again.

"Let us begin with introductions," Mengyao said after a few minutes, breaking the awkward silence. "I am Mengyao Yang. These are Haipeng Hsieh, and Junlong Kao. I was the captain of our voyage. Junlong is a pilot, and Haipeng our ship's engineer." Junlong was the distrustful one, still sitting a distance away from the others, although at least no longer lurking over us with an assault rifle.

Zub quickly began introducing the four of us, leaving himself for last. Mengyao reacted to Zub's name.

"Ezekiel ben Zahav? Of Zahav International? Your company received the contract to build the first American transplanetary vessel, did it not?"

"That's me," Zub said. "Always nice to meet a fan, I guess."

"Did you also design the ship that brought you here?"

"It's called the *Johannes*. And yes."

Mengyao nodded. "Your expertise may be of some use to us, then. Hsieh is a capable engineer, but there are many problems he has not solved."

I noticed, I thought. Chief among those, no doubt, being *Get us the hell off of Mars*.

Mengyao sat for a moment, considering the four of us carefully, then began speaking again. "We are survivors of the *Shenzhou XIV*, the first manned human mission to Mars. We beat your American astronauts by over a year."

All four of us gasped. The three of them had been living on Mars for over *three years*.

"How..." Zub breathed.

"Planning," Mengyao replied. "We had always planned on a lengthy stay on Mars and were provisioned for several years. But, as you will soon see, simple survival on the planet proved less complicated than we had initially expected."

"Where is your ship?" Celeste asked.

"Patience," Mengyao answered. "Our government had resolved to keep our mission a secret, at least as much as possible, until we actually arrived on Mars and were able to transmit messages from the planet's surface. I am sure that your government was aware of the launch, but the Chinese citizenry were not to be informed until we were successful in our voyage. In January of 2022 we entered orbit around Mars after a trip of over a year."

"You didn't use a Hohmann transfer," Celeste said. Windows for Hohmann launches only came about so often; there was a reason the *Tycho* had launched in February and not, say, June. No Hohmann window would have had them arrive in January of 2022.

"We did not," Mengyao agreed. "It was deemed more important to beat the Americans to Mars than to take the most efficient path to the planet. No matter; we arrived without incident. It was then that we received the transmission from the Martian surface."

"No green spots?" Zub asked.

"Not yet," came the answer. "We did not understand the signal. To this day we are not certain what the source was, or how it was that we were even able to receive it. But it was unquestionably coming from the planet beneath us. Moments later, we found ourselves descending to the Martian surface through no initiative of our own."

Zub spoke up again. "You crashed?"

"No. We *landed*. We cannot be certain, but our best guess is that the *Shenzhou* was caught in some sort of tractor beam. We were pulled down to the planetary surface. We sent an emergency transmission back to Earth, but never received a response. Our communications appeared to have been cut entirely. The ship was brought down into one of the caves on the planet's surface-- the one you call Nikki. We were pulled down at astonishing speed; it took perhaps a minute for us to descend from orbit, yet we landed without incident or injury in a hangar underneath the skylight. Our ship was the only vehicle present. But the *Shenzhou* was not designed to take off from the Martian surface. It was never meant to land. We were stranded."

He paused, then had a quick exchange in Chinese with the other men.

"We exited the ship, not sure what was in store for us. We were provisioned with a small number of weapons. We had joked about them during the trip. None of us were certain why anyone had wasted the fuel to transport them. But we brought them with us anyway. We stepped out into the hangar, not certain if we were going to be met by alien life."

He paused again, scratching his chin.

"None of us are certain how best to describe what happened next. The word I will use is *scanned*. But that implies a beam of light or some other energy being washed over us, something passive. The world went blue, and it felt as if we were being disassembled at a molecular level and rebuilt. It was, at the same time, exhilarating and quite exquisitely painful. And then, nothing. No one came to meet us. No further mysterious signals were received by our ship's communications array. As we explored, we came to discover that we were completely alone."

"Mengyao, what is this place?" I asked.

"We have a number of theories," he replied. "We have had little to do for several years but debate them. Certain things, however, became clear over the first months of our stay. First, that the subterranean complex was slowly acclimating itself to our presence. There was no more atmosphere underground than on the surface when we first landed. Within a month, there was breathable air in certain areas. It was thin, but it was there. And then we found water."

"We've known there was water on Mars for decades," Zub interjected.

"Not from taps," Mengyao corrected. "There are areas nearby that have been producing much of the food and drink we have been consuming since we have been here. They--"

"*Producing?*" Celeste spat out.

Mengyao sighed. "I had forgotten how much Americans like interruptions. Please believe that I will try my best to explain anything that may be confusing, and let me finish."

"We're sorry," Zub said.

"We believe that this entire facility is a giant terraforming plant," Mengyao said. "It appears to be both ancient and abandoned; we do not believe that anyone or anything has been here since soon after the construction was completed, and we suspect that that time may have been at least many hundreds if not *thousands* of years ago. Much of the facility appears to be automated. The scan that we experienced when we landed seems to have initiated a process of adapting the facility to the needs of human beings. The atmosphere slowly became more and more consistently breathable, and we eventually learned how to access machinery that produced food and water for us."

He said something in Chinese to Haipeng, who retrieved a package of some sort of grain from one of the crates and set it in front of us.

"That looks like rice," I said. "That's..."

"Expected?" Mengyao finished my thought. "Stereotypical? Perhaps. It had occurred to me, if perhaps not to my native-born colleagues, that our food might look like cheeseburgers and pizza if our crew had been American and not Chinese. But I doubt it. It looks like rice, and it can be cooked like rice or eaten raw, but it is not rice. I suspect that its appearance is merely coincidence. The machines produce nothing but this grain, so our diet has been much lacking in variety. Or, at least, we do not know how to make them produce anything different."

He stopped talking again, thinking carefully.

"We spent much of that first year exploring Mars, investigating what we could of this facility, and learning as much as we could about whoever or whatever created it. Soon after we landed, it became clear that the facility's purpose was much larger than simply to accommodate itself to our presence. It was to accommodate the entire *planet* to our presence. However, it appears to be malfunctioning."

"The green spots," Kathryn said.

"Yes. It took a month for the first plant life to appear. We were able to open some of the vats on the production floors, and discovered that they contained primitive, monocellular plant life within them. We suspect that the plant life was actually being created or generated by the machinery, as opposed to something that was in storage somehow and was being nursed into life. The first explosion happened soon afterwards, as the mechanism began breaking down. We lost our first comrade to one such explosion, in fact. What you view as a green spot from orbit is the tanks all venting themselves at once. They pump out an incredible amount of superheated air into the Martian atmosphere as well as many tons of plant life. The plants die almost immediately, and the cycle begins again. Lately, it has begun speeding up. At first, these events happened once every few months. Recently, it happens once every few days or sometimes even hours. We cannot imagine how this could have been the intent of the creators. It makes no sense unless the machines are beginning to deteriorate."

He looked at Zub. "Were you responsible for the detonations earlier?"

"I... uh... I might have pushed some buttons," Zub said.

"It is not the first time that has happened. There is a factory floor producing water, Earthlike air, and the plant life under each of the skylights except for Nikki and Abbey. At least one other has exploded."

"Can we talk about the dead bodies we found underneath Chloe yet?" Zub asked. "Because I have to admit I'm really curious about what happened there."

Junlong jumped to his feet and began shouting at Mengyao in Chinese. The two of them argued for a minute, with Hsieh inserting comments from time to time. Junlong, clearly losing the argument, picked up his gun from the floor and strode out the door, slamming it behind him.

"We should lock him out," Haipeng said. It was the first words of English he had spoken in our presence. Mengyao spoke another sentence in Chinese and Haipeng nodded and fell silent again.

"My apologies," Mengyao said. "Junlong is not a scientist. He is military, and accustomed to doing things a certain way. He is not accustomed to being outvoted."

"Or being disobeyed," Haipeng added.

"We had certain orders that we were to follow in the event that we encountered living beings on Mars," Mengyao continued. "Our superiors were... well, I will say that our orders were rather comprehensive. Nonetheless, Hsieh and I do not believe that we were intended to murder people who could perhaps help us escape from this place."

"Junlong disagrees?" Zub asked. "He can stay if he wants."

"He does not necessarily disagree. He simply wants to be more in control of our situation than we are at the moment. He would have wounded one of you to keep the rest of you under control, and he does not believe that we should share information about our losses. I disagree, but I understand him."

"About those losses," Zub prodded.

"I will have to ask you to continue being patient for now," Mengyao said. "As I said, we lost our first comrade to a tank explosion. That was, sadly, not the last. Our numbers have been reduced by more than half since we landed."

"Eight's an awfully large crew for a ship like that," Zub said, doing the math. "All my engineers were trying to convince me to take no more than four."

"There were ten," Mengyao said. "We are not all present. The first year was spent exploring and learning, trying to discover a way off of Mars, or at least back into orbit, where we might contrive a way to send a signal back home. We never considered what might happen if another ship happened to enter orbit around Mars. As I said, the *Shenzhou* was not built to take off from a planet under its own power, and while it is capable of taxiing on a runway we never saw a reason to move it once we were forced to land."

"The day the *Tycho* arrived, all of that changed. We were not initially aware of its presence in orbit. Our assumption is that the same thing that happened to their ship happened to ours. They were caught in the tractor beam, their communications went out, and they were pulled down into the hangar. As I said, the descent from orbit happened at astonishing speed. And we had not moved the *Shenzhou*."

"Something went wrong with whatever forces power the descent of the ship. Where ours had glided into place, your ship *fell* the last several hundred meters; the tractor beam seemed to give out or run out of power at the last minute. The command portion of the *Tycho* landed directly on top of the *Shenzhou*. The impact crushed the *Shenzhou* and demolished the crew portion of the *Tycho*. There were no survivors."

Everyone looked at Zub. Saving the survivors of the *Tycho* had been our reason for making this journey in the first place. They'd been beyond rescue since before we had even left; likely since before Zub had even conceived of the rescue mission in the first place.

"I'm so sorry, Ezekiel," Kathryn said. Zub was staring at the ground, the expression on his face unreadable.

"Where are the bodies?" he asked. "You didn't just leave them where they fell, like your buddies who were cut down by the robots, did you?"

Mengyao winced. "They were... dealt with honorably," he said. "I can show you the location if you wish. But first--"

"Never mind," Zub said, his voice affectless. "At least none of them suffered."

"Wait," I said. "The rover that picked us up was *from* the *Tycho*. How'd you get your hands on that if the ship exploded?"

"It did not explode," Mengyao said. "A portion of the ship was destroyed in the crash, but the crash happened in an atmosphereless hangar. There was no oxygen to cause an explosion. If it had exploded, we would not even know the ship's name. We were able to salvage a substantial amount of supplies from the ship, including the rover we sent to collect you."

Before he could begin another sentence, both yuhangyuan jumped to their feet, Mengyao with the telltale glassy-eyed look of a man who is reading a blink and not looking at the people in front of him.

"We need to leave," Mengyao said. "Junlong says Dr. Liang is missing."

EIGHTEEN

"Who's Dr. Liang?" I asked. The yuhangyuan ignored me, putting their helmets back on and checking their weapons. Zub, apparently suddenly feeling defiant, planted himself in front of the door, his arms crossed in front of him.

"Let's try that again," he said. "Who's Dr. Liang?"

"Dr. Liang is the man who tried to blow you up," Mengyao replied. "I apologize for that. We did not find out about the bomb until very recently, although we did notice when your supply unit landed on the surface. He also sent a simulated distress signal to attempt to lure you into the Chloe skylight. He has... not reacted well to the isolation on Mars. We thought that we had him confined. Apparently we were wrong."

"You *apologize* for him trying to blow us up?" Zub asked.

Mengyao picked up another gun, handing it to Zub.

"Dr. Liang is not dangerous any longer, I assure you. He suffered a psychotic break soon after the arrival of your supply ships that he has since recovered from. We think that the stress caused by the possibility of rescue triggered the event, believe it or not. He believed that Mars was Chinese territory and that your presence here represented an act of war. Somehow, and I do not think even *he* knows how this happened, he managed to activate the sentry robots throughout the complex. I do not know if he somehow influenced them to be hostile to humanity or if they somehow know that the facility was not built for us, but the machines have treated us as unwelcome interlopers, to be destroyed on contact, ever since. Five of us were killed by the guard robots the first time we encountered them. He has not been the same man since. He cowers in his room, and refuses to speak most of the time. I believe that he accidentally turned the robots loose on us, and that his guilt over that is tearing him apart. He may have shifted into another manic phase, however. We cannot let him wander about alone."

"The guns aren't for him, then," I clarified.

"I do not know how he will react to the presence of foreigners. But no, they are not. He is likely trying to deactivate the sentry robots again. We will try to find him before they do."

Ezekiel moved. Mengyao barked another command in Chinese, and Haipeng handed Celeste, Kathryn and I weapons. We took them, repressurizing our Flye suits as we checked the guns out.

"These are designed to fire in the absence of atmosphere," Mengyao said. "The modifications make them somewhat inaccurate outside of short distances. We have little ammunition left. Do not waste it." With that, he turned and sped through the door, bouncing down the steps in the light Martian gravity.

I had only fired guns under strictly controlled circumstances in the past. From the looks on Celeste and Kathryn's faces, they had less experience than I did. I looked at Zub, who appeared much more comfortable than any of the three of us.

"Israeli, remember?" he said, demonstrating his uncanny ability to read my mind again. "We're practically born with semiautomatics in our hands. How do you think they figured out we were on the planet in the first place, by the way?"

"There's more he's not telling us," I responded. "You think he knows if Zvi's okay?

"Only one way to find out," he said, and followed the yuhangyuan out the door.

*　　*　　*

The cell the yuhangyuan had left Dr. Liang in turned out to be located only a few flights of stairs below us. We'd passed several doors that the men had ignored on our way to the storage room we'd eaten in, and I'd made the rash assumption that they hadn't been able to get into those areas for some reason. On the way down I discovered I was wrong-- two or three of the floors we'd ignored sported the telltale palm locks. I wondered just how many of those Hsieh had managed to scavenge. It didn't seem like the type of thing that one could just MacGyver together from potato peels and duct tape.

Junlong was waiting outside the room when we got to it. Dr. Liang's room was small, perhaps a quarter of the size of the room we'd dined in above. There was a cot in one corner. Alarmingly, the walls and part of the floor were covered in Chinese writing.

The yuhangyuan were having an animated conversation, but they were having it over their private connection and probably in Chinese anyway. I saw Zub saying something, and abruptly I could hear their argument as they pulled us into their global feed.

KUDOS TO THE ENGINEER, I blinked Celeste. I'M SURPRISED THAT OUR SUITS CAN TALK TO EACH OTHER THIS EASILY.

STANDARD COMMUNICATION PROTOCOL, she responded. TAKES ABOUT A MILLISECOND TO HANDSHAKE ANYTHING WITHIN REACH AND THEN WE'RE GOOD. YOU CAN ADD THE THREE OF THEM TO THE LIST OF FRIENDLIES IF YOU WANT, TOO. I did, pulling up the interface, and all three of the yuhangyuan were obediently labeled with their names and outlined in healthy green.

Mengyao turned back to us. "Junlong and I have both attempted to contact Dr. Liang, by blink and by the suit radios. He is not responding. That is typical in these situations, unfortunately. He is most likely heading for the security station. Or, at least, that's what we think it is. It was where he initially activated the sentry robots. It seems likely that they could be deactivated there as well."

"So where is that?" Zub asked.

"The space beyond this stairwell is a wide open oval-shaped room. We aren't sure what it would have been used for by whoever created this place. We suspect it may have been planned as some sort of mess hall or meeting place, since the equipment that creates our food and water is nearby. The security station is near where we came in, at one of the narrow ends, by the tunnel to the factory floor. We will retrace our steps."

Hsieh and Junlong were already moving. The rest of us followed them.

*   *   *

The second dash across the empty floor was much the same as the first, only with somewhat less fear that we were about to be machinegunned to death. We all had our suit lights on, as well as the flashlights on the guns, but they were useless. The room really was just a big empty space, and if it was capable of the same sourceless lighting that had illuminated the factory floor then it had apparently been turned off. We passed the palm-locked door where we had entered from the tunnel and continued on past it for a few minutes, at which point Junlong raised a fist in the air and called us to a halt.

"It might be best if our guests hid themselves," Junlong suggested. "We don't know how he will react."

Fair enough, I thought, and killed the lights on my suit and the flashlight. I could see the other three doing the same.

The entrance to what the yuhangyuan were calling the security station lay some fifty feet ahead of us, an open portal with metal-shuttered windows stretching for a few yards on either side and up for a few floors. If the room was a wide ellipse, as Mengyao had said, this room would command a view of the entire chamber with the windows open and would be virtually impenetrable with them closed and the door locked. They gestured for us to stay where we were and crept inside.

"Too bad we can't slave our suits to theirs," Zub said. "Celeste, I command you to go back in time and sell your technology to the Chinese." It was the first thing resembling a joke he'd said in a while. Celeste did not bother to respond.

"I don't like being out here so exposed," Kathryn said.

"I'm sure it's--"

"Don't you *dare* finish that sentence, Ezekiel ben Zahav," she said. "God Himself is in awe of your sense of ironic timing."

"--fine," Zub finished anyway. "What's the worst that could happen?"

"Oh, God," Celeste said.

Oh, God, I thought.

We all waited for the world to explode.

The world did not explode.

GET IN HERE, came a blink from Mengyao. THEY'RE ON THEIR WAY.

"See! *See!* This is *your* fault!" Kathryn shouted, as we all wheeled around and darted into the entrance of the security station. There was a tremendous roar from south of us as we slammed the gate shut.

"They have a bulldozer," Zub said, watching a giant machine smash its way into the mess hall. "Why do the robots have a bulldozer?"

"Because *you* said everything was fine, you idiot!" Kathryn screamed.

"Katie, hon, you're a scientist, you *know* that's not--" Zub said, and then didn't finish his sentence, choosing instead to catch the machine gun Kathryn had thrown at him.

"Let's not throw machine guns," I said. I looked around for Mengyao and spotted Hsieh instead, who was heading down from a stairway at the opposite end of the room. He waved us to follow him, and we chased him up the stairs. If this was a security station, it didn't much look like one. Other than the reinforced door and walls it looked much the same as the room we'd been in earlier, with more banks of alien computers against both of the side walls, behind what I would have thought was a teller's counter had I been back on Earth. It didn't say *security station* to me. It said *bank.*

I had about three seconds to wonder if aliens still used banks before whatever had just burst into the mess hall hit the wall behind me. Amazingly, the walls held. They were made of sterner stuff than it appeared. The room shook, and I lost my footing for a moment, crumpling onto the stairs and tripping

Celeste in front of me. We picked ourselves up and sprinted the rest of the way up the stairs, spilling out into the upper floor.

"Good news!" Zub was saying. "The robots are smarter than we thought they were. And they have a bulldozer."

There was a fourth yuhangyuan ahead of us, working feverishly at an activated console that sat at the front of the room. The other three stood around him, weapons at hand, watching whatever he was doing. There was a crackle of static as someone added him into our global audio feed.

He was chattering on in Chinese, apparently oblivious to everyone else's presence. I moved closer, looking at the images on the console in front of him. What we had taken for a touchscreen was actually some sort of hologram generator, which he was manipulating with his hands. The screen in front of him was lit up with dozens of tiny rows of the alien characters, all scrolling by at a rate I found it impossible to believe even its extraterrestrial creators would have an easy time comprehending.

"Mengyao, can you translate for us?" Zub asked.

HE'S BABBLING ABOUT VIRUSES, Mengyao blinked back, not wanting to talk over the doctor's voice. HE SPEAKS ENGLISH. I ASKED HIM TO TALK TO YOU, BUT HE'S BARELY RESPONDED TO ANY OF US.

Outside, the thing slammed into the walls again. The crash was audible even through the suit, and the floor shook again.

Whatever sort of interface the doctor was interacting with, it looked impossibly complicated. All ten of his fingers appeared to be involved, sliding little bits of light here and there, sometimes flicking them outside the range of the holoprojector, where they dissolved into nothingness. Occasionally something would resolve into an image, or a diagram of some sort, and at more than one point he appeared to select something from some kind of menu. I saw nothing that remotely looked like English or Chinese.

"His eyes," Kathryn said. "Look at his eyes."

I hadn't even looked at his face yet. Dr. Liang looked thirty years older than any of the other yuhangyuan, with an Einstein-like shock of iron-grey hair that was visible through his mask and a painfully thin, lined face. His eyes were open, fixed, and staring at the text on the monitor, and his hands worked apparently independently of his body. He didn't appear to have any idea what he was doing, and he mumbled incoherently to himself while he did it.

HE'S STILL TALKING ABOUT VIRUSES, Mengyao blinked. SOMETHING ABOUT THE IMMUNE SYSTEM.

"The system's trying to purge us," I said. "We're the viruses."

Acting on a hunch, I pulled up the external sensors in my HUD. For most of the time we'd been underground, the air around us had been roughly Earthlike. It sometimes had lower pressure than we were used to, granted, and was much colder than would have been comfortable almost everywhere except in the room the Chinese slept in, which they'd managed to keep heated somehow. But the conditions were rarely entirely foreign. There were plenty of places on Earth that were low-pressure and cold, even if most of them were located inconveniently on top of mountains.

The air was now twenty degrees colder outside than I'd ever seen it before, and the balance of gases appeared to be tilting back towards methane and carbon dioxide. It was already too toxic to take off my helmet if I wanted to stay conscious for long.

"Uh, guys," I pointed out. "The place doesn't seem to want to be friendly any longer."

"I think it's finally figured out we're not supposed to be here," Mengyao said.

"Or he *told it* that," Celeste said. "What the hell is he *doing?*"

Opening the shutters appeared to be the answer, as the protective barriers in front of us slammed open, revealing a host of robotic sentries gathered in the space in front of us. The lights had been turned on, too; the better to see our impending doom ahead. They had somehow commandeered one of the earth-moving machines we'd passed in the long tunnel from Chloe: it was that, and not a bulldozer, that had bashed in the barrier the Chinese had erected in front of the doorway.

"That's not good," I said.

There was a loud crash from below, as they successfully tore the door out of the way and entered the security station.

"That's worse," Zub said. The yuhangyuan spread out, pointing their weapons at the stairwell, which-- luckily for us-- was the only point of entry into the room we were in.

"EMP?" Celeste asked.

"We've got a half-dozen left. They don't work on the guard robots. And they don't care about flashbangs, either," Mengyao said. Then we saw the first of them at the top of the stairs and everything was gunshots and explosions for a time. We turned the stairwell into a killing field. The robots lacked anything in the way of long-distance weaponry, and at any rate weren't being given a chance to use it. In moments, the stairwell was clogged with defunct robots, leaving no room for new ones to get to us. They'd have to clear the stairway first. Or find some more horrible way of dealing with us. Behind us, Dr. Liang continued spinning his hands through the alien console interface.

"All they have to do is wait us out," Junlong said. "We're going to starve. They aren't. We've got to fight our way out." He moved closer to the stairs, only to be greeted by a storm of whirring blades as the nearest robot body was abruptly hauled out of the way. He only barely dodged away, emptying a clip into his attacker to little effect. A whip-thin manipulating arm shot out of the smoke and chaos and grabbed his ankle, tossing him onto his back.

It was Kathryn who saved him, pushing her gun into his hands as she hauled him out of the way. The second clip scored where the first had not, incapacitating the sentry robot and causing the arm that had grabbed him to release its grip.

There was another shuddering *boom* from beneath us, and the ground underneath our feet began to buckle. I could see the stone floor starting to crack in one of the corners.

"They're coming through the floor," Zub said. "Or just bringing us down on top of them. Any ideas?"

I looked out the window again. Bringing the floor down on top of themselves didn't seem like a brilliant idea. Most of the robots had moved into the security station, and only a few remained outside.

"We could go out the window," I said, aiming my gun and preparing to shoot one of them out. There was a clatter of gunfire behind me as another sentry robot rushed the stairs.

"NO!" Several voices shouted at once. Celeste actually went so far as to rush over and grab the barrel of my weapon, pushing it down toward the floor.

"The glass is probably bulletproof," she pointed out. "Very bad idea. You'd kill one of us." Indeed, the glass hadn't cracked despite the number of heavy impacts the walls and floor had been taking.

"Yeah, okay," I said, feeling foolish.

Suddenly the room was plunged into darkness as the lights in the mess hall abruptly winked back out. At the same time, the ambient sounds of angry sentry robots beneath us ceased. Everything was eerily dark and quiet, the silence broken only by Dr. Liang's continued mumbling over the comm.

"I think he turned them off," I said.

"Wait here, all of you," Junlong said, and moved into the stairwell, weapon at the ready. There was a crash as he shoved wreckage out of his way. I watched his outline in my HUD move down to the lower floor of the security office and pick his way through the sentry robots.

"He says nothing's moving down there," Mengyao said. "They're all frozen in place. I think Liang finally managed to deactivate them."

The doctor was continuing to manipulate the interface in front of him. The flood of letters on the screen suddenly dimmed, replaced with what was clearly a map of the complex. Dr. Liang disengaged from the console for the first time and took a few steps back.

There as a bright green dot glowing on the map inside a small box hanging off of the bottom of a large ellipse. One other part of the map was marked, with what was clearly a miniature picture of a ship.

Dr. Liang had found the *Johannes*. Or, at least, he'd found *something*.

"Damn, we need to copy this," I said. "Mengyao, do you have any paper or writing utensils with your stuff? We need to--"

My suggestion was interrupted with chuckling.

"Something funny, Zub?"

He certainly thought there was. "Well, I'm wearing a thirty million dollar space suit. It's got these things on it called *cameras*. And I've already used them to take about two dozen pictures of that map. You, apparently, flew to Mars in your pajamas."

I had no defense for myself. "Shut up, Zub." Even the yuhangyuan were snickering at me.

Except Dr. Liang, who chose that precise moment to collapse to the floor. Mengyao reached him first, pulling a thin cable from a recess in his glove and connecting it to a port in Liang's helmet.

"His vitals are all right," Mengyao said. "I think he's just exhausted, and I bet he hasn't had much to eat or drink lately. We should get him back to the supply room, and plan our next move."

"Do you think you can follow the map to wherever the ship is?" Kathryn asked.

"That's part of what we need to plan through," Mengyao said. He pointed to a portion of the map. "This is the hangar that the *Shenzhou* and the *Tycho* landed in. I don't think I've ever actually seen this one that's indicated on the map here, so it probably is your ship. Here's the problem. See this area?"

He pointed to a sequence of rooms next to the hangar.

"This is the only way to reach the hangar, at least according to this map. The reason we've never seen that hangar is because this area is rubble. This is the first of the production floors that we visited. It's also the first one to overload. According to this map, I can't guarantee that there's actually a way to get to that hangar through the complex."

"I can think of a way," Zub said. "Sajad."

"Who is Sajad?" Mengyao asked. I realized with a start that I hadn't seen the little monkeybot since the yuhangyuan had found us.

"He's a *what*, technically, not a *who*," Zub said, as Sajad came bounding up the stairs and pounced at his owner. He'd apparently gotten past Junlong without ever being seen. "You weren't looking for a monkey robot when you grabbed us, and he was a bit of a ways away from us when you guys showed up. You never noticed him, and I had him stay away until I had a better idea of what we were dealing with."

"And how can this monkey help us?" Mengyao asked, sounding like he was trying his best to be patient.

"Monkey *robot*," Zub corrected. "Who has somehow gotten out of the *Johannes* and back to us once, which means that there's a way to get to the *Johannes*. Celeste, do you know where that hangar should be overland?"

"Directly underneath Jeanne," she said. "We're idiots. We went to Chloe because it was the closest and we figured Sajad had come from there. Jeanne was only a few miles away. I'm surprised we didn't see the *Johannes* landing when it came down. We went to the wrong goddamn skylight. Chloe was a vent for the terraforming, not a hangar."

"Let's get him back to the safe room," Zub said, indicating Dr. Liang. "Then let's find my uncle and my ship and get out of here."

NINETEEN

For the second time in a few days, the low Martian gravity worked for me as I helped carry an unconscious body to safety. The most difficult part proved to be getting him out the door. The sentry robots had packed themselves rather tightly into the bottom floor of the security room before Liang had succeeded in shutting them down, and even at one-third Earth's gravity, navigating the pile of sharp-edged robot statues while towing an unconscious old man in a relatively delicate space suit had all of us panting before we got back to safety. Zub proved entirely unhelpful, commenting at one point that he hoped that Liang had managed to shut down all the sentry robots in the entire complex and not just the ones nearby. Unfortunately, he had a point. We would be foolish to let our guard down at any point until we made it back to the ship.

Once we wrestled him out of the security room, I let Junlong and Hsieh take over carrying duties and decided to take a look at the sentry robots. I'd not actually had a chance to examine one up close, since my previous experiences with them had mostly involved running and shooting. Mostly running, to be honest.

"Zub," I said. "Why do you think none of them have guns?"

We'd managed to come up with a reason why the robots in the factory rooms had been coming after us mostly with blades: the danger of a spark in that kind of atmosphere had been amply demonstrated when the room blew up behind us. But as far as I was aware, we were far from anywhere with an atmosphere that volatile, and I couldn't come up with a good reason why none of the guard robots we'd encountered appeared to be carrying long-range weapons, much less something concussive or explosive.

"I'm not sure," Zub said, joining me. As I examined the deactivated robots, a few differences between them became clear. It turned out not all of the robots wielded blades, for example. They weren't all the same size, either; the ones we'd been attacked by earlier had been larger than us, but many of these were man-sized or smaller. They all had the same general shape, and nearly all of them had four arms, but not all of them had bladed arms. Some appeared to have blunt instruments instead, and others appeared to be fitted with tools of other kinds.

Wait a second. "I got it," I said.

"Enlighten me, please," Zub responded, grinning.

"We've been calling these things sentry robots, like their job was to patrol around and look for things to kill. That's not it. Look at the different configurations they're in. They're for *construction.* I'd bet you a year of your salary that they *built* this place. That they're just now getting repurposed into killing people is a coincidence. That's not what they were made for."

"Good for us," Zub said. "The not-built-to-kill-us-bots are still dangerous enough that they wiped out half the Chinese and damn near us a couple of times."

"I didn't say they were pussycats, just that they're not kill-bots."

"Maim-bots, then."

"Build-bots. But you can drive a nail with a hammer or smash a skull in, you know? They're multipurpose." I felt like I'd figured out something important, but Zub was back in a mocking mood. We left the robots behind and followed the others back to the safe room.

Once we got back to the supply room, Dr. Rosansky and the yuhangyuan busied themselves with examining Dr. Liang while the rest of us analyzed the map.

"It's about 110 miles between here and Jeanne," Celeste said. "Another 35 or so beyond that to the base camp, if we end up needing to take care of the external fuel tanks manually, but if we can take off with the ship that shouldn't be a problem."

"I thought you said we'd have trouble landing the *Johannes* on Mars?" I asked.

"We will," she responded. "It'll be dangerous, but the area around the domicile unit is literally as safe as we're going to be anywhere on the planet. If Zvi is still on the ship, he should be able to do it."

"If Zvi's still on the ship, and *if* we can get the thing out of the hangar," I added. "He got tractor-beamed down. Don't you think that if he could get the ship out of there, he'd have done it by now?"

"Pointless to worry about it now," Zub said. "If Dr. Liang can figure out the alien systems enough to shut down their security, I can figure out how to shut down their tractor beam. I'm pretty sure I still have that Mad Genius certificate somewhere on the ship. Besides, if Zvi's with the ship, we need to find him, even if we can't use the *Johannes* for anything other than comfy bunks any longer. Only important question now is how we get there."

He hooked his suit into Sajad again. "Now, we've got a couple of options here. We can travel through the complex or we can travel aboveground. Problem is, we'll need another transport either way, and that's only if the bulldozer didn't wreck the rover the Chinese scavenged from the *Tycho*. It's a hundred miles to Jeanne, and a hundred and sixty back to Chloe, and I don't know about you but I don't feel like walking any farther than I have to. Question is, now that we *have* a map, whether or not we can use Sajad here to find out how he got out of the hangar. That might be a way for us to get back *in*."

"Could we use the bulldozer?" I asked.

"Well, the robots could," Zub said. "I guess that-- oh, wait, we aren't robots. And I can't hotwire a car on *Earth*."

"I can," Celeste said.

"Can you hotwire an alien bulldozer?" Zub said.

"I can try," she answered.

*   *   *

Celeste could not hotwire an alien bulldozer. The machine did not appear to have any provision for a living driver at all, as a matter of fact. There was nothing resembling a steering wheel, much less an ignition or even any sort of console to interact with.

By a great stroke of luck, however, the *Tycho's* rover had sustained only minor damage when the bulldozer smashed the barrier out of the way, and a half hour or so of clearing rubble allowed us to drive the vehicle back to the safe room. By the time we returned, Dr. Liang was awake. The good news was the presence of foreigners did not appear to alarm him. The bad news was that he did not appear fully aware of anyone around him, and continued to babble meaninglessly to himself.

"He's gone," Kathryn said, "and yes, that's my official medical diagnosis. I can't do a thing here without a brain scanner. I don't know if interacting with the alien console damaged his mind, or if he was already so far gone that a psychotic break was guaranteed no matter what happened. We got him to eat and drink something, and his suit says he's in decent shape anyway-- all four of them are a little malnourished, and they could all stand to put on weight. The weak gravity's affecting him pretty seriously, too. All four of them are going to have major problems when we establish Earth gravity again on the Johannes. For someone who's been stranded millions of miles from home for three years he's in as good shape as we could expect."

"What's he saying, Mengyao?" Zub asked.

"Nonsense," the yuhangyuan replied. "It's not even Chinese. No language that I recognize. Occasionally there's a word or two, but he's said some words that sounded vaguely like English and Spanish, too. I think it's mostly coincidence. Your monkey appears to need something, by the way."

Sajad had apparently had time to digest the map and had managed to find something. We slaved our suits to his, and found a new glowing spot on the map, just outside of Jeanne's crater.

"I'm guessing that's an entrance," Zub said.

"So why didn't Zvi come with him?" Kathryn asked.

"This is *Zvi* we're talking about, Katie," Zub said. "I don't see any way he's going to leave that ship where just anything could happen to it. We didn't leave another rover on the *Johannes*, and it would be crazy for him to try to walk however many miles it is to the base camp by himself. I think this tells us that the ship's locked in place, though. He's probably waiting for Sajad to bring us back."

"I'd be a lot happier if we could communicate with him," I said.

"So would I, but I don't think it's as sinister as we've assumed," Celeste said. "These suits are designed for pretty decent long-range communication, but talking to Zvi right now would require throwing a signal through a hundred miles of rock. I'm not surprised that's not functioning. Or it could be that whatever keeps the ships from communicating is also blanking out any kind of long-range communications from the suits, too."

Hsieh spoke up. "I think you are correct," he said. "Many times, while exploring, we strayed too far from one another. Our communicators do not work over very long distances in this place."

"Is there another transport nearby?" Zub asked.

"We do have one," Mengyao responded.

"That's enough for everyone, then," Zub said. "Here's what we do, then: we use the transports to get as close to Jeanne as we can. If we end up hitting a place where we can't go any further, we try and find a way to go *up*. The map Liang gave us is useful, but it doesn't have a lot of detail to it, so it might be that there are a number of exit points to the surface that just aren't marked on here. Either way, once we get to Jeanne, we find a way to free the ship and then skip town."

"I would like to know exactly when you were put in charge," Junlong said, a bit of his temper showing again.

Zub stood up, bowing theatrically. "My apologies, *General God-King Lord Super Leader Kao Junlong*. Do you have a better idea?"

Junlong opened his mouth, then closed it again and shrugged. For a moment, a smile crossed his face. It was enough to crack the rest of us up, the first laughter I'd heard from anyone in a while.

"Get to work, then," Zub said, addressing it to everyone. "We need to take as many supplies as we can fit in the rover."

"That's an order," Junlong said, and we all started laughing again.

*   *   *

We split up into mixed groups in the rovers. Kathryn insisted on riding with Dr. Liang in case he had another attack, so she rode with him, Junlong, and Hsieh. Zub, Mengyao, Celeste and I, along with Sajad, took the *Tycho's* rover and the lead. Most of the trip would be through an access tunnel similar to the one we'd used to get from Chloe to Abbey and Nikki. It seemed that each skylight had its own complex underneath it-- most of them, like Chloe, dedicated to the terraforming factories, with Nikki and Jeanne being used as hangars for incoming spacecraft instead. Jeanne apparently also had a factory, since the first of the explosions had happened there, but it was much smaller than the others and apparently vented somewhere else.

"So what's your theory?" Zub asked, passing the time. "You decided this place was a terraforming station for Mars. Who put it here? Why was it abandoned? Why build something this large and then never use it?"

"We do not know," Mengyao said. "Many nights of talk were dedicated to unraveling this mystery. What is perhaps the most interesting is the suggestion that the facility is, at least when working properly, able to terraform the planet to *any* specifications. When Earthlings landed, it began producing Earthlike atmosphere, Earthlike food, and providing us with a source of water, as if it knew we would need it. We were scanned when we first arrived, remember. It implies that the race or culture that built this place had many members with different needs, and that the facility was built to be prepared for any of them."

That was sobering. Constant evidence that aliens existed had already blown my mind and put it back together. I was used to the idea. The thought of a *confederation* of aliens of some sort, multiple races working together, wasn't something I had considered before.

"Or perhaps it was left *for* us," Celeste said. "Maybe we're being watched, and the facility was constructed so that it would be here when the first human beings landed on Mars. Maybe the aliens are... I don't know, trying to help us along somehow."

"Its current level of hostility seems to put the lie to that," I pointed out. "I take it you never found any bodies anywhere?"

"Not a one," Mengyao said. "Nor, interestingly, is there any artwork or any visual depiction of what the beings who constructed this place might look like. Consider for a moment how many times in a day you see stylized representations of the human body on Earth. Even our bathrooms give a vague impression of what we look like. There's nothing like that here. The only trace of culture of any kind is the writing that appears periodically, but the only one of us who was able to make any headway with that at all was Dr. Liang. And it may have driven him mad."

"Didn't you say he was the one that set the robots loose?" Celeste added.

Mengyao nodded. "We saw them for the first time only a few months ago. The arrival of your support vehicles set off alarms across the facility, and we went to investigate. That, sadly, appears to be when Dr. Liang set the explosives in your habitation module. None of the crew who were with him were aware of the sabotage, and he only confessed to it much later. He had apparently already activated the robots somehow. The soldiers he was with tried to take a short cut through Chloe, which was when they encountered the robots for the first time. Only Junlong and Dr. Liang survived."

"We never found the rover they took," Zub said. "Did they leave it outside Chloe?"

"I believe so," Mengyao said. "There is a stairway on the far side of the crater. They likely left the rover there. They also attempted to back some robotics that Hsieh thought we could repurpose to some other task. They were pursued from the terraforming factory at Chloe all the way back to the mess hall, where the rest of us were able to fight off the robots coming after them. It was then that we constructed the barrier. We left the *Tycho's* rover on the other side in case we needed to reach Chloe again for some reason."

"That's how you knew we landed," I said. "Our ship set off alarms again, right?"

"And Dr. Liang had set a proximity sensor or two around your camp," Mengyao said, nodding. "We didn't know where the *Johannes* was going to land when and if it was pulled down-- we were worried that it was going to come down on top of the other two ships. I know of no other reason than luck that it was pulled down to Jeanne and not Nikki. We knew you had arrived, so we programmed the rover to head toward Chloe in case you came that way. Dr. Liang had also arranged for the distress signal. That was also without my authorization. I told him to send a signal for you to come to us, but not to send you into a trap."

"Nice to hear," I said.

*   *   *

Mengyao was right about one thing. As I watched the scenery fly by as we drove through the underground complex, one thing became perfectly clear: this facility was empty. *Absurdly* empty. Other than the functioning factory floors that we'd entered first, it was rare to see a room whose purpose was immediately clear. Most of the facility was huge, featureless rooms with nothing in them. It took a couple of hours of driving before we arrived at what had been Jeanne's factory floor. Half of that was through another grey access tunnel, which gently sloped toward the surface as we traveled. The facility we were heading toward was going to be much closer to the surface than the one at Chloe had been. Eventually we reached the end of our trip, pulling up to a closed gate similar to the ones we'd seen in the other tunnels.

We got out of the rovers and Zub tried the control pad next to the door. There was a shrieking sound as the machinery inside the door engaged and the gate lifted about four feet off the ground before grinding to a halt. Red dust spilled out onto the floor from the other side.

"Huh," Zub said. He gestured at the gap, and Sajad ran through. A moment of borrowing Sajad's visual input showed plenty of room on the other side for the eight of us so long as we didn't mind getting a little dirty crawling underneath the gate.

I opened a private channel to Kathryn. "How's Dr. Liang?"

"Shaky," she said. He'd slept for part of the trip, but spent most of his time while he was awake continuing to babble quietly to himself. They'd gotten him to eat something, but something had broken inside him at the security station and he hadn't been able to get over it yet. While the rest of us simply crouched to get underneath the jammed gate, he crawled on all fours like an infant, and had to be coaxed back to his feet afterwards.

I wasn't sure what I had been expecting to see on the other side, but it certainly wasn't what I saw. The detonation of the terraforming equipment had transformed the room from a pristine, almost hospital-like environment into a chaotic, shattered mess. It had also blown a hole clean through the ceiling, which accounted for the tons of Martian surface dust that covered the floor-- several feet deep in places- and coated every exposed surface.

"Dust storm?" Celeste asked.

"Had to be," Zub said. "Maybe a couple of them. Everything boils up over the hole, any dust that falls through gets stuck, no air currents to pull it back out again. This place would probably be completely buried in another few years."

"The map has the exit to the hangar over here," Mengyao pointed out, picking his way carefully through the wreckage to a point on the far side of the chamber. Walking was a challenge, since the layer of dust and dirt on the floor concealed any number of sharp-edged pieces of machinery. We had to move carefully to avoid injury or a torn suit. After a few minutes of laboriously picking our way over and around the obstacles in our way, Zub gave up and sent Sajad ahead again. The little monkeybot, made of sterner stuff than us and with no need to worry about putting a hole in his suit, covered the distance much faster than we would have been able to.

"That's not what I wanted," Zub said when Sajad reached his destination. If the doorway to the hangar was even still there and still functional, it was buried underneath tons of wreckage and Martian soil. The walls in this room were ringed with catwalks and balconies just as the other factory floor had been, and a huge section of them had collapsed right in front of the door, then been buried in the dust storm. It might be possible for us to dig our way through, but there was no way of knowing if we'd ever be able to get the door open on the other side.

Zub described the situation to the Chinese, who were unable to simply hook into Sajad's visual feed, and I watched Mengyao's face fall as he processed the news.

"Disappointing, but not surprising," he said. "We will simply have to find another way. Perhaps--"

He was interrupted by a screech from Sajad.

"He's found something," Zub said. And he had. There was a hole in the wall near the doorway, too small for us but exactly the right size for something Sajad's size to squeeze through. He leapt up to it and scrambled through, eventually turning on his suit lights to show us how the little opening eventually came through to a hole in the wall of the entryway to the hangar.

"I'll be damned," Zub said. "That's how he got out. Celeste, how far can he throw us a signal from those cameras?"

"Depends on how long that tunnel is," she responded. "I didn't design the suit networks to be good at transmitting signals underground. Version 2.0, though, I promise."

"Go find my uncle, Sajad," Zub said. "And my ship. We'll wait here."

The feed from Sajad's suit faded out as he ran down the tunnel.

"Okay," Zub said. "We know he got in here, and that he got up to the surface from inside this room. That means--"

"We go up," Kathryn said, pointing at an unbroken stretch of catwalk on the near side of the room. "That gets awfully close to the hole in the roof. I bet we can get to the surface from there, and then back into the hangar from aboveground."

"Let's start looking, then," Zub said. "Katie, you think we can get the doctor to do a little bit of climbing?"

"We might need to encourage him a bit, but yes, I think so," she said.

"Okay," Zub said. "Let's hold over there and see if the catwalks will still hold everybody's weight."

*   *   *

Sajad caught up with us about fifteen minutes later, as we were just starting to pick our way up the first set of scaffolding around the outside of the room. He leapt onto Zub's shoulder.

"He's got something," Zub said, taking a wadded piece of paper from the monkey's hands and unfolding it. A moment later, he exploded into laughter.

"What's it say?" I said. Zub handed me the piece of paper, which had a single Hebrew word written on it.

"It says 'You're late,'" Zub translated. "Uncle Zvi is apparently doing quite well on the other side of that pile of junk down there. Give me a minute, guys." He said something over a private channel, and Sajad took off again, heading back toward the crack in the wall.

"I should have thought of that the first time," he said. "I just recorded an audio message for Zvi. I told him what we're doing, and to hold on to the monkey. Hopefully we'll see him in a little while."

*   *   *

It took nearly an hour of zig-zagging back and forth along the walls, climbing staircases, and occasionally helping each other across gaps before we reached the surface. Dr. Liang, as expected, had the hardest time. He was able to negotiate much of the climb by himself, but there were points where Junlong or Hsieh simply carried him piggyback-style. Luckily for all of us, making the final move from the room to the outside world proved to not be as difficult as it could have been; Junlong and

Mengyao gave Zub and I a boost up to the hole in the ceiling, and the two of us were able to pull everyone else out.

We hadn't been aboveground in a couple of days. It was darker than I expected. My chronometer showed that it was midafternoon, but the sky was obscured and dark.

"Look there," Celeste said. "To the south."

The summit of Arsia Mons was behind us, dominating the skyline and stretching off to infinity to the east and the west. But the sandstorm building behind the mountain dwarfed even it. I had seen pictures from the Dust Bowl on Earth in the late nineteen-thirties, where the huge swirling storms of dust yanked up off of the depleted plains buried entire towns and choked animals in the fields to death. This looked worse than that by an order of magnitude. There was a huge wall of earth and sand swirling behind the mountain-- a mountain, mind you, that was already the *second-largest in the solar system*. Mars' dust storms were known to cover the entire planet. This one looked like it might aspire to that.

"We'd better hurry," Mengyao said. The storm was miles away, but who knew how fast it was going to move. Luckily, Jeanne wasn't that far away, and ten minutes of admittedly fast and vaguely nervous travel had us staring into another of the skylights. Jeanne wasn't as big as Chloe, but staring into the *second*-largest hole I'd ever seen wasn't really that different as far as the overwhelming vertigo and near-panic went. The only real difference was that, unlike Chloe, Jeanne's walls went straight down, rather than curving back out underneath us. The astronomers who had first noticed the skylights had noticed this feature of her right away, and hey'd gotten a great picture of light reflecting off of one of her sides, which was enough to show that she went straight down but still didn't provide any evidence of how deep she was.

Chloe had been a hundred and fifty meters or so deep. When Zvi suddenly blinked back into my HUD a few moments after looking over the edge, I discovered that Jeanne was even deeper-- 213 meters straight down.

"Welcome back to the world, Uncle," Zub said.

"Welcome back? I have gone nowhere," Zvi responded. "I have remained here and loyally guarded your space ship while you were nowhere to be found."

Yeah, he's fine, I thought.

"There's an entryway over there," Celeste noticed. It looked much the same as the one I'd scrambled into just before being roasted on Chloe. It would look like a rock or boulder from above, but there was a door set into it on one side that we could enter.

"Zvi, we found an entrance up here," Zub said. "We should be able to get down to you. Any idea where the other end of the thing is?"

"There is a door down here I have not been able to open," Zvi said. "Directly underneath where you are standing. Perhaps you will have more luck from the other side."

There was no lock on the door, which swung inside easily. I checked my environment sensors, wondering if I'd be able to take my helmet off and breathe outside air for a few minutes. This time, though, the tunnel wasn't pressurized and warmed like the first one had been. The complex had apparently given up on providing us with warmth or breathable air, and while it was warmer than it had been outside, forty below zero wasn't something I really wanted my face exposed to.

We headed down the rampways for what felt like several dozen stories. This wasn't fair. We'd just climbed *up* out of a hole, and while the hangar was considerably farther underground than the destroyed factory floor had been, we were all exhausted by the time we reached the bottom. Dr. Liang, in particular, was practically whimpering, and for the last part of the trip we'd had to take shifts carrying him again.

"We had to cut through this door the first time," Junlong said.

"Still have the torch?" I asked.

"I do," said Junlong, producing it from the satchel of supplies he'd been carrying.

"Zvi, we're at the door," Zub said. "We're cutting through. You probably don't want to stand too close to it."

Junlong fired the torch, causing a bright flash that darkened my visor momentarily. The lock was mechanical, not magnetic, and within a few minutes he'd gained us access to the hangar.

The *Johannes* sat fifty meters away, undamaged, looking as new and pristine as she'd looked when I'd first seen her back on Eunostos. The ship's bright running lights illuminated the hangar space nicely, and she glowed like a small sun in the distance.

"There's my baby," Zub said. A ramp dropped from the ship's side, and Zvi emerged. I surprised myself and actually choked up a little bit upon seeing him. It was possible, maybe just a little bit, that we were all going to survive this.

Shut up shut up shut up, my brain said, as Zub embraced his uncle. The rest of us settled for handshakes, as Zub introduced the yuhangyuan, to Zvi's great surprise.

"These are the men who attempted to kill you," Zvi said, his bass rumble even deeper than usual, "and you bring them to the ship?"

"We'll explain in a few minutes," Zub said. "Let's get in orbit first. Now is the time for you to tell me that taking off is impossible."

"Taking off is impossible," Zvi said. "You will not be surprised to learn that I have already thought of that. The *Johannes*... it is as if she hits a ceiling once the wheels get more than an inch or two off of the ground. The first time I tried, it nearly caused me to destroy the ship. She hit the ceiling and then slid to the side, and nearly crashed into the wall before I regained control. There is some force keeping her on the ground. I do not know how to disable it."

"Let's worry about that in a little while," Zub said. "For now, I want to spend a few minutes not wearing a space suit, and take a shower, and eat something. Life support's still working, right?"

"Everything is as you left it," Zvi said.

"Excellent," Zub said. "Come on, guys," he said, waving to the yuhangyuan. "Want to see the advances we've made in spaceship design since you left Earth?"

TWENTY

It was a few hours before much of anything else got done. We relaxed a bit, changing into regular clothes, the yuhangyuan using spare outfits. I found that it was surprisingly pleasant to wear underwear again. We filled Zvi in on where we had been and what we had discovered about the strange happenings on the planet, and he interrogated the yuhangyuan thoroughly about Dr. Liang's attempts at sabotage before letting the old man out of his sight.

WE'RE LUCKY IF HE DOESN'T LOCK HIM IN THE CARGO BAY, Zub blinked me at one point.

"There is not much for me to tell you," Zvi told us when it was his turn. "Soon after you sent me the video from the destroyed domicile unit, I received a signal from somewhere on the planet. It was, as you said, indecipherable, but I found that soon afterwards I could only broadcast or receive signals on the wavelength that I had been contacted on. Communications were not precisely cut off, but with no one listening, there was no point in broadcasting."

"Alien air traffic controllers," Celeste said.

"Cool," Zub said.

"It was not 'cool,' Ezekiel," Zvi said, glaring at his nephew. "A few moments after receiving the signal, the ship began descending toward the planet's surface. Nothing I could do would change our trajectory, and at the speed the ship was moving, I thought I was about to be smashed to bits. But then it became clear that we were headed toward one of the skylights, and once we passed its perimeter we slowed down and the ship touched down. Since then, I have been here. I was not able to get out through the stairwell you entered through, and the tunnel to the rest of the complex was blocked. There are no other ships here. The hangar is ringed with rooms with nothing in them. They may be offices or dormitories. One has a bank of consoles that may be similar to the security room you describe, as it overlooks the entire hangar. I did not attempt to activate it. It may be that you will be able to release the ship from that room, however."

"That's where we'll start, then," Zub said. "Katie, wake Dr. Liang up. We're going to need him."

"We may not be able to convince him to use the consoles again," she said, and Hsieh and Mengyao nodded in agreement. "He didn't react to them very well at all last time."

Zub shrugged. "If he can make them work, I can make them work."

"He had *years* to try, Ezekiel."

"Don't make me go get the Mad Genius certificate, lady. Go wake 'im up. Everybody who's coming along, suit up."

I suited up.

*   *   *

Zub stared at the console, trying to figure out how Dr. Liang had managed to turn the thing on.

"This is *not* fair," he said. "I wrote an operating system for fun when I was *eight*. This guy is *not* smarter than me." Liang, for his part, was standing aside, regarding the console with a mix of fascination and horror. As near as I'd been able to tell, the thing had turned on as soon as he had touched it. If he'd pushed a button or anything like that, he'd done so without me noticing it. But he didn't seem up to the idea of actually interacting with the thing again, and Zub couldn't get it to do anything at all. The console was lit up, powered on, but there was nothing on the screen and the hard-light touch interface that Dr. Liang had been manipulating in the security room was inactive.

Kathryn stood next to him, speaking to him in a soothing tone of voice I'd never heard from her before. I hadn't heard Liang speak a single word of English since we'd first encountered him in the security room, but according to Mengyao he did understand us. The three of us had come up to the command room, plus Mengyao, along to act as a translator in case Dr. Liang decided to say something intelligible.

"Please, Doctor," Dr. Rosansky said, letting her accent come through more than usual, "we just need to get the ship freed, and then we can go home. You can help us, can't you? You saved everyone before. You just need to do this one thing more, and then you can rest." She stroked his arm with one hand, the other in the small of his back. I wondered if she was trying to push him toward the console or if she was rubbing his back through the suit.

For the first time, Dr. Liang looked at her, making direct eye contact. I hadn't seen him react that way to anyone before. He said something-- I wasn't sure if it was Chinese or the strange gibberish he'd been mumbling for the last several hours-- and then, haltingly, stepped to the console and held his hands out.

The machine burst into light, the alien writing scrolling on the screen again and the hologram interface forming around his hands.

"What the hell? I just *did* that!" Zub shrieked.

"You're so cute when you're jealous," Kathryn said.

Dr. Liang's face froze into a grimace, his lips pulling back from his teeth in a rictus of stress and pain. I could hear whimpering over the comm, and for an awful moment considered cutting the feed so that I didn't have to hear him. In the hangar, the lights flickered on, illuminating the entire room with ghostly white light.

And then, suddenly, we could *see* the force holding the *Johannes* captive on the hangar floor, as a lattice of delicate, shimmering blue light spiderwebbed itself across the room, hanging in midair only a foot or two above the ship. The lights brightened at first, then flickered, then disappeared altogether for a few moments, only to come back as bright as ever again.

"Come on," I found myself mumbling. *You can do it...*

And then, without a sound, Liang keeled over. As he broke the connection with the console, the lights went back off and the spiderweb over the *Johannes* disappeared again-- invisible, yes, but likely still there.

Dr. Rosansky was at his side as he hit the floor.

"Oh God," she said, "I think he's had a stroke. I can't-- *shit*, there's nothing I can do while he's in that suit, we've got to-- all of you, help me move him." Mengyao moved quickly to Liang's side, picking him up off the ground and throwing him over his back in a fireman's carry.

Zub took a step forward and put his hands into the light interface, which Dr. Liang's stroke had not deactivated.

"NO!" Kathryn and I both shouted, but he was already in. He reacted to the system very differently than Liang had, though. Where Liang had clearly been in pain, Zub's face, if anything, took on a look of serenity as the crawling mass of alien letters reflected off his face.

"I'll stay here with him," I told them. "Get Liang back to the ship."

"Zvi, medical emergency," Kathryn said, as she and Mengyao hustled out of the room. "Get to my clinic and get *everything* prepared. Dr. Liang has had a stroke. I repeat, I'm bringing a stroke victim back to you..."

I tuned her out and directed my attention back to Zub. The lights came back on in the hangar, a feat that Zub acknowledged by wincing slightly. Seconds later, the blue light spun its way across the room, glowing steadily and clearly even in the lit room.

Damn, he's pulling it off, I thought, and then the web silently blew apart, the thin strands of light evaporating into billions of blue motes and then dissolving.

Right about then was when the sirens started going off.

Naturally.

At first, I was afraid that I was going to have to pull him away from the console. Zub didn't react to the sirens at all, continuing to stare into the screen of text ahead of him, his fingers still in the interface. Then he grimaced, blinking hard, like there was something stuck in his eyes, and started trying to pull his hands out of the hologram. He only managed to disengage himself from the computer with what looked like great effort, pulling one hand free at a time and then slumping to one knee. He stayed there, swaying slightly, then gestured to me to help him up.

"You all right?"

"Wegahgonow," he slurred, his eyes rolling around crazily in his head. "I tol' em... I said... no... *he* tol' em..." he trailed off. I could see a thin line of saliva trickling down from the side of his mouth through his visor. In my HUD, his outline shifted to yellow from green, his heartbeat accelerating and blood pressure rising.

"Can you walk?" I hooked one arm around him, prepared to carry him if necessary. He nodded, and with my help we staggered out of the room, down the stairs, and back to the ship. The alarm horns continued booming, forcing me to turn my external audio feed almost all the way off. Even then, I could *feel* them through the suit.

I opened a private channel to Kathryn. "Better make room for two in sick bay. Zub will make it back to the *Johannes* but he's not in great shape."

"Zvi," Zub said, his voice thick and hoarse. "Get ready. We gotta... we gotta leave *now*." I could see that the ship's engines were already beginning to rotate to allow the ship to take off vertically. Hundreds of yards above us, the Martian sky beckoned.

I half-pulled Zub up the rampway to the ship and pulled it closed behind us. As soon as the locks engaged, I could feel the *Johannes'* engines kick in and the ship leap from the ground. I lowered Zub to the floor, not willing to try and walk with him we were taking off, and not completely sure that it was safe for *me* to be standing around either.

I hadn't any reason to be worried. As it turned out, the *Johannes'* vertical take off was smooth as butter after that first initial bump, and I could barely tell the ship was moving within thirty seconds.

At least I hoped that was what was happening; the alternative was that something else had gone wrong and the ship *wasn't moving.* Zub's eyes were closed, but I thought he was still conscious.

I heard a rattle from around the corner, and Hsieh and Kathryn shoved a gurney around the corner. Hsieh and I lifted Zub onto the bed, where she began methodically stripping off his suit and examining him at the same time.

"What happened?" she asked.

"He freed the ship, and then he got woozy," I said. "That's really the best I can do to describe it." She hopped up on the gurney, continuing her examination as Hsieh pushed, so I followed.

"How's Liang?"

"Dead," Hsieh said.

"And I'm not going to lose two of us to that thing today," Kathryn said. "Get up to the front of the ship and see if Zvi can use you for anything. We'll take care of Zub."

I stopped, watching as they moved into the lift to the second floor, and turned and headed to the bridge. Unsurprisingly, Zvi's command center was an oasis of calm, with Zvi and Celeste quietly communicating with each other about coordinates and headings. I slid into my seat and waited for someone to notice me.

"How is my nephew?" Zvi asked.

"I think he'll be okay," I said. "He got knocked for a loop turning off the tractor beam, or whatever it was that was holding us here, but I think he'll get over it soon enough."

"Good," Zvi said. "Did you need something?"

"I think Kathryn wanted me out of her way while she checked Zub over," I said. "She sent me up here."

"That works out," Celeste said. "We have a problem."

Of course we do.

"What is it?"

"That," she said, as the ship turned to change direction.

That, as viewed through the main viewport, was the sandstorm from Hell that we had noticed during our brief stay on the surface. Unfortunately, it had gotten closer since then— in fact, we appeared to be heading directly into it.

"It's right on top of the base camp," Celeste said. "Probably beating hell out of the base camp, as a matter of fact. The fuel tanks aren't responding to the command to disengage and meet us in orbit. Either they've been sabotaged or the sand is gumming up the works somehow. So guess what we have to do?"

"Land the ship and fix the fuel tanks?"

"Got it in one," she said.

"In a sandstorm," I said.

"What? No, are you nuts?" The look she shot me was perhaps a bit more scornful than it needed to be, but given the circumstances I didn't see a reason to make an issue about it. "Zvi says he can still land the ship in a sandstorm. He says he can still *fly* the ship in a sandstorm. I believe both of these things."

So did I, for that matter. I recalled Zub saying that his uncle could fly a cantaloupe if the need struck him, and I figured I'd believe him if he said that he could land in a sandstorm.

"But that doesn't mean that *we* go out in the sandstorm," she said. "We wait on the ship until the sandstorm blows over or at least lessens. It's not going to throw so much dust at us as to bury the ship, and even at a hundred and fifty miles an hour the dust out there isn't going to abrade the ship's outer coating. And the atmosphere isn't thick enough to lift us off the ground, which would be a problem on Earth. It's still too dangerous for us. We wait."

"Ten minutes," Zvi said. "I'll put us down about a hundred meters outside the base camp."

"Let's fill the others in," Celeste said. "We've got some time to relax."

We almost collided with Zub, clad in a hospital gown, who barreled into the cockpit at top speed—- or, at least, what looked like top speed, since he was still lurching a bit.

"We're in trouble," he said.

"We knew that already," I answered.

"No," he said, collapsing into his chair, as Kathryn and the remaining yuhangyuan appeared in the entryway behind him. He put both hands on the sides of his head, rubbing his temples. "I know... I know what happened with Liang, now. He didn't mean... he didn't want any of that to happen."

He paused to cough, a thick, wracking sound, as if he'd been battling pneumonia for months.

"I think... that he... no, that *we* aren't supposed to ever be here. Their tech... too far beyond us. The consoles knew he wasn't supposed to be there. I feel like he... he blew a password, or missed a code... or something. That's what brought out the robots. Supposed to clean us out, like we were a virus. Or a *stain*. I have no idea how he ever... turned them back off. Willpower. I dunno."

He put his head between his knees, breathing heavily and trying to pull himself together.

"Tsvika... how close are we?"

"No more than six minutes, nephew."

"Scan for electronics near the camp. Not *at* the camp. *Near* the camp."

Zvi pushed a few buttons, and a million lights started blinking on an overlay through the main viewscreen. Zub looked at the screen and moaned.

"The robots. Left through skylight... Annie. Been heading to the base camp for hours, even in the storm. They... they figured out where we were, somehow. Maybe Liang told them. He probably... he probably never had a choice."

Celeste spoke up first. "If they get to the fuel tanks before we do—"

"We're stranded," Zub said. "No way back. We all die here."

I looked at the overlay on the screen.

The robots were less than two kilometers from our camp.

*   *   *

"Tell me exactly what we need to do," I said to Celeste as we made our way back to the exit. Zvi had promised to put us as close as possible to the base camp, and we were due to land in seconds. Hsieh was already there, and handed each of us a gun as we finished adjusting our suits.

"First priority, get the solid rocket boosters attached to the *Johannes*," she said. "That gets us into orbit, and isn't going to be as complicated as it sounds. We just get them nearby and the rest of the process is actually automated. That way, worst case scenario, we get into orbit, grab the ERSV, and we have a year and a half to figure out what to do next."

"Second priority?"

"Fixing the external fuel tank. Hsieh and I will try and figure that one out. All we need it to do is launch; I'm hoping it's just not receiving the signal correctly and we can give it instructions manually. It launches, we follow it into orbit and grab it, and we're back to Earth."

"All this in a sandstorm," I said. "And before the army of alien robots gets to us."

"Yep," she said, and the ship touched down.

*   *   *

Sandstorm, as it turned out, didn't really properly describe what was happening outside. Ordinarily, Martian wind was constant and virtually undetectable. The atmosphere was just too thin. However, when combined with the low Martian gravity, which made dust particles easy to pick up, the storm we were walking into was like nothing ever seen on Earth. My virtual environment inside the suit activated the moment we stepped outside, and the inside of the *Johannes'* airlock was covered with dust the second the external doors opened.

The winds were not full-strength, maybe fifty or sixty miles an hour. The wall of sand and dust nearly knocked me off my feet anyway. An overlay on the virtual environment showed the SRBs about thirty yards to the northwest. The *Johannes* had landed just south of the base camp. My job was to get those to the ship while Celeste and Hsieh dealt with the fuel tank. I could see their outlines to my right in my HUD. I couldn't see the two of them at all. Even with the virtual environment on, I was nearly blind.

I stumbled toward the rocket boosters, my arms out in front of me like an extra in a zombie movie. The rocks on Mars could be sharp, and stumbling right now could be disastrous. Just keeping my balance was enough of a challenge. The wind could change direction at a moment's notice, meaning that one minute it was propelling me toward the boosters and the next it was slamming at me from the side, knocking me off course.

The SRBs were mounted on a huge piece of industrial equipment, sort of like a Y-shaped flatbed truck, or a forklift with wheels at the end of the forks. It was designed to be driven up to the *Johannes*. So long as I got one of the SRBs on one side of the ship and the other on the other side, Zvi could lock them into place from inside the cockpit. All I had to do was get them there.

The door to the driver's seat was ripped out of my hand as I pulled it open, nearly knocking me to the ground again and swinging crazily in the constantly shifting winds. The seat was already filled with dirt even before I got myself into position.

Thank God for automatic starters, I thought as I pushed the button to turn the thing on. Manipulating keys in the suit would have been annoying enough on a clear day. It was flatly impossible in this wind. I felt, rather than heard, the machine roar into life around me, and a few lights on the dashboard penetrated the gloom.

"Zvi! I've got the truck running!" I shouted over the comm. We were already facing the right way, luckily. I wasn't at all sure how good of a job I would have done had I had to turn the thing around.

"Bring it forward slowly," Zvi said. There wasn't that much distance between me and the ship-- maybe a hundred feet-- and I could see Zvi's outline in my HUD suspended weirdly above ground, but this ship itself was nearly invisible.

"Get all the external lights on," I said. "I can barely see you, and I don't want to hit the ship." I aimed the center of the truck at Zvi's outline, figuring that since the cockpit was in the center of the ship that was probably my best bet.

Suddenly the window of the driver's compartment blew in, as something heavy smashed into it. I stomped on the accelerator in a panic, throwing the truck into a lurch. Outside, I could just barely see the outline of three glowing photoreceptors.

The robots were starting to reach the camp.

I switched to global. "The sentry bots are out here, people. One of them damn near just took my head off. Hsieh, Celeste, you two okay?"

There was no response. *Shit.* The *Johannes'* lights flared into visibility as I finally got close enough to the ship for them to penetrate the black. Wind and Martian soil were swirling around in the driver's compartment from both sides now, making visibility even worse than it had been before.

"Stop," Zvi barked. "That's close enough. Get out of there and onto the ship."

"Not yet!" I shouted. "Celeste and Hsieh are still out there!" In the distance, I could just barely see their outlines. They were still green, but I couldn't tell if they were surrounded by the robots or not. Nor could I see the one that had taken a swing at me earlier.

I turned and started to sprint-- if that was even the right word-- to the fuel tank. I slipped and fell almost immediately, and warning lights began blinking all over my HUD. There was a tiny hole in the suit, and I was leaking air.

No time to worry about that, I thought. I was still okay on oxygen, and even a big leak wouldn't run my supplies out before I got back to the ship or the robots killed me.

I scrambled to my feet and started moving again, only to pull up short when three robots suddenly appeared in front of me. I skidded to a halt, hoping they couldn't see me any more than I could see them, and carefully moved around them. In the distance, I saw Hsieh leap to his feet and run toward something.

Damn it. They'd found them. Celeste, still bent over the computer interface, was still working on the release for the fuel tank.

"Can you two hear me yet?" I shouted over private channels.

"BUSY! I was ignoring you!" Celeste yelled. "The goddamned thing's password-protected! Why in the name of *hell* did Zub put a goddamned *password* on here?"

"So ask him what it is!"

"I can't! Rosansky says he's *seizing!*" she yelled back. "Help Hsieh!" The yuhangyuan was to my right, trying his best to distract a robot from attacking the tank.

"Don't shoot!" he said. "Too close to the tank! We don't want a ricochet!"

Wonderful, I thought, and threw a rock at the thing instead. It pinged off one of its photoreceptors, causing it to turn and wheel toward me. I backed up, cursing, and tossed another rock. This one missed. As it began rolling in my direction, Hsieh leapt into it, hitting it hard and knocking it spinning away.

At least it was one of the smaller ones, I thought.

"There's more on the other side!" he shouted, and I saw his outline moving again.

"The SRBs are attached," Zvi said over global. "We can leave at any time. I suggest you get back to the ship *now.*"

"I *got it!*" Celeste screamed triumphantly. I ran around the backside of the tank, shoulder-to-shoulder with Hsieh, who I could barely see. There were faint shapes moving around in the dark ahead of us. We both emptied a clip into the distance, hoping to hit something important.

"Get over here," Celeste said. "I can't activate the burn with you two standing right next to the goddamned rockets, now, can I?"

We both moved. Celeste's hands were flying over the keyboard, punching in commands. The fuel tank's machinery groaned as the heavy tank was lifted into a vertical position.

"You figured out the password?" I asked. I couldn't believe it.

"It was his goddamned *birthday,*" she said. "I don't know whether to kill him for choosing something so obvious or kill him for his sloppy security or kill him just for the sheer hell of it."

She hit a final button, and the rockets roared into life. *That,* I could see.

"Running now," she said. "They'll fire in twenty seconds. We should probably be on the *Johannes* when that happens."

We turned, the wind at our backs, and fled back to the ship. Zvi already had the *Johannes* moving, taxiing around so as to take off away from the domicile. We encountered more of the robots on the way and simply blew past them, Hsieh stumbling just in time to avoid a blade aimed at his head. When we reached the ship, we threw ourselves up the rampway and locked the airlock.

"Put your backs against the wall and hold on," Zvi said. "We're launching. This will be uncomfortable."

* * *

Forty-five minutes later, we were comfortably in orbit and headed for the rendezvous with our extra fuel and the ERSV. We got out of our suits, then made our way-— carefully, since the ship hadn't established gravity yet—to the sick bay to check on Zub. He was conscious, but Kathryn had actually gone so far as to restrain him to his bed.

"He tried to come out and help you," she said. "That's when the seizure hit him. He's not going anywhere until I tell him it's okay."

"We're safe, man," I said. The trip back to Earth would take much longer than we'd planned, since we didn't have the right timing for a Hohmann transfer, but we had plenty of food and fuel to get there unless something else went critically wrong.

"That's it," Zub said. "We're not."

"What's that mean?" I asked, suddenly expecting a horde of angry robots to come boiling out of the floor or something like that.

"Need to warn Earth," he said. "They're coming."

"Who's coming? The robots have a way off of Mars? You think they'd chase us all the way back to Earth?"

"When I was using the console," he said. "I think I found what finally cracked Liang. The robots-— the reason the whole site's automated-- they were sent there *first*. To prepare the planet for their masters. They wanted it ready when they arrived."

My blood froze. "Who are their masters?" I asked.

"No idea," he said. "But I found something. A signal, a message, I don't know, buried in the computers. As clear as if it had been written in English. Arrival dates. A schedule. They're on their way. The robots told them the place was ready, hundreds of years ago. And they're almost here."

"Who, Zub? When?"

"Two years," he said, and collapsed back onto his bed. *"They'll be here in two years."*

THE END

AFTERWORD

Skylights is Warren Ellis' fault. Hopefully you enjoyed it, so this feels like I'm giving him credit instead of blame.

It's the truth, I swear it. The skylights on Mars are real things, if probably not filled with alien terraforming devices, and I first found out about them through him, soon after their discovery-- either in one of his newsletters or on his website. I believe he made a comment about how he thought they'd make a great story.

Can't wait to read what you come up with, I thought.

And then he didn't write the damn story.

And then, with NaNoWriMo 2008 fast approaching, the prologue for *Skylights* jumped into my head. It's probably obvious that it's the truest part of the book; other than the grade level(*) (I was in fourth) it's a more or less autobiographical description of that day in 1984. I wrote that section in about fifteen minutes, and it's seen less editing than any other section of the books, and even that was just altering dates a bit. I won NaNo that year, and got the first draft done in January of '09, at 106,000 words or so. It's seeing the light of day now because I think it deserves it-- if you as a reader had half the fun with it that I did, it's going to be massively successful-- and because I finally realized I could just put it out there myself.

I want to take a moment to thank Warren for (sort of) letting me steal his idea, and Dr. Robert Zubrin (who, much like Ellis, has no idea who I am) for providing the inspiration for most of the science in the expedition itself. His book *The Case for Mars* should be required reading for everybody. I have no reason to believe he's anything like Zub. I'll let you decide if that's a good thing for him or not.

Thank you for reading.

Luther M. Siler
Somewhere in northern Indiana
September 29, 2014

(*) Well, okay. I *might* have stolen the name of a person I know for the biggest butthead in the first grade. She may or may not be an immense butthead in real life. I ain't saying.

THANK YOU

for reading SKYLIGHTS. If you enjoyed reading it, please consider leaving a review at the sites of your choice online.

ABOUT THE COVER

Skylights' amazing cover was created by the art duo of Casey Heying and Andrew Hibner. You can see more work by Casey on his DeviantArt page at ozwonderland.deviantart.com or visit his comic shop at buymetoys.com. More artwork by Andrew Hibner is available at achibner.deviantart.com.

ABOUT THE AUTHOR

Luther Siler was born in 1976. He lives in northern Indiana with his wife, three-year-old son, two dogs, and two cats. In his spare time he teaches middle school. *Skylights* is his second commercially available work.

He only occasionally refers to himself in the third person, and writing this is making him slightly uncomfortable. He is also godawful at smiling for pictures.

Luther Siler's blog: infinitefreetime.com

Follow Luther on Twitter at @nfinitefreetime

ALSO BY LUTHER M. SILER

THE BENEVOLENCE ARCHIVES

Troll evictions! Dwarf pirates! Daring rescues! Angry gods! Impossible technology! Oversized bars! Pissed-off ogres! Disrespectful spaceships! All this and a mild disregard for proper wound treatment!

THE BENEVOLENCE ARCHIVES, VOL. 1 is a novella-length collection of six short stories set in a common universe. Combining elements of space opera-style science fiction and high fantasy, THE BENEVOLENCE ARCHIVES tell the adventures of Brazel, Rhundi, and Grond, a gnome/halfogre team of smugglers.

THE PLANET IT'S FARTHEST FROM: A simple job in a saloon goes poorly for Brazel.

THE CLOSET: Brazel and Grond are hired to teach someone why gambling can be a bad idea.

YANK: Dwarven pirates. 'Nuff said.

REMEMBER: Brazel and Grond are hired by one of the galaxy's most powerful people for a suspiciously easy job.

THE CONTRACT: Rhundi tries to get through a simple business negotiation without anyone being shot.

THE SIGIL: Brazel and Grond encounter something horrifying on a frozen rock in the middle of nowhere.

THE BENEVOLENCE ARCHIVES, VOL. 1 is available anywhere ebooks are sold.

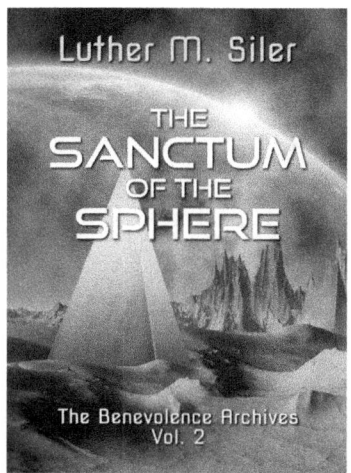

THE SANCTUM OF THE SPHERE: THE BENEVOLENCE ARCHIVES, VOLUME 2

"Go rob that train." Nice, normal. An everyday heist.

But nothing is ever normal for Brazel, Grond and Rhundi.

A simple act of motorized larceny quickly explodes into a galaxy-spanning adventure for the two thieves. Blade-wielding elves, a fast-moving global war, a secret outlaw space city, incomprehensible insectoids and one impossibly lucky human are just the start of their problems. And that's before they learn that someone from Grond's past has gotten the Benevolence involved...

What is happening on the ogrespace moon Khkk?

Who are the Noble Opposition?

And what is the secret of THE SANCTUM OF THE SPHERE?

www.ingramcontent.com/pod-product-compliance
Lightning Source LLC
Chambersburg PA
CBHW071308200626
46813CB00015B/643